USA TODAY BESTSELLING AUTHOR
K.C. MILLS

YOU COULD DO DAMAGE *TOO*

BLACK
ODYSSEY
MEDIA

WWW.BLACKODYSSEY.NET

Published by
BLACK ODYSSEY MEDIA

www.blackodyssey.net
Email: info@blackodyssey.net

YOU COULD DO DAMAGE TOO. Copyright © 2025 by K.C. MILLS

Library of Congress Control Number: 2025902596

First Trade Paperback Printing: November 2025
ISBN: 978-1-957950-85-3
ISBN: 978-1-957950-86-0 (e-book)

Cover Design by Ashlee Nassar of Designs With Sass

10 9 8 7 6 5 4 3 2 1

Manufactured in the United States of America

Distributed by Kensington Publishing Corp.

The authorized representative in the EU for product safety and compliance is
eucomply OU, Parnu mnt 139b-14, Apt 123
Tallinn, Berline 11317, hello@eucomplianceprtner.com

Dear Reader,

I want to thank you immensely for supporting Black Odyssey Media and our ongoing efforts to spotlight the diverse narratives of blossoming and seasoned storytellers. With every manuscript we acquire, we believe that it took talent, discipline, and remarkable courage to construct that story, flesh out those characters, and prepare it for the world. Debut or seasoned, our authors are the real heroes and heroines in *OUR* story. For them, we are eternally grateful.

Whether you are new to K.C. Mills or Black Odyssey Media, we hope that you are here to stay. Our goal is to make a lasting impact in the publishing landscape, one step at a time and one book at a time. As always, we welcome your feedback and kindly ask that you leave a review. For upcoming releases, announcements, submission guidelines, etc., please be sure to visit our website at www.blackodyssey.net or scan the QR code below. And remember, no matter where you are in your journey, the best of both worlds begins now!

Joyfully,

Shawanda Williams

Shawanda "N'Tyse" Williams
Founder/Publisher

CHAPTER 1

KINCAID.

Nari followed me through the lobby, fuming, but I understood. She and I had just discovered details that completely complicated everything about us.

"You're right. We do have a lot to discuss, starting with how you know my father and knew I was here. Are you following me?" She folded her arms across her chest, firing bullets through a heated stare while I ignored her, hitting the locks on my car so that we could leave. There was no way in hell we were about to have this discussion in the middle of the sidewalk, in plain sight, after what the hell I had just found out.

"It's my job to know where you are at all times, now more than ever." While my hand rested on the open door of my vehicle, my eyes lowered to her stomach, and she laughed under her breath.

"You're not going to use this baby as a way to control me."

"How am I controlling you, sweetheart?"

"Let's start with the fact that you've known all this time who my father was, and you didn't bother to tell me because the two of you are in some dick-swinging contest. How is that *not* control?"

"Nari, I'm more than open to having this discussion with you, but before that can happen, you need to get into the car. We're not doing it out here."

"No, I'm not going anywhere with you until you explain why you conveniently left out the very important detail that you knew who my father was."

"I didn't leave out a damn thing. I didn't fucking know. Imagine my surprise the moment I got word that my wife was alone, sitting at a table across from a man who would take her life and not think twice, so we're both at a crossroads here, now get in the fucking car."

"You expect me to believe that you *didn't* know? You, the almighty Kincaid Akel, *didn't* know who my father was?"

"No, sweetheart, I didn't fucking know. Now, get in the gotdamn car. If you want to have this discussion, we can, but again, we will not have it out here like this."

My stance widened at the same time my shoulders expanded. My chin dipped so that our eyes leveled to ensure she understood just how serious I was. If she didn't move in a matter of seconds, I would physically move her myself.

"Fucking tyrant," she muttered under her breath, but at least things between us didn't have to get physical. After she was seated, she slammed the door before I got a chance to close it myself, which had me taking a cleansing breath before I scanned my surroundings for any signs that someone was watching us. Once I determined nothing seemed out of place, I got in and pulled away from the curb with Nari shooting daggers through me.

"If you didn't know, then why make the point of telling my father that he should know that you wouldn't let me anywhere near him?"

"Because I didn't have to know he was your father to make that determination."

"And you don't think that's control? He's my *father*."

"He's a killer."

"So are you."

When my eyes met hers, she didn't back down. I laughed arrogantly. "Lucky for you I'm invested in keeping you safe. I'd be willing to bet my life that's not a sentiment he and I share."

"He's my father. Why wouldn't he want me safe?"

"Because that's not who he is. Regardless of whatever dream he sold you, Eli Manchester will always put his agenda ahead of yours. That means if it serves his purpose, then you don't fucking matter."

"Sounds very familiar." Her heated gaze landed hard on me, and I snorted.

"Not even fucking close."

"You sure? Because what you're describing sounds a lot like you."

"The fact that you would insinuate that we're the same lets me know just how fucking naive you are. We're *nothing* alike."

"What makes you so sure?"

"Because I fucking love you, and he loves the potential that he sees in the prospect of using you for whatever sick fantasy he's dreamed up in his head after learning that you exist."

"You love me?" Her tone was accusatory and snide, which I didn't fucking appreciate. I cut my eyes at her but didn't respond.

"Answer the gotdamn question, Kincaid. Do you love me?"

"More than you will ever be capable of comprehending."

"Then why the fuck did you sleep with another woman?"

Again, I didn't answer, and it triggered something because before I could process what was happening, she slapped me so hard that it took everything in me not to break her fucking jaw from an instinctive reaction. When our eyes finally met again, I could see the moment it registered what she had just done, but she didn't fold.

"I will never in my life put my hands on you, but I promise I can make you suffer in ways that you can never even imagine without ever laying a finger on you. Show me the same respect that I show you."

She snorted. "Fine. Then I'll just go fuck another man because, apparently, that's how we're showing respect."

The best thing Nari could have done at that moment was shut the fuck up. As much as I loved her, she was engaging in a dangerous war with me. One she wouldn't be able to win, so it was a small blessing that she chose to ignore me *silently*.

When we arrived at the house, she and I went in different directions. She climbed the stairs, and I headed straight for my office. I needed time to process what the hell had just happened.

Nari's father was a man who I wanted nothing more than to silence with a bullet. He wanted me on the receiving end of one as well, preferably from his gun. How fucking small did the world have to be? The first thing I did was wrap one hand around a bottle while the other gripped a glass, which I filled to the brim, taking down half in one motion before I landed in the chair behind my desk and refilled it. I wasn't sure how long I sat there repeating the process, but half the bottle was gone by the time I had control of my thoughts.

I finished the last of what was in my glass, gripping the fine crystal snifter in my hand before I sent it flying across the room. Glass shattered against the wall, landing in shards on my office floor. My head met the back of my chair just as my eyes closed.

"That bad?" Darius's voice caused me to snort through my frustration.

"That fucking bad." My fingers massaged my temple before I dragged them across my forehead. A migraine was inches away, hindering the ability for me to think as clearly as I needed.

"What's up? What do we need to do?"

"Kill Eli Manchester," I muttered before lifting my head to see Darius. His expression was pensive, which I understood. Three simple words would tip the scale and cause a rift. *Kill Eli Manchester*. It wasn't as easy as it seemed, not just because of the DNA he had provided my wife.

"I'll stand by whatever call you make, but what you're saying will start a damn war."

"And not just in the streets."

His frown drew deeper. "I don't get it."

"He's Nari's father."

"You're shitting me, right?"

"This mess would be a lot less complicated if I was."

"Damn, how did that get by you?"

A good fucking question.

I prided myself in knowing all the details so I would never get caught with my pants down. The best business strategy was to know every player and the weight of their importance. This one small detail changed the gotdamn game.

"If I had to guess, I didn't know he had a daughter. His name was never listed on any documents. There was no connection to be made. Nari's mother was sixteen when she had her, and her parents handled everything because she was a child. When they found out she was pregnant, they made her give Nari up for adoption, only she was never adopted, so it wasn't necessary to get relinquished rights documented from the father. It's likely why she landed in foster care. There was no contact from her mother or father throughout Nari's life. Nothing at all to point to Manchester before now."

I had done my research because that's who I was, so it was really fucking with me that that one very small, yet important, detail somehow remained unknown until today.

"And what evidence is there now?"

"He confirmed after ambushing Nari today."

"He pulled up on your wife?" Darius's eyes lowered, expressing his feelings on the matter. He didn't like Manchester's stunt any more than I did.

"She was at the penthouse. I'm sure he had people watching once he connected the dots and realized who she was. It would be the smart thing to do because he knew I wouldn't openly welcome him into her life."

"The penthouse? What was she doing over there?"

Running from me!

"Story for another day. I just need to decide what the fuck I'm going to do about this."

My decision was already made. That muthafucker's days were numbered. Nari didn't understand whose blood she carried. Even if I exposed the type of man he was, she wouldn't easily handle the idea of me killing her father. A presence she's wanted in her life from early on as she understood the role of a father. Her emotions would get in the way of logic, and I would end up the bad guy for ridding her of a cancer that would ultimately destroy her heart. It was inevitable. Regardless of Nari being his flesh and blood, she would be handed over as a sacrifice without a second thought if she got in the way of anything he wanted.

"I already know what you're thinking, and that's not an easy call to make." Darius's voice had me exhaling through my frustration.

"He's not worthy of her time or her heart."

"I agree, but he's her father. You can't—"

"I can, and I *will* without hesitation if that's what it comes to."

"At what cost?"

"*She* is the cost. It might take time, but she'll eventually see that I prevented an inevitable disappointment . . . or even worse, placing her life in danger."

"You willing to bet your marriage on that?"

We shared a look of understanding. Darius was issuing a warning. One that I had already tossed over in my head a million times. Killing my wife's father could be the end of us. "I might not have a choice."

"Don't move irrationally. Sit on it. See what his plan is."

I snorted. "His plan is to divide and conquer. Giving him time only strengthens his ability to do so."

"Nah, man. Y'all are solid. It won't be that easy."

I exhaled a sigh and brushed my hand down my face. Darius was astute and immediately picked up on what I wasn't saying.

"What the fuck did you do?"

"Not a damn thing." My eyes cut to him, but his expression didn't change. "Val."

"Come on, Caid. You're still fucking with Val?"

"No, I haven't in months, but my wife believes otherwise."

"How did she come to that conclusion?"

"Val popped up on me in New York. We had words. I made clear I wasn't breaking my vows, not even for her. Apparently, that didn't sit well because her mind crafted a much different picture of what we really were. I'm assuming she found Nari through my social media pages and sent a recording of a call we shared while I was engaged to Aila. The clip makes it seem as if she and I had an agreement about my wife's lack of importance, or rather her role in my life. It was Aila who I was referencing in the recording, not Nari."

"Why the hell was she recording your calls?"

For this exact reason.

"Women like Val thrive when they feel they have leverage. I'm sure it was her way of guaranteeing some type of retribution or control if I ever decided to cut her off."

"Only you can't be controlled."

"I weigh every decision I make, including the consequences. The potential for Val to threaten me with details of our relationship would never matter."

Darius shook his head, laughing under his breath. "Until now. How the hell did you manage to fuck up your marriage before the ink's even dry?"

"I didn't. She only thinks I did because she's too damn emotional to hear me out."

"That's your fault."

"How the hell is that my fault?"

"I hear pregnancy hormones are a bitch. You were the one fucking like a sport trying to make a baby. Now you got one and an emotional-ass wife as well."

And a way to permanently stay connected to Nari!

"I seriously need to stop telling you shit," I groaned, remembering the conversation we had after confirming that Nari was indeed pregnant. He questioned my position with having a kid so soon, and I made clear it had been my intent, which I'd been diligently working toward since the first time I lay between her thighs.

"You don't trust anybody else, so I'm all you've got, but since that's a role we're playing for each other, I wanted your opinion on something."

He seemed uneasy, which let me know it was something serious.

"What's up?"

"I've been tossing around the idea of Lish and I having kids." His eyes hit the floor before he gripped the back of his neck. It took a minute for him to look at me again.

"You two have discussed adoption before." I'd been privy to their conversation about possibly adopting children, but it was never discussed in a way where they decided to move forward.

"We have, but I was thinking about possibly doing in vitro. She can carry a baby; it just wouldn't be hers."

Ahh, now I see where the conflict lies.

"So, how would that work?"

"My sperm and a donated egg."

"So, technically, it would be your kid and not hers?" He nodded. "Have you discussed this with Alisha?"

"Not yet. You think I should?"

"If it's something you're considering, then yes. Open communication helps prevent misunderstandings on both sides. I feel it's vital in all negotiations, but more so in a marriage."

He laughed sarcastically, brushing his hand over his head. "This isn't a business deal. It's about our future, our family, or the potential to have one."

"But a negotiation, nonetheless. I'm curious, though, why now?"

"It's not new for me, you know that. I've always wanted a family, but it's something I was willing to sacrifice if I had to. Shit, man, I love that girl to death. I would give her the world if it were within my power."

"So, if she says no, that it's not something she's willing to do, you can move past it?"

It took him a minute before he responded with a slow nod that wasn't very convincing.

"This is important to you?"

"It is, but it's not a deal breaker. I love my wife, and nothing will change that. Even if she decides kids aren't for us—"

"Kids or having a kid that's yours?"

When he didn't answer, I offered my honest opinion. "If you truly love her like I know you do, then have the conversation and decide together, but you have to be honest and prepared not to get the outcome you want. If that's the case, then you'll have to decide where that leaves the two of you."

"Together. No matter what, that's where it leaves us."

"Then that's all that matters."

He tossed his chin and moved on. "Where do we stand on this thing with Manchester?"

"As of now, I keep Nari away from him. We also keep an eye on what he's got going on. This was intentional and has nothing to do with building family bonds."

"I would agree, but there's a slim chance that he really wants—"

"Not happening. He won't get near her again."

Darius removed his phone and squinted at a message on his screen. When I had his attention once more, his face seemed tense. "This is not the time to get sidetracked. You're taking on a lot and need to be focused."

My position with The Families.

"You don't think I know that. If I could set this on the shelf, I would, but if he pushes the issue, I'll have no choice but to push back. It makes more sense to get ahead of things before it turns costly."

"The price is already inflated, Caid."

Nari.

"I need a few days to get back on the same page with Nari. We'll revisit this then."

He tossed his chin. "Yeah, I need to get going anyway."

I sensed his urgency and understood right away. I recognized the same urgency in myself lately.

"Tell Alisha I said hello."

He chuckled and nodded. While Darius let himself out, I traveled upstairs to check on my wife. She had been distant since we left the penthouse, and it was time for me to make clear that she was and would be my number one priority.

When I found our room empty, my next stop was the guest room at the end of the hall. It was the only one that had an entrance to a balcony, which I learned my wife loved indulging. Sure enough, she was there, curled up in the egg swing, staring out into our backyard. The tranquility was pleasant, but considering the tension between my wife and me, I could not enjoy the lush greens and rainbow of colors sprinkled about.

"We need to talk."

"No, we don't. Not until I'm ready, and I'm not there yet. Please also call whoever the hell you had dismantle the beds unless you want us sleeping on mattresses stacked on the floor."

"Our bed will do just fine. I'm not sleeping on the gotdamn floor, and neither are you."

"So fucking arrogant, but I'm not surprised. When I said *we*, I meant me and my child."

I moved from where my shoulder was anchored against the frame of the French doors, which separated the room from the balcony, and stepped out into the evening air. My eyes roamed briefly before I rounded the front of the swing, blocking Nari's view. "*Our* child and I know exactly what you meant. You seem to forget that there is no running, sweetheart. Not to the penthouse and not down the hall to another room. We sleep together in the same bed, even if you have to resort to childish measures by building walls with pillows to assert your authority."

Her eyes lifted to mine with a vengeance. They blazed with anger, further filtering into her expression with a clenched jaw and tight muscles around her brown orbs.

"Our agreement is that we sleep under the same roof. *Not* in the same bed."

"Fuck that agreement, Nari. It's no longer relevant . . ."

She laughed snidely, untucking her legs from beneath her butt, slowly lowering them over the edge of the swing. Once she was upright, her hands gripped the edge, her fingers so tight that her knuckles drained of their natural color. "It's *very* relevant. You have the best lawyer in the state, possibly even the country. *You're* the one who told me that, remember?"

"I do, and it's true, but he does what I tell him to do—always. I can call him now to confirm if you'd like. If I tell Nathan to burn that shit, he will. What proof do you have that it ever existed?"

"I have a copy."

"Do you, sweetheart? If I'm not mistaken, you threw it at Nathan this morning just before demanding that he amend our terms to permit you to sleep with other men." My eyes lowered to hers, and Nari's lips parted as if she were tempted to speak; however, she decided against it when her mouth slammed shut. I was sure she felt she could trust him. She could. Hell, he damn near cursed me out when he called to inform me that my wife was demanding changes because I cheated on her. I spent twenty minutes convincing my lawyer, whose salary *I* pay, that I hadn't been unfaithful. How the fuck did that turn of events occur, where I had to explain myself to a man *I* cut a check for? "You want to sleep with other men, baby? Am I not enough for you? I guess I truly *am* losing my edge."

"Maybe I do, or maybe I'm simply following your lead. I'm making a judgment call for my sanity."

Which you will pay for later.

"You're testing my patience is what you're doing. Unfortunately, Nathan knows better."

"He promised," she snapped.

I was positive that was his intent. Not many are immune to the spell my wife could cast on the strongest and most determined. It was the craziest shit I had ever seen because she had no clue about the power she held. My good pal Nathan didn't see her coming. Those sinful eyes, paired with her innocence and tortured spirit, were enough to bring any man to their knees and have them risking it all.

I could bear witness.

"I'm sure he did, and he would have stood by the decision had I actually been in the wrong."

"You were. You had sex with another woman." Her voice was just below screaming, but I wasn't alarmed, nor did I match her level of intensity. One of us needed to remain levelheaded.

"No, baby. I didn't."

"I heard you inviting her over after expressing I was a *means to an end*. That call—"

"Wasn't about you. I was referring to Aila."

"You expect me to believe that?"

"I expect you to believe the truth."

"Were you with her in New York?"

"Yes, but not the way she's insinuating. When I'm in town, people talk. She knows my habits and showed up at my place because she's familiar with it."

"But she is the reason you had to call me back." The memory weakened my case.

My pensive gaze remained on Nari. I didn't falter, and I wouldn't lie, never to her. "Yes, but not to have sex with her. It was simply to get a handle on the fact that she showed up in the first place, which I couldn't have done if I had you on the line. She and

I talked, and I made clear that my situation with you wasn't the same as my arrangement with Aila. That, of course, didn't make her happy, so she left with a bruised ego and the need for vengeance. She sought you out to hurt your feelings like I had done to hers."

"You were with her the night you proposed to me."

My patience was wavering. I understood her position. The facts pointed toward what she believed was true, but images were easily altered and twisted to produce favorable results. That was precisely what Val had done.

"I was with Val the night I proposed to *Aila*. *Not* you. The recording she sent you is a call we had before you and I ever met. There are very few things that I value in this world. My word is at the top of that list. The only thing which ranks above my word is you. I have not, and I will not ever, disrespect you by being with another woman, mentally or physically. I won't entertain anyone's advances but yours. I can't be any clearer on my position with you and our marriage."

My phone signaling a call was the only thing that pulled my eyes from my wife. Noticing that it was Cast, I answered immediately.

"Yeah?"

"They just found Knotty with a hole in his head."

"Okay." I frowned, needing him to get to the point.

"In your zone. It was done to send a message—"

"From whom?"

"You."

"The fuck does that mean?"

"Somebody ran up on his guys while they were carrying. Stole the product, dropped three of their guys, and word is they heard that whoever did it said to tell Knotty's boss that 'Kincaid warned him about being on his blocks.'"

"Why the fuck . . ." My eyes lowered to my wife's. She was watching me intently. "Meet me out there in an hour."

"Got it, boss." Cast ended the call, and I returned my attention to Nari.

"I'll be back in a few hours. Don't leave the house. We have a lot to address."

"I'm not a child."

"No, sweetheart, you're not, but you are carrying ours. One thing I refuse to debate is the safety of either one of you. If you have ever believed anything I've ever told you, believe this: you will not *ever* again put your life or our child's life in danger without serious consequences."

Her heated glare remained on me until I left the balcony. I hated to force her hand, but my wife was still learning the importance of trusting my leadership. Until she was clear on what that meant, I would maintain complete control.

"They left the bodies?"

"Yeah, three. I got them loaded up and out of here."

My jaw flexed as I stood with my hands submerged in my pockets, allowing my eyes to move up and down the blocks.

"They took the product too?"

"Yeah. Not sure how much, but it was enough to add to the problem. Knotty's Haitian."

I nodded, understanding. He was family to Toussaint; therefore, a layer of protection extended to each member, regardless of the affiliation. It muddied the waters with potential problems for me if people truly believed I was the one who put in the order to have him killed.

"He's trying to put me in the middle of a war with Toussaint."

"Who is?"

"Manchester."

"That's a lot of work just to come at you about two low levels. Those men you tagged were muscle at best."

"This isn't about Gains and Taylor," I made clear.

"Then who is it about?"

"My wife."

"You're gonna have to make that make sense for me, Caid." Cast's brows pinched as he stared at me.

"He's her father. I just found out. Shit, we both just found out. It's very convenient that hours after the discovery, Knotty ends up with a hole in his head, and my name is attached to it. This could be just to fuck with me or, at the very least, complicate my life because I shut him down with Nari."

"Hold the fuck up. Let's circle back to Eli Manchester being your father-in-law."

"He ain't shit to me, and neither is he anything to my wife. Blood doesn't give you a pass. I just need time for her to catch up and understand he's not worth the time she so desperately wants to give him."

"So she wants to get to know him?"

My eyes lifted to his, delivering my answer.

"That isn't the type of weight you need on your shoulders."

"You're right, which is why it's not happening."

"So, what now?"

"I'll reach out to Toussaint to set up a meeting to make sure he understands this isn't me."

"What if he don't hear you?"

"Then I do what I need to do."

"Knotty is family to him. Things aren't always black and white when it comes to family. Those gray areas are a bitch."

There was a double meaning in his statement. Cast was warning me about handling Manchester. I didn't give a damn what anyone thought. My only concern was my wife and our child. I would do whatever was necessary for them to remain untouched.

"When I get it set up, I'll let you know. And, Cast, be clear; there's no room for anyone to make decisions about the well-being of my wife but me."

He offered a nod, understanding I wasn't trying to hear his thoughts on how I needed to move where she was concerned. Cast wouldn't take offense because he knew me well, but he also wouldn't intervene with his thoughts on what needed to be done regarding Manchester. My word would be the only one that mattered.

CHAPTER 2

NARI.

My body warmed at an alarming rate. I felt him in my dreams, smelled his scent, and absorbed his energy. *My God, I'm so weak for this man.* Even as angry as I was and as hurt as he rendered me emotionally, my body still craved him, even *needed* him.

My fists gripped the sheets as my thighs spread wider. When my groin began to roll over and over again, I lost the battle and took flight. My hips left the mattress, thrusting forward, and were met by the vicious assault of his tongue. That's when it registered. I wasn't dreaming. Kincaid was here, in bed with me, his head between my thighs, his lips and tongue rendering me useless.

Through heavy lids, I peered at my husband's handsome face. His eyes were fastened to mine with a determination that I could feel just as strongly as the wave of pleasure still moving through me. It bubbled in my core, then shot like lightning bolts, reaching every inch of my being.

I had no choice but to brace and allow it to happen. He was in control . . . always in control. That caused a sob to escape. The first one was soft, followed by another, which caused my chest to cave and my spine to tremble.

He was on me quickly, pushing between my thighs, using his body to spread them wider. Pillow-soft lips collided with mine, but the kiss was sensual and tender.

"Don't cry, baby. If you want the truth, all you have to do is shut off your mind and allow your body to pull it from me." Kincaid thrust forward, landing deep, long, and thick, forcing me to bear down from the intrusion. My body jolted from the force used to penetrate me, but when he pulled back and returned, it was gentle and slow. He was still deep, but his movements were calculated and purposely slow. "Haven of truth, remember?" His eyes were on mine, peering with a pleading that caused tears to creep into the corners of my own, threatening to escape. When I closed them, he pulled back and pressed forward, penetrating me deeper.

"Look at me."

I turned my head and refused, which granted me a hand on my chin, forcing me back. "Nari, look at me, baby." Soft kisses peppered my cheeks and then my lips. I peeled my eyes open slowly. "Haven of truth. Anytime I'm here with you, in you like this, I couldn't lie even if I wanted to. I didn't cheat. I wasn't with her. Only you. Only us."

I stared, not saying anything, and he grew agitated, thrusting into me with a little more aggression. "You believe me?"

I did. I couldn't explain it, but with him here in me, connected the way we were, I could feel his truth. He wasn't lying.

My eyes closed, and I nodded, but he growled, hitting me deep again.

"Then say it. Tell me you believe me."

"I believe you."

Kincaid got what he needed because his lips met mine again. This time, they attacked me in a needy manner. He had my mind, body, and soul. There was no defense against how he made me feel, which terrified me.

I loved the way he left me completely useless, powerless. I was sure I couldn't even deliver my name if asked. Everything about me disappeared and became Kincaid when he was in me this painfully deep, finding my spot repeatedly before he left that one and discovered another. This had to be the epitome of delirium. The lines were blurred because I couldn't decide what was real from fake, pleasure from pain. It all blended to perfection while he stroked me with purpose, marking me in a way that would erase any doubts that might still linger behind.

He was communicating. *I. Did. Not. Fuck. Her.*

His gaze weighed heavily on my face, and his eyes fastened to mine while he eased into a steady rhythm that was euphoric. The muscles in his arms and shoulders strained with the controlled movements that he delivered.

"*Uxor Mea. mea agendi ratione.*" (My wife. My inspiration.)

A smile ghosted his lips before they collided with mine. Kincaid pulled out and returned harder, repeating the motion. His body was demanding my attention, and without hesitation, I gave in, hanging on to every ounce of pleasure and pain he provided. He was embedded in me, but not just physically. The man was in my soul, and the reality of him had me terrified again. He could destroy me. This man could permanently damage my entire existence. I wasn't allowed to linger with the thought too long because a few more seconds passed before I shattered into a million tiny little pieces that managed to bind again, making me whole, when he spilled himself into me, burying his face into my neck. His heavy body weighed down against mine, blanketing me in his heat, in his promise, in his love.

When the high settled, my body began to tremble again. I opened my mouth, but the words seemed stuck. Lost. What was I trying to say? What did I need to say?

"I . . ."

His lips gently rested against my forehead and his tone was low and soothing. "Tomorrow. We'll talk tomorrow. Tonight, we sleep." Kincaid shifted to his side, bringing me with him, pulling me closer as if there were any space between us that he could demolish. I closed my eyes, inhaled his presence, and drifted off to sleep.

The next morning, my body came alive when my husband found his way between my thighs again. I was still tender from hours before, but I welcomed the connection. His touch, his feel, his scent felt like home.

I moaned deep within, and it remained lodged in my throat because I was still in a haze and groggy from sleep. When my eyes peeled open, his were waiting, telling of his mood. Dark and possibly angry. I frowned, trying to make sense of what the issue was.

"You think about other men being where I am, Nari?" His voice was eerily calm but icy. My eyes went wild before I rushed my answer.

"No."

Kincaid's head lowered, and I felt a pinch on my nipple. His teeth grazed it once more before biting down again.

"You sure because that's what you insinuated."

"I did not . . ."

That's when it registered. Our argument yesterday before he left. It must have been playing on his mind, spiraling through his thoughts in the worst ways. My husband was insanely jealous and equally possessive.

"Maybe I do . . ." He repeated my words, and his pace increased to a faster rhythm with more intensity. In a movement so unexpected and quick that I didn't have a chance to react, he pulled out of me violently and flipped me over. I landed on my stomach, and he entered me from behind, just as violently as he had withdrawn. Kincaid bound my hands over my head one by one. His long fingers connected them both into one of his large hands with so much strength I was sure they would bruise.

"I asked you if you wanted to sleep with other men. It was a yes-or-no question, sweetheart. *Maybe* is a dangerous response to provide when it comes to you and other men."

His movements were calculated. Hard and deep. I struggled to keep up, to breathe, to deny the pain he caused, but enjoyed the feel of him reaching my depths. Kincaid was making a point. He was issuing a warning and reminder about who I belonged to. No other man was even allowed space in my head and most definitely not allowed access to my body. A body he commanded and controlled, which he reinforced each time he sank into me.

"I was angry."

He snorted and bit my shoulder. "Well, now, so am I."

I felt him, every inch full and hard inside me. His anger made me delirious because it felt good being delivered through deep, purposeful strokes. He drove into me like a madman but with a type of control that he executed with precision.

God, I'm addicted to this man.

His body was heavy against the back of mine, and I surmised it was because he was using his weight to thrust as deep as he possibly could. "Loving you makes me murder with no remorse, no conscience, no discretion. Loving you makes me lose all sensibility. Loving you makes me hurt in ways I can't even imagine because

I haven't experienced the pain yet, but I know it's coming. All of these things will be *your* burden to bear if the word *maybe* ever lives on the tip of your tongue again when I ask you about another man. Understood?"

"Yes." I could barely release that one word because I felt the danger in what he just proposed. He would never lift a finger to hurt me, but anyone who crafted a thought to have any part of me had better be damned.

He took me so fast and hard I was barely able to hold on. The best part was that I loved the feel of his possessiveness wrapping around me, thrusting in me. He was so deep it hurt but in the best way. When I plummeted over the edge, he was right there with me, that last thrust so forceful and intense I felt his muscles tense against me while he grunted through his release.

Heavy breathing was the only sound that danced around us until he calmed enough to regain focus. The insanity subsided, and soft, gentle kisses grazed my skin. "We don't fight dirty. That's not who we are. You don't have to create images in my head to see me, Nari. I do enough of that on my own each time I'm reminded that I don't deserve you, and there's a possibility that I could lose you because I don't."

He was raw, vulnerable, and confiding in me one of his fears . . .
Losing me.

It wasn't until that moment that I realized how deep we both had fallen. We were lost to each other in such a dangerous way that our thoughts cut deeper than our realities. The same way I tortured myself imagining him with another woman, he'd done the same imagining me with another man.

"Come, let's shower. We need to talk."

Another kiss met my shoulder before my body instantly chilled from his absence. It wasn't just the warmth of his body but also the warmth that his connection to my soul created. How the hell was I going to survive this man? *How?*

I sat on the island in the kitchen, scrolling through my notifications while Kincaid rummaged through the refrigerator, looking for something to prepare for breakfast. I offered to cook, but he insisted that he had it covered. I was grateful because there wasn't an inch of me that didn't seem to ache with a reminder of the past twenty-four hours. Catching sight of him out of the corner of my eye had my attention, leaving my phone seconds later. I visually devoured his body, which was bare from the waist up. It was impossible not to enjoy how his arms and back muscles flexed with the simplest motion. His abs bubbled subtly under his beautiful brown skin, and that deep, defined V guided my line of sight to the weight that bounced about against the cotton sleep pants that sat low on his waist, hanging loosely over his long legs.

His appearance was sinful, and he knew it based on the arrogantly smug grin that seemed to linger each time he caught me enjoying the visual. My body betrayed me like it always did by way of my stomach taking flight and my thighs clenching. The act was yet another reminder of how much virility this man released between my thighs. I flinched, and he eyed me suspiciously before his regard trailed down my body, pausing at my inner thighs. They were already bruised from the pressure of his body being wedged between them. I watched him inspecting me and noticed how his face softened with regret.

"I don't break easily." I tried my hand at humor, but his jaw tensed, and I could see the veins in his neck pulsing. "You cook?" I tried again. It took a minute before his posture relaxed, but he let go of the thoughts that seemed consuming him.

"Some, but I can't promise I'm good at it."

I grinned, shaking my head. "Maybe I should take over."

He laughed in a way that was light but edgy. "I won't kill us." I was grateful when his attention left me because it allowed me to clear another message from Joey. I had already blocked him several times, but he would make a new account when I did and keep trying. With the way my relationship was all over the place with Kincaid lately, the last thing I needed was another reason for him to fly off the handle, and I didn't want to be the reason why Joey ended up on a missing person's report. Placing my phone facedown, I focused on Kincaid.

"I hope not. What are you making?"

"Eggs and toast. I don't know if I can manage waffles."

"I'll survive."

He moved through the process, and I watched. We didn't speak much other than me commenting on his remedial cooking skills while he playfully warned me to be grateful for his efforts. When he finished, we both had a plate of cheese eggs and toast with butter and jelly. Orange juice filled both our glasses while I added a cup of hot tea.

"So, how does this work?" I asked, filling my mouth with eggs. After I swallowed, I added, "This talking thing?"

"Ask what you want, and I'll tell you what you need to know."

"Of course."

He delivered a visual warning, and I returned one. Kincaid exhaled a harsh breath, lowering his fork before he allowed both hands to rest outside of his plate. His knuckles cracked when his fingers curled into a fist.

"Ask."

"Why don't you and my father like each other?"

"His older brother and my father have a history. I'm unsure of all the details because it wasn't necessary. I've always relied on my father's leadership with whom I needed to trust."

"So, you two are at odds because of issues that linger between them?"

"It's not that simple, but at the root of it, yes. Loyalty dictates the choices you make. His was to his family as mine was to my own. That put us against each other in the past. There was already bad blood, but he pushed, and I pushed back. It's not anything I will ever go into detail with you about. Just know that what he presents to you will never be the heart of who he really is. I also realize that regardless of what I tell you about him, there will always be that question lingering in your mind about whether I'm trying to sway your opinion because of my feelings about him or if I'm simply attempting to protect you from a threat."

"A threat?"

"Yes, sweetheart. Make no mistake about it. DNA or not, he is a threat to your well-being. The reality of his intent might not surface immediately, but it's inevitable. His objective is to do you harm or use you as a weapon against me. My position is to prevent that from happening."

"So then, where does that leave me?"

"Untouched."

Kincaid's teeth raked across his bottom lip and with intense eyes, he stared across the table at me in a way that had me struggling to maintain their harshness.

"I've never had a family. I wanted it more than anything I can ever imagine in my life, and now, he's right here at my fingertips, and you're promising that we'll never have a chance to get close. How am I supposed to feel? What am I supposed to do?" I was falling. My emotions rushed through me like a raging bull charging toward a red cape. My breathing became labored while my body attempted to regulate the chaos swarming at the base of my emotions.

"You're my wife, the mother of my child—two reasons why I will never apologize for my decisions about your safety. I can't be moved on this, not right now. Until I have a guarantee that you come out of this with not so much as a harsh breath against your skin, then I do what I feel is best."

I pushed my chair back and stood. He moved at the same time I did, closing the space between us, but he didn't touch me with his hands—just his chest to mine. "You've never had a family. I can't begin to imagine what it means to be alone in the world, but I know with certainty what it feels like to have you in mine. *I'm* your family, Nari. *This* is your family." His hand moved between us and pressed against my stomach. Kincaid kissed my forehead before he stepped around me, leaving me with my thoughts. How could something so simple feel like such a betrayal? To have my father in my life, I had to be disloyal to my husband.

We were both dressed and out of the house a few hours later. I didn't bother asking where we were going because things between us felt off and tense. It wasn't until we reached his parents' property that he finally spoke up.

"I have a few things I need to do. I figured you could use the company."

"Or you could use the peace," I shot back. Instead of responding, he got out, rounding the car to open my door, but I didn't wait. I was out and moving to the front door before he reached me.

Kincaid was on my back, his chin resting on my head while he reached around me to enter the code to let us in. As soon as the keypad flashed green, his arm circled my waist, and his hand gently pressed my stomach. "Anger doesn't bother me. I can handle your anger as long as I know you're safe."

He moved around me and stepped into his parents' home without giving me a chance to respond. His mother bent the corner with a huge smile until she picked up on our energy. It was impossible not to feel the divide between us because when we were in accord, our connection was palpable to the point where it was all-consuming and suffocating.

She approached me first with a tight hug before she moved to her son. They were still healing, but she was better and rebuilding their bond. She smiled after he enclosed her in an embrace, which ended with a kiss on the cheek. "I wasn't expecting you."

"Oh, so you didn't know you were babysitting me today?" I shot my husband a heated gaze, but he brushed it off.

"I have a few things to take care of, and I figured you two could use the time to catch up."

"Absolutely. I'm sure we have plenty to discuss." His mother had years of knowledge and experience from being a wife to a man who moved with hidden purposes and agendas. She wasn't protecting his feelings. She was in favor of mine. The look she delivered was proof.

"I'll be a few hours." Kincaid hooked my chin, landing a kiss before he was out the door.

"You feel so distant. I've missed you." She slipped an arm around my waist, briefly allowing her head to rest at my shoulder before we moved to the kitchen. She made tea, and we talked about the baby and how I felt. Her eyes were illuminated with the joy of being a grandparent. Then sadness covered her mood like a dark cloud when she thought of experiencing her grandchild alone without her husband.

"I miss him so much." She smiled as her eyes ghosted. "So much it hurts sometimes."

"I can imagine." It was odd, but I could be raging with anger, ready to slit my husband's throat, but the thought of being without him would steady my hand so I wouldn't actually consider lifting the knife. I couldn't fathom not having him, even when he pushed me to the point of having murderous thoughts.

"You can." She chuckled, her smile increasing after a bit of silence. "Being loved by an Akel man is like floating on air. They consume you completely, taking all you have to give and filling you with their essence. The power, the strength, the pride they feel from having you by their side. I know my son. He's a carbon copy of his father. Selfish and demanding, but when you have him, you have all of him. He implanted his heart and soul in there after stealing yours for safekeeping. It's deliciously scary how skilled they are. My husband is even selfish in his absence because he refuses to release me." She shrugged. "But I'm his to keep and always will be."

"Kincaid's complicated in a way that I'm struggling to keep up with, but I do love him."

She laughed hard before sipping her tea. "Indeed you do, sweetheart."

I expelled a cleansing breath. "However, because I love him, I can't love my father. I can't even get to know the man who's a part of my existence."

Her eyes narrowed just a bit. "What do you mean?"

"I know who my father is. I just found out, but there's bad blood between him and Kincaid." I scoffed. "*That's* why I'm here. You're babysitting me because your son doesn't trust me to make the right decisions. He thinks I'm going to do something dumb."

She frowned a little more. "Who is your father?"

"Eli Manchester."

The color drained from her face and her eyes closed. I watched as she swallowed hard before her eyes slowly peeled open.

"You know him?"

"Come with me. I need to show you something."

She was suddenly anxious and it had something to do with my father. This was only getting worse. We moved through the house to her husband's office. The look, the smell, and the feel reminded me of both Kincaid and his father. The space mirrored the office Kincaid kept in our home, but that wasn't the only memory that surfaced. My mind drifted to the day of his father's funeral, and my mood soured a little thinking of his ex.

His mother opened a drawer and lifted a key she had used to unlock another. After digging through files and folders, she handed me a stack of photos. My stomach grew queasy at the sight of a woman who had been beaten. Her face was bruised with black and purple marks, and her eyes were swollen to the point of being unable to open. After sifting through several of them, I noticed a label printed in the corner of the last one.

Corinne Akel

"Is this . . ." My eyes lifted to meet hers, and she nodded.

"Yes. The history between the Manchesters and Akels is torrid and entangled. Everett, Eli's older brother, and Yusuf were close. They came up together, but the two were different and always would be. Yusuf's life was laid out for him. His father and grandfather were connected, which meant he would be too. I met Yusuf in college. I was an undergrad while he was in the last year of gaining his master's. Everett didn't attend, but he was always around because they were good friends. I was struggling, barely able to keep my head above water. Being a product of a system that wrote me off seconds after my eighteenth birthday wasn't always easy." We shared a look of understanding before she continued.

"Yusuf says I was a fighter; always had been. He fell in love with me, and that was that. Things were good . . . until the time came for Yusuf to take his place officially. I had no idea what the hell was going on between them, nor had I any idea of the type of man who stole my heart. Everett did and wanted to be a part of it. He assumed his friendship with Yusuf would grant him acceptance, but The Families are very selective. There are so many layers of how things work. I still don't fully understand. I damn sure didn't back then, but what I knew was that Everett would never be what my husband was. When the time came, he would be left behind. Everett tried to convince Yusuf that they could be great doing things independently. His father had his hands in a few ventures that he deemed worthy of praise. Guns and enforcement. They strong-armed businesses to pay for their protection. The Manchester name was tainted and he wasn't respected. The Families do illegal things, but they maintain a certain level of honor. They have rules. Their members own businesses and build legacies to balance the dark side of things. That's what Everett didn't understand. There was no comparison to his family and the Akels. With Yusuf, there was no choice to be made. His destiny had been decided before he ever took his first breath."

Her eyes met mine, communicating what I already knew— *the same as Kincaid's had.*

"I was out with friends late one night. After they drove me home, he caught me at the door, forcing his way in. Everett wore a mask to hide his face, but I had been around him enough to know his eyes, his scent, his voice. He beat me until I was barely conscious, then told me to tell Yusuf that if he took his place with The Families, I would always be a target."

I felt my body tremble from the thought. I was now in the same place she had been all those years ago. Loving a man whose existence placed me in harm's way.

"Everett was desperate and assumed if he couldn't convince Yusuf to deny his place, the threat of losing me would decide for him. He wanted my husband to believe my being attacked was connected to The Families. Everett knew how much Yusuf loved me. What he didn't count on was that I could identify him."

"What happened?"

"Yusuf married me and took his place with the syndicate. Everett went missing. They found his body months later. Someone shot him in the head and cut out his heart. The heart was delivered to Everett's family before his body was found. From what I understand, Eli is the one who found what was left of his brother at their parents' home."

"Did he do it? Was it Yusuf who killed him?"

She nodded softly.

"Does Kincaid know?"

"He knows I was assaulted right before I married his father. He just doesn't know by whom and he never will if I can help it. He found the pictures and demanded answers. His pride wanted to end the person who put their hands on me. I know what my son is and what he's capable of. There's enough darkness in his life, and I refused to add to what already exists. I never told Kincaid what Everett had done to me all those years ago. His father wouldn't either. The Akel men are black and white with some things. For the women they love, they lose all sensibility. Everett was no longer breathing, but his brother was. Eli would have been a target for the anger that Kincaid couldn't extend to Everett. I didn't want him in that position. Neither did his father."

"If he didn't know, why are they at odds?"

"He felt his father's hate for their family. He understood the silent warning, even if he didn't know why it had been given. Kincaid never questioned his father about certain things. Yusuf's word was law. Over the years, Eli and my son simply became enemies because that's how life plays out sometimes. The universe's cruel little joke, I suppose. Things are different now. Eli found a way in. He became a useful resource. He changed the legacy his father built, and instead of strong-arming businesses, he presented the business owners with an offer they couldn't refuse, and they paid him willingly. He's connected by default. I don't know all the details, but he can't be touched without approval from the syndicate. If you push, Kincaid will break the rules. He'll lose everything, but he won't care. He won't think straight because all he'll see is you. Yusuf didn't think when it came to Everett; he moved off rage and regretted not being there for me. My son is his father in more ways than one, the same as Eli is also his brother."

She was telling me this as a warning to stay away from Eli.

"I know your heart is at odds. There are holes you yearn to have filled, but trust me when I say Eli is poison of the worst kind. Some men don't deserve the love of others because they're not capable of giving it in return. They're also not capable of handling others with care. That man will hurt you one way or another if you let him get close, and that will destroy my son. So I'm asking you to trust him, please."

I nodded. She lost her husband and was begging me not to be the reason why she lost her son. The only problem with making that promise was that I would never know *my* father. I wouldn't necessarily say that I wanted to after what I just learned, but I couldn't deny that a seed had been planted, a sprouting possibility of having a connection. I now understood the consequences and refused to be the person responsible for doing damage to Kincaid or his mother.

CHAPTER 3

KINCAID.

I sat in my car, flipping the business card Eli had left for my wife. The sleek black cardstock moved through my fingers, feeling as if it weighed a ton when, in reality, it was featherlight. Things were changing. I didn't know how they would end, but I knew who wouldn't be a casualty . . .

My wife.

I placed the card in the center console before my eyes landed on the multicolor building. Nari's mother was in there. She wouldn't be expecting me, but that was my plan. After leaving Nari with my mother, I drove straight to the airport and got on my jet to make the hour-and-a-half flight to Miami. What happened while I was here would depend on what her mother told me.

The minute I stepped inside, she frowned, pointing to the table we used when she met my wife for the first time. She whispered something to the young girl behind the counter before wiping her hands on the towel tossed over her shoulder. She placed it on the counter before coming to join me.

"Is she with you?"

I stared at her face, inspecting every inch. I could see what Nari would look like years from now. Her mother was beautiful. They shared that in common.

"Is she?" Her voice elevated because I hadn't answered, making her anxious.

"No."

Her frown grew deeper.

"Then why are you here?"

"To see you."

"About?"

"Before I allowed you to meet my wife—"

"*My daughter* . . ." She cut me off, and my fist balled, causing my knuckles to crack. She didn't know me, so she wasn't aware of what lines not to cross. I would give her a pass.

"*My wife*," I reiterated before continuing. "I asked you to promise me she would never be placed in harm's way by your doing. Not with her physical being or emotional state."

"And she hasn't." Her spine straightened, causing her shoulders to square a little more. I was sure she was on the thin side due to her condition. I knew a little about depression and its ability to steal your appetite. The mood swings and medications were the reason.

"Eli Manchester." The name had her visibly shaken even though she attempted to hide the reaction. I noticed everything. Maybe it was because I had become an expert on reading my wife, which gave me insight into her mother, or possibly I was just talented in the art of reading people in general.

"How-how do you know that name, that he's—"

"Nari's father?" My expression remained even, but hers fell fast. "You sent him to her. That means you sent harm her way. Something you promised me you wouldn't do."

I studied her again. Trying to read the reaction that followed my words and I had my answer before her mouth delivered it.

She doesn't know.

"I would never. He doesn't even know he has a daughter. I refused to allow him to know about her."

This proved what I had already assumed. Eli lied about how he knew of my wife. Now, the question was, how had he found out and what the hell did he want? He might have recognized Endia when he looked at Nari's face. It was hard not to see the striking resemblance if you knew the two. Maybe he'd gone to her family for answers. They wouldn't be able to provide much other than confirmation that she did indeed have a daughter. He would assume she was his by doing the math. It wouldn't be that complicated to piece together a timeline.

"Has he reached out to you?"

"No. I haven't seen or heard from him since I found out I was pregnant. The man was toxic. I was young and dumb for falling in love with the devil."

The way she looked at me exposed her darkest secrets. She was afraid of Eli. Whatever he had done wasn't something she wanted to remember.

"Do your parents know?"

She shook her head quickly. "No, I never told. I didn't trust them to protect me. In their eyes, I had a bastard child with a nameless, faceless man."

She snorted, looking off into blank space, likely lost in her thoughts. "It's why they refused to let me keep her. It's also why they lied to me about who would have her." Endia's eyes met mine again. "I would never send the devil to my child's front door. Even if I know one lives behind it and will protect her."

My eyes danced with amusement. "Are you calling me a devil?"

She shrugged. "You are in some ways. I can feel it. Just not the kind that would hurt my baby. Others, yes. I knew the day you came to see me that you would end my life to protect hers. You love Nari, and that's good enough for me to trust you."

"I do."

I wondered if she had the same gift as her daughter. She said she could *feel it*. That meant she was perceptive to things about me I hadn't revealed. Some had the gift to see and feel what others couldn't. I had that with my wife, but only her. It was a dangerously calming sensation.

"So, now what? Eli now knows I kept her from him. That man doesn't want to be a father. He's incapable of loving anyone but himself. I wasn't the only woman he took advantage of. There were several, and he shared them with others in his circle. He passed women around like it was nothing. I was lucky enough, if you can call it that, that he was partial to me. Eli refused to allow anyone else to touch me. There's no way I would want my daughter to be a part of his life and I'm positive he only cares that she exists because he feels like I stole from him. He had a thing about that: *stealing*. The thought of anyone taking what he believed to be his made him crazier than he already was, which was dangerous."

She's referring to Nari when she referenced stealing from Eli. That doesn't sit well with me.

"He won't touch you. Tell them you're leaving for a while." I tossed my chin to the counter.

"A while?"

"Yes, a few months."

"I can't do that; they won't hold my job, and I need it."

"They won't need to. You'll be fine, but you have to trust me."

We were at war. Our eyes battled; neither of us prepared to surrender, but she retreated first. "Where am I going?"

"To spend time with your daughter."

I couldn't allow my wife to forge a relationship with her father, but I could offer a compromise . . .

Her mother.

I stood, and she hesitated briefly, but followed. I posted up by the door while she disappeared in the back, then joined me, carrying a fabric purse and a jacket. We drove to her tiny apartment and she packed the little she had before we went to the airport. She was quiet, not saying much because she was deep in thought. I studied her for a while, wondering what plagued her thoughts before I decided to finish some work. I made calls and checked financial reports, which allowed time to pass quickly. After we landed, her things were loaded in my car and I drove to our home to get her settled before I went to pick up my wife. I wasn't sure how she would react to what I had done and I didn't want my mother there to witness if things didn't work in my favor. Lately, the two of them were as thick as thieves, which would make me the bad guy regardless of whether I was right or wrong.

I sat on the balcony, enjoying the quiet. With a glass in my hand, I stared into the evening sky. It was rare I was allowed a minute for my mind to slow down and settle into a state of peace. I had to force it this time, but I managed. It was a struggle, but I was learning to be in tune with everything around me, which was how I sensed her before she spoke.

"Why is she here?"

"You don't want your mother here?"

"Yes, but I didn't think *you* would. She's the reason he found me."

"Your mother didn't send Eli to you. He lied."

"How do you know?"

When my wife came into view, I lifted my eyes to hers and took in her appearance. She had a fresh face, and her hair was in its natural, curly state, parted down the center and tucked behind her ears. She had changed from the jeans she wore to my mother's house and was now in a cotton dress hanging loosely around her body and reaching her ankles. Her nipples were hard, pushing through the fabric, giving away that she wasn't wearing a bra. My dick swelled.

"I asked." I placed the drink beside me and reached for Nari, pulling her between my legs. She frowned, still partially angry, but didn't back away. Angry about what, I didn't fucking know. She was always at odds with me for one reason or another. Although I preferred her heaven, I was used to feeling her hell.

"And you believed her?" When I looked up, curious eyes were waiting, mocking me. She knew me well. I didn't trust people, hardly ever.

"I believed her reaction more than her words. I'm good at reading people. I find their truth in the simplest things, like a shift of their eyes, the tone of their voice, the vibration of their heartbeat, or the tempo of their pulse. It's how I know you're angry with me about something."

"I'm not."

My hands gathered the material of her dress, bringing it high enough to ease my hands beneath it so I could feel her skin. I loved how it felt like silk on the pads of my fingers.

"You are, but I'll fix that later."

She cracked a smile, and I gripped the back of her thighs, bringing her closer. When she leaned into me, her arms cradled my head, and I pressed it against her stomach.

"You sent me to your mother's house like I'm a child."

"Nothing I do is intended to hurt or mishandle you."

"I know." She exhaled a short breath. "It just feels that way sometimes. You hover and hold on so tightly that it suffocates me."

"That's love, sweetheart."

"I'm still trying to understand what that means. It's hard to think clearly when you're all over me and in me. Give me space to navigate."

There is no space between us.

I pressed kisses against her stomach, wishing the fabric wasn't between me and her skin. If I changed that, I'd be inside of her without a doubt.

"I'll give you whatever you need as long as I know it won't harm you."

"I've decided not to push when it comes to Eli."

Honestly, I hadn't expected her to concede so quickly, but I decided not to question her reasoning. I would take what I could get.

"Good. It won't do you any good."

He will never know the beauty of you because he will never get close enough to get the chance.

"All my life, I've felt incomplete. There was so much of myself I didn't know because I didn't have my parents. You have to understand that a part of me won't feel whole without him. You had your parents, while all I could do is miss the presence of mine. It won't make sense to you, and I can't explain it, so I won't try."

I understood the void. Maybe not to the degree she experienced his absence, but I understood. Regardless of that understanding, it fucking hurt. She was telling me I wasn't enough, and for a man like me, her words were a knife in my chest, twisting and turning, inflicting the worst type of pain.

"I'll spend my entire life doing whatever's necessary until you feel whole."

Until you realize I'm enough . . .

"Why do you hate him?"

"I don't hate him. For me to hate him, I would have to care first. He's never been important enough for me to care about. I simply don't respect his kind. There's no honor in a man who has no moral compass. Our grievances in the past have been monetary. A dick-swinging contest from inflated egos. When he pulled you into the equation, things became personal. Once he crossed that line, there was no coming back. I meant what I said. Nothing touches you—ever, not even a man who shares your blood."

Nari delivered a look that expressed curiosity; however, understanding kept her words hidden.

"Thank you for bringing my mother back with you."

"You're welcome."

"I'm going to make sure she's settled."

"I'll wait up," I promised. Bringing Endia to our home was a way to maintain balance in my home, but it wasn't until this moment that I realized it meant I had to share. I didn't like to fucking share . . . especially not my wife.

She stepped away, and I didn't bother to watch her leave our room or her mother would have been on her own, settling herself into the new accommodations we provided. Nari dividing her time was about to test my resolve. I could already feel it.

CHAPTER 4

NARI.

"**W**hy are they here?" I pointed to the men standing near the door. I remembered them from the night we attended the fundraiser. They drove us there and back home that night. My husband was fully dressed in a suit, similar to the ones they wore. However, as always, his fit in a tempting and dangerous way. Theirs were . . .

Just suits.

"I'm heading out. If you leave, they'll drive you."

His eyes were serious and dark, challenging me to contest his decision. I wouldn't win. We both were clear on that, but he expected me to engage in a verbal sparring match. Not today. I was mentally exhausted with the weight of my new life. I didn't have the energy to instigate an argument I wouldn't win.

"How long will you be gone?"

Kincaid met me at the bottom of the stairs, which put me about a foot above him in height since I paused on the last one.

"Most of the day, but I'll be home in time for dinner. Will you cook?" His teeth raked his bottom lip. It was presented as a question, but he wasn't asking.

"Yeah, I can. Any requests?"

"Whatever you make will be fine."

"Got it, boss." It was my way of showing my compliance sarcastically. Truthfully, I didn't mind cooking for my husband. I just didn't like how much control he'd had over my life these past few days. I was beginning to feel suffocated by his existence. He continued studying me, silently assessing my mood. I hated when he did that because he was somehow always spot-on. We both could read each other expertly, and I was positive it wasn't normal.

"Our wedding." His arm encircled my waist, lowering me from the last step. I tilted my head back to meet his eyes while his chin dipped, giving me complete access.

"What about it?"

"We've had a lot going on, but maybe you can focus on the planning. I'm sure your mother and mine would love to map it all out with you."

"What's the point? We're already married. Everyone knows."

That taunting smile slipped into place. My body tensed with reminders of how he'd explored every inch of it last night. "Of course, they do. However, I feel it's necessary to present my wife to the world properly. You deserve a grand entrance." He pressed a kiss to my lips, triggering my body. I leaned into him, moaning slightly when his tongue began to explore.

"You just want me busy and preoccupied." My eyes rolled and his lowered in a hooded manner.

"Agreed, but I also want you to have the wedding you deserve."

"I already did." I shrugged.

"Not even close." Kincaid's lips brushed mine again and his hand at the small of my back brought me closer. He was hard against my stomach, and I was tempted to delay his departure but decided to push past the thought. I was abnormally addicted to this man in ways that had to be unhealthy. Instead of getting lost in my lustful thoughts, I focused on the topic at hand.

"Can we compromise?"

"In what way?"

"How about we just do a reception? Maybe a big dinner and make it a formal event instead of a wedding."

"We can do whatever you want, sweetheart. I just assumed you would want a proper wedding."

"Our wedding was perfect, and there's no point in putting on a show that will overshadow the memories of the real thing. That's the one that matters most to me."

Kincaid stared for a long moment, attempting to be sure I was being truthful. Once satisfied, he nodded, confirming that he agreed to my request.

"I'm okay with whatever you decide. Call me if you need me." One last kiss was granted before I felt his fingers brush across my stomach. He looked down then stepped away.

After he left, I entered the kitchen where I found my mother sitting at the table with a book and a mug of coffee. She smiled when I entered, whispering good morning. I returned the greeting. It felt weird having her here. Something I'd wanted all my life, and now that it was tangible, my spirit felt conflicted.

"How did you sleep?" I asked after I dropped a bagel in the toaster and removed the orange juice.

"Like a baby. It's quiet here, but not the kind of quiet that makes your heart race because you don't know what's lurking in the dark. It's the type of quiet that covers you like a cozy blanket. It's been a long time since I've had that type of peace. You're blessed."

Her smile was soft, but something behind her eyes expressed the type of darkness she had experienced throughout life.

"Why did you leave home?"

My mother still gripped her mug with both hands. I watched her fingers create a rhythm against the light gray ceramic piece while she tossed the question around as if deciding on an answer. I added more of what I knew. "Shayla said you were depressed."

My mother's eyes squinted slightly. "Your niece."

I could see the *oh* flash through her eyes.

"You didn't know about her?"

"No. I haven't seen or talked to my parents since the night I left."

I nodded, removing my bagel in search of the cream cheese. Once I was done, I joined my mother at the table, sitting to her left and taking a huge bite.

"She told me that too."

"She?"

"Shayla. I've never met her mother or your parents." I should have said my aunt and grandparents, but they weren't that to me. They were just people who knew I existed and didn't want to get to know me.

"Are you close?"

I snorted, shaking my head. "No. We met, lived together for a few months, then she stole what little money I had and disappeared. I wanted a connection; she wanted someone to split bills with."

"I'm sorry."

"Don't be. Not your fault or mine. Some people just are who they are." I shrugged. "But why didn't you go back? Hell, why did you leave in the first place?" I was desperate for anything she would share to help me better understand her life.

"Have you ever felt like you were drowning? Like everything around you was restricting your ability to think, to feel, to breathe?" Her eyes were distant.

"I kind of feel like that now. I'm new to all this." I tossed my hand in the air. "It's a lot to take sometimes."

She laughed, shaking her head. "I can imagine, but it's not the same. Your husband loves you. He's not trying to suffocate you, and if by default it happens, he pulls you to the surface so you can breathe again. I had no one to pull me to the surface, so I left."

"Were they . . ."

"No." She shook her head softly. "They weren't bad people. My parents didn't understand me. They refused to believe I was lost in a way that I couldn't find myself without help. My parents loved me. They just didn't know how to love me the *right* way, which is how I ended up spending my entire life searching for anyone who could." She laughed vaguely. "Never happened, though. I embarrassed them when I got pregnant with you. I think it was hard for my parents to move past the shame, although it was my decision and no reflection on them."

"But your sister did the same thing. She had Shayla."

"I'm guessing by then, they'd given up on clinging to the false image of what their daughters should be. Who knows? I wasn't there. The reason I didn't go back is because it would hurt too much. There would always be reminders of you. I was young. Too damn young to be somebody's mother, but I still loved you regardless. You weren't with me, but you've always been a part of me. Being there with them wouldn't allow me the space to remember what I lost. They wanted me to forget it happened, to forget there was a piece of me somewhere out there in the world." Her soft gaze shifted to me. "I couldn't do that, so I left and didn't look back." She stilled before lifting her mug, sipping while lost in her thoughts.

"What about my father? Why didn't you go to him?"

Her eyes turned dark. "He's not the kind of man you hand your life over to without consequences. I realize you want to know him and feel like he's a part of you, but he's not. You don't want that type of darkness in your life. He's toxic."

"But you loved him, right?"

She laughed in a way that was void of humor. "I fell in love with the devil. Eli was a grown man who had no business with a child. A young, dumb kid searching for something I couldn't define. What I found was a monster that lurked in the dark. He was the worst kind."

"He hurt you?"

"Emotionally, yes. He never had to lay a finger on me because his words were enough." She tapped her temple. "He got in here with the intent to destroy and control." My mother drifted somewhere for a minute before she continued. "What grown man lies with a child? And yes, I did so willingly, but he knew better even if I didn't. He saw the weakness, the longing, and he used that to make me believe he was there to save me from the pitfalls of life, but mostly, he managed to make me believe he could save me from the loneliness I struggled with.

"When I found out I was pregnant with you, I almost told him. I showed up at his house with the test in my purse, but found out just how much of a devil he really was. There was another woman there. She was young too. Probably only a few years older than me, at best. The door was open and I peeked in. She was curled up on the floor and Eli was kicking the woman in her stomach. She did her best to prevent the inevitable, using her hands to cover her body protectively while he yelled that no bitch was gonna have his kid without his permission. He said she 'stole' from him. He felt that her getting pregnant was stealing when he knew what the hell he was doing. Eli never used protection. Ever.

"God has a way of showing you things. It's up to you to make sense of them. That could have been me. It probably would have been had I stayed, which is why I never told him about you. I refused to tell my parents either for fear that they would find him and try to hold him accountable. Kincaid is right to keep that monster away from you."

"That's why you wouldn't tell me about him when I asked. You protected me from him then and you're protecting me from him now."

She laughed, this time with light in her eyes. "Your husband is protecting you. Well, actually, he's protecting both of us."

"That's kinda his thing," I grinned, and she nodded.

"I'm aware. He's the kind that loves hard. Don't judge him too harshly. He only knows one way, and that's *his* way. It's what he trusts."

I frowned a little and she smiled wider. "You give him a lot of shit."

That time, I was the one who laughed. "Maybe."

"You do, but he lets you because you hold more power over him than you know."

"You must know secrets that I don't," I mumbled. She smiled brightly, lifting her mug.

"I know what you know."

Deep down inside, I understood. In ways that I had yet to master, I did control my husband. It was just that my control was overshadowed by his because Kincaid had a handle on maneuvering in his world. I was still trying to figure it out.

"So, since you're here . . ." I lifted my bagel, allowing my teeth to sink into it. The cream cheese melted against my tongue. ". . . You can help me plan this fancy dinner. Kincaid seems to think it will keep me occupied enough to keep me out of harm's way."

The smile started with her eyes before her lips curved. "Or maybe he simply wants you to have the type of introduction to society that you deserve as his *wife*." She shrugged, and I rolled my eyes.

"You heard that?"

"I did, but I would be honored to help. However, I'm not sure how much I can." She paused and waved her hand the same as I had done earlier. "This is new to me too."

"Then I guess we have a lot to figure out." She nodded softly, her expression matching mine. We didn't have to exchange the words for them to pass between us.

This has been a long time coming!

I spent the day with my mother. We did a little surfing and got ideas for the dinner reception, but mostly enjoyed each other's presence. We both asked questions, attempting to move closer to each other. She would occasionally show the remorse she felt from not being in my life, and when that happened, I reassured my mother that she should have no regrets. Being around her now, getting to know the woman she was, I understood the motivation behind her decisions a little more. She did indeed want me. My mother had loved me from the day she learned of my existence, but a child raising a child wasn't ideal. Especially not one who suffered from the demons my mother struggled with. I experienced the pain and resentment from not having family, but I was also able to forgive. I made that clear when I hugged her tightly and released the words several hours ago before she retreated to her room. *I'm not angry or resentful.*

She stayed with me while I prepared dinner for Kincaid, then mentioned she was tired. I knew my mother was only attempting to give us privacy after the call she overheard between Kincaid and me. I mentioned I would have dinner ready when he got home. He promised it wouldn't be past eight and that he had been looking forward to spending time alone with me.

Once she was in her room, I showered and changed. I raked through my closet, attempting to find something appealing, but ended up settling on one of his gray T-shirts. They were my favorite things, and I realized they were his too, primarily because of the easy access when I wore nothing beneath them. But also because I mentioned that it made me feel like he was wrapped around me even in his absence.

By 7:45, he was walking through the door. His handlers left after a brief conversation with Kincaid. They had been there all day but were experts on staying out of the way. So much so that I forgot they had been there until one came in to request water. I offered them lunch, which they refused—just water.

After a quick shower, Kincaid joined me in the kitchen. He was dressed in a crisp white tee and navy shorts trimmed in white and hanging loosely around his waist but still fitting in a way that didn't look oversized or sloppy. Always put together. That was his thing.

"Did you make dinner or are *you* dinner?" Kincaid pressed behind me, his hands moving beneath his shirt, up the sides of my thighs, resting at my hips.

"Possibly both."

A low, throaty growl slipped through his lips before they made contact with my neck. "Don't tempt me."

I smiled, allowing my neck to fall to the opposite side, giving him more access. He didn't waste the opportunity because his lips were all over me. Soft kisses abounded, causing my skin to tingle like he was delivering electronic pulses. That's what it felt like, or maybe I was just hypersensitive to this man.

"You're going to have all my clothes smelling like you." His nose glided down the curve of my neck before he pinched my skin with his teeth.

"Do you want me to stop wearing your things?"

"No, I like it."

"I know." I grinned, turning to face Kincaid. After sliding my arms around his waist, I pushed against him.

"Truce."

He chuckled and nodded. "Truce, even though we're not at war."

"Maybe we were a little bit."

"You possibly, but not me. Either way, I'm used to your rejection."

I pouted, inching closer. "I don't reject you."

"That's what it feels like when you leave me out here alone."

I eased my arms from around his waist and slipped my hands beneath his shirt, allowing them to graze his warm skin, moving up his chest.

"I apologize, and I will work on doing better, but I offer a truce for now—no more talk about my father. I will follow your lead. I just can't help but wonder about the possibilities. The curiosity has been there all my life and will take time to get over, but I trust the family I know I can count on enough not to worry about those I can't."

He stared at me in the way he always did when he was reading my mood, like he had to measure my words against what he could physically see and feel.

"Family?"

My cheeks hiked and my lashes fluttered. "Mm-hmm."

"Which is?"

"Well, first of all, you." I lifted onto my toes and brushed my lips across his. "And then there's your mother and mine."

I actually kissed him that time. "And then there's the extended family like Alisha and Darius."

I kissed him again. "Oh, and Cast. Definitely can't forget him."

He grunted, muttering, "Careful."

I laughed just before one of his hands fisted the side of my shirt and the other tangled through my hair with a tight grip as his tongue met mine. He explored my mouth while I leaned into him a little more.

I felt him growing hard against my stomach before he pulled back, his eyes darting around the kitchen. "Where's your mother?"

"*Tired*, which is code for 'I'm giving you two some alone time.'" I smiled, and he laughed under his breath.

"I don't want her to feel like a stranger in our home."

"Oh, trust me, she doesn't. She's at peace."

He frowned a little, and I pecked his lips. "She's comfortable here. Shall we eat?"

I attempted to step away, but he held me firmly, his hand on my hip. "I missed you today."

"Good."

Kincaid smiled, kissing my temple before he let me go so I could fix our plates. We ate, enjoying a light conversation. He told me about his day. It was a busy one, but I expected nothing less. The man always had a thing or ten on his agenda. Today was no different. I learned that the paperwork for the renovation to begin on the Margaux properties had been finalized. We would be taking a trip to Paris at some point to tour the original one. It was the first established, and while Kincaid wanted to completely gut and renovate the properties, I convinced him that they should maintain some of the original authenticity and charm that played a hand in its success. He countered that he purchased Chateau Margaux after the company took a dive, losing its appeal, but I reminded him that this was hundreds of years in the making. He agreed and decided I would have the final say in what stayed and what would be revised.

I discreetly attempted to hand him the task, but he refused. I had somehow become a partner and not just an owner by way of marriage. It was exciting and terrifying simultaneously, but like always, Kincaid convinced me that I had to be the force he knew I could be.

After dinner, we ended up in the bedroom. I sat Indian style on top of his solid frame, my ass seated just below his waist, while my legs crossed at the ankles, resting on his abs. I was comfortable, staring down at his carved chest since he'd shed his shirt before we settled in. His arms were folded behind his head. I hadn't experienced this Kincaid since Tulum. He was relaxed and seemed at peace, and my God, he smelled so damn good. I wanted to talk and not get swept into the abyss of his looks and charm . . . Hell, just him.

"What's on your mind, sweetheart?"

"Hmm," I hummed, realizing that I had been in my head.

He smiled. It was charming and salacious. "I see you thinking. I feel it too."

"Is this the life you want?"

"With you, yes." He gave a sexy smile.

"It better be," I threatened with a squinted stare. "But I mean with everything, *not* just me."

"I don't know if I understand the question."

"When I was talking to your mother yesterday, I realized you didn't have much say in what was expected of you. You were born into all this with set expectations as to who and what you would become. That makes me wonder if you're happy. Like *truly* happy, or if you're only playing a part in a script created for you versus by you."

His teeth raked across his bottom lip. *Sexy.* I was aroused but attempted to remain focused.

"I guess you could say both. I never really put much thought into it. I've always known my role in The Family, even as a young child. I was groomed to think, behave, and perform in a way that would pattern me for the man I am now. There are days when I feel the weight of my life and wonder what it would feel like only to have to worry about simple shit that most men debate but likely take for granted."

"Like?" I arched my brow, and he offered that charming smile again.

"Like how to kick game to a beautiful, sexy woman such as yourself." I blushed.

"Versus?"

"Deciding if the head of a Haitian, Dominican, or Cuban cartel deserves to go home to his family after he's tried to skip past the rules that were agreed upon and bonded by their Family ties."

His eyes were serious, dark, and hard as stone. They remained fastened to mine while he waited for my reaction. I wouldn't fold. He expected me to, but I knew who my husband was regardless of whether I had proof. I didn't have the fine details of what kept him from enjoying restful sleep at night. Those weighted decisions had his face tense and the muscles around his eyes tight even as he slept, but I knew who he was. I could feel it so deep in me that it was like the marrow that filled my bones. And I accepted all of him. Even the darkness he suppressed when he held me against his chest at night, trying to find a reason to believe he wasn't a monster.

"You're good. Even if only to me. That still counts."

"Does it?"

I deserved that. I'd called him a killer.

"It does if I say so, and my vote is the only vote that matters. I'm your wife."

A smile surfaced. It was subtle and easy to miss, but I studied him the way he studied me. "It's a lot easier to recognize that you're mine when you're not stubborn and fighting me on everything."

I laughed, throwing back my head before I lowered my eyes, offering a soft gaze. "You make me crazy, making me feel like I'm losing control. When I lose control, I fight because it's all I know to do. It's my way of remembering who I am." I shrugged with one shoulder. "It's not really about you. It's about me holding onto the little pieces I still have."

His eyes moved, taking in my features like he was trying to understand my thoughts. My words only scratched the surface. I could sense he felt what was beneath them.

His control was about molding me into someone good enough to be in his life, by his side, in his bed.

"I'm not trying to change you. My only goal is to help you realize your potential, but . . ." He paused, sitting up, using his arms to lift us both, moving his back against the stack of pillows positioned behind him. "If that doesn't happen, and this person before me is who you choose to be, then it's enough. You're enough. What you see as control I see as love."

I blinked several times, but my eyes refused to focus. I felt him shifting both of us and we ended up sinking into the mattress. His arms were around me, his face buried in my hair while my back met his chest. Kincaid inhaled, releasing his breath slowly before I felt his chin rest atop the crown of my head.

"This is my favorite thing."

"What's that, sweetheart?" His voice was slow and lazy, like he was already in the space between deep thought and the lull of falling into the unconsciousness of sleep.

"When you're here with me like this, just us. It feels like nothing else matters."

"Because it doesn't."

"You're enough." My voice was low and timid. I wasn't sure why, other than that I felt raw and vulnerable. That's the effect he had on me.

"Hmmm?" The vibration of his deep tenor rumbled through me. I cleared my throat and spoke more confidently.

"You said I was enough. I just need to be sure you understand you're enough for me too."

His body tensed, but only for a second or two. The act was followed by his arms tightening around me. He shifted a little, adjusting me so I was closer.

There already existed no space between us, but he moved me closer to make sure.

"Good. As long as you always remember that, I'll die a happy man." His face sank deeper into my hair, then I felt his breathing even to a slow, steady pace. Sleep took him that fast. I smiled, closing my eyes, knowing I wouldn't be far behind.

CHAPTER 5

KINCAID.

"What kind of kid were you?" Nari lay next to me in the double lounge. Her body was sideways to mine while I was positioned on my back. Her small hand rested on my abs just above the waistband of my shorts. The feel of her fingers grazing my skin was soothing to the point of lulling me to sleep.

"A disciplined one," I muttered, which had her eyes hard on me. Mine remained closed, but when I smiled, she groaned.

"Disciplined? That's it?"

"For the most part, yes. I was a typical kid, though. Always into shit, curious about life, which drove my mother crazy." I paused at the memory, momentarily stuck on my next thought. "My father used to always be in the background, demanding she let me be, while my mother fussed that I would end up killing myself from the dumb stunts I used to pull."

"Like?"

"Like jumping from the balcony on the second level of our home into the pool. I was six." I laughed at the memory of how insanely crazy my behavior had been. "I thought my mother was going to beat me senseless when she yanked me out of the pool by one arm, but she didn't. She hugged me so tightly I couldn't breathe. I remember the look in her eyes. *Fear.* I didn't like the way it made me feel."

"Did it stop you from doing dumb shit?"

I grinned, peeling my eyes open. Hers were waiting. "No. It only made me more cautious about getting caught. I made sure she was never around to witness my stunts." I winked and she rolled her eyes.

"Typical man."

"I was a kid. I needed to explore, feel fear, and test the bounds of my abilities. My father said it would teach me how to push beyond limitations. My mother's rebuttal was that I would kill myself, or at the very least, evoke irreversible harm. My father argued back that my walk on the wild side would prepare me for life and make me a man."

"Who won?"

"I suppose they both did. I'm still alive, and I'm definitely all man. Being curious about life teaches you to push limits you wouldn't normally test. Kids are fearless. They have that thing that burns in their eager little minds, making them feel as if anything is possible if they believe it to be. It's why they do dumb shit. That's why *I* did dumb shit."

The memory had me temporarily suspended in my thoughts. It was frustratingly disheartening that no one had gotten any closer to finding out who had gunned down Razi and my father. Not one lead had surfaced, and I feared that it was a question that would remain unanswered. The thought of never finding out canceled the ability to seek retribution was a concept that I wasn't sure I could be at peace with. However, I might not have a choice. For now, I was left with knowing that my father's life was cut short, which made missing him hurt a little more.

"I don't know if I'm prepared for that type of stress." She groaned. I kissed her cheek reassuringly, allowing my mind to move into a happier space.

"You'll be just fine."

My hand eased up her thigh, sliding down her stomach, but she stopped me before I could reach my true destination. Nari lifted her chin just a little to look across the pool, where her mother was seated at a small table under a patio umbrella. Her feet were kicked up in a chair, crossed at the ankles while she held a book in her lap. I gazed at her face, which belonged to my wife with a little more maturity to it. She seemed at peace, reading whatever book had her currently captivated.

"It's crazy how much the two of you look alike."

"I know. I have to catch myself from staring. It's odd seeing your face on someone else. I wonder if that's how twins feel."

"Possibly."

She settled into a heavy silence. I could feel her brain moving.

"What's on your mind?"

"It's like I'm all her. He doesn't exist."

"Is that good or bad?"

It's a fucking bonus in my opinion.

My eyes remained on my wife. She was still in that space of longing. Regardless of the things she'd learned about her father, she still felt the void of the unknown. He was her unknown.

"Neither, I guess. If he's as bad as everyone says—"

"He is," I made clear. There was no room for negotiation where he was concerned. The smallest crack would allow her to see something that didn't really exist. Humanizing a degenerate.

"I believe you, but if that's the case, then some of that is in me. It could be passed down to our children. Traits tend to skip generations. I've heard that a lot."

I pushed out a harsh breath and kissed her forehead. "You're good enough to cancel anything negative. Even my demons. Our baby will own the light that you bring."

"I don't want our child to be all me. There should be a good blend of both of us."

"As long as it's the good things, but if not, I'll be perfectly content with a replica of you."

"Even my stubbornness?"

I chuckled, nodding. "Most definitely your stubbornness. Our child will not be a pushover. *He* or *she* will be tough as nails like their mother. Life tends to be harder on those who have a weak resolve."

She stared at me until I gave her my eyes. "What?"

"Did you have friends when you were a kid?"

I laughed at the thought. "Yes, sweetheart. I had friends, plenty, I might add. I played in the mud, rode bikes, and threw rocks at little girls because I thought they were cute. I wasn't a six-year-old wearing a suit while a gun was strapped to my side. Get that idea out of your head. I had a typical childhood."

"But you had men in suits with guns hovering."

"Sometimes, but it became a part of my life, so I tended to forget they were there."

"That's the life our child will have." It wasn't a question. She was more or less thinking out loud. "I don't see how anyone gets used to that."

"It's a necessary evil, but I promise, it will never be so overbearing that you feel trapped."

Nari nodded and smiled. "So, can we talk about these little girls who you threw rocks at? I don't like the idea of my husband crushing on anyone else. Even as a child."

I threw my head back and laughed before sitting up. "A story for another day, but if I tell my secrets, you must tell yours." I narrowed my eyes, and she smiled harder.

"Fair enough."

"Remember, you said that, but for now, go spend time with your mother. We'll be out late tonight."

Nari frowned, which meant she forgot that we had plans.

"The function I mentioned yesterday."

"Oh, that's right." She was pouting. As adorable as it was, I didn't want her to be uncomfortable or dread events that she and I would be required to attend.

"It won't be that bad. Alisha will be there as well, if that helps."

"An ally when your past decides they want to rip me to shreds."

"Not possible." I gripped the front of her neck, landing a kiss. "Nothing touches you, agreed?"

"Agreed."

I left her there to make a few calls. She still had a lot of settling to do, but I would give her time. She need not fear anyone crossing lines without the type of consequences that would make them regret the day they spoke an ill word against the woman who now owned my heart. *That was my promise.*

That night, I waited in the foyer for Nari to finish preparing to leave. I was dressed before her, handing over our room to her and her mother. Their bond seemed to grow, and after only a few days, they had settled into a routine. It wasn't quite mother-daughter yet, but it bore a close resemblance. Endia was eager to be a part of her daughter's world, and Nari was open to the idea. At times, however, I could see she retreated as if still on the fence about her feelings. I didn't think it was intentional, but if I noticed, Endia did too.

I could read my wife better than anyone. The downfall to that was she had the same ability where I was concerned. We often communicated without words. Like at that exact moment, I felt her presence, which had me looking toward the top of the stairs.

"Shit, baby." It rushed out so quickly I wasn't able to curb my response. She stood at the top of the stairs, looking down— *my angel*. Although I preferred her in red, her formfitting black dress was equally pleasing. It hugged her body, exposing those dangerous curves. Nari's hand rested on her stomach while the other hung softly at her side. There were no signs yet of our baby, but she always seemed to have her hand protectively resting where our little one was hidden beneath the surface. A constant reminder that we were forever bonded.

"See? I told you he'd like it." Her mother whispered the response, but it was not low enough to remain between them because I caught it.

Nari was a beautiful woman in her natural state, but the light touch of makeup she wore brought her features to life. It was as if someone were shining a spotlight to enhance the qualities I'd fallen in love with. She took the stairs slowly. It was torture because I couldn't wait to have her close enough to feel, smell, and taste. My dick jolted at the thought. My arm encircled her waist when she reached me, resting at her hip while I brought her in for a kiss.

"Your hair is straight." Her fingers lifted and raked through the silky tresses that brushed her shoulder. I was sure it was a nervous reaction to my statement.

"You don't like it?"

Her naturally curly look was my favorite, but she was stunning, regardless. I would never complain.

"You're perfect. In fact, you look so damn good that I want to make you change."

"Why?"

"*Sanguis in manibus meis.*" (Blood on my hands.)

"I'm not wearing red." She blushed, and I held her closer.

"Doesn't matter. You're wearing sin. You're going to tempt even the most controlled man."

"Do you want me to change?"

My eyes did another sweep. "No, they can look, but if anyone touches . . ." My gaze grew dark.

"I'm untouchable, remember?" She grinned, and even that was sinful. My fucking wife.

"Will you be okay here alone?" I pulled Nari into my side and addressed her mother.

She smiled and nodded. "I'll be fine. I'm not really alone, am I?" She motioned to Conner and Floyd, who would be stationed here while we were out. I was driving us and didn't feel the need to have anyone shadowing. The dinner would have security just in case anyone grew some balls and decided to try their luck. It was always a precaution when it came to high-profile events like the one we were attending tonight.

"Consider them invisible. If you need anything . . ."

"I won't; have fun. You both look stunning."

I offered a dip of my head before leading the way to the door.

Dinner was at Gian Monelli's home. He lived in a gated property just outside of town. The Monellis owned a chain of exclusive jewelry stores that had been in his family for centuries—the pieces they custom-made created bidding wars. Tonight was to showcase some of those that had been recently crafted. A select group was invited, which included several members of our syndicate.

Gian's home sat on six acres and was roughly 14,000 square feet. Overkill, in my opinion, but it suited his lifestyle. Gian had a wife and no children. From what I knew, he wanted them, but his wife was barren. That had me glancing down at Nari's stomach as we walked down the winding hall escorted by one of Gian's staff. I wasn't sure how I would handle being with a woman who couldn't bear my children, but love was love, and no situation mirrored the next. What they had worked for them.

As we reached the area where cocktails were being served, Nari's hand tightened in mine. She was anxious. I didn't like the reaction, but understood, so I kissed her shoulder.

"Relax."

Her eyes met mine just before we entered. A server at the door dressed in a tux greeted us with a smile before speaking. "Drinks for you and the lady, sir?"

She couldn't have alcohol, but I was sure they had others, so I waited until she shook her head softly.

"No, thank you," I responded as we moved deeper into the room. I was approached by several people who greeted me before acknowledging my wife. I made introductions but kept her close. I could feel the stares from those still uncertain about why she was by my side and not Aila; however, they wouldn't dare speak about it. Our marriage was now public knowledge. But the history behind our union remained our personal business. That baffled those who understood Aila was in line to be my wife.

"*Finalmente. Conozco a tu hermosa esposa. La has mantenido oculta, pero no te culpo. Ella es impresionante.*" (Finally, I meet your beautiful wife. You've kept her hidden, but I don't blame you. She's stunning.)

Saulo was in his sixties and his wife was in her thirties. She was his second marriage and gave birth to their first and his sixth child on the day of my father's funeral, so he wasn't there. He flew in days before to provide his condolences, and I met him alone, so this was his first time meeting my wife. He reached for Nari's hand, but her eyes drifted to me, unsure. I nodded, and she allowed him to take hers, planting a kiss on her knuckles.

"I am Saulo Perez." He grinned. "An associate of your husband, and you are?" He arched his brow, waiting, although he already knew exactly who my wife was. He likely had a file printed and on his desk as soon as word reached him that I had chosen Nari as my wife.

"Nari Akel," she offered with a soft smile. The word "stunning" did her no justice. My wife was extraordinarily breathtaking.

"Mrs. *Nari Akel*, it is a pleasure to make your acquaintance. Your husband is a well-respected man, and you are in good hands."

"I hope so," she returned lightly. His smile expanded when she cut her eyes at me.

"I give you my word." He paused, locking his arms behind his back. "Now, explore, enjoy. There are some beautiful pieces that should suit your taste. Make this man empty his pockets for you. It's only right for a woman as beautiful as you to be donned in expensive jewels." He winked, and I chuckled. Nari blushed. Saulo's hand came down on my shoulder as his eyes met mine and he offered a subtle nod. He approved. Not that it mattered one way or another, but I did take pride in his acceptance of my wife.

"Have a good evening, both of you." He walked away, and she turned to me, her eyes expressive as she watched him cross the room.

"What did he say to you?"

I offered a warm gaze. "That you were stunning and he understood why I kept you hidden."

"Hidden?" She frowned. "Are you hiding me?"

"No, but I have turned down a few invitations because I didn't think you were ready to be exposed to this part of my life again."

"Are you sure that's why?"

"What other reason would there be, sweetheart? The fundraiser left you feeling uneasy. You didn't have to say the words for me to know you weren't in a hurry to attend another event."

"But we're here tonight?"

"I wasn't able to turn down the invitation. It would have presented as rude, almost disrespectful."

"Agreed. I would have been seriously offended." Gian approached with his wife at his side. "Kincaid is a good friend and business associate. Had he declined, I'm not sure how I would have taken the rejection very well."

"It's good to see you." Gian extended a hand, which I shook before he turned to my wife. "And this is the lovely wife. She is gorgeous, Kincaid."

"Careful, *amore*." (Love) Cella's narrowed eyes landed playfully on her husband, and he grinned, joining in on the amusement.

"Just an observation, *mio angelo*." (My angel.)

"Mrs. Akel, this is my wife, Cella."

"Nari," she began. "Nice to meet you." She extended a hand, which Cella accepted.

She smiled softly before returning the greeting. Her regard focused on eagerly taking in my wife from head to toe.

"Pleased to meet you as well. You are gorgeous. Good job, Kincaid."

"Glad you approve."

"Oh, I do. She's lovely. *Peccato per mio marito che i tuoi voti siano sacri.*" (Too bad for my husband that your vows are sacred.)

Gian shot his wife a look, and I chuckled. *You're damn right they are. I will not be sharing my wife with anyone—ever.*

"*Ah, una donna così gelosa.*" (Such a jealous woman.)

Nari's nose crinkled a little and she inched closer. She had no idea what was happening and I wouldn't tell her. Gian was attracted to my wife. If I would allow it, he would sleep with her. He and Cella had an understanding about their marriage that included "outside" relationships. I didn't see how either was okay with the agreement to see others, but hey, to each his own.

"Welcome to my home, Mrs. Akel. Spend lots of money tonight." He winked at her before taking his wife at the small of her back to leave.

"What was that? It felt like a private joke."

"Nothing of importance, I assure you. Let's go see what they have." I kissed Nari's cheek and led her to the outside perimeter of the room, where glass enclosures housing the custom pieces were on display.

"These are beautiful." I watched as she fell in love with a necklace and bracelet set. It was loaded with tiny diamonds assembled to look like little flowers. The creation would be hers. I'd make sure of it. "They make them?" She lifted her eyes to me then lowered them back to the glass case that held her new addiction.

"His family, yes. Gian no longer does as often as he used to. He's getting old and claims his eyes aren't as reliable as they used to be."

She flashed a smile over her shoulder. I was directly behind her, my hands in my pockets, but I kept my wife close. Touching her in any way gave me life.

"How much are these? I bet they're expensive."

"Don't worry about the bottom line. You're married to a capo." Alisha eased beside Nari, and the two shared a warm, silent greeting.

"What did I tell you about that shit, Lish?" Darius stood behind her, mirroring the proximity to his wife that I shared with Nari. Alisha always referenced our life as a Mafia family. We were so far from it; however, it was the only way her mind could process what we were a part of.

"What? It's true," she fussed before turning to Nari. "No red?"

"I decided to switch it up." She glanced at me, and I winked.

"Well, I approve. You're wearing this dress."

"So are you." They went back and forth, doling out compliments before dragging each other to the next display. Darius and I gave them space, but not too much.

"Anything new?"

"No, but we have an understanding about Manchester."

"Does that include you killing him?"

I shrugged. "If it's necessary, but I won't ask for permission."

"I didn't expect you to."

"Kincaid?"

I turned to my left and noticed Mya smiling seductively. The first thing I did was locate my wife, then her husband, who was across the room, brownnosing. He had cornered Saulo. My regard made it back to Mya, and I spoke.

"You look well."

"*Well?* Damn, Caid. You say that shit to your mom's ugly friends." Mya shot Darius a nasty look, and he chuckled and stepped away. I would have preferred he stayed. Nari was still very sensitive about my association with other women. We both had a nasty, jealous streak, but my reactions were slightly more refined than hers. I glanced across the room and noticed she was occupied with Alisha, enjoying the pieces on display.

"So, that's her? Your wife?" She seemed disappointed, but I wasn't sure why. Nari easily outshined almost every woman in attendance, and Mya was married, so the woman who belonged to me shouldn't have been any concern of hers. Maybe that was the issue . . .

Nari is my wife . . . not her.

"You shouldn't ask questions you already know the answers to. It presents as arrogant or ignorant, talking just to be seen or heard." My intense gaze met with her seductive one. She didn't bother hiding her lustful feelings.

"That's never been an issue. You always see me. *All* of me."

I chuckled and turned to walk away. "It was good to see you, Mya. Tell your husband I said hello." He was here. I could do that myself, but I wouldn't. He wasn't relevant to me, and my acknowledgment wasn't necessary. I was simply making a point, which she didn't bother to receive. She did, however, catch my arm just before I got away.

"*Ella es bonita. Incluso le daré hermosa. Me pregunto si ella puede manejarte de la manera que yo puedo.*" (She's pretty. I'll even give her beautiful, but I do wonder if she can handle you the way I can.)

"*Esto es difícil de decir. En el momento en que se convirtió en mía, no existían recuerdos de la mujer antes que ella.*" (That's hard to say. The minute she became mine, no memories of the women before her existed.)

The minute she released me, I could feel my wife. Alisha shot me a dirty look before she joined her husband, but Nari's face expressed what she heard. Only she wasn't sure of what the exchange was.

"Nice to meet you. Love that dress, girl," Mya delivered in a snide tone before walking away. My eyes, however, never left my wife.

"What did she say to you?" Nari hissed the second we were alone. I could see Mya now watching us from across the room. The pleased grin on her face created tension in my shoulders.

"It's not important."

"It most definitely is. What the fuck did she say?"

"That you were beautiful, but she wonders if you can handle me the way she could."

I wouldn't lie. There was no point.

"And what did you say?"

"That it was hard to tell because I had no memories of any woman who came before you."

"You had sex with her?"

"Yes, I did. Years ago. It was before she married her husband. Long before I ever met you."

"Apparently not long enough in her mind if she's reminiscing just from being in your presence. My God and she's here, whispering about the things you've done, grinning in my face, sarcastically complimenting my dress."

"Sweetheart, I have a past just like you—"

"My past isn't here taunting you and challenging whether you're good enough now, are they?" Her eyes narrowed into slits, heated with the thoughts of me and Mya. When Nari released me from the deadly rays, they made it to Mya, who blew us both a kiss, then pushed her breasts up a little higher before allowing her hands to glide down her curvy frame. When I realized Nari was about to head in that direction, I caught her by the waist, bringing her into my chest.

"I've had sex with plenty of women. Some you will never lay eyes on and others you'll sit across from at functions such as these. Most you will never know have been in my bed because I have always been clear about their role in my life. There are those who have just been fucks, some companions, but none have ever been my wife."

My eyes leveled with hers in a way that left no room for uncertainty. "That role will only ever belong to you, baby. The reality of what you are and what she is not is why she's standing next to her husband, reminiscing about when she was in my bed. She is very clear about what she will never be, what she could never be, and that's causing her to lash out at you. She wants what you have. You have me. The only way that changes is if you decide you no longer want this, and even then, I'll still be yours because no one can ever reverse the damage you've done. You've ruined me, sweetheart. I'm no good to anyone but you, so there's no point in me trying."

Her eyes softened, but her body was still tense. "Now, can we join everyone, or are you going to allow someone irrelevant to make you question your rightful place..." I allowed some space, extending a hand, motioning for her to move. "...by my side?"

Our eyes were at war for a long moment before she cut them toward Mya, who pretended not to notice while easing closer to her husband.

"You were right to turn down those invitations. I'm not ready for these people," she gritted and attempted to walk away. I was on her after the first step, leaning around my wife to press a kiss to her temple while my palm lay flat against her stomach.

"These people don't mean shit to me, which, in turn, means they don't mean shit to us. My only concern is you, as should yours be me. Only us. Just us, agreed?"

"It would be a lot easier to believe it's just us if there wasn't a new woman at every turn reminiscing about when it used to be you and them. No matter what I know you feel for me, it's not easy having what used to be constantly thrown in my face."

"Key words, 'used to be,' as in the past."

She shot me a look when I stepped around her but didn't respond. I kissed Nari and smiled before I took her at the small of her back to go see the rest of the pieces.

The remainder of the night went well. There were heavy hors d'œuvres and drinks while everyone gathered to explore the pieces. About an hour into the evening, the bidding war began. It wasn't necessarily an auction but a silent promise. Those with status would be granted first rights, even if that was unspoken. Price wasn't an issue or discussed because you could afford the pieces if you were in the room.

When they got to the set I knew Nari wanted, my chin dipped, offering a slight nod to let Gian know we would purchase it. Mya watched me so closely that she noticed, sending an evil glare to Nari, who was so caught up that she missed it. Thank God.

Nari's mouth fell open when she realized what I was doing. I winked at her, and she smiled softly, mouthing, "Thank you." *Imagine that. Diamonds landed us back on good terms.*

At one point during the evening, Mya dragged her husband our way to engage in conversation, although she did most of the talking, attempting to exert her familiarity with me. Poor bastard didn't have a clue that he was being used as a pawn in his wife's sick obsession with me. I wondered if she ever told him about our past. Likely not because he was too cordial and eager to be in my space. Not the type of behavior for a man who knows another is well versed in what his wife's body was capable of.

Nari kept her cool, which surprised me. Alisha joined at one point, and the two had a sidebar conversation, leaving Mya and her husband to me and Darius. I quickly shut that down, excusing myself and pulling Nari away.

I noticed after the showcase that Mya sent her husband to Gian. When he shook his head and motioned to me, I chuckled. She wanted him to purchase the set promised to Nari. Gian wouldn't do it. He didn't know the history between Mya and me, nor would it have mattered. For one, he was sweet on Nari, and two, I made clear I wanted the set, so he would ensure it was mine. I shook my head, amused by the argument that took place when Mya's husband returned empty-handed.

"Is that about you?"

"No, sweetheart. That's about you. She wanted the set I purchased."

"Before or after she realized you were buying it for me?"

I smirked and lowered my eyes, easing my hands into the pockets of my slacks. "Does it matter? It's yours, and after they package it so we can leave, you'll wear it for me tonight while I see how many times I can make you come."

Her cheeks flushed and her eyes lowered. "Maybe I'll be the one who's keeping count," she shot back, and my dick inflated to an uncomfortable degree.

"That's a challenge I'll willingly accept. Let's say good night to everyone so we can get started right away."

Her smile was seductive and teasing, but she didn't disagree. On the way over to Darius and Alisha, Mya locked eyes with Nari, who smiled cunningly but lifted her middle finger before the rest surfaced, and she wiggled them, delivering a wave. Nari's hand then ended up moving down my chest below my belt, but I caught it, lifting her fingers for a soft kiss. Mya's eyes widened, not expecting the reaction she received. I kept quiet. There was no point. Nari was staking her claim.

My sweet Nari has her claws out, and it makes my dick even harder.

CHAPTER 6

NARI.

We were approaching the fifth day of Kincaid's absence. He traveled to Chicago for a day, another in New York, then it was off to Dubai. He wouldn't be home for another two days, and I missed him terribly. Kincaid extended the invitation for me to travel with him, but I didn't want to leave my mother. He further extended the invitation to her as well, stating we could shop and spa hop while he worked. I declined. It didn't feel right, dragging her with me just because I didn't want to be apart from Kincaid. While he was away, I spent the time with her, Alisha, and Corinne, pulling together details for our reception dinner.

I attempted to include Kincaid, but the only input he gave was red. I was instructed to incorporate his new favorite color into whatever we were planning, but he didn't provide input on how. *"I'll leave that up to you, sweetheart,"* was his response.

Since he had been responsible for our original union, I decided to emulate our actual wedding, but on a grander scale to include him in the planning. I was okay with keeping things simple, but his mother and Alisha both insisted it be a grand production.

My mother seemed to agree, but remained quiet about most of the planning. I assumed it was because she wasn't well versed on this lifestyle and what was to be expected. Hell, I wasn't either, which was why Alisha and his mother did most of the planning. They seemed to get lost in the details. I agreed with most of what they suggested, and when I didn't, I would express my feelings, but truthfully, I already had the husband, so this part was simply for show. It did, however, seem important to Kincaid, so I played along.

Kincaid's handlers remained behind but worked shifts so that someone was on guard twenty-four hours while he was away. They didn't come inside, but instead were stationed in front of the house in their vehicles. Cast traveled with Kincaid, so I didn't know these men. Their faces became familiar over time, but they didn't speak much other than a programmed good morning or good evening when driving me around. My mother and I both offered them food, but they always refused. Eventually, the one known as Conner made clear that it was against the rules. I expressed concern with Kincaid one night when he called, asking when the hell they were supposed to eat, and he made clear that their meals were scheduled only when they were off duty. I guess the team had that all worked out because neither looked like they missed a meal. They were solid framed, always in suits with their faces set in a pleasant scowl. Due to the hardened looks that remained on their faces, I assumed they took their jobs seriously. Today would be no different. After being out of bed, showered, and dressed, I traveled downstairs. I peeked outside, and sure enough, two black-on-black SUVs were parked where they had been all week.

My next stop was the kitchen, where I found my mother drinking tea. After a few days here, I quickly learned she was an early riser, but she never made a peep or requested anything. She had become familiar with the kitchen, so she would fix a small breakfast, have tea, and enjoy quiet time until I was up and moving. Then we would enjoy the remainder of our day together. Today, I planned on getting out of the house. I was beginning to feel restricted being stuck at home and needed a bit of fresh air.

"How long have you been up?"

She grinned, motioning to the refrigerator. "For a little while. I cut you some fruit."

I returned her smile at the same time my stomach growled. My little one created quite an appetite, but aside from constantly wanting to stuff my face, I was having a reasonably decent pregnancy.

"You feel like going out today? I figured we could do a little shopping or something. Maybe get our nails done." I held up my hand and squinted at the growth of my nails. I wasn't the type of person who religiously created a routine to pamper myself, but Kincaid made a point of stressing the issue. Deep down inside, I felt it was more about him than me, but then again, I didn't take offense. It was simply his nature. The man was always put together from head to toe.

"Whatever you want to do is fine with me. I'm just happy to spend time with you."

My eyes lifted to hers slowly, and she was watching me with a warm smile in place. Having my mother around made it hard to keep my emotions at bay. I found myself staring sometimes, trying to remember every moment. Between her and Kincaid, I was always at a loss attempting to manage feelings I wasn't used to experiencing.

"I want you to enjoy your time here. I know it gets cramped being stuck inside for days at a time."

She laughed hard, shaking her head. "It's impossible to feel stuck in this beautiful home. Don't waste time worrying about me."

"Can I ask you something?"

"Anything you want," she confirmed.

"Do you ever miss them? Your family, I mean. You left and never went back."

"Sometimes, I do, but most of the time, I don't. It's hard to explain, but after so many years have passed, you tend to forget what it feels like to have anyone but yourself. With all the time we've missed, I don't know them, and they don't know me. Well, at least not the person I am today. I've learned that sometimes it's easier to leave things as they are."

"Do you think they want to see you, at least to know you're okay?"

My child wasn't born yet, and I still couldn't imagine them walking away without me giving my all to find them.

"Truthfully, I don't know, so it's hard to care. When I first left, I lived on the streets, worked odd jobs for cash, and did whatever I could to survive. After I was eighteen and old enough to live on my own, I used my real name. I got licenses, used my Social for jobs, and even applied for state assistance. It's how I found out there was a missing person's report for me. They filed a month after I left, but that's all they ever did. If my parents really wanted to find me, they could have." She shrugged. "I guess that's why I understand your resentment toward me for not looking for you."

"Were you curious . . ." I paused. "About me?"

"All the time, sweetheart." She covered my hand with hers. "But in my mind, you had a good life. I didn't want to interfere. I also didn't know if I could handle being rejected. Just because I wanted to be in your life didn't mean you would want to be in mine. I'm sorry for not trying. I apologize for not being strong enough, but I'm here now, and I pray we can build something that we both need."

"Me too."

There was no point in being overly emotional about things I couldn't change. I had her now, and that would have to be enough.

"I don't think I've ever been that pampered in my life." My mother laughed as we left the nail salon. It was the most posh and upscale place I had ever experienced. Of course, it was recommended by Kincaid, who set up an account for me. I had only been there twice before our visit today, and each time was an experience. Apparently, my mother agreed.

"I'm still getting used to this life myself, but some of the perks are kinda sweet," I grinned, playfully leaning into her side. "Some, not so much."

I glanced over my shoulder at Conner, who moved with us but allowed a safe distance. He waited outside near the door, where he had a visual the entire time. "I agree, but at least Kincaid makes the effort to keep you safe."

"He does, so I try not to give him too much shit. What about lunch?" I asked as soon as we reached the car where Floyd waited. He'd stayed behind and had the door open, ready for us as soon as we stepped out into the sun.

"I'm easy to please."

"You are, but sometimes, I'm confused about whether you're just being polite or if you're truly happy." I found myself pouting, eager to please the woman who had recently come into my life. What daughter didn't want love and approval from their own mother? Regardless of her being absent most of my life, I was still needy and starved for the closeness I'd imagined in my mind over the years.

"Oh, sweetheart," she turned, touching my cheek, "anything that includes you makes me truly happy. Never question my motives or intent, but if it helps, how about we explore a simple menu today, maybe sandwiches or something?"

My smile was wide as I nodded. "I know the perfect place."

Kincaid owned a lot of restaurants—thirteen and counting. The ones we had visited so far were upscale, but I'd recently learned that one of my favorites was a café he owned in Midtown. After I handed over the address to Conner, who was driving, we were on our way. It took a little under an hour to get there, and as soon as my eyes took in the logo, my stomach began to do its own thing.

Once we were out of the truck and heading to the door, I heard a voice that set my blood on fire. It had been months, and yet, I still felt the fury like it had only been days, possibly hours.

"Cuz, is that you?"

My head turned toward the high-pitched tenor and Conner cautiously flexed beside me. His body somehow grew bigger in seconds, possibly from how he widened his stance and rolled his shoulders back.

Easy, big guy.

"Damn, you're looking like new money. Unless the purse you're holding is a knockoff, that's ten stacks hanging from your shoulder, and shit, you got the matching sandals too. Bitch, who're you fucking?"

I swear I heard Conner growl from above me. He wasn't pleased by the way my cousin addressed me.

"Ma'am, we need to head inside," he demanded like Kincaid would, not leaving any wiggle room for debate.

I guess the hubby gave direct orders to protect me from a physical attack and verbal lashings as well. That's when my mother stepped up to my side. Her eyes narrowed at Shayla. The two stared at each other in a way that incited feelings of violence.

"You found her? Oh, shit. Mama, look. It's your sister." A woman who resembled Shayla only in body type and complexion stepped up beside her. My mother's regard moved from my cousin to who I assumed was my aunt.

"Damn, Endia, that's you?" She squinted with a frown, not waiting for an answer before she continued. "Where the hell you come from? Wait 'til I tell Mama and Daddy I saw you."

"Don't bother." My mother spoke firmly, which had my aunt's face twisting.

"What you mean, 'don't bother'? You up and left, not even caring what it did to them. They made my life a living hell because you was gone. Mama was always worried I would leave too. How you gon' tell me not to bother?"

"Easy. *Don't* bother. Now, if you'll excuse us . . ." She looked at me, and my eyes bounced between the two of them.

"We should go," I said, narrowing a heated glare at Shayla, who returned the gesture.

"Oh, so you're fucking some rich guy and you're too good for family now?" She stepped closer, but Conner moved between us. "Who the fuck is you?" She looked him up and down, and I rolled my eyes, stepping around his big body.

"Who I'm with has nothing to do with me not wasting my time on you. How's life been? Steal from any other family members lately?" I sneered.

"Girl, ain't nobody steal from you. That money was mine anyway. You owed me—"

"I didn't owe you a damn thing, but you know what? I'm glad it happened. Taught me a valuable lesson about *family*. If family means being connected to people like you, then I'm better off alone."

"She's disrespectful just like you, Endia. I'm not surprised." My aunt sucked her teeth, glaring at my mother. Shayla shifted beside her with anxious limbs, balancing her need to attack.

"Family can whoop your ass too. Maybe that's what I should have done instead of trying to baby your ass." Shayla lunged forward, extending a fist like she would hit me, but Conner caught her wrist with one hand and pushed me behind him with the other.

"Get your hands off my baby. Who the fuck you think you are?" my aunt growled.

"Mrs. Akel." Floyd extended his phone to me, and my eyes shot up to his, but all he did was toss his chin toward the device. I already knew the deal. Kincaid was on the line, so I took the phone.

"What?"

"Get in the truck, now."

Oh, he's big mad, but so am I. I'm also not his child, regardless of me carrying one.

"No, I'm not doing that. I'm fine. I don't know why he called you."

"Did she not just attempt to put her hands on you? I thought I made myself clear about the safety of our child. Get in the gotdamn truck now."

Damn, how long has he been on the line to know she tried to hit me?

My eyes shot up to Floyd, who didn't so much as flinch. I was positive Kincaid had clear instructions on the dos and don'ts when it came to me. If ever unclear on what decision to make, they were instructed to contact him, which was what had happened.

"We're here for lunch."

"Give Conner your order and he'll get it to-go. Get in the truck, sweetheart." There were two ways he used that endearment and this wasn't the one I preferred. It was the warning before his ugly side surfaced.

My eyes lifted to Floyd before they bounced over to my aunt and cousin, who were still arguing *at* Conner. I couldn't say *with* because I hadn't once heard his voice, only their verbal lashes demanding he give them access to me. There was a brick wall dividing us: Conner and Floyd. I was sure Kincaid could hear their loud mouths in the background, and I wasn't in the mood to begin a verbal match with him, so I gave in.

"Fine."

"Give the phone to Floyd."

I rolled my eyes, almost throwing it at him, listening while he tossed out a few "yes, sirs," but didn't end the call. I was sure my very overprotective husband wanted to remain on the line until I did as he demanded.

"We're leaving," I said to my mother, who nodded, not asking any questions.

"You running again, Endia? You been gone for years, and it's fuck your family? You were selfish then and you're selfish now."

"I'm selfish, but you raised your daughter. I wasn't allowed to raise mine. Why don't you ask our parents about *that* before you go judging my decisions? Maybe then you'll understand why I never came back. It's not like they cared."

"You had a choice—"

My mother snapped quickly. "No, I didn't. Regardless of what they told you, I was never given the option to keep my child, but apparently, you were, and what an amazing job you've done. She's quite lovely. So much like you."

"Don't you dare act all high and mighty. At least I know who my kid's father is. Can you say the same? Maybe if you did, then they wouldn't have given her away. Who the hell wants to explain about their daughter's bastard child?"

"I got your fucking bastard!" I yelled and attempted to be on the move again, but Conner put a quick stop to that. My mother remained calm, speaking her final thoughts.

"I can say a lot of things, but I won't. It's really not worth the energy. *You're* not worth the energy."

My mother stepped around me, sliding into the backseat. I was about to follow but paused when I heard Shayla still verbally attacking.

"Forget her, Ma. Ain't neither one of them worth the time. She thinks she's something 'cause she done opened her legs for one of them men at the club. I told you she wasn't shit." She laughed sarcastically. "Yeah, I always knew yo' ass wasn't no better than me. Hell, you're worse. You let some nigga pimp you out just 'cause he got a few commas in his bank account."

"Possibly, but if you're gonna let a man *pimp you out*, at the very least, get something out of it, right? Isn't that what you told me when it came to your ex?" I arched my brow while her eyes narrowed, causing me to return a smug grin before I continued. "I got a ring *and* his last name. What can you claim other than being passed to your man's homeboys because you were so desperate to keep him around that you'd do anything he asked? How did *that* work out for you?" I tossed my hand up, making sure she could see the massive diamond on my finger, and her eyes doubled in size.

"Bitch, I will beat your ass—" She lunged at me and my chest expanded because I was so angry. I hadn't realized I was moving in her direction until Conner stepped in front of me. "Ma'am . . ."

That was his subtle warning. His boss had given instructions, and they weren't about to allow me to break them. I got in the truck, and while Floyd stood guard, ending his call with Kincaid, Conner left to get our order after I rattled off a few items. I knew who I was, but that didn't mean her words didn't bother me. Kincaid hadn't "pimped" me out, but she didn't know the truth. I hadn't decided if my truth was any better than what she had already assumed. Why the hell I even cared was beyond me. This was the same person who used me, stole from me, then had the audacity to talk down to me when she had done far worse things than I would even consider. I was sure she was kicking herself from admitting during a drunken rant that she'd slept with three of her ex's friends one night while they all got high. "*Baby, if you love me, you'll hook up my guys,*" he told her. That was a few weeks before we were getting kicked out of our apartment and probably when he ended things.

While I was stuck in my thoughts, my mother was stuck in hers. We were both quiet until we were about halfway to the house and I asked about my aunt's comment.

"She said you didn't know who my father was, like she had a secret about him."

My mother's eyes left the window, where she had been staring blankly since we left the parking lot.

"There's no secret. It was easier for me to pretend like I didn't know than it would have been to deal with the consequences if they ever found out. My sister and I were never close. I couldn't trust her to keep it from my parents, so I lied and said I had been with multiple guys. I knew she would tell my parents and that's exactly what happened."

I didn't question my mother any further. I believed her, but regardless, it didn't matter one way or another because he would never be a part of my life.

"It's why I said sometimes it's easier to leave things as they are." We shared a look before she turned to the window again. The topic was dropped and I wouldn't bring it up anymore. She was all the family I needed outside of my husband.

The rest of my day moved in a blur. Everything around me ignited the sting I felt from my cousin's words. *Pimped out.* Technically, I married for money. Even if the terms weren't as simple as that, the foundation of my decision was money. It was why I agreed. Neither did it matter that I was now in love with the man whose last name I carried. I craved him like an addict who chased a high. He had become a part of me in a way that made me feel incomplete in his absence. Not having him around most days altered my mood. It wasn't that I couldn't be happy without him. I could, which had been proven over the past week. I enjoyed time with my mother and his. I laughed hard and smiled big when spending time with Alisha, but there was always a void I felt, like I wasn't whole. He was the reason. That man had implanted himself so deeply in me that I didn't feel whole unless he was within reach.

Nights were the worst. Our bed felt cold and lonely in his absence. For that very reason, I kept myself busy until I knew I would pass out from exhaustion before climbing underneath the sheets. Tonight had been no different, which was why I felt him as soon as he was near. The bed dipped, and it seemed like I had just closed my eyes, so it took me a minute to open them. Kincaid wasn't due home for another day and a half, so I had to be dreaming. I fought against the urge to find out for fear of being disappointed, but the feel of his hand covering mine, which rested on my stomach, had my eyes slowly peeling open.

"What are you doing here?"

He snorted. "I live here."

That grated me. Regardless of how tenderly his large hand and lengthy fingers rested atop my own, I could feel the aggression radiating from those broad shoulders and solid arms.

Kincaid is angry.

"I know you live here, Kincaid. I'm reminded every second of every day because this place reeks of you, but my question is more about day and time. You're not supposed to be back for another day and a half."

"Reeks?" His eyes lowered to meet mine. I shifted beneath the covers, sitting up and scooting back. The disconnect caused the muscles beneath his beard to flex, sharpening his angular jawline.

"You know what I mean. It wasn't meant in a derogatory manner." My voice was clipped. This man confused the hell out of me. He could move between so many personas that I struggled to keep up. My words caused him to feel offended, which initiated a pout of sorts, but Kincaid was too damn alpha to really pout, so the more appropriate terminology was more along the lines of brooding.

"I just traveled almost fifteen hours by flight only to arrive here and spend the rest of the day and evening getting brought up to date on the million and one things I had to push aside while traveling. I'm exhausted and not looking to argue with my wife."

"I don't want to argue with you, either. I was only asking why you're here so early."

This too felt out of sorts. I didn't know his every move. However, he made clear the importance of his business while being away. He made a point of pushing up several ventures on his calendar to lend himself to me with more flexibility around the time I was expected to deliver. We had discussed his plans at length because it would mean excessive travel to settle his affairs over the next few months.

"It's my duty to make sure my wife is okay."

He's worried about me? Why?

"You were traveling for business. It wasn't an emergency."

"I made some minor adjustments to ensure I could be home a few days early. I will always put you first, sweetheart. The concept is never a debate in my heart or my head."

"I'm fine. Your handlers did what you paid them to do then ushered us to the safety of our home." I wasn't sure why I was so upset, but something about his coming home early felt . . .

Controlling versus caring.

Not to mention, I was still angry about being treated like I was a child. The luxury of my new life came with an overseer.

"As opposed to what? A physical altercation with a woman who throws insults at you?"

I shrugged. "Sometimes you have to put your foot in people's asses for them to realize you're not to be fucked with." My eyes narrowed and warred with his.

"And while you're putting your foot in someone's ass, how does the care and well-being of our child fit into that equation?"

Ahhhh, now the truth comes out. He's not worried about me. Just the precious cargo I'm carrying.

He was yet again coddling me, and I didn't like it. Being pregnant didn't make me handicapped, and of course I would have considered my child. At the present, my words would have been enough to get my point across. What I didn't appreciate was my husband not trusting me to make good decisions about myself or my child.

"Why are you with me?"

"Excuse me?" His eyes squinted slightly, but I could see the irritation dancing behind his pupils. One thing I learned about my husband early on was that he had very little patience. Kincaid made demands and people obliged. It was one of the things that attracted me to him—his ability to command.

"You're always there, protectively hovering. Even in your absence, you manage to do so. I thought it was endearing at first, but now I see things for what they really are. You're always hovering because you're waiting for me to fuck up. You don't trust my judgment with things in your life or with this baby. Why be with someone you have to coddle like a child? How is that even remotely appealing for a man like you? Why wouldn't you want a woman who has it all figured out and doesn't need you to dictate how she looks, thinks, or acts? I had a disagreement with my family and you made the call to control the outcome. Christ, I can't even have a simple argument without you expecting me to do something reckless."

My emotions were all over the place. I was spiraling, which forced my insecurities and caused me to self-sabotage. I just didn't know how to get a handle on being in his space, in his life, or worse . . .

His wife.

Kincaid snorted, his eyes narrowing a bit more. "She's *not* your fucking family. Your family wouldn't offer to fuck me and keep it secret. *I'm* your family. *Endia* is your family. Hell, my mother, Darius, and Alisha are *your* family. What's reckless is you using that term so loosely about a woman who would insult you by minimizing your marital union to something as degrading as me pimping you out."

My eyes expanded, but I settled quickly.

He heard that.

"Who offered to fuck you?"

"The same woman you felt the need to prove yourself to and reference as *family*, and for the record, I declined the offer. I have no interest in disrespecting our vows."

When the hell did Shayla offer to fuck my husband?

"Do you think I care what she assumes about us?" I didn't. She couldn't say a damn thing about me or the man I married. The problem was what I felt bubbling in the pit of my stomach most days. My own insecurities were sometimes more acute than what people on the outside assumed them to be.

"Don't you?" He was searching my face for a reaction, and if I wasn't mistaken, I noticed a slight moment of uncertainty.

"No. I don't give a damn because I know better, even though a part of me knows I married you for money—"

"Don't—"

"Don't *what*, Kincaid? Regardless of where we are now, neither of us can erase how this began. I may not appreciate her accusations or delivery, but technically, she's right. You pimped me out. I just got a ring and a title out of the deal."

"Is that *all* you got?"

No! I'm simply struggling to find my footing with my new reality and what I have known all my life. Everything comes at a price.

I stared at him hard, not responding.

"I said, is that *all* you fucking got?" This time, his voice raised, and his sentence came out in a growl. However, I still refused to answer. He stood, leaned over the bed, and pressed a palm into the mattress to brace himself while bending toward me. I flinched, not sure why. This man would never send a finger in my direction with the intent of harm. The reaction caused something to move behind his eyes, but he still pressed a kiss to my forehead, allowing his lips to linger while he whispered, "Get some rest."

His voice was low but firm. I watched as he left our room, closing the door behind him. My mind moved a mile a minute as I sat motionless, processing what the hell that meant. There was no argument. He just left.

CHAPTER 7

KINCAID.

My eyes shot open at the sound of something crashing in the kitchen. I sat up on the sofa in my office and bent forward over my knees, pressing my elbows into them. After a few moments of resting my face in my palms, I exhaled a cleansing breath. I had suffered a long night of uncomfortable sleep and the need to be near my wife. I'd grown accustomed to having her body wrapped around mine, creating a position of peace.

This battle with Nari had me at my wits' end. I struggled to prove that she was safe with me. I only wanted what was best and sometimes that meant being ahead of things. What she saw as control was my way of ensuring that she remained untouched. My world was new, as were my overprotective feelings for my wife. I was attempting to find balance in navigating through this adjustment like she did.

Exhaling through my frustration, I reached for my phone, which buzzed with the notification of a call the second I had it in hand.

"Yeah?"

"You sound like shit. Rough night?"

"What do you want, Dee?"

Darius chuckled. His voice was light and crisp, meaning he'd been up for a while. The flight home was quiet. He spoke to his wife then slept. I was up working through the struggle in my mind about how to handle my wife, and still, I came up empty.

"We still meeting today?"

"Yeah. I'm about to get moving. I'll hit you back when I'm heading your way. There are a few stops I need to make first."

"A'ight." Darius wouldn't question me. If it were something he needed to know, I would tell him. After ending my call, I tossed the phone on the sofa and stretched, allowing my eyes to mindlessly roam my surroundings.

I slept in my fucking office, but I could see now that the only way to make my point was to show better than to tell. Before Nari was up, I showered, dressed, and made my way out of the house, only stopping because I crossed paths with Endia once I reached the bottom of the stairs. She smiled politely before assessing my attire.

"You arrived late and you're leaving early." It wasn't a question, more of an observation.

I nodded, taking her in. She was fully dressed in sweats, a T-shirt, and running shoes. Her shirt was lightly misted with sweat.

"You worked out?"

Her cheeks hiked, broadening her smile, reminding me of Nari.

"Figured I'd do something to bide my time. I hope you don't mind."

"Not at all. This is your daughter's home, which also makes it yours."

"And yours?" She arched her brow and I nodded. "She up?"

"Not yet."

"Oh." I could see her mind spinning. "Do you mind if I share something with you?"

"Not at all."

"You're a strong spirit. Confident in a way that makes others refuse to challenge your authority. It's a force that takes time to understand and get used to."

"I love your daughter," I made clear. Endia was always quiet, watching and observing, but she didn't say much, at least not to me. I wasn't sure if she understood my position as well as she needed to because a part of me didn't truly care. I had never been the type of man to explain myself to anyone nor did I apologize for my decisions. One of those decisions was claiming her daughter. She was mine. Mine to love, mine to protect, and mine to handle how I saw fit. Endia's approval wasn't anything I required or that would change the course of things between my Nari and me.

"Oh, I know you do." A teasing smile danced behind her eyes while her lips curled slightly. "But what you don't do is see *your* world through *her* eyes."

"I do . . ."

Her head gently motioned side to side, pausing my thoughts. "No, you don't. You see the world you want her to accept and feel safe in. You know your intentions, and as strongly as she feels that she's safe with you, there's always that small bit of uncertainty that makes her question."

"I will never hurt Nari, ever."

"Intentionally, no." My eyes turned hard and she smiled brighter. "You push because you know what's best and understandably so. Your experience far outweighs hers. You're stubborn by nature and are used to being in charge. This . . ." She paused, allowing her eyes to roam. "She doesn't care about any of it, and that's a good thing because money doesn't make your problems disappear. No matter how much you give her access to, she still has to grow into her own and find security in *you* as a man and as her husband. Her heart longs for a connection; to have people she can depend on."

"I give her that."

"I agree, but on your terms. You also make clear that she will only ever have *you*."

I snorted, feeling the tension in my shoulders. "Your family and her father will never be a part of her life," I warned, being clear that there was no room for negotiating.

"They don't deserve to be, but you must understand that all she sees and feels is you pushing. You have good reason, but it creates the illusion that she doesn't have a voice, that she's simply here in *your* world, living by *your* rules. Let her find her footing. Give her time to make decisions about her life because she knows what's best and not because you forced her hand. She will make the right decisions if you allow her space to do so. She's your wife, not your child."

My eyes narrowed because I wanted to argue that I wasn't treating her as such, but I understood. My control took away hers. We had to meet somewhere in the middle.

As if she sensed my revelation, Endia's face brightened with another smile, and her hand rested on my arm, offering a gentle squeeze. "Find the balance between the two of you. Sometimes, that's the hardest part. Compromise. You both struggle with it. She's more like you than you give her credit for."

Endia took the stairs and I watched her for a minute before I snorted at the thought of being put in place. My first thought was, who the hell was she to tell me a damn thing, but it was quickly clarified by the reality of things . . .

My mother-in-law!

When I stepped into the building, I did a quick sweep. The crowd was slim, but that made sense, considering the time of the morning. Yet, there was still a need for places such as this to function around the clock.

As I moved through the dimly lit space, I felt eyes on me. I stood out for two reasons: one, I exuded the look of money, and two, I didn't belong with the crowd sprinkled about. It was also why the women watched versus approaching right away. They wanted to see if I would give the reason for my appearance in their seedy establishment. Either I had money to waste and wanted to remain under the radar or I had a specific person I intended to spend time with. I damn sure wasn't about to spend my money on any of the women who were currently on shift.

My focus remained on the stage. She watched me with eager eyes and a subtle grin. One, I assumed, she thought was seductive. When I stood next to the stage, she began performing. That only annoyed me because, as nice as her body was, she didn't have a clue what to do with it—a complete waste. My mind drifted to Nari and the way she yielded to me when my dick was deep, but even the simplest actions from her, like the softness of her smile or the whisper of her voice, made my dick hard. This woman, who had her entire body on display, only wearing a gold G-string while gyrating to whatever song was playing, hadn't so much as caused my dick to twitch. When she realized her best efforts weren't prompting a reaction, she moved to the side of the stage, taking the stairs until she reached me.

"My cousin know you're here?"

Of course not. She doesn't have a clue I even know who the hell you are.

"No."

"You don't need to come throwing your weight around. I didn't tell her that you and I have our little thing."

A grin eased in place as she reached for me, but I caught her wrist, my fingers tightening to the point I knew it was painful, but her smile only stretched wider.

"Unlike Nari, I like it rough, and you look like the type that's into kinky shit." Her tongue pushed through her heavy-coated, gold-glitter lips and swiped them slowly. I laughed under my breath, releasing her.

"We don't have a damn thing other than me warning you to stay away from my wife. You don't seem to understand the severity of crossing me."

Those big-ass eyes of hers rolled. I squinted a bit, attempting to see any of Nari's features on her face. There weren't any. This woman likely took after her father.

"You might have her trained, but I'm not the type to jump on command. However, the offer still stands if your money's right."

She attempted to walk away, but I caught her arm with a little more force, bringing her closer but not close enough to get her smell on me.

"As does mine. Stay the fuck away from my wife and you get to exist."

Her eyes went wild for a minute before she tried her hand at pretending that she wasn't afraid.

"I know who you are, but that don't mean shit to me. You can't just go around—"

"Take a minute to think before you finish that sentence," I warned.

My smile eased in place but there was nothing pleasant behind it, which she quickly picked up on because she swallowed hard. After finding Nari's family, I kept tabs on them. Still did, in fact, but I never approached any of them other than Shayla and hadn't planned to unless I deemed it necessary.

Shayla made it necessary once she found her way to me after Nari began posting our lives on her page. She reached out, presenting herself as family. I made clear that she wasn't and wouldn't be allowed in Nari's life. The next communication I received was a message propositioning sex with a promise to keep it from her cousin. She was willing to fuck me on the low if I agreed. I received those types of offers often, but having it come from someone in Nari's so-called family had me seeing red. I pulled up on Shayla that night to make clear that if she reached out again or so much as breathed my wife's name, she would become a news story.

Those types of promises were better served in person, which was why I sought her out. Needless to say, she got the point and hadn't been in touch since. It was also why I was confused by the fact that she would engage in a shouting match with Nari after I made my position clear. The only thing I could come up with was that she wanted to possibly appeal to Nari's need for family and work her way into her cousin's life again so she could, by association, benefit from the privilege I provided Nari. But that wasn't an option either.

Shayla attempted to wiggle out of my grasp, but I held firm and moved closer to her face.

"Apparently, you need a refresher course on what 'stay the fuck away from my wife' means."

She swallowed hard and her eyes shifted. "I didn't go looking for her. We just happened to run into each other and—"

"And you decided to try to devalue her place in my life. Maybe I wasn't clear before. She is my wife by *choice*. *Not* some piece of ass . . ." I paused, allowing a minute for my eyes to travel the length of her body before they met hers again. ". . . that I'm pimping out.

The lifestyle I provide Nari is strictly because I love and cherish the woman she is. There's nothing within my power I won't do to ensure her happiness, and that goes far beyond monetary things. The concept may be hard for a woman like you to understand, considering your only asset is between your legs, but I would advise you to try harder to find some clarity. Understood?"

"Yeah, I hear you," she mumbled, her eyes blazing with anger and embarrassment.

"Smart girl. Now run along, *Passion . . .*" When I used her stage name, her face hardened even more. ". . . Looks like you have a willing customer."

I let her go, and she quickly moved the same arm to her chest, rubbing the spot where my hand had just been. As I gave her my back to leave, I heard the anger in her voice when she addressed the man who took a seat.

"You want a dance, daddy?" She was in a place befitting a woman of her stature.

An hour later, I sat in a cigar lounge with Toussaint. He had six men in the private room eyeing our every move, ready to react at the slightest twitch of a muscle that appeared threatening. Darius sat to my right and Cast stood just inside the doorway. He too was ready for gunplay if required.

"Ya know I can't just turn a blind eye." His accent was thick regardless of his years in the States. Toussaint was born and raised in Haiti and split his time between there and the U.S. He had men sprinkled across the entire East Coast, pushing the drugs he secured from us.

"I'm not asking you to turn a blind eye. I'm only asking that you use your head." A finger tapped my temple, which caused his already narrowed eyes to squint more while his lips pressed into a straight line, expressing offense. I didn't give a fuck. I was here for a specific reason, to make my case that it wasn't my men who took out his family, Knotty. He must have considered the obvious, but one could never be too sure. There was nothing to gain from me moving so recklessly. Had Knotty continued to ignore my terms, I would have dealt with him, just not in the manner that was executed.

"Ya questioning my intelligence, Akel?"

"No, because that's not necessary. We exist in peace with each other. I don't fuck with you, the same as you know to stay out of my way . . ."

"But Knotty was on your blocks in zones that weren't approved, aye?" His hand lifted and a finger tapped his knee. "Disrespectful. I tell him no good, but his head is hard as stone, ego too big. Ya two had words."

"I issued my warning. Had the disrespect continued, my next step would have been to place the responsibility on you. Had you not handled the situation, my issue would then be with you, not a boy trying to play a man's game."

Toussaint stared hard for a minute before he nodded and brushed his hand down his face. I was a man of integrity. I would have given Toussaint the chance to deal with Knotty. Reckless killing wasn't good for business on either side.

"Meh product is gone. That's a lot of money. Whoever 'tis wants it to be ya issue. Dat means I lost money 'cause of ya."

"You lost money because your family didn't follow the rules. That's not my debt to pay, and I won't. I will give you my word that once I have a name, you'll have it too. I'll give you time to collect, but that's all you're allowed. To collect what you're owed."

I was making it clear that the final call was mine.

"I'm owed blood. He killed one of mine. The retribution is on me to make right."

"Understood, but that can't happen, not this time. I'm the only one who ends this."

Again, he stared for a moment before he offered a nod. "Ya have my word long as I have yours." He wanted assurance that I would take the life of the person who killed Knotty.

I stood, adjusting my jacket. Darius was on his feet seconds after, followed by Toussaint. We shook on the terms, and just as I was about to leave, his voice stopped me.

"Ya wife . . ." There was a long pause before he continued. ". . .'da streets are whispering."

I turned to face him while Darius stepped forward, his hand resting at his waist. Cast did the same, placing him next to me. Toussaint's men moved into position, but he held his hand up, pausing their reaction. "Easy, Akel. I respect the rules because I have my own family to consider. Just passing the word for ya to keep her close. Not all men understand what it means to dance with the devil." His face remained stoic while referencing me as the devil. *Smart man.*

On occasion, I could be considered a monster, but there was no doubt in my mind he understood that no one had come close to experiencing the worst of what I was capable of. However, it would be unleashed for public record if anyone managed to touch my wife.

I tossed my chin before leaving, with Darius leading the way and Cast behind me. Our discussion would happen when there weren't any unwanted ears listening.

"Why the fuck didn't you ask for a name?" Cast glared at me through the rearview mirror. He was driving the SUV we left in while Darius was beside me.

"He wouldn't have given one." Darius spoke my thoughts before I got a chance to. We shared a look of understanding. Cast didn't have to question my intent because he too was clear on the rules. His anger came from the fact that Nari had also worked her spell over him. She was family, which created a sense of obligation for him to protect her, the same as he was sworn to protect me. Only with Nari, it was more of a loyalty to the woman who had managed to steal his heart without trying. It was what had him asking a question he already had an answer for. Toussaint wouldn't be labeled as a snitch; however, he wanted me to know that a weakness had been identified . . .

Nari.

As much as I hated that my life put hers in a challenging position, I was fully prepared to ensure she was never fully affected. For now, that would have to be pushed aside. My priority at that moment was leveling us again. She and I needed to be on the same page and I was fully prepared to do whatever was necessary to ensure that happened.

CHAPTER 8

NARI.

"**W**hat's on your mind?"

His voice settled something in me, even though I had been in my feelings all day. I didn't react right away. My focus remained on the backyard even after I felt his hands rest on the balcony and his body gently pressed against mine, locking me in. I knew Kincaid. The move was strategic. He wanted me close without leaving me the ability or space to deny him.

Like he denied me all day.

"Not you," I muttered, granting me a smile before a kiss landed on my temple and Kincaid's chin rested on top of my head. He leaned into me, his breathing relaxing a little more with every passing second.

"You're still angry." Statement, not a question.

"No, I don't have a reason to be." He laughed lightly and smiled again. I hadn't seen his face yet, but didn't need to, to feel his smile. It was that potent.

"You never need a reason, sweetheart, but somehow, I find myself on the receiving end of that sharp tongue of yours more than I like."

My eyes rolled, but I didn't respond. After a few more moments of silence, he pulled away, but it was only enough to give him leverage to move me with him. His large hands met my hips and we both ended up in the egg chair. It took a minute to adjust my position, which ended up being my shoulder against his chest and my feet tucked beneath the cushion that lined the back of the chair. I sat sideways across his body, my knees resting lazily on his solid frame.

We stared at each other briefly before Kincaid pressed a soft kiss on my lips then his forehead to mine. "Truce."

"We're not at war. That doesn't apply."

"But you're angry, and I don't like you angry."

I grinned, narrowing my eyes. "This conversation sounds eerily familiar."

"It worked for you, so I figured it might work for me."

His shoulders relaxed when he sank deeper into the cushion. One arm encircled my body, pulling me closer, and the other hand rested on my calf. His fingers moved across my bare skin, creating a soothing rhythm.

"You didn't sleep in our bed last night. What happened to 'no running'?"

"I was up late and ended up crashing in my office."

"And then you left before I was up and ignored me all day." I'd called twice and sent several texts, neither of which were answered.

"It's been a busy day and I needed space."

"You can have space, but I can't?" My eyes narrowed once more.

"I was working, so technically, it's not the same."

"If you're ignoring me, it most definitely *is* the same," I warned.

"Agreed, and I apologize. I don't want to argue with you, Nari. In fact, I want to take you to dinner to try to work through a few things."

"Like?"

"You'll have to agree to our date to find out." His smile was smug, which struck a nerve. This man was always in control, but I decided to play along.

"Dinner where?"

"That's also a surprise, but I promise you'll enjoy it."

"So. . . . date with my husband?"

"If you'll agree."

"I'm hungry, so, yes."

He laughed lightly and kissed me again. "I'll take what I can get. Now, go get dressed. I need to make a few calls, then I'll shower and change."

"How do I need to dress?"

"However you want. Tonight is casual." He tapped my thigh, signaling that I needed to get up. After I climbed from his lap, Kincaid was on his feet as well, stopping me before I got too far. He lowered his head and I felt the warmth of his breath against my skin before his lips brushed my neck then landed gently in the same spot. "No arguing tonight, okay? We can disagree, but we won't argue."

When his eyes reached mine, I nodded slowly. There was something about this man that I couldn't shake. The way he owned the ability to make my body react with just a look and a few words. It was dangerous but in a good way.

"Good. We need to be out of here in an hour." Kincaid stood upright and pinched my chin between his fingers before he leaned in, delivering a kiss. I moved in one direction to get ready and he moved in another to leave our room. I was hopeful that tonight would be good. It was my goal to ensure that it was.

"Where are we?"

"One of my favorite spots." He smiled down at me, sensing my unease. The place didn't fit the class of those I had been accustomed to frequenting with Kincaid. The building was a standalone covered in artwork layered in spray paint over the years. Some colorful designs were well thought out images; the others were tags and random things from known local gangs. I eased closer to my husband's side. His hand gripped mine firmer as we crossed the parking lot to reach our destination. I noticed several groups of people filling the metal benches near the doors and others scattered about, but all were clearly waiting to enter the establishment. We, of course, bypassed the crowd.

Stepping inside, I relaxed a little. The atmosphere felt warm and cozy, even with the rush of bodies moving about and the buzz of conversations humming from the various tables filled with patrons. Every seating area seemed to be occupied, and judging by the clientele, I was glad I'd chosen to dress casually. But even still, the expensive strappy heels on my feet, ripped jeans, boyfriend silk top, and burgundy blazer almost felt like too much. Kincaid was in jeans, Ones, and a designer crewneck sweatshirt. Although he wore labels, he fit in better than I did.

"You said casual?" I warned, and his soft brown eyes swept my body lingeringly before he smiled.

"I'm the only one who needs to be concerned with what you're wearing, and I like it, so don't worry about what anyone else thinks."

Before I could respond, an older gentleman approached us with cheeks as fluffy and round as his belly. He smiled generously and I noticed Kincaid's expression matched his.

"Well, look who decided to show his face around here."

Kincaid extended a hand, but the man waved him off, pulling him into a familiar hug.

"I'm sorry about your pops, son. He will be missed." I sensed the sincerity in his voice and noticed it mirrored the humility in his expression. Kincaid only nodded, then the mood quickly shifted. The man's smile was back as he moved on to me.

"*Mrs.* Akel. It's about time he brought you around. I was beginning to think I was no longer family."

I frowned a bit. My regard then moved to my husband, who only chuckled under his breath before making a formal introduction.

"Nari, this is Roosevelt Taylor. One of my father's dearest friends and an extended part of our family."

"It's nice to meet you." I offered a hand in Roosevelt's direction, but the same as he'd done with Kincaid, I ended up in a tight embrace.

"Easy, Roosevelt, that's my wife," Kincaid warned playfully, but there was a hint of seriousness to his demand. He wasn't keen on sharing anything about me, not even an innocent hug to potential family.

"You worried this old man's charm might be enough to steal her from you?" Roosevelt grinned hard while his stumpy hands landed roughly on his round belly. "I might not be tall, dark, and handsome, but I know how to charm a pretty lady. Never forget, looks fade, but the ability to put a smile on her face is a gift."

I was moved into Kincaid's side while he made sure one of his corded arms draped protectively around my shoulders. He kissed my temple before addressing Roosevelt. "I agree, but I'm just as skilled in that department, or so I hope." His eyes lowered to me and I couldn't hold back my smile.

"You do okay, but this one is hard to resist." My regard landed on Roosevelt, who winked mischievously. It was clear to me that he found pleasure in taunting Kincaid.

"She's a keeper, son. This one's going to give you trouble. She's just as full of the bullshit as you are, but I blame your old man. He made you a clone of him when it came to ensuring the ladies fall hard and fast."

A laugh burst from my gut because I hadn't been expecting that. He'd rendered me completely speechless, but apparently not Kincaid, who came back quickly.

"She might have fallen for me, but you have no idea the hell this woman can put me through. Either way, it's all worth it."

"Better be. Let me go get you a table cleaned up. We've been really busy tonight. Still got a crowd out there waiting. Good thing you're in good with the owner."

He scurried away, and I noticed he moved with a slight limp, favoring his left side.

"He was attacked years ago. They shot him in his chest and leg several times; killed his wife also, all over a few thousand dollars."

My eyes shot up to Kincaid, who had been watching me watch Roosevelt. "How do you know that?"

"It's how he and my father became close. He used to bring me here when I was a kid. The two would talk cordially, but nothing more than Roosevelt tending to his customers with quality service. My dad was a busy man, so a couple of months passed without us showing up. During that time, the place was robbed, and Roosevelt's wife was murdered that night. We came by a few weeks after the botched robbery and the restaurant was closed. Roosevelt and his wife ran it together. So with her passing, and his condition, they had to close up. When my father asked around and found out what had happened, we went to see him at the hospital. I was young, but I understood the conversation they had that day. My father made him a promise to set things right. About a month later, the place was open again, and my father occasionally brought me here again for dinner, the same as he always had. I learned years later that my father took care of the people who robbed Roosevelt and the debt he owed on this place."

"You own this too?"

He shook his head gently. "No, Roosevelt does. My father never wanted to take the business from him. Only ensure that it would always be his."

I smiled at the thought just as a younger woman who couldn't help but blush and steal glances at Kincaid approached us.

"We have your table ready, Mr. and Mrs. Akel."

"Kincaid and Nari are fine." His tone was light and her cheeks lifted higher from his attention.

"Yes, sir. Please follow me."

Kincaid nodded and his hand lowered to the small of my back while we navigated through the maze of tables until we reached the corner in the back where ours was. Our setup was a small, round wooden table topped with menus wedged between condiments and a tea light candle in a small glass enclosure. There were only two weathered wooden chairs, but the spot was cozy and private compared to the rest of the establishment.

After my chair was pulled out and I was seated, Kincaid settled in across from me.

"I hope this works. We're swamped tonight, and it's all we have."

"This is perfect. Thank you," I offered, and she flashed a smile before taking our drink orders and hurrying away, stopping at several tables before disappearing in the back.

He picked up a menu and began a visual sweep until he felt me staring.

"What?"

"You're different here. You were different with *him*," I stated in reference to his mood tonight and his interaction with Roosevelt. I could tell the two were close and truly considered each other family.

"Different, how?" His brow lifted just a little, but his stare remained intense.

"I don't know; less high class."

Kincaid laughed under his breath and tossed his chin dismissively, delivering that sexy, cocky grin of his. "Maybe it's because I'm not in a suit."

"Nope, that's not it." I shook my head, smiling softly before I lifted my menu.

"Then what do you propose warrants this so-called change?"

"I don't know. Maybe you feel at home here, like you can just *be*."

He laughed again before his eyes found mine. "Or maybe I just want *you* to feel *at home* with me and I'm letting my guard down to allow you space to do so."

"I feel at home with you, Kincaid."

"Occasionally, but lately, things between us have been a bit disjointed."

"True, but that doesn't mean I don't feel like I have a place with you or in your life. I'm simply trying to define what that means to me."

"It means that whatever you want, need, or desire will be yours, even if it's space from me while you work through things. It's been brought to my attention that my pushing isn't always the best way to get the results I seek."

"Which are?"

"For you to trust me with all of you and to know there's nothing in this world I wouldn't give or do to ensure your happiness."

His eyes were intense, but his declaration didn't waver.

"It might not seem like it, but I believe you."

"Good, then that's all that matters. Would you like me to suggest something or would you rather decide on your own?"

Ahh, his way of giving me space.

This was new. Usually, he wouldn't have asked. He simply would have offered his suggestion.

"You order. You know better than I do what's good here."

Kincaid nodded. "Everything here is good. It's just a matter of what type of damage you're looking to take on. As good as it tastes, I can't guarantee it's good for you."

Dinner went smoothly. I learned that soul food was Roosevelt's specialty by way of the fried chicken, mac and cheese, greens, and homemade cornbread we both had piled on our plates. Our conversation was light while we demolished our dinner. I updated Kincaid on the reception plans, to which he only nodded and offered a lot of mm-hmms before he discussed minor details of his business trip with me. It felt encouraging to be in a good space with my husband. I longed for the type of connection we shared tonight.

"You look happy."

"I am." One shoulder lifted into a shrug while Kincaid studied me closely.

"What can I do to ensure you stay that way?"

"How about you promise me that no matter how bad things get between us, you will never, and I mean never, sleep with my cousin."

"I would have to assume you're joking because there's not a chance in hell that will ever happen."

"I'm so not joking. Did she really proposition you?"

"Yes."

"How?"

"Through social media not long after we returned from Tulum."

I sat silently processing, wishing I had actually been able to put my foot in her ass. Apparently, she deserved it for more than one reason.

"Please do not let this be another issue between us." Kincaid stared at me, waiting, and I decided to let it go. I honestly didn't believe he had any interest in Shayla, the same as I also did not doubt in my mind that she actually extended the offer. *Fucking bitch.*

"I refuse to allow her any more space in my life."

"Good, so can we get back to my initial question? What can I do to ensure that beautiful smile remains on your face?"

"Nothing. You do enough."

He lifted his beer, taking down some, but his eyes lingered, still absorbing me. "*Enough* doesn't exist where you're concerned. You're my responsibility, and that starts with making sure I'm not taking away any parts of you."

"You're not."

"Not even your control? That seems to be a point of contention between us. Even your mother mentioned it."

"She has?" That was news to me. I hoped she hadn't overstepped.

"She has. We shared a brief conversation about my propensity to overlook your pending needs. And as much as I didn't like being called out on my shit, I had to agree. My need to give you the life I feel you deserve has left me a little singular in my understanding of what that might feel like from your perspective. It seems I've been a bit selfish, and Endia made a point of bringing the issue to my attention."

"She shouldn't have—"

"Your mother has every right to protect your best interest, even where I'm concerned. I might not have appreciated how it felt for Endia to *put me in my place*, for lack of better phrasing, but I respect that she cares enough to step up for you, even if it meant going against me. I'm not the most pliable with my expectations, which I'm sure you'll agree." His tone was teasing, even if his expression was void of a smile.

"You have good intentions."

"Agreed, but execution is sometimes far more important than intent. I don't want you to feel like you're just existing in my world. It's important that you feel you belong and on your terms. Unfortunately, there are some things I can't bend on because there are measures in place to ensure your safety, but I also understand that you have to have a say in certain aspects of your life. I'm willing to allow you space to find your footing and I'm also willing to trust you'll make the best decisions for our family."

I was taken aback. This wasn't exactly the confession I was expecting tonight, but I appreciated that he was, at the very least, attempting to understand things from my perspective. It was only right that I offered the same.

"You make it sound like I see this marriage as a nightmare. You're not some abusive, controlling asshole who's holding me hostage."

A smile split onto his face. "I would hope not, but I do understand it was a lot of change in a short time. I simply expected you to adjust without truly allowing you time to do so."

"And I promised to trust you without running every time I got scared or something didn't feel right. I apologize. This part is new for me . . ." I paused, taking a moment to regroup. "The whole 'having someone in my corner.'"

"Understood. All I ask is that you trust me. I belong to you and only you. I'm never going to lie to you and I damn sure won't share any parts of me with another woman, ever."

His gaze was stern, demanding, and leaving little room for me to question the validity of his affirmation. It was crystal clear. *I'm yours, you're mine. There is no question about our bond, nor is there room for anyone else to fit into the equation but us.*

"As much as I know and believe that truth, it's still not easy to be faced with your past—especially when that past is insistent on aggressively reminding me that they existed at one point or another. Even the most confident women allow their insecurities to get the best of them occasionally."

He simply sat poised; his body relaxed, but his posture was just as confident as the intense stare that penetrated me for a long moment. "I understand, and I will do my best to keep the past from landing in your lap, but in the event that something slips past me, promise we'll talk about it before you jump to conclusions or forge assumptions that my dick gets hard for anyone *but* you, agreed?" His eyes squinted just a bit before they issued a smile of reassurance. Again, he was confident, his stance resolute. *I only want you, sweetheart!* It was so clear that I could nearly hear his voice in my head.

"Agreed." My tone was breathy because, somehow, my sick mind focused on one part of that request . . .

"Let's go. I see we're now on the same page."

This man knew me so well that it was scary. Unfortunately, I had to consider that a blessing because, right now, I wanted exactly what I knew he was about to deliver.

CHAPTER 9

KINCAID.

She shifted in her sleep, adjusting her body while inching closer to mine. I had just eased back into bed after a trip to the bathroom since I couldn't force myself back to sleep. I, however, had no complaints because the warmth of her bare skin against mine felt nice. This was the part I loved the most, waking up to her scent and the silky feel of her skin against mine, her body tangled in the sheets, tempting me and testing my willpower. Nari was the best part of my day.

Our date last night was successful. We both promised to do a better job of being on the same page with our marriage, which meant being in tune with each other's emotional needs. I must admit I'd failed somewhat regarding what my wife needed from me.

She had a bit of a jealous streak, which, in a weird way, I liked. What man didn't want his woman to feel possessive over him, regardless of whether he would choose to betray her trust? I never would, but it felt good to know Nari cared enough to be cautious of any and all relationships I had with other women—past or present. I felt the same about her, but unlike Nari, I wouldn't react by running. My resolve would be to cancel the threat, if any existed—permanently if that was what I felt was necessary to maintain my peace of mind. Joey was lucky I hadn't taken such measures with him. He hadn't been around, so I assumed the message was received: *stay the fuck away from my wife.*

When we arrived back home, I physically reminded Nari just how much she belonged to me, and I belonged to her. There wasn't an inch of her body I hadn't delivered a reminder to, bringing her to the edge of delirium until she ultimately submitted, allowing me to provide the ultimate pleasure. I lost count of how many times she orgasmed before I eventually released my own. Nari was out within seconds after we showered and climbed back in bed, naked and exhausted. I watched her sleep peacefully, seemingly completely content until my body could no longer fight, then I was out myself.

My phone alerted me to a call. I gave Nari one last glance before I eased away to connect with Cast. I didn't want to wake her, so I moved through the bedroom to the sitting area and stepped out onto the balcony.

"Yeah."

"Still no activity at the grandparents' house. Just them coming and going every so often and the aunt. Looks like she's living there now."

"Keep the live feed. If you see anything that looks suspect, let me know."

"He's been extremely quiet. More than usual, but I think you'll find this interesting."

"What?"

"He visited Salacious. Only once, and he never went inside."

"Then what the fuck was he doing?"

"Meeting with an old friend of your wife's."

"Joseph?"

"You got it. I wanted to see if it led to anything, but so far, nothing has happened. You can't see much other than Joey getting into the car with him. They talk for about fifteen minutes, then he leaves. The only time they've met I know of was at the club, but two of his guys have been seen there multiple times. Each visit is the same. Joey meets them out front; they have a few words, then they leave. Whoever they are, they know how to remain anonymous. Those fuckers avoid the cameras every time and I can't lock them down to any of the vehicles coming or going. I'm sending you the footage from Salacious's security system. What do you think it means?"

"Could be a number of things. Joseph still works for Darius."

"He still pushing that shit after everything that happened?"

"He doesn't have a choice. The man is marked, and he's also not stupid. At least not when it comes to his obligation."

When it comes to Nari, he has no fucking sense.

Which is going to get him killed.

Keeping Nari safe meant keeping tabs on those who could harm her. I arranged to have cameras set up to keep an eye on her grandparents' home, the strip club where Shayla worked, and her apartment. She latched onto some wannabe drug dealer who was pretending to be her boyfriend. At the same time, he actually had a pregnant live-in girlfriend two blocks over from the complex where he occasionally shared a bed with Shayla.

And she had the nerve to accuse my wife of being controlled with money.

"Manchester can't figure out a way around me to get to Nari or her mother, who I'm sure he now knows is under my protection. He may try to lure her to him by using anyone she was connected to. It wouldn't be hard to do some digging to find out Joseph might be an option. Keep me posted on how frequently his people end up anywhere near her family or Joseph. Anything new on the Knotty situation?"

"I might have something, but nothing solid yet."

"I feel like it's Manchester, but something's off about it. I refuse to make a move until I have the evidence. I can guarantee that Saulo and Kafi will wait to see what I do. Everything's a damn test with them."

"And if you fail?"

"Doesn't matter. I do whatever is necessary when it comes to Nari. They will do what needs to be done on their end, but either way, the decision is mine, and I don't give a damn what either of them think. I refuse to allow my wife to get caught up in any of this any more than she already is." Arms encircled my waist just before I felt her cheek press against my back. I covered her hands with one of mine.

"Maybe it won't be an issue."

"It's already an issue. I have to go. Call me if you come across anything worthwhile."

"Will do."

After ending the call, I slipped my phone into the pocket of the shorts I tossed on and turned to face Nari. She likely got out of bed shortly after I did because her hair was now pulled back into a ponytail and her face was freshly washed.

"I figured you would sleep in." I pressed a kiss on her forehead and she groaned in a gruff voice.

"I tried, but you left me."

"What does that have to do with you sleeping in?"

"I'm used to you next to me. When you're not, I can tell, and I can't sleep peacefully."

"Flattery will get you everywhere."

"Good to know." I was blessed with a cheeky grin while she angled her head back to look up, her eyes transitioning to something serious when they met mine.

"I heard part of your call."

"Yeah?"

She nodded slowly. "What am I caught up in? Was that about my father?"

I tensed at the term *father*. Regardless of whether I preferred the reference, he was indeed the man partially responsible for the existence of the woman who now owned my heart.

"Yes. It's possible he's been in touch with your aunt and likely your cousin. It's all the more reason I need you to promise to keep your distance."

The warning was delivered with the look I offered, which had her face tensing.

"I said I would."

"Good. It's what's best until I get a handle on things." My thumb brushed across her lips and along the outline of her jaw before I sealed the deal with a kiss. "Now, let's get dressed. I want to spend the day with you, starting with breakfast."

Nari searched my face for answers before asking the question on the tip of her tongue. "You're not working today?"

"No. If you'll allow my company, I'd like to be with you instead."

Her eyes narrowed slightly and sparked with amusement. "Oh, so you need permission to spend time with me?"

My expression eased into a confident grin. "I'm sure you know better than that. I'm simply being partial to formalities and issuing a request instead of my usual demand."

"Right. Whatever Kincaid wants, Kincaid gets." She spoke with a light bit of sarcasm that contradicted the curl of her lips exposing a smile.

"As do you, Mrs. Akel. And today, you get me. I pray that I don't disappoint."

"Not possible," she said, seductively allowing her eyes to take me in.

I winked, landing one last kiss before we separated to get dressed. Nari finished before me, and while I stood in the center of the closet deciding what to wear, I caught a glimpse of her in a strapless dress that hugged her chest and flowed loosely around the rest of her body. It was red and some type of silk material that stopped at her ankles. There was nothing sexual about it. However, the color and my knowledge of what was beneath it had my dick inflating. While I was lost in my lustful thoughts, she mentioned something about her mother, which I missed because my mind was on another mother. The one whose legs I had been between all night.

Deciding to keep things casual for the day, I dressed in jeans, a graphic tee, my Presidential watch, and no other jewelry besides my wedding ring. When I reached the kitchen where Nari was waiting, I found her chatting away with Endia, who smiled and greeted me the minute I entered. She was dressed for the day as always. Since her time here, I learned she was an early riser who retired each night no later than nine unless Nari kept her up beyond her regular routine. I wasn't sure if it was her routine or if she was attempting to stay out of the way. However, I planned on addressing that at some point. I had grown selfish with my wife's time, but I was also mature enough not to allow my needs to get in the way of her relationship with Endia.

"We're heading to breakfast if you'd like to join."

"No thanks. I already ate."

"Then we'll do dinner tonight as a family," I offered as an alternative, stepping behind my wife, encircling her waist so I could allow my hand to rest on her stomach. There were still no signs of the life that grew there, but we had an appointment in a few weeks to learn the sex of our first child.

"If you're home in time, that will be fine."

"We'll be here. I'll have Chef come by at five to get started. We can have dinner by seven."

"Then it's a date," she offered with a soft smile and nod.

"Good. I look forward to the evening." I began a trail of kisses down my wife's neck to her shoulder, speaking against her soft skin. "You ready?"

"Yep."

I stepped back, allowing her space to move, noticing she lifted a jean jacket from the counter before telling her mother goodbye and heading out of the kitchen. I lingered behind to have a few words with Endia.

"Floyd and Conner are out front. Eli is still lurking, which could potentially be an issue. He may attempt to use your family to reach the two of you. I don't know if this needs to be addressed, but—"

She shook her head softly before she held her hand up to stop me. "No. I understand, and you don't have to worry. I have no interest in speaking to or being around my family. She's all I care about." She motioned toward the entrance to the kitchen.

"Understood. I'm just making sure we're clear on expectations. Have a good day, and we'll see you tonight."

"We are. Take care of my baby," she warned playfully, like a loving parent would.

"Of course," I assured Endia. She seemed comfortable with my response and returned to her book and tea.

Nari chose the location where we dined, a bistro in Buckhead Alisha recommended that I had never heard of. Since it was just the two of us and no security, I wasn't too keen on unfamiliar places, but I decided not to object. Today was her day, and it turned out the food was pretty good, and the place was relatively empty. We both had omelets and fresh fruit. While Nari sipped hot tea, I chose black coffee. It was an indulgence I didn't engage in often, but occasionally, I craved a good brew.

"Do you know why I run so much?"

"Excuse me?" The question caught me off guard. For the most part, our conversation was light and about random things. I attempted to keep the mood light after having such an intense discussion about our relationship the night before.

"You said, 'I run; do you know why?'"

I kept my expression neutral but maintained steady eye contact. She was sharing, and I needed her to feel a connection so she felt comfortable doing so. These moments from Nari when she was exposed were rare but appreciated.

"I have my assumptions, but I would love to hear your thoughts."

Her fingers continuously brushed across the cloth napkin that sat beside her plate. She was nervous and it was cute.

"You're always so poised and in control. It's like nothing upsets your balance. You know what you want and don't hesitate to stake your claim. I'm a prime example of the practice." This time, her nervous energy was expressed by way of shifting in her chair. I remained quiet, not interrupting, so she could say what she needed, and she continued. "I've only been with a few men . . ."

My eyes narrowed, but I decided not to react, even though the last thing I wanted was to hear about her past relationships, especially if this would turn into a confession about their physical nature. I briefly understood my wife's low tolerance when it came to my past sexual encounters, which was like a proverbial slap in the face. I relaxed when she exhaled and kept going after faltering from my stern glare.

"Well, not really *men*, per se. I wouldn't truly classify them as such. Especially not after experiencing you." Nari grinned, but my expression remained neutral until I was sure where she was going with this. It was inching dangerously close to a topic I wasn't prepared to explore.

My wife having sex with another man.

"Sweetheart, I don't think I'm prepared to discuss the men you've been with."

Her eyes rolled softly. "Imagine Kincaid Akel having an insecure moment, but that's not where this is going. I just wanted you to know I've never experienced this before . . ." Her hand lifted and she flicked her wrist between the two of us.

"This?" I questioned, still unsure what we were discussing.

"A serious relationship. You're my first." She shrugged with a slight grin. "First with a lot of things, apparently, and that's intimidating because you have it all figured out and I'm simply fumbling through all of this."

I snorted at the thought. "Not even fucking close," I found myself mumbling. My wife was frustratingly unpredictable, which kept me second-guessing. I might not have been fumbling, but I struggled to understand the woman I married.

"We both know I don't mean first sexual experience, same as we clearly know I'm nowhere near close to yours. I do, however, mean my first with all the other heavy stuff. Even if you don't have it all figured out, it appears that you do. The men I've been with—"

"Boys." I smirked and she shook her head.

"The *boys* I've been with didn't put much thought into me and you put too much thought into me and *us*."

"Is that so terrible?"

"Yes and no. For me, it's intimidating as hell because I always feel like I'm struggling to keep up with you, your life—shit, even with sex. You're so confident with everything."

"Nari, sweetheart, no one's keeping score. This isn't perfect. It would be foolish of either of us to expect perfection. I simply want you to be happy."

"But that's the thing. You want me to be happy, which is a lot of damn pressure because I feel like I'm going to fail when it comes to *you* being happy."

Ahh, finally. Some truth.

"You are all I need, baby. If I have you, I'm happy. I'm not putting pressure on you to be anything other than who and what you are. I don't want you to put that type of pressure on yourself either." I paused for a minute, relaxing my shoulders. "I'm at an advantage. I've lived and experienced things you haven't with relationships and life. You're still young, and part of my responsibility is to give you space to grow and figure things out. All I ask is that you're confident in your role in my life. We're both going to fuck up. I'm sure, in time, I will. . . far more than you. However, right now, I know I have the advantage. Trust me. You'll get there as long as you stay in this with me."

"I don't want to make a big deal out of it since, after last night, we're in a good space, but I felt like you needed to know why I run. I'm not necessarily insecure with you, but more so with this entire thing. A part of me feels like you're too much for me, but I want this, and I deserve this . . ." She paused her gaze, pinning it to mine. "I deserve you."

Oh, sweetheart, far more than I deserve you! My biggest fear is that you'll one day realize the truth.

"You deserve better than me, but it's too late because, as you've stated, I've staked my claim, and there's no going back."

"Good, I kinda like being claimed by you."

"*Kincaid* . . ." An overly animated voice almost sang my name, forcing me to peel my eyes from Nari to see who it belonged to.

"Gwen." I offered a smile and hers grew wider.

"My God, I'd know this body and handsome face anywhere. It's been a few months. How are you? Today must be my lucky day running into you."

Over the fucking top. All that wasn't necessary, but I was sure it was aimed at Nari, who sat patiently, watching our interaction.

"Great, actually. Let me introduce you to my wife . . ." I paused and motioned across the table, watching as my Nari sat up straight, squaring her shoulders while peering smugly at Gwen. She didn't, however, get a word in because Gwen spoke up immediately.

"Your wife? Wow." She fumbled over the words. It was a shock, considering she and I had a few dinners with the intention of getting to know each other before my engagement to Aila. She saw us out one night, noticed the ring, and threw a bit of a tantrum after I explained my inability to offer my time any longer. It should have been evident with the unanswered texts and calls. I supposed women had their own version of what certain things meant, just like I could see her mind working at the present moment, attempting to make sense that Nari wasn't Aila. Hence, the confusion on her face.

"Yes. His *wife*. Nice to meet you, *Gwen*." Amusement danced in my expression when I noticed Nari purposely lifted her left hand, resting it on the table. That wasn't a coincidence, which Gwen also picked up on because her regard remained on the ring longer than it should have before she finally found her voice.

"Same, although I am a little confused, Kincaid." Her unsettled eyes landed on me. "This isn't the woman you introduced to me as your fiancée."

"But I *am* who he introduced as his *wife*. Now, if you don't mind, my *husband* and I would like to finish our breakfast. Enjoy your meal. The omelets are phenomenal if you're undecided about what to order."

Easy, sweetheart. No need to show your claws to prove ownership of what already belongs to you.

Gwen's lips parted slightly before they pressed together firmly and her eyes bounced between us. I decided to make it clear that it was time for her to keep it moving—no point in leaving room for her mind to wander down the wrong path.

"Take care, Gwen."

She scoffed and walked away gracefully, or at least attempted to. I was simply grateful she didn't push. It wasn't like she had a reason to, but most women didn't need a reason to overstep their bounds.

"Gwen seemed overly excited to run into you." Nari's fork dove into her fruit and a strawberry slipped between her lips. I chuckled at her chill demeanor. Not what I expected.

"I assure you, I didn't sleep with her, so relax whatever twisted thoughts are going on over there."

Nari laughed lightly under her breath. "I don't really care if you did. The past is the past, right?" She arched her brow, paired with a smug grin. I wasn't sure if I believed her amicable reaction to the whole Gwen thing.

"It is."

"See . . ." She shrugged, lifting another strawberry. "Growth." The way it moved past her lips while her eyes remained fastened to mine had my dick twitching.

"So it seems."

We settled back into casual conversation and even though Gwen made a point of sitting at a table that gave her a perfect view of ours, not once did Nari seem bothered. I wasn't sure if it was really growth or if I would hear about it later, but for now, she seemed happy, so I decided not to dwell on the thought. She had nothing at all to worry about when it came to these women. Gwen was beautiful, smart, and extremely successful, but the truth was she could never compete with my wife. I now truly understood the heart wanted what the heart wanted, and mine only desired and craved the woman across from me.

Having dinner with Nari and her mother became one of my new favorite things. Quite often, the two got lost in their own little world and forgot I was there, allowing me to experience their candid conversations about random things. Tonight was no different, but this time, I appeared to be the center of their private discussion, which occasionally meant allowing my input. The two were discussing men and how some demanded submission. It wasn't something I would admit to demanding, but I did prefer Nari to be submissive in certain situations. I was intrigued to hear their thoughts because my wife's views were extremely important regarding how she functioned in our union, and her mother's were as well, considering the magnitude of how they were bonding. Endia's new connection to her daughter had the potential to shape the way Nari functioned in our marriage, and at the moment, they were both waiting for my response. Right now, Nari was eager to see if I would argue against the fact that she insisted I was very much a dominant personality.

"There's a difference in standing firm on my views versus being dominant. I'll agree to not bending in most situations. However, I'm always open to discussing the topics I stand firm on," I offered as a compromise. Endia chuckled and my eyes left Nari and landed gently on her.

"What you're saying is true; however, I beg to differ, Kincaid. Your personality is very much dominant. You don't leave any room for negotiation once you've taken a stance on something."

"The man controls every aspect of our lives, even in the bedroom," Nari mumbled, which caused my expression to shift briefly in amusement before I managed to regroup. The comment wasn't one I would guess Nari meant to vocalize out loud. I wasn't comfortable discussing our sex life in front of her mother and prayed we weren't about to travel down that rabbit hole.

"I'm not surprised. Men like your husband can rarely turn that part of their persona off. Nonetheless, I have my experience with the type, and I assume that works in your favor."

You have no idea. My dick jolted at the thought.

Nari's cheeks flushed, and this time, her eyes widened in surprise. I chuckled at her reaction because we had somehow jumped over the topic of our sex life and landed on Endia's. Neither was a subject I felt comfortable broaching, but Nari seemed a little out of sorts with the comment, which Endia picked up on.

"Stop looking at me like that. I might not have had any other kids, but I've had ample experience with the practice of what leads to making them. I was alone but not always lonely."

My wife gasped, but then smiled, staring at her mother. "I don't think I care to hear about that part of your life."

"Good, because I'm not open to sharing. But my point is, I know plenty of men like your husband. I suppose we both have a type." She lifted her glass and drained the wine she was drinking. "And it's not always a bad thing to have a man who takes charge, *even* in the bedroom."

"This just got extremely uncomfortable," Nari mumbled, shoving a forkful of salad into her mouth.

"You only have yourself to blame, sweetheart. If I recall, it was your slip of the tongue that landed us here."

"Then let me hurry and move us in a different direction." Nari cut her eyes at me and her warning was met with a smug grin. She was adorably embarrassed and I was relieved this was where the subject ended.

"So, I was thinking . . ." she began slowly, and I waited, almost holding my breath. Nari's *thinking* could lead to complications for me. She was still very unpredictable when it came to us.

"About?" I questioned in an easy manner not to set off any alarms and Endia was also waiting.

"You mentioned in Tulum that I should consider launching a business of some kind. It's been on my mind. As lavish as you make my life, I need more than shopping and spa visits. I need to pull my weight around here."

Cute but not necessary.

She offered a soft smile, which I accepted as reassurance that she was not complaining about her current disposition.

"I did, and whatever you need, let me know."

"Well . . ." She straightened her spine. "I need money for resources. I was this close to becoming a millionaire, but I foolishly wrote a check to this strikingly handsome guy, leaving me in a financial deficit."

"I can offer with the utmost confidence that he never cashed it. It seems the bulk of this strikingly handsome guy's business ventures are doing quite well, so it wasn't necessary. And besides, what's a man who goes back on his word?" I winked at her and she rolled her eyes.

"A very wealthy one, apparently, but moving on, I've been thinking that since you're here, you could help me. I'm sure you would appreciate doing more than sitting around here all day." She turned to her mother, who seemed confused about what was happening.

"I'd be more than happy to help you with whatever you need, but I promise my time here is well spent, even if I never leave the house."

"Good to know, but maybe if you help me launch this, you wouldn't mind hanging around for a while or at least visiting once you decide to go home."

Shit. How the fuck did I miss this?

Two things became clear at that moment: Nari was attempting to settle into her purpose and find a way to keep her mother attached to her life. She was not only insecure about her place with me but also with her mother. I watched, praying this didn't go terribly wrong. Endia loved her daughter. I thought she was even partial to me, but that didn't mean she was looking forward to sitting under us for the rest of her life. She had one of her own, and as mundane as we might have assumed it to be, it was hers. Nari was connected to me and this world by the rings on her finger, the vows we exchanged, and the baby she was carrying . . .

And the fact that I would never give her the option to leave me.

But Endia wasn't. I naturally assumed she would want to remain a consistent part of her daughter's life, but then again, it was still an assumption. She was here because I showed up and forced her to get on my jet, not because she'd asked to come be a part of her daughter's life.

"Nari, baby, I know we've missed a lot of time, and you're likely still dealing with the rejection from me not looking for you all those years, but I promise, I'm not going to disappear on you again. I'm here for as long as you want me to be and I pray that you want me here. You don't need to attach me to a business to ensure a connection with us."

And there it was. I noticed the reaction even if it only existed for a brief moment . . .

Relief.

Nari mentally exhaled the tension and fear she had been carrying, which I hadn't recognized or been privy to.

"I want you here."

"*We* want you here," I added, just so there was no misunderstanding.

Endia nodded and Nari began explaining what she had in mind for her business. I was thoroughly impressed to hear the plan to open facilities that would be available to those kids who aged out of the system and weren't quite prepared for life. She expressed the frustration of turning eighteen and being thrown into society, unable to depend on the state anymore. She didn't have housing or support, which sent her down some dangerous roads, attempting to survive the best she could.

Nari wanted to create dorm-style housing for those in the transition period, as well as services that either helped them find and prepare for jobs or assisted them in getting into college. She also wanted to provide services to help them find family members who could be vetted to serve as a support system. I was thoroughly impressed by her passion for creating a safety net for those who would ultimately experience the highs and lows she suffered after foster care. Nari planned on being an agent of change to hopefully prevent others from struggling the way she had. My mother focused on those still in the system, while Nari focused on those who would age out of the system. She was excited about partnering with my mother, who I knew would be all over the idea of her daughter-in-law wanting to work that closely with her for a cause they both believed in.

Endia also seemed genuinely interested in being a part of the project, which created a sense of pride in Nari I knew could only exist from receiving the admiration of a doting parent. It reminded me of things I took for granted since I'd always had my parents' love and support.

That night, I enjoyed my second meal, the haven between my wife's thighs. I feasted like a famished man and not one who had just enjoyed a three-course dinner by a world-renowned chef. My tongue made good on the promise I delivered to make her come multiple times before I explored with my dick, which remained painfully stiff until it found its way home.

Home. My wife was home . . . everything about her, but at that moment, my focus was her body. I aimed to please, which shifted my mind to the earlier conversation about my dominance. It was true. I typically controlled things during sex. Tonight would be no different. I currently had my wife's wrists secured with one of my hands while I plowed into her with deep, penetrating thrusts. She didn't seem to mind because with each one, she opened a little more, moaning deeper in a way that had my dick expanding further.

When I felt her body experience its first round of tremors, I released her wrists but she kept her arms above her head, watching me in a lust-filled haze while I pushed her limits to expedite her undoing. This was more like fucking. My deep strokes were steady and strong. I was starved for the connection somewhere deep within and she worked with me as if searching for the same. Each time I landed hard, she pushed against me, matching my intensity, but thrust forward, eager for more. Something about the neediness she displayed with her mother sent me spiraling. She often pointed out that I had it all together and nothing seemed to leave me unbalanced. For the most part, that was true. However, Nari was the exception.

You weaken my resolve, sweetheart.

The insecurity of not being enough for her ignited something primal in me. I didn't understand where it came from other than the desire to be everything she needed when others refused to be. It was imperative Nari knew that I could make her whole and fucking her until she was full of me and unraveling was the only way I could do so at the present, so that was my intent.

"Uhhhh," she hummed, attempting to fight the feeling building in her core. I not only saw it, but also felt it in the way she pulsed around me in a quick concession that heightened my pleasure. But I kept it together, needing her to reach her peak before me or with me.

When her eyes found mine, she understood because her teeth sank into her lip and she let go. The first wave hit quickly. Her eyes panicked briefly in surprise before settling. I felt her tightening around me, which had me driving deeper, faster, and harder. Nari was a soldier, so she took it all in stride . . . until she lost the battle and unraveled. Her head sank deeper into the pillow and her sex thrust forward, allowing me to go deeper. I slammed into her a few more times before she completely took flight and I began drowning in my haven. I continued stroking long and hard while she grinded against me, attempting to heighten her experience. I was allowed to thrust a few more times before exploding, and she drained me until I completely emptied my load. I rolled us both onto our sides, mindful of the baby, and we remained that way until we summoned the strength to crawl out of bed and shower.

I changed the sheets while Nari curled up on the sofa in our sitting area. After I finished, we both climbed in, her back to my chest while I rested my chin on her head and massaged her stomach. I was still amazed at times that she was carrying my child. And I could guarantee it would become more of a reality when I physically saw the changes, but for now, the idea of us creating life still felt unreal.

"You were needy." When Nari's voice pulled me from my thoughts, I smiled into her hair and nodded against it.

"I'm always needy when it comes to you."

She laughed, squirming a little, searching for comfort. "I still feel it." I couldn't help but smile. She continued, not allowing me to get stuck there. "Where did that come from?"

"I didn't know you were not just doubting things about me but with your mother as well. I suppose I hadn't considered the possibility and I wanted to reassure you that you had all of me, regardless of what others couldn't provide."

"I'm not doubting things with either of you." She stiffened a little but relaxed when I kissed the top of her head and continued brushing my fingers across her stomach in a soothing manner.

"You are, but it's okay. Nothing to be embarrassed about."

She was quiet for a long moment. "My God, you must think I'm such a big-ass baby."

"No, sweetheart, I don't. I think you're incredibly strong for having to survive on your own for so long, and now you're overwhelmed with new feelings of attachment for people who promise to love you. That's a lot for anyone, but that doesn't make you a baby or weak. It makes you human."

"Thank you."

"For?"

"For being patient with me and not calling it quits when I act insane. I'm working on it."

"I know you are, and there is no calling it quits. I thought I made that clear."

"Oh, that's right. I'm married to a very demanding and uncompromising man. What the hell was I thinking?"

"You weren't, which has worked in my favor. I told you from the start I negotiated terms that would always put me in a position to win. And for the record, I'm extremely proud of you and can't wait to see your vision come to life."

I could feel her smile, which made me offer one as well. I felt confident Nari would blossom into her full potential from the beginning. This was only the beginning and I was sure there was no limit to how much she would accomplish when she allowed her confidence to lead.

"Thank you. It will take a lot of work, but I'm excited and can't wait to start. But, of course, I'll wait until after we get through this reception. Once we get that out of the way, I'll dive right in to get as much done as possible before the baby comes."

"We'll figure it out; whatever you need is as good as done. We'll make it work," I mumbled, feeling my body settling. I didn't have much fight against the comfort of my wife in my arms and the subtle scent of her body wash and shampoo. The combination was a natural sedative.

"Good night."

"Night, sweetheart." I inched Nari closer and allowed my mind to drift.

CHAPTER 10

NARI.

"I hate this part," I groaned as I watched Claudia hang several dresses on the wall of my dressing area. This one was modest in size and had two ivory leather sofas, a three-way mirror centered on the wall across from them, and two private rooms that could be closed off with an off-white curtain matching the internal design. The entire space looked as if it was the result of a silk, pearl, and crystal explosion. Although it was very chic and exquisite, it was the type of place that made you cautious about touching or disturbing anything.

"I love this part. How on earth are we friends?" Alisha's tiny frame stepped out of one of the rooms with a smile that consumed her face while she smoothed her hands down the black dress she wore. It was a floor-length number that hugged her petite body, secured around her neck with an attachment that resembled a beaded choker.

"Because even though I hate shopping, you love everything else about me."

Her smile grew more expansive, but this time, she exposed teeth. "I do. You're like the sister I never had. Flawed in the worst way, yet my go-to for any and all things good and bad in my life."

"How the hell am I flawed?" My eyes narrowed on her and she shrugged.

"Because you were born without the shopping gene, although technically, that's not your fault. I should probably take that up with Endia." She circled me once then tugged at the side of my dress I was holding in place with one hand across my chest.

"How's that going, by the way? You two seem like you haven't missed any time."

Our eyes met in the mirror and I smiled. "We're good. I'm glad she's here."

"Me too. Suck it in so I can zip this." She balled up her mouth and tugged harder before continuing. "I wouldn't know what to do without my mother. We're not exactly best friends, but she's always there for me."

After she managed to get the zipper all the way up, I released a short breath, working my hands down the sides of my waist and over my hips.

"It's too tight."

"So what? It's sexy. I really hate your height. I'm so jealous." She pouted slightly. "This dress is perfect, though." We both eyed my curvy frame through the mirror. My dress was strapless with silk and satin material covered with tiny crystal beads. It was similar to the one I got married in but swept the floor, with a split up on the left side that stopped midthigh.

"If I gain even half a pound, it won't work." I pressed my palm into my stomach and frowned. "And these things." My hands moved to my breasts, which were pushed up higher and on display due to the cut of the dress.

"Those *things* deserve to be presented to the world. You're sexy, Nari. The dress is perfect. No one will even notice you're pregnant. It looks like you ate one too many doughnuts and that's about it. How far along are you, anyway? Shouldn't you be showing?"

"Nineteen weeks. Dr. Chandler said it's my first pregnancy, so I may not get that big. She said that with my body type, I'll carry differently, mostly all up front and all baby."

"So you get the whole pregnancy experience and still get to look like this in a dress like that. You know, I secretly think I hate you."

"You love me too much to hate me." I stuck my tongue out and she rolled her eyes just as Corinne and my mother rounded the corner with champagne flutes in their hands. They both chose their dresses after one fitting while I was on my fourth and Alisha was on her third.

"Oh, wow, you look hot." Corinne approached with a sly grin. "Kincaid might not approve, which is precisely why you must go with that one."

A laugh burst from the pit of my stomach, which had them all smiling as she sipped from her glass, peering at me.

"So, you know he won't approve, but this is the one you want me to get?" I arched my brow, and she shrugged, issuing a mischievous grin.

"Husband or not, you have to remind him that he still needs to invest the time. You're not just his wife. You're his very *sexy* wife, who's carrying his child while still owning the ability to turn heads." Her regard lowered to my mother. "Isn't that right, Endia?"

"The dress is perfect. He wanted to show you off, so give them a show," my mother added with a slight shrug.

"While giving him a heart attack at the same time." I raked my fingers through my hair, turning to face the mirror once again.

"Nonsense . . ." Corinne flicked her wrist, unbothered. "My son will be just fine, and I can't wait to see those hateful women's mouths drop and see the envy in their eyes when you step into the room. Serves them right. I heard about the little performance Mya put on at Gian's event. She was certainly out of line."

"You heard about that?" I frowned, and she nodded, sipping her champagne.

"I hear about everything, dear." She winked and smiled before addressing my mother. "Let's get one more refill before we head out. You two hurry so we can go eat or you're fully responsible for my behavior after drinking on an empty stomach."

The two of them walked off, leaving me with Alisha. "All eyes will definitely be on you in that dress."

Once we were changed back into our clothes and arrangements were made to deliver the dresses to everyone the following morning, we all climbed into the waiting SUV. Floyd hurried out of the driver's seat to open the door on his side while Conner, who had been with us guarding the door, opened the one on the passenger side. We had a short drive to the restaurant, one Kincaid owned and happened to be his mother's favorite. A table in the back was set, waiting. Not long after our arrival, shareable plates were brought out, causing my stomach to do a happy dance. There were several arrangements of appetizers for which I was grateful.

"Good thing I called ahead," Corinne teased.

"Joke all you want." I pointed to my loaded plate before I continued. "This is all *your* grandchild's fault."

"Well, you barely fit into the dress that you chose, so you might want to tread lightly until this weekend." Alisha grinned before forking a cheddar-topped scallop in her mouth.

"Such a good friend," I taunted, which made her face split into a grin.

"I'm hating that you're tall, pregnant, and still look like a runway model." She stuck out her tongue then popped a jumbo shrimp into her waiting mouth.

"You are absolutely stunning, Alisha." My mother felt the need to deliver a compliment, which I thought was sweet, but I also knew if Alisha lacked anything, it wasn't confidence.

"You would be correct. I'm simply stunning *and* height-challenged." She blew my mother a kiss and winked at me. The table circled through a round of laughter before everyone began loading their plates with appetizers, the same as I had.

Lunch and conversation were amazing, as always, but I was exhausted and ready to get home. It seemed we were all on one accord, so Corinne motioned for the server to bring the bill, and that was when things took a drastic turn. Our server, Dalia, offered a polite smile when she stood at the end of the table, her hands folded in front of her as she explained the bill was covered. Based on his mother's quick eye roll, I assumed Kincaid had handled things as did the rest of us.

"I bet those handlers reported where we were having lunch," she mumbled, referring to Floyd and Conner before addressing Dalia. "Well, since my son covered the bill, let me at least leave a tip."

Dalia's face twisted slowly into a frown. "The tip is covered as well, but it wasn't Mr. Akel who covered it."

"Well then, who?" Corinne's frown now matched Dalia's.

"Mr. Manchester. He said his wife and daughter were having lunch here with family and he wanted to cover the bill."

Wife and daughter? What the hell?

"He was here?" I was sure the color had drained from my face because my voice was unsteady and my hands were shaky.

"No, ma'am." Dalia's nervous eyes moved around the table before they landed on me again. "He sent someone with cash to cover the bill and deliver his message since he couldn't make it as planned." She then perked up and dug into the pocket of the apron tied at her waist. "He also asked that I give this to Mrs. Manchester." She smiled before her eyes landed on my mother, whose identity she likely assumed, considering she was familiar with Corinne. Her frown surfaced again when I snatched it from her before she could place it into my mother's hands.

"Is there a problem? Have I done something wrong?" She was likely reading the table as I was positive we all shared the same sentiment . . .

Alarm!

"No. No." Corinne was on her feet quickly. "Absolutely not. We'll be leaving now. Thank you, the food was lovely as always."

"Are you sure there's not a problem?"

"No, everything's fine," I said to her, but I was trying to convince myself more. Dalia nodded and hesitantly walked away.

"What does it say?" My mother's voice was low. She removed the note from my hands when I didn't speak.

There's nothing worse than a thief and a liar. Your time is coming. Enjoy what's left of it. Eli

We shared a look, knowing exactly what that meant. It was a threat. He planned on doing something terrible. The thought had me nervously looking around while I removed my phone to call Conner.

"Hey, are you okay?" Alisha was on me quickly, placing a soothing hand on my back. I nodded and addressed Conner when he answered.

"Yes, ma'am?"

"Can you come to the door? We're ready to leave."

"Is everything okay?"

"Yes, just hurry, please."

It seemed he had ended the call and appeared not even a minute later. While Conner shuffled us out of the restaurant to the waiting SUV, my eyes nervously bounced around. I had an eerie feeling we were still being watched. Had to be and it made my skin prickle with uncertainty.

The ride to the house was quiet. From the look in everyone's eyes, it was clear we all shared the same sentiment but refused to have the discussion out loud. He was watching. He could have been watching all morning, but either way, he had been close, or some of his people had, at the very least. Lunch was at one of Kincaid's restaurants, so this move was bold. The man was sending a message, one that didn't sit well with me. He wasn't presenting as someone who wanted a warm and fuzzy reunion with his daughter and the woman he once shared a relationship with. He wanted my husband to know he had the power to get us, which had my stomach sinking.

Eli threatened my mother.

Once we reached the property, Kincaid and Darius were waiting for us outside on the porch, their expressions hardened with anger, their eyes introspective. Kincaid took me in from the bottom of my feet to the top of my head, slowly observing every inch of me as if he needed to reassure himself I was unharmed. He knew I was. Conner delivered confirmation the minute after he and Floyd were filled in on what had happened. Darius's reaction to Alisha mirrored Kincaid's to mine before he pulled her into his tall frame, hugging her tightly then ushering her to his waiting car. She and I shared a look that served as a goodbye. My mother didn't speak. She simply passed everyone and hurried into the house. Corinne followed. They had become friends and I could tell she was concerned. I was also worried because I sensed her nervous energy, but Kincaid stopped me with a stern look and a firm hand on my hip when I attempted to follow them. He and

Darius shared a few words before he and Alisha left and we ended up in the foyer.

"You okay?" Kincaid's large body engulfed mine. His arms were firm as they kept me tight against his solid frame while he kissed the top of my head.

"I'm fine, just a little freaked out."

"He won't touch you, sweetheart. That's my promise. He knows better. Today was simply about him attempting to get under my skin."

"I know and I don't like it. He threatened my mother. I'm wondering if this was ever even about me. What happens next?" There was no way in hell Kincaid wouldn't react. That was who he was. Darkness that consumed him, which made it easy for him to settle into the killer I knew him to be. As much as that frightened me, it soothed me as well. When he made a promise that I would remain untouched, there was no doubt in my mind it was one he would give his life to keep. If I were honest with myself, the only reason I was remotely frightened about the man I knew Kincaid to be was because I feared it might one day be the reason I would have to live without him. I was afraid those things he wanted to protect me from would eventually get the best of him. No matter how capable he proved to be, he was only one man.

Before he could respond to my question, his mother came down the stairs wearing a tight expression.

"Is she okay?" I questioned about my mother. Regardless of what Corinne's answer would be, I would check for myself.

"She's fine, sweetheart. Just a little shaken up, but that's understandable. Your mother's no pushover, so don't worry about Endia." Corinne offered a soft smile and gently rubbed my arm when she was close enough. "I'm going to head home."

"No, stay here tonight and maybe for a few days. I can have my guys run by the house to get what you need."

She narrowed her eyes at Kincaid, shaking her head. "I'll be fine."

"Ma, no. I don't want you in that house alone until I get a handle on this."

"I said I'll be fine. I need to be home," she stated firmly. The two shared a look that I understood. It was the home she shared with her husband and being there allowed her to feel at peace. She'd discussed that with me once when Kincaid was away and she spent the night at his insistence.

"I'll have some guys on the house. They'll be there waiting for you. Let them sweep the place before you go in and they'll post up outside for the night." His word was final. She and I both knew he wouldn't move on any other orders but his own with this. She hugged me, kissed her son, and was gone shortly after. I headed to my mother's room to check on her while Kincaid headed to his office, promising not to be long.

By the time I joined her, she had changed into sweats and a T-shirt and was sitting on the side of the bed staring into blank space. I noticed two medicine bottles on the nightstand and a half-empty water bottle.

"What are those?" I sat next to her, and she smiled, patting my leg.

"Nothing for you to worry about. They just keep me balanced. When I don't take them, that's when you worry. I can be a bit of a handful and I'm sure that husband of yours is enough as it is." I appreciated the attempt at humor to lighten the mood, but I didn't want my mother to feel obligated to protect my feelings at the cost of not dealing with her own.

"Are you okay?"

"I am. It's just been so long. The thought of him being close makes me anxious."

"He won't touch you or me. Kincaid won't allow it. You're safe here."

"I know, baby. It's just a reality I have to get used to being a *reality* again. He exists. It brings up old things, fears, you know, but I'm okay, so please, don't worry."

I smiled and allowed my head to rest on her shoulder. "I can't help it. That's what you do for your family. You worry."

She laughed softly and nodded. "You do, but just know, I'll take a life before I lose mine or allow anyone to harm you. I guess that's why Kincaid and I have such an understanding."

When I lifted my eyes to hers, they were waiting with a seriousness I hadn't seen in my mother before.

"It won't come to that."

"Let's hope not. I'm gonna catch a little nap. That champagne is catching up to me." She patted my leg again and after I stood, I kissed her cheek. "I'm going to cook tonight; you can help if you want. I think Kincaid is kinda getting used to the whole family dinner thing."

"We all are. I'll be down later," she promised, and I left the room, traveling down the hall to ours. After changing into shorts and a T-shirt, I sat on the bed for a while but got anxious waiting on Kincaid and decided to go to him. He was exactly where he promised, finishing a call when I pushed open the door. Since I stopped in the doorway, he waved me over, saying he'd be in touch with whomever he had been speaking to before he pulled me down into his lap.

"Did you find a dress?"

"I did. It will be delivered tomorrow morning. You didn't answer me."

His hand slipped under my T-shirt, resting on my stomach, while the other made it to my bare thigh. Warm fingers began a soothing rhythm against my skin.

"About?"

From the stern look delivered, I knew he was well aware of what I was asking, but I indulged anyway.

"What's next?"

"That's not for you to worry about. It's handled."

"He's using me and my mother as pawns and he actually threatened her. How can you tell me not to worry?"

"Because I can. He can't use you. He can't do a damn thing remotely related to you, and I will make sure he doesn't get to your mother either. Get that thought out of your head, sweetheart." There was no denying the confidence in his tone, but I still pushed.

"But he—"

"Nari . . ." The warning was delivered with finality . . .

Let it go.

Discussion over.

The two of us remained in a war of wills before he gripped my chin and pulled my face to his for a kiss. Those pillow-soft lips did just what he planned—distracted me.

"I missed you this morning."

"I missed you too."

His smile was beautiful. Everything about the man was beautiful, sexy, edgy, and alluring.

"I'm sure you did."

"So arrogant."

"Which is one of my best qualities, so I've heard."

"From whom?" I arched my brow and pursed my lips.

"My wife."

"Mm-hmm. Good save."

Kincaid chuckled. "Now, about this dress. Should I be worried?"

"Yes, very much. Your wife is sexy."

"You sure you want that on your conscience?"

"Nothing will be on my conscience because you know I'm all yours the same as I know you're all mine."

"Finally," he teased, which had me shoving his chest gently. This had been a journey for me, but I was settling into my confidence about us and our marriage.

"You're a lot; this life is a lot. You can't expect me to be implanted into all this without some type of hesitation and uncertainty."

"Agreed, but as long as you know who owns my heart, I'm at peace and the world's safe."

"Safe?" I frowned and he navigated my mouth to his once more.

"When you run, the world is not safe. I'm a dangerous man, sweetheart. For you, I know no bounds, understand no limits, and employ no control."

He tapped my thigh, requesting I stand, which I did. His hands pushed my shorts over my hips, and as soon as they reached my ankles, he tossed his chin toward the desk behind me. "Up there."

I wasted no time and neither did he. As soon as my bare ass met the polished wood surface, Kincaid pushed forward in his chair and large hands landed between my thighs, forcing them open.

The way his eyes devoured me had my sex throbbing instantly. By the time his tongue glided between my folds, I was already on edge. While his mouth did its own thing, his thumb strummed my clit over and over again. All I could do was arch my back and moan, but I managed to thrust forward when he added a finger and began enticing me with it as well.

His pace increased, and when he lifted his eyes and caught me watching, I noticed a hint of a smile curve on his lips before his free hand pressed against my back, bringing me dangerously close to the edge at the same time he added another finger. The man's speed and talent made me delirious. My hands landed hard against the desk, my palms flat while I attempted to brace for the first round bolting through me. In the seconds that followed, my vision went blurry with an orgasm so intense I felt the muscles in my stomach lock up. That had me lifting one hand and placing it under my shirt protectively. The act sent a wave of alarm through Kincaid, which was expressed through his intense eyes.

"*I'm* . . . I'm fine."

"The baby?" His voice was hoarse with need yet still very much concerned.

"Is fine, keep going," I demanded, bringing another devilish smile to his handsome face. Soft kisses trailed my inner thighs while he maneuvered below me, undoing his jeans. Before I could regain my composure, I felt the thickness of his head grazing my opening before he pushed in with one hard thrust, groaning under his breath while he adjusted and I wrapped my legs around his waist.

I needed more, so I pushed forward, which had his eyes on me and his dick easing out before he returned, landing harder and deeper.

"Easy, sweetheart. This is my rodeo." He moved slower, but with more purpose, and I swear I felt every vein that pulsed along his thick, long shaft, adding additional intensity to what was already building. He was a lot to take regardless of how turned on I was, but my body craved him, all of him, which he knew and delivered.

I groaned his name, allowing my hands to clench the edge of the desk while he focused on hitting the perfect spot with a trained focus. That was intentional because he smirked when it began happening again. Those pulses were building at an alarming rate and my groin was rolling. His pace increased and the muscles in his arms flexed while his fingers dug into my hips, waiting for me to take flight. I did.

"Fuck, baby," floated around me in a low growl right before he came. Kincaid lifted me around his waist and I pulled his face to mine for a kiss and could taste myself on his lips. While we both allowed our energy to settle, his eyes bored into mine with an intensity that allowed me to feel his internal struggle. What he didn't say vibrated between us. My father was an issue and my husband needed to feel close to me. I loved Kincaid even when I was conflicted. I'd kill Eli my damn self if it meant never being without Kincaid.

CHAPTER 11

KINCAID.

Nari looked back at me over her shoulder and offered the biggest smile. She was beautiful. No one could compete as far as I was concerned and that damn dress she wore . . .

Dangerous!

I winked and she blushed. I could tell she was over having to play nice with everyone in attendance tonight, but I was proud of her for powering through. This was a part of my life. And the people here also played a role regardless of whether I liked it. My eyes roamed the large crowd, which had to be close to a hundred and fifty guests. All five head members from The Families were in attendance as well. They had all expressed their approval of my wife and were pleased with how she complemented me. Nari handled their conversations well, smiling the entire time. She was articulate and smart, regardless of her lack of postsecondary education. Nari had never gone to college, but one would never know based on how she carried herself so intelligently, being able to compete with those who had multiple degrees.

When Kafi made his toast, expressing his thoughts about the beginning of a loving and powerful union between us, she smiled, leaning into me while I stood behind her with my hand resting on her stomach. We both agreed not to announce the pregnancy formally, but I was beaming on the inside after learning this morning that our firstborn would be a boy—my *son*. Nari was blessing me with a namesake—the first of our legacy. I couldn't be more pleased nor could I be more in love with her.

"She's beautiful and it appears she's also smart." I kept my eyes on Nari but nodded at Angelo Ricci. His English was perfect regardless of his thick Italian accent. Ricci was the quietest and unseen member of all the families. We typically only saw him at the quarterly meetings or if a problem required his presence. Outside of that, he was a ghost who moved in the shadows. Rumor had it his son would soon be taking his place. I never asked. It would be confirmed when needed and the decision didn't affect me one way or another.

"You never know your true value as a man until the right woman is by your side. She gives me purpose beyond anything I could have ever imagined." It took a minute for me to grant him my full attention. When our eyes met, a grave expression covered his face. He subtly glanced at Nari before nodding and offering a smile.

"I would have to agree. Anna Marie is my world. She makes me a better man. I'd shed blood for her honor and her happiness." His regard moved across my yard to where his wife talked to a group of women. As if she felt his stare, their eyes met and she offered a soft smile before waving. His smile expanded while I dipped my chin in acknowledgment and she returned to her conversation.

He spoke of my arrangement. "It was not traditional, but you love her, aye?"

"It wasn't, but I do. She was meant to be mine." There was not a doubt in my mind that Nari had always belonged to me.

"Ahhh." He smiled. "You will be a good husband to her, no?"

"As best I can. I'm sure I'll fuck it up at some point, but maybe not so much that she'll second-guess taking this ride with me."

Angelo chuckled and nodded. His hand came down on my shoulder at the same time. "You're an honorable man. Smarter than most. You will be okay. Congratulations, Kincaid. Many blessings to you and your wife. I know your father is proud. He loved you and I know it's hard to reach these milestones without having him here by your side."

"It is. Speaking of, has anyone gotten any closer to knowing who was behind the shooting?"

At that moment, Angelo's expression presented a mixture of compassion and remorse. "No, and believe me, we have extended all of our resources. As much as I hate to consider it a possibility, we may never know. However, we will continue putting our best efforts forward. I assure you, it's just as important to us as it is to you and your family."

I nodded. "I know, thank you," I offered with sincerity before Angelo stepped away. Nari was on her way to me right after. She leaned into my chest, circling my waist with her arms, and I placed a kiss on her forehead.

"It's almost over."

"I'm tired, but this wasn't so bad. Even with *her* here." She pointed with her forehead to where Mya was across the yard. She was watching us, had been all night, but knew enough to keep her distance. I was sure she would have attempted to steal a moment when I was alone, but she never tried. I was grateful for not having to hurt feelings or embarrass her by requesting that she leave. Mya's invitation was a formality due to her father's status. I did, however, clear it with Nari. Her sentiment mattered more to me than the opinions of those who only had an investment in my position. My leadership was solid, and I would forever fulfill my obligations, but Nari was off-limits. If a choice had to be made, I would always choose her.

While sharing a private moment with Nari, I searched the faces, attempting to locate those who were under my watchful eye. My mother was with two women she shared a charity with and Endia was with Cast. She smiled widely at whatever he said and her hand rested on his forearm. She appeared to be relaxed and happy.

"It looks like your mother has a suitor." I grinned, watching as things unfolded. Nari looked in the same direction and her eyes went wild before they landed on me again.

"Him? Cast?" Panic was laced in her tone, which had me responding quickly and clearly.

"No, shit, no. Over there." I motioned in another direction. "Abisai Sinclair." I smirked when I noticed her body relax. The idea of her mother with Cast seemed to create an internal panic. I could understand why. He was the type who kept women in rotation and was considerably younger than Endia.

"Who is he?" Nari watched intently as he approached with both hands behind his back before he bowed his head, speaking to Cast first then extending a hand to her mother. From how things unfolded, I assumed he introduced himself and requested a moment of her time because Cast instinctively stepped in front of Endia protectively when Abisai approached, but nodded and moved out of the way after the verbal exchange.

"A colleague, retired, but he's a good guy," I offered, keeping it vague instead of going into detail about Abisai's history of being the most valued enforcer in our organization at one point in his life.

"Retired from what?" Nari pushed.

"He used to be an enforcer," I tried again. A little more detail, but nowhere near the specifics outlining the blood he'd shed in his active years.

"And he's a good guy?" She watched as the two interacted. Her mother's posture was friendly and she smiled a lot.

"A very good guy. I trust him with her, if that turns out to be anything."

She lifted her eyes to me, but I continued watching their exchange a few moments longer before I gave her mine.

"Well, at least he can keep her safe. I know what enforcer means." She delivered a pointed stare, and I grinned, kissing her softly.

"He can."

About an hour later, the last of our guests were gone. Endia was in her room and Cast volunteered to take my mother home before the second shift of his evening began. He had *personal* plans, which meant some woman or women would end up in his bed, or he would end up in theirs. I finally had my wife alone and we had both survived our reception.

"I shouldn't be this tired." Nari's voice was laced with exhaustion when she spoke. I tugged at my tie while I watched her step out of her heels. She had been in them for hours, and I wasn't necessarily happy about that, but she looked terrific. The dress she wore hugged every curve of her body, which was already fucking amazing but had filled out quite nicely since being pregnant. Her hips expanded, and her breasts were fuller, which had me on edge all night because I could see both men *and* women checking her out. They were all respectful, but that didn't stop them from stealing glances at Nari's body . . . a visual which had my dick hard all night.

"It's been a long day and I appreciate you suffering through this for me." I made my way to her. My chest brushed against her back before I forced her hard against me with an arm around her neck and the other firmly circling her waist. I delivered a trail of kisses from just below her ear to her collarbone, and she settled into me, moaning softly.

"It was important to you."

"It was, but mostly because I wanted to show off my beautiful wife." I kissed her neck again before lowering both hands around her waist, moving them up her stomach then to her breasts, which I cuffed in my palms. "But this dress made that incredibly hard." I brushed my nose against the soft curve of her neck, inhaling her scent before continuing my thought. "Amongst other things." I pushed forward and she angled her head back on my shoulder, delivering a smug grin.

"What's new?" she teased, covering my hands with hers. "I just want to get out of this dress, shower, then crawl in bed."

"Let me help you with that." My fingers scaled her side, searching for the zipper I had helped secure in place earlier that evening. I tugged it down and Nari expelled a sigh of relief, which had me frowning, wondering if the dress had been too tight.

"As tempting as you look in this dress, you're done with it and anything remotely close until you deliver our son. From now on, I must approve your formalwear." My lips grazed her shoulder before planting a soft kiss. Nari didn't object. She only stepped out of her dress, turning with it in her hands before she placed the silk beaded material in mine.

"I'll start the shower while you undress."

With a nod, she walked away, and I watched her thick, curvy frame, cheeks spilling out of the bottoms of the black lace panties she wore, until she entered the bathroom. I moved toward the closet, undressing down to my briefs, laying our clothes from the evening across the massive marble-topped island that separated the space. I would deal with our things in the morning. Right now, I was about to soothe Nari's body and put her to bed.

When I reached the bathroom, she was already in the glass enclosure. The waterfall showerhead was on, as well as the ten jets lining the wall on the other side. I approached Nari, pulled her to me, and immediately enclosed her in my arms. She already smelled of coconut and lime from her body wash.

"You started without me." I allowed my mouth to explore her skin, moving down her neck and across her shoulder.

"I told you I was tired." I could hear the smile in her voice, which turned to a soft moan when my fingers reached her left breast and I rolled her nipple between two of them.

"That feels good."

"*You* feel good. At least you can rest tomorrow."

"I wish. I have to finish the paperwork Nathan sent me to trademark my business name and logo and the documents to open the business account. I still have to find a building and . . ." She paused, enjoying the feel of my exploration of her body before chirping, "Oh, and I've been invited to join the cult."

My head lifted, tilting slightly to the side. "The cult?"

She nodded softly. "One of the committees. Some of the ladies insisted I join and host the next meeting here. Mostly Cynthia." Nari exhaled a short breath, likely because my fingers found her clit.

"Oh yeah, and what did you say?" I was curious. Nari was reluctant to connect with these women. Mya was a big part of that. They weren't all bad, or like her, and she was the only one I had a sexual history with. Some were pretty nice, but most were entitled and not welcoming. And with a few, she had a position they wanted but would never qualify for . . . as my wife. They also weren't partial to Alisha because she was considered an outsider. Nari would be placed in the same category, but their eagerness to kiss my ass and please me would give my wife more leeway and acceptance. I owned the ability to control their husbands' positions with the syndicate, which forced them to be kind to Nari.

"I said I would have to speak to you first." I frowned at the thought. I didn't want her to feel like she had to clear every move with me or that she needed permission to connect with them. I trusted and valued Nari's opinions about what was best for her and us.

"Why is that?"

"This is our home. I wasn't sure how you would feel about having them here."

I relaxed at the reasoning behind her decision.

"They were here tonight, sweetheart."

"Yeah, but that was different. Me hosting a meeting would be more intimate. They were mostly outside, you know, with everyone else. I'm not sure if I like the idea of having them here. This is our space."

I grinned and kissed her shoulder. "It's your decision. I'm okay with whatever you decide. Just let me know so I can plan accordingly. It's a good thing. It represents acceptance. Don't overthink about their intent."

"Acceptance?" I could hear the accusation in her tone paired with how her body stiffened.

"Not for me, Nari. I don't give a shit if they accept you. You're mine, you're here, and you're not going anywhere. I meant acceptance in the sense that you're finding your footing with the things I'm involved in. That's all." She relaxed again.

"I'll think about it."

"Again, sweetheart, it's your decision. I'm okay with whatever you decide. Now, enough about that. Let me help you relax a little more so you'll sleep well tonight."

Firmly grabbing ahold of myself, I guided my length between her legs, easing into her slowly. She was ready and welcoming, causing my eyes to close briefly while I released a slow growl. Once I had my bearings, I lowered one arm around her waist to steady Nari while the other lifted her leg, holding it out to the side, resting across my arm.

"Is this comfortable?"

"Hmm?" Her voice was barely audible, but enough confirmation for me to process. I slowly made love to my wife until we both came together, then I washed her body, and mine, before we got out, dressed for bed, and climbed in. Nari was out in a matter of minutes, and after checking a few emails on my phone, I wasn't far behind.

Some hours later, in a hazy state, I reached for my ringing phone, too exhausted to check the name before answering.

"Kincaid," I mumbled, my face tight from being awakened from a peaceful sleep. Nari shifted next to me but didn't get far when she attempted to inch away. I had her locked against me, but she didn't seem to mind because she quickly settled against my side.

"I . . . I . . . need you." The voice on my line was female. It sounded as if she was crying, which sent an alarm bolting through me. My mind was still attempting to awaken, which had me sitting up to shake the haze I was under.

"Who is this?"

"Val. *Kincaid*, I *need* you!" she screeched, sounding like she was in pain.

My eyes immediately lowered to Nari while my jaw tensed. "Have you lost your damn mind? Do you know what time it is? Don't call again," I hissed before ending the connection. My body radiated with anger and Nari shifted again. When my phone rang once more, she sat up immediately afterward.

"Answer it."

"No," I stated firmly. Her heated gaze on me was stern when she pointed to the phone, which was still in my hand. Our room was dark, so Val's name was evident as the call illuminated the space around us.

"You want me to trust you, then don't give me reasons not to. Answer the damn phone, Kincaid."

I wasn't in the mood for this shit. I hadn't spoken to Val since she'd reached out to Nari with that bullshit accusation that caused Nari to believe I was foolish enough to cheat. I called and issued a warning I assumed she understood, but apparently not if she was calling me in the middle of the night. With little option but to comply so I wouldn't feed into her insecurities, I did as Nari demanded.

"What the fuck do you want?" I growled when I answered this time, tossing my legs over the side of the bed, bending at the waist, giving Nari my back. I felt her move behind me, and she rounded the bed seconds later, her arms folded across her chest, her eyes blazing.

"I need you."

"Val, I don't have time for this shit. I thought I made myself clear—"

"I was attacked. It's your fault. I need you. I get it. You love your wife, but don't I mean enough that you'll at least make sure I'm okay? I need you, *please*."

"Where are you?"

"Our hotel. Our suite. Are you coming?" Her voice perked up, which let me know this was bullshit.

"No, but someone will, just not me."

"Kincaid, please—"

I ended the call and immediately dialed Cast. He answered on the second ring, his voice lively, meaning he was still awake.

"Yeah, boss?"

"I need a favor. I'm going to send you an address. Val's there. She said she was attacked. If it's true, take her to the hospital and get her checked out. Stay with her. No cops."

"Attacked by who?"

"She didn't say, but I also didn't give her a chance. She said it was because of me." I brushed my hand down my face before lifting my eyes to Nari, whose stare was still heated. She was pissed, but that was understandable. This looked bad.

"You think it is?"

"Not sure; it could be a setup. Let me know what you find out."

"Got it."

I didn't need to tell him to be careful. This was his thing. It was what he was trained to handle. After I ended the call and reached for Nari, she pushed my hand away.

"Shouldn't you be the one going?"

"No. She's not my concern."

"But she said she was attacked." Nari didn't want me to go and was pissed that the call happened, but she was a good person. Val insinuated that she was hurt.

"Still not my fucking problem." I was already irritated but understood she also had the right to be.

"Not even if it's true and it was about you?" She did a fairly decent job of camouflaging her emotions, but the way she chewed the corner of her lip told me she was unsure of what to believe. I couldn't blame her.

"No, not even then. Cast can handle it. If she's in danger, he'll get her somewhere safe. That's the most I'll offer, and even that's too much. She's no longer my concern. Now, are we going to fight about this or go back to bed?"

This moment would be pivotal in proving whether Nari truly trusted me like she promised. I never lied; I wasn't now, but this was yet another situation that would allow her to doubt me.

She remained still and quiet momentarily as our eyes warred with each other before she eventually gave in and retreated to her side of the bed. She did, however, leave space, which I wasn't having, and when I pulled her close, she didn't object.

"That call was Val's reaction to me cutting her off. I haven't seen or talked to her since I made clear that she was to stay the fuck away from both of us."

"Okay," was all I got, but I felt the tension in her body dissipate.

"Nari . . ."

"I promised to trust you. This is me trusting you. Just don't make me regret it." She spoke softly and I placed a kiss on the back of her neck.

"You won't."

She fidgeted beside me briefly but eventually drifted back to sleep. I remained up, unable to allow my mind to settle. If Val truly had been assaulted because of me, I would make sure it was handled and ensure she was safe, but I would keep my distance. Val had proven she wasn't emotionally stable enough to separate me doing the right thing from her weird obsession, which led her to believe she could make me fall in love with her. Either way, I knew how this needed to be handled, and that wouldn't be by way of me disrespecting my wife.

The next morning, I was up early after only sleeping for a few hours and not peacefully. While Nari slept, I worked in the study. It was Saturday morning, and I planned on spending the day at home, which meant shutting out the rest of the world. So I was grateful when Cast eventually called to fill me in on Val so it wouldn't come up later. I answered, looking across the room at Nari, still sleeping peacefully. I decided to take the call on the balcony, unsure of what he was about to tell me.

"Morning, boss."

"Morning. What do you have for me?"

"You're not gonna believe this shit. . . or maybe you will." He laughed lightly before continuing. "The doctors think the bruises are self-inflicted. They're pretty bad too. If that's the case, she really did a number on herself. She's crazy, Caid."

"So this wasn't about me?"

"No, it was *definitely* about you, just not as she implied. The woman is fucking loony."

I felt Nari's presence before she reached me. Her arms encircled my waist and her face pressed against my bare back while Cast continued.

"But that's not the worst of it. She's pregnant. Kept yelling at me to call you since they took her phone. She was acting so erratically they almost sedated her. No one could calm her down until they promised to do a pregnancy test so I would call and tell you. She made them do the ultrasound and everything so you could have a picture of *your* baby." He chuckled, but I wasn't sure why the hell he thought this shit was funny.

"It's not mine."

"Oh, trust me, I know. She's barely six weeks. Timelines don't add up unless you've been lying."

"That's not my kid."

Nari's head popped up, and I lowered my hand, placing it on hers to hold it in place.

"What do you want me to do?"

"Call Chandler. See who he knows in the psych ward and tell him I need a favor. Maybe if she spends a little time there, she'll stop with all this bullshit. Hell, sounds like she really needs to be there."

"You have no idea. This chick is out of her fucking mind. I'll handle it."

"'Preciate it."

"You owe me *again*," he made clear.

"I pay you well."

"Yeah, but this shit is extra."

I chuckled and nodded even though he couldn't see me. "I always cover my debts."

Once I ended the call, I turned, leaning my back on the railing and pulling Nari into my chest.

"She's pregnant?"

"Six weeks and it's not mine. I've never cheated on you. She's also lied about being attacked. The doctors feel like the bruises were self-inflicted."

I stared intently at Nari, watching her process what I was saying. I could see her thinking hard and prayed this wouldn't be an issue.

"And just like that, you can keep her locked away in a psych ward?"

I can do much more, but I won't. That baby she's carrying saves her, even though it's not mine.

"Me personally, no. I do, however, know people who have the authority to do so, and based on what I just learned, she's not only a danger to herself but also to the child she's carrying. It seems necessary, and hopefully they can manage to do what I haven't and convince her she needs to move the fuck on with her life."

We remained in a silent standoff for a long moment before Nari spoke again.

"I'm hungry. I'm going to find something for breakfast."

"Nari?"

"I'm fine. *We're* fine. You said it's not yours, and I believe you, but if that bitch calls you again in the middle of the night, you both better do some heavy praying because I'm not about to keep playing nice with this thirsty lunatic." Her warning was firm. I offered a nod and kissed her forehead.

"I'll be down in a minute."

"Okay." She turned and walked away and I blocked Val's number. Part of my promise to love my wife was ensuring she remained untouched. That meant emotionally as well as physically. Val was a threat to her happiness and I refused to fuck that up . . . again.

CHAPTER 12

NARI.

The weekend had been perfect. Neither of us left the house and we barely left our room. My body was sore but thoroughly pleased, so I had no complaints. It was now late Sunday evening, and Kincaid had received a call he had to take, so my mother and I decided to start working through the gifts from our reception. It hadn't been requested or necessary, but no one showed up empty-handed.

Some boxes were filled with imported crystals, rare artwork I googled to find was worth seven figures, and envelopes that held island trips to exclusive tropical places I had never heard of.

"Who the hell are these people?" I mumbled, and my mother smiled, handing me yet another box. She and I were sitting on the floor after moving most of the gifts for easy access. They now surrounded us while we both opened them one at a time.

"Wealthy people who like to impress." She grinned, untying the ribbon to a rectangular Tiffany box.

"Another vase. It's different than the other two, but still a vase." I flashed her an amused smile before lifting the lid to the box that sat in front of me.

My eyes widened in surprise and I quickly shoved it away, gasping at the contents. The silver box was lined with plastic, and inside were two severed hands. I threw mine over my mouth and kicked the box farther away with my foot before scooting back to get up.

"That's . . ." I shook my head, not even able to finish the thought.

"I'm going to get Kincaid. Don't touch it again," my mother instructed, quickly leaving the room. She returned moments later, following Kincaid while pointing to the floor where the box was.

"Shit! Fuck!" He cursed before turning to me. "Are you okay?"

I was still staring at the severed hands, so he grabbed my face and forced me to look at him. "Nari, are you okay?"

"I'm fine. Stop asking me if I'm okay." I knocked his hands away and pointed at the box. "That I can handle. What I can't handle is knowing the person who delivered it was in our house. How the fuck did that happen? What if it was one of your people? What if you can't trust them? What if—"

He cuffed the sides of my face again, focusing my eyes on his in an attempt to force me to calm down. "Sweetheart, you're okay. We're okay. Let me figure this out. We had a lot of people in and out, and no matter how tight security was, this was always a possibility."

I nodded slowly, and he pulled me into a hug, removing his phone at the same time.

"I need you at my house now. A box was delivered. It's one of Medina's men. He's wearing the Gallardo crest on his pinky finger." I listened as Kincaid spoke to someone I assumed was Cast or Darius. After the call ended, he was on me again.

"Let's go." His regard then moved to my mother, who shook her head, understanding the silent request to know if she was all right.

"I'll be by the pool. I have a book I'd like to finish." She looked at me before turning to leave.

I stepped away from him and pointed in the direction she'd gone. "I'm going to go with her. I'm sure you have to figure this out."

"Stay with me for a little while."

"No, I just need a minute, okay?"

He stared hard before nodding but watched me until I was no longer in sight. I stepped out into the back and took a cleansing breath before joining my mother. I sat next to her on the edge of the lounge and she lowered her book and turned to face me.

"This is his life, I get it. I'm sure much worse will happen, and truthfully, I'm not all that affected by what was in the box. Maybe that means something's wrong with me." I closed my eyes for a brief moment and shook my head. "What bothers me the most is that I feel violated. They were here in our house. What else could have happened while they were here? Who was it? They managed to move around without anyone knowing. That bothers me."

She nodded but remained silent for a minute longer before she sat up, placing her feet on the ground and the book she was reading beside her. After propping my elbows on my knees, I lowered my face into my palms.

"What do you need me to do?" My mother's voice was soft. I laughed sarcastically, lifting my eyes to hers.

"Can you somehow transform the man I married into something basic like a lawyer or a doctor? Hell, he could be a gotdamn city worker collecting trash for all I care right now."

She flashed me a smile, softly shaking her head. Soft, thick coils that matched mine bounced over her shoulders and around her face.

"No, baby, I can't, but that's not who you married, and I can't imagine that it's who he wants to be."

"I just . . . shit. I don't know. I don't want to start feeling afraid in my own house."

"And you won't." His voice was deep, vibrating with confidence. Kincaid spoke from a few feet away, standing just outside the door. His stare was confident, firm, and intense, communicating the promise he'd just delivered before he turned and walked back inside. He seemed angry. Certainly not with me, but he was indeed angry. How the hell had such a perfect weekend ended so terribly?

The rest of the day moved fast. Kincaid spent most of his time in his office. Several people were in and out of our home, all professional looking one way or another. Most were dressed in suits; some were in black-on-black cargo pants, long-sleeved shirts, and combat boots. They all shared the same stature: tall, solid, ripped bodies. A few carried the build of football players: massive, bulky, and wearing permanent scowls even when their features softened when I was around. Yet, they still appeared unfriendly in a way that relayed their purpose for being there. None of them spoke to me outside of Darius and Cast. They both carried on conversations, keeping things light, but I could see the tension behind their expressions and playfulness.

Kincaid was quiet when it came to me. He was watching me though, and his thoughts were heavy. I could feel them. And the way his eyes followed me when I was near told of his mood. He was worried, but I wasn't sure about what exactly. After hours of being barricaded in his office, I entered with food because he hadn't eaten a bite all day. There were two men in there with him. I didn't bother to offer them anything because I learned from experience they would decline. Obviously, they were working.

Kincaid stood and rounded his desk when I entered his space. He thanked me softly with a kiss on the cheek before he accepted the plate, placed it on his desk, and watched me as I left. Again, that strange feeling took over, letting me know his mind was working and his thoughts were still weighted.

That was how the hours passed after I discovered the severed hands hiding amongst the wedding gifts that we received. At some point, my mother and I found places for the opened gifts, and the rest were placed in the garage for Kincaid's men to sort through. I had no objections because I wasn't interested in locating more body parts. My mother retired to her room right after dinner. At first, I assumed it was from the day's stress, but after checking on her, I learned it was because she had a FaceTime date with Abisai. She had been texting him throughout the day, and that put a smile on her face, which made me happy as well. While I showered, Kincaid took a call on the terrace and joined me just as I finished. He made sure to make me come several times before I stepped out and he finished showering then joined me in bed after making me a cup of lemon ginger tea while he enjoyed Cognac. The bottle made it to the room with him and rested on the nightstand beside the bed.

After finishing the last of my tea, I muted the TV and crawled across the bed, straddling my husband's waist. He took me in slowly, tossing back the last of his drink before placing the empty glass next to the bottle. I stared down at his bare chest and arms, watching the muscles move like choreographed waves with the slightest motion. His hands eventually made it to my hips and rested there.

"You've been quiet all day. Are you ready to tell me what's wrong?"

"Nothing's wrong. I've just been dealing with the shit that happened earlier." It was a partial truth, but I felt him holding back, so I pushed harder.

"You have, but it's not just that. The way you've been watching me today is like you're worried, and that makes me anxious."

"There's nothing to be anxious or worried about. Watching you is simply my way of remembering everything about you. Your smile, the way your eyes lower when you need me, and how your hands cover our son protectively without you even thinking about it. I need those memories. They're important."

His words sounded cryptic before he settled into a silence. They lingered between us in a palpable way and combined with the heaviness of what I felt him holding onto. I closed my eyes, exhaling, wanting to get this over with, whatever the hell it was.

"Just say it, please. I can't take these weird spaces we find ourselves in, one you're in right now."

"You can't leave me, Nari." My eyes shot open, narrowing to find his waiting. They were fearful and needy. Nothing like the man I knew Kincaid to be.

What the hell has him afraid?

Certainly not me leaving.

Why would he think that?

"I know I said you can't because I wouldn't let you, but truthfully . . ." He paused as if needing a minute to regroup. "I love you enough to let you go if that's truly what you wanted or needed to be happy. I just . . ." He shook his head and moved one of his hands to my stomach. "It'll fucking ruin me if that's what you decide. My heart tells me to hold on tight and never let go, but my rational side understands I'm asking a lot by keeping you here. I'm afraid of what that means for me. I'm afraid of the person I have the potential to become without you here to remind me I need balance. You're my balance, baby. Today, what you saw—"

I lifted a hand, allowing it to rest on the side of his face while I leaned closer, my fingers brushing the smooth texture of his beard. "I'm not going anywhere." I laughed before my lips curled into a smile. "How can I? Who the hell can come behind you?"

He snorted and pulled me closer, covering my mouth with his. That skillful tongue I had grown addicted to began to explore, eliciting a soft moan from me.

"Not a damn soul. I'd kill anybody who tried."

I playfully rolled my eyes, even knowing there was nothing playful behind his words. He meant exactly what he expressed.

He would take the lives of anyone who thought they could have me.

"How the hell is that fair? You can't tell me that you'll let me go if it was what I needed to be happy in one breath then say you would kill any other man who wanted to be with me."

His smile was slow to form and also deadly, but still sexy, nonetheless. "I said that I would let you go, but not once did I say I would allow another man to have you. Sorry, sweetheart, that's not a possibility. You can be without me, but you will never be with anyone else. That's the best I can offer."

"Wow." I laughed under my breath and his smile expanded.

"You know who you married, Nari. Don't you dare act surprised."

"Correction, I *now* know who I married. Before I agreed to this, I only had an *idea* of the type of man you were. You knew exactly what you were doing." My eyes narrowed on him, but I paired it with a smile. I might not have known I was marrying a man who would receive severed hands in a box, but I damn sure knew he wasn't a saint.

"I did, but it's too late for either of us. You're in me and I'm in you." His hand rested on my stomach again before his other gripped the back of my neck, pulling my mouth to his.

"I'm carrying your baby, but what are you carrying of me?" I lifted my brow and he stated with not one ounce of uncertainty . . .

"Your heart. It's mine and solely belongs to me. I keep it safe and right here." He winked when his finger pressed into his chest just before our mouths collided again. The kiss was intense and sealed the promise, both spoken and unspoken. He was mine and I was his. There were no outs for either of us and I was okay with the declaration. I cuddled up to his side moments after and enjoyed the feel of his arms around me. Everything about us felt right, even the things that were dangerously wrong. It wasn't perfect, but it was indisputably us.

Two days later, we all received a much-needed break from the stress of what was lingering around us. Kincaid was still dealing with whatever the hell landed that box in our home, which meant men in and out, calls and meetings in his office. So when we received a surprise visit from an unexpected guest, it shifted the energy in our home.

Abisai stood in our living room with Kincaid while I was by his side and my mother sat quietly on the sofa, a barely-there smile teasing at the corners of her lips. The entire scene was odd but adorably cute at the same time.

"My apologies for the unannounced visit, but I felt it necessary." Abisai's accent was strong, but I could tell he'd been raised in the States based on how perfect his English was. My mother had informed me that Abisai was Jamaican but had been in the US since he was a teen. He was now in his early fifties.

"It's not a problem, but I'm curious why you wanted to speak to me. I would assume you were here to see Endia." Kincaid glanced over his shoulder, smiling, clearly amused by how uncomfortable she appeared.

Abisai also glanced at my mother and smiled, but he reflected a sentiment different from Kincaid's. He was smitten.

"I am, but considering she's family and in your home, I humbly request your permission to spend time with Ms. Endia."

"Ahh, I see. She's grown, Abisai. She doesn't need my permission to spend time with you. You possibly should be having this conversation with Nari instead." He cut his eyes at me before they landed on Abisai again.

"I agree, and I pray Mrs. Akel extends her blessing as well so I can spend time with her mother. However, you are the man of this house and Ms. Endia's extended family. Her *only* active family, as she has informed me, so I wanted to be sure you understood my intentions."

"Which are?" I cut in, shifting his attention to me.

"To get to know her better, allowing her the opportunity to do the same with me. Then hopefully, she will entertain the idea of allowing me to be a more permanent fixture in her life." He glanced at my mother and smiled charmingly. She did the same, which, again, was adorably cute.

Oh, he's laying it on thick.

"Permanent fixture?" I arched my brow. "Like *marriage?*"

"If she so pleases," Abisai answered quickly.

"That is none of our business at the moment, but you have my blessing to spend time with Endia, not that you needed it. I trust you in my home, and I assume I can trust her in your care when she's out with you?" Kincaid questioned, waiting. Abisai nodded and followed with his response.

"I will offer my life in exchange for hers."

Well, damn.

He spoke with a certainty that mirrored Kincaid's sentiment when he made the same promise to me. Abisai then looked at my mother. Their eyes fastened for a long moment, which ended with another nod.

"You have my blessing too," I offered with a smile, which prompted Abisai to chuckle lightly.

"Shall we?"

He extended his hand to my mother and she wasted no time accepting the offer, moving to his side after he pulled her in and kissed her fingers. Then Kincaid's phone rang and he stepped away to answer.

"You're leaving?"

My mother shook her head softly. "No. We're going to hang around here tonight if that's okay. I thought maybe Abisai wouldn't mind joining us for dinner."

"I'd be honored."

"Works for me." They left the living room just as Kincaid ended the call and joined me.

"They're gone?"

"Nope. Hanging out here. Abisai's staying for dinner."

"You okay with that?" His eyes lowered to me, waiting.

"Yeah, I'm happy for her. She deserves to be happy and you said he's a good guy."

"He is." Kincaid pulled me into him and kissed my forehead. "Conner and Floyd will be here in a minute. I'm about to call them. They'll be outside. I have to run out to take care of something, but I shouldn't be long."

I wanted to object because I could feel this had something to do with the night of our reception, but I didn't need Kincaid leaving here worried about me. There was no doubt in my mind he was going, regardless of how I felt.

"Okay." I attempted to step away, but he pulled me back again.

"Hey, we okay?"

"We're fine. This is a part of being with you. I get it. Go." I lifted enough to reach his lips, delivering a soft peck that he held longer.

"Now I can go."

CHAPTER 13

KINCAID.

"**W**hat do we know about her?"

"Basic shit. Name, background, family, work history. She's a college student. The catering gig is part time to help with expenses. She's in law school and lives with her boyfriend. He's a DJ at Bleu."

"That piece-of-shit club?" I said, but more so speaking my thoughts out loud.

"Yeah, same thing I said."

"This place is decent. Not exactly cheap."

"They both drive nice cars and you know he's not making shit at Bleu. My guess is he's using it to build a name for himself so he can move onto one of the bigger clubs."

"You question them yet?"

"No. I figured you'd want to do it, but it's definitely her. The same woman who was there at your house. She's supposed to work tonight, so she's in her uniform now."

I nodded and brushed my palm down my face before following Cast into the apartment. After doing a sweep, I located the woman in question sitting in a chair near the kitchen table.

173

Her eyes landed on me the second I was in the room. The man, who I assumed was her boyfriend, was in the living room on the sofa with one of my men in front of him, gun in hand. Instead of aiming it at the guy, the weapon rested beside his thigh.

When I walked over to her, I placed a small recording device on the table and kneeled down to get eye level. Her hazel orbs went wild briefly before they settled back into the worried expression she had when I walked in.

"We need to talk."

"Talk? Why the fuck you need guns to talk?" her boyfriend based from the living room. With the location of where he was sitting, there was a clear view of the kitchen, which meant he could see my every move. I glanced over my shoulder but didn't acknowledge him. I wanted him to feel disrespected and unsure of my motives.

"Name?" I didn't have to look at Cast for him to know who I was talking to. He quickly rattled off the woman's identity.

"Darian Blakey."

"Darian . . ." I began slowly. Her eyes bounced around before connecting with mine. "I'm not here to hurt you, but I will." Those hazel orbs, already uncharacteristically large, expanded again before she looked past me at her boyfriend. He gritted his teeth but didn't say anything.

"Darian, look at me. He can't do shit for you. I'm the only chance you have, okay?"

She nodded quickly with anxious energy. She kept smoothing her hands down her thighs and shifting in her chair.

"You work for Elegant Eats."

She nodded again.

"You were also at my house on Friday."

She hesitated, as if weighing her options on how to answer. But before she could lie, I told her it wasn't necessary.

"You were there, Darian. We've pulled up the footage from my surveillance system and know for certain you were. It's taken us a few days to decide how to handle this, which is why you're just now seeing me. My guys have been watching you to get a more vivid picture of who you are. From what I've learned, you seem to be a decent person. Both of you. Wouldn't you agree?"

"Yes." This time, she used her voice.

"Good girl. Now, let's get down to business." I stood and pulled an empty chair closer to the one she was in, positioning myself right in front of her. I rolled my shoulders back, resting my hands in my lap. I stared at Darian for a few minutes, not saying anything. That made her even more antsy because she did not know my intentions. Her eyes bounced around the room and she shifted in her chair. I allowed this to go on until I was sure she was close to losing her composure, so I eased slowly into the reason for my visit.

"Who paid you to leave that package at my house?"

Her eyes went wild again, revealing she knew what I was talking about. However, she denied any acknowledgement verbally.

"I didn't leave a package at your house."

I flashed her a smile that didn't help her anxiety. "Sweetheart, my time is very valuable. Let's not waste any more of it than you already have." I lifted my hand, motioning over my shoulder, and Clay's gun met with her boyfriend's forehead. I didn't bother looking behind me for verification. The way she gasped and the alarm in her eyes was proof enough.

"He will shoot him and it will be your fault. Now, let's try again. Who paid you to leave that package at my house?"

"I don't know. The man didn't give me a name. Just paid me five grand and told me to mix it with the other gifts and not to open the box. I swear I don't know the guy."

I studied her face a little longer, attempting to decide whether she was lying. Darian was telling the truth, which I already assumed. It would make sense for whoever paid her to keep their identity hidden. At this point, she was desperate to save her boyfriend, which meant she understood how serious the situation was.

"That box you left at my house contained the hands of a man I'm sure is dead. He was likely murdered by the one who paid you. These are not typical bullies or thugs you're now connected to. They're very dangerous men who don't mind taking lives to protect their interests. You made an extremely bad decision when you accepted the money and did what they asked. My wife is the one who opened that box, and the fact that it was in our home, our private space, left her feeling violated. That leaves me angry, and like the men who paid you, I'm also a very dangerous man. The good thing is, I don't want to hurt you, but if I can't find a way to ensure my wife no longer has to worry about feeling violated in our home, then make no mistake about it. Anyone who played a role in the reason why . . . *will* suffer." My eyes fastened to hers and she began to sob lightly while her body trembled.

Threat received: smart woman.

"Don't tell him shit, baby. He's not going to hurt either one of us. The cops will be all over his ass. Trust me, D. Don't cry, baby. We gon' be straight, I promise."

Clay snorted behind me, and Cast chuckled, removing his phone. He made a call and put the phone on speaker.

"Nine-one-one, what's your emergency?"

He took the call off speaker and began playing a role, changing his voice so he sounded panicked and not like a six foot-something, 200-pound Black man.

"There's a guy in my apartment. He has a gun to my girlfriend's head. I think he's going to shoot her. Please, send somebody now. I don't know what to do. Yes, that's my address. Please, hurry. I'm gonna hang up now so he can't hear me. Please, hurry." A moment later, "Okay, thank you. No, I'm not staying on the gotdamn phone. If he catches me, he'll kill us both."

My eyes lifted to his, and he shrugged, likely knowing I was thinking what the fuck with the whole white-guy voice.

"They'll move faster."

I shook my head before staring at Darian again. Cast moved to the door, pulling it slightly open while we all waited, none of us saying a word. I was good with silence. It forced people to have to deal with their thoughts, and right now, Darian's were haunted by just how badly she'd fucked up. About ten minutes later, two officers arrived, creeping in with their guns drawn. I had never seen either of them before because knowing their faces wasn't my burden. With all the dirty money we shelled out to the city, their superiors needed to ensure they knew mine.

"What the hell is going on—" the first officer started but was cut off by the second who shoved him in the arm.

"Shit, man, shut the fuck up. I got this." The first officer didn't recognize me, but the second did. "Mr. Akel, is there anything we can do to assist you with this situation?" He squared his shoulders and both officers returned their weapons to their holsters after speaking my name. They may not have always known my face, but they damn sure knew the name.

"No, not at all. Just making sure my money was well spent with you gentlemen. Enjoy your evening, officers. We've got it from here."

They both tipped their heads to me and left, closing the door behind them.

"Now, let's get back to business. As you can see, the cops can't do shit for you, but I can. So I need you to search deep inside that pretty little head of yours and try to remember *anything* that will help me."

Her eyes moved past me. I was sure she was searching for confirmation from her boyfriend. I didn't know why because the little shit had proven he wasn't too bright. He obviously gave her what she needed, though, because she started talking.

"I swear I don't know his name or anything about him. I can barely remember what he looked like because I didn't care. He gave me five grand to deliver a box. All I can tell you is that he was Spanish or something. He had an accent and his English was broken. He also had a bunch of tattoos."

"Think harder, Darian. You're going to have to do better. That's not helping me solve the problem you played a role in creating." I kept my tone even, but my stare was icy. She needed to provide more. None of what she had said so far would be enough.

"The tattoos, he had them on his face too. There was a cross on his left temple. Oh, and when he was leaving, he called some guy named O'Neal and told him it was done. That's all I heard because he was walking away from me while he finished the call."

My eyes shot up to Cast's and we both had the same thought. Initially, we assumed this was Manchester, but it turns out it was a little less complicated.

Fucking O'Neal.

"Good girl. Now, I need you to listen closely." I waited while she shifted in her chair and straightened her spine. Satisfied that I had her full attention, I delivered my instructions. "The only way you remain unharmed is by doing as I say. If O'Neal finds out you're the one who led me to him, he will kill you both. I have already proven the cops can't do shit for you. All you have is me." I glanced over my shoulder to make sure the little fucker behind me understood this as well. His jaw flexed, but he nodded and looked at Darian.

"She's gon' do whatever you need her to."

I was on Darian again. "For the next couple of days, stay here. Don't leave your apartment. I'll give you a number. If you need anything, call that number and they'll get it for you, no matter what it is. Understood?"

"I have work and school."

"I'll take care of both. Don't leave the apartment, either of you."

"We got bills. You gon' cover those too?" the boyfriend gritted from behind me.

I stood and turned to face him, tilting my head to the side briefly before moving closer. Clay stepped out of the way, allowing me the spot before him.

"You're a DJ at Bleu, correct?"

"Yeah, why?"

"They're not paying you shit. I have a friend who owns several clubs. You want a better position with a bigger audience that pays ten times more than what you're making now?"

"You gon' do that for me? Why?" He was skeptical of my offer, which was good. If a man was too trusting, they were usually naive or not very smart. I needed him to be neither, although I had my assumptions.

"Because I'm not a bad guy. Darian did something stupid, but she had no clue how severely stupid her decision was. She needed money, likely because you're not making enough to do your part around here. I'll help, but if you so much as think about making a wrong move where I'm concerned, this ends badly for both of you. Your life, as well as hers, is now in *your* hands. You can either choose to be the man she, for some reason, thinks you already are or be the reason why this ends permanently for both of you. Your call. What's it gonna be?"

He flexed his jaw and looked past me at Darian. The minute I noticed his expression soften, I had his answer.

"Yeah, I'm down."

"Good. Someone will be in touch."

Once we left, I made plans to have two of my guys on their apartment until I mapped out what was next. Cast and I then posted up between our vehicles to discuss what the hell had just happened.

"This muthafucker has bigger balls than I gave him credit for." I felt the muscles in my arms flex when I balled my fist, causing my knuckles to crack.

"Yeah, we've been looking at this shit all wrong. You think Knotty was O'Neal too?"

"Possibly. It would make sense why we can't find anything on who actually killed him. We totally missed the fucking mark. Our direction was completely off."

"Well, now we know, so we handle it. What do you wanna do?"

"Nothing tonight. I have dinner with my wife, her mother, and her new boyfriend."

Cast grinned, shaking his head. "Damn, that shit sounds domesticated as hell. Better you than me."

"You should consider finding a wife or at least a steady girlfriend. The benefits are immeasurable."

He laughed harder. "Nah, I'm good. You keep that shit."

I brushed my palm down my face. "We head to Miami soon. I need to do this in person and the element of surprise is necessary. O'Neal killed a high-ranking member of Gallardo. The pinky held the crest. Medina is in charge; Martinez isn't far down the line. If I had to guess, Martinez knows nothing about it or he would have slit O'Neal's throat. He's not loyal to him. Martinez uses O'Neal to allow his people to maneuver how they want. O'Neal damn sure didn't like how I pointed out that he was Martinez's puppet. This won't play out well for O'Neal. All I have to do is put the pieces together and let Medina and his guys handle the rest."

He nodded, following what I was planning. "Got it. Just let me know when and I'm there. But if he really is the one, that also changes the angle on Manchester. All he's doing is fucking with Nari to get under your skin."

"I'm not positive it's about Nari anymore. He seems more invested in Endia, considering the threat he issued. Based on how he's been playing this, he has no interest in building bonds with Nari. However, regardless of his focus, I'll still end him if he pushes things to the point where it's necessary."

Cast gave me a look of understanding. He would stand by my decision, backing me no matter the repercussions. It didn't need to be discussed. If Manchester had indeed been the one behind Knotty and the death of a Gallardo leader, then I would have more pull with The Families to get rid of him. Without it, they would expect me to deal with the matter civilly. Civil wasn't an option and I didn't give a fuck how it played out. He was hiding in the shadows right now because he knew better than to be where I could get my hands on him. But it would be happening sooner rather than later.

CHAPTER 14

NARI.

"Are you sure she'll be okay?"

I watched the city pass as we traveled to Kincaid's beach house. The trip was last minute, and although he mentioned he had a few business things to handle, he insisted that most of our two-day stay would be focused on us.

"There will be guards on the property until we return and Abisai has promised to keep her close. She will be fine."

I smiled briefly at the thought of my mother and Abisai. Turns out he had proven to be just how Kincaid described him: a good guy. He adored my mother based on my conversations with her, and she was feeling partial to him as well, even though she pretended there was nothing between them but a budding friendship. As much as she attempted to downplay what was between them, the way her entire spirit lit up when she spoke of Abisai and the smile planted on her face when he was around was proof of something more between them.

"And what about us?"

He frowned slightly. It was a subtle shift, but it didn't get past me. "What about us?"

"You didn't travel with security, not even Cast?"

He arched his brow, delivering a barely-there smile. It was cocky but teasing at the same time. "Am I not enough? You don't feel safe with me, Nari?"

"I do, but you're here on business." I shrugged at the thought.

"Not all of my business ventures pose a threat that requires the presence of security. Sometimes, it's simply an exchange of signatures. No one needs to watch my back while I'm negotiating terms of an acquisition."

"So this is *that* type of business?" This time, I was the one offering a cocky grin. I knew better, and so did he, but if Kincaid felt secure being our sole protector for this trip, then so did I.

"You focus on our time once business is done. Let me worry about the rest."

Diversion!

"I can do that."

"Good." He offered a slight nod then changed the subject. "I've had Annalise pull a few properties. If she hasn't already, she'll be emailing you a list. I know you're ready to move forward."

I wasn't able to contain my smile. With everything going on in his life, I had no idea how Kincaid possessed the ability to be still in tune with the things going on in mine, but he was.

"I have it already. I just haven't had a chance to go through the listings."

"Make sure you do as soon as possible. Many of those properties are in high demand and will move quickly."

"I will."

"So, what would you like to do while we're here?" The question felt odd. I wasn't sure why he was asking me. Kincaid never *asked* much of anything from anyone. He was the type who was well organized and moved with specific plans. From the time I'd known him, I'd learned he wasn't a wing-it type of person.

"This was your idea, so I'll leave that up to you. Besides, I don't know much about the city. Since you're the one with a residence here, I'm sure you would have a better handle on what our plans should be."

He stared at me introspectively. Those beautiful brown eyes of his communicated the complexity of his thoughts, but I couldn't quite determine what currently plagued him. After a few additional moments of silence, he offered a nod. That was it.

I frowned while he focused his attention back on his phone. "Is something wrong?"

"No, sweetheart. Why would there be?" He didn't give me his eyes, but he didn't have to in order to let me know that something was off between us. Just that quickly, we'd transitioned from a place of happiness to one of those weird spaces I hated. I did not know what the hell I had done to upset this man.

Instead of pushing the issue, I removed my iPad from my purse and began a superficial surf of the properties Annalise sent. I decided to use my time wisely while Kincaid had settled into yet another one of his moods. I was still learning to navigate his complex personality. Regardless of the connection we shared, there were still some gray areas I was working my way through.

By the time we reached the beach house, the sun was setting. I couldn't wait to strip out my clothes and relax on the beach for a few hours. There was something so serene and peaceful about the sound of waves creeping toward the shore and the gentle breeze misted with saltwater, prickling my skin. As much as I loved our home, I'd have to say the beach house was a close second and possibly even a tie for my favorite space simply because of the location.

While Kincaid removed our luggage from the car and gave instructions to the driver, I keyed the security code to let us in. I was in such a rush to disarm the security system that it took me a moment to take in the space. First, there was silence, then a sweep of emotions . . . then the floodgates opened. I felt him behind me, his cologne soothing my emotional state seconds before his arms created a cocoon of security.

"Happy birthday, sweetheart." His voice was just as soft as his lips when they brushed my temple and landed in a gentle kiss.

"You did this?"

"I arranged it, yes. I hope no one else is as invested as I am in ensuring that today was special." I heard the smile in his tone, even though his voice rumbled in a low murmur.

It all made sense for some reason and I turned quickly into his embrace. "Is this why you were upset on the ride over?"

"Not upset, just a little confused about why you hadn't mentioned what today was. I have been waiting for you to at least acknowledge the day, but you never did, so I took a chance, praying there wasn't an underlying issue that created bad memories."

My eyes closed briefly, allowing me a minute to regroup. "I hadn't really thought much about my birthday. However, I should have known you'd make a big deal out of it."

"You're my wife. Your milestones are just as important to me as they should be for you. Why haven't you given much thought to today?" His eyes narrowed a little, and his expression was filled with concern. I knew Kincaid. He assumed the worst, that some tragedy had possibly happened on my birthday. I was positive he was already plotting the downfall of anyone in my past who had ruined the occasion.

Exhaling a short sigh, I prolonged the conversation he wouldn't let me bypass. I hated to explain the reasoning. It wasn't anything detrimental; truthfully, it felt childish to hold onto things I couldn't change.

"I've never once celebrated a birthday."

His face twisted in surprise before slipping into what could only be translated as anger. "Never?"

My head shook lightly as the weight of embarrassment behind my confession felt even heavier. "Nope, not once. In my world, birthdays were more of a nuisance than a luxury. A luxury I was never granted. I moved from family to family, and no one had ever been invested enough to remember or care when my birthday was. Some even made clear that I wasn't allowed to celebrate because that's for 'families.' I wasn't their family. I was a paycheck and an obligation. I sort of got used to it, and birthdays eventually became just another day."

He pulled me in closer and kissed my forehead, mumbling his apologies as he held me in only the way he could. That started another round of tears that threatened to fall, but I pushed them away and refused to be that person, the sad little girl nobody loved. I wasn't her anymore. I had my mother and my husband. No need for tears, right?

"This is beautiful. Thank you." I turned, moving deeper into the room. My first stop was the three massive crystal vases holding exotic red flowers. They had six to eight petals that looked soft as silk and opened into a blossom that mirrored a small bowl. The delectable scent of rich chocolate tickled my nose when I leaned in closer.

"Oh, wow. These smell amazing. Like chocolate." I grinned over my shoulder, where I found Kincaid a few steps behind me, his hands submerged in the pockets of his track pants. His beautiful smile was on display while he watched my every move.

"Good because they're supposed to. It took me a lot to get those here. Cosmos Atrosanguineus or Chocolate Cosmos. It is one of the most beautiful, rare flowers in the world. Their fragrance only adds to their mystique."

"Well, I love them. Thank you."

"You're welcome, and there's more." He pointed his forehead toward the table where two black leather boxes were waiting.

I could tell right away they held jewelry. I lifted the first, about three inches in height and a foot in length, pressing the small gold button on the front. I gasped when I noticed a delicate platinum chain with a pendant hanging from it. A plethora of small, strategically placed rubies surrounded an oval diamond. It was the most beautiful thing I had ever seen.

Before I could turn and face Kincaid, his chest was at my back while he peered over my shoulder. "I pray that smile on your face means you like it."

"I do. This is beautiful."

He kissed the top of my head. "The bracelet is in that one. You have no idea how frustrating it is to have access to just about everything in the world but still have no idea what to purchase my wife for her birthday."

I rolled my eyes, turning to face him. "I'm not that complicated."

"Oh, indeed you are, sweetheart. You're not impressed by much, regardless of your humble beginnings. I've quickly learned that you don't give a damn about price tags or labels."

"You make me sound unappreciative. I like nice things."

He grinned and lifted my chin, delivering a kiss. "Quite the opposite. You're not impressed by *things*, making it much harder to surprise or impress you."

"Well, you most certainly delivered." My eyes lowered to the necklace.

"Twenty-five carats for the center stone and twenty-five rare ruby chips were used to make this. The same applies to the bracelet. Gian sent a personal note, which is at the bottom of the case. Please make sure you read it, or I'll never hear the end of it."

I grinned, nodding. "So, twenty-five is the magic number? I assume that's the count for the flowers in each vase." It didn't take much to piece together the recurring theme.

"It is. Happy twenty-fifth birthday, Nari. As much as I'd love for this to be a celebration of you, it's more mine than yours. I'm blessed to share this with you—your first celebration of life on your official day. I never want you ever to feel as if your birthday is a nuisance or a luxury. Your gift has twenty-five precious and rare stones because you're precious and rare to me. I love you more than words can express."

"Thank you."

"No need for thanks."

"So. . . now what?"

"That's up to you. I can order us dinner, or we can go out if you'd prefer." His eyes lowered to mine, waiting.

"I kinda would rather stay in if that's okay with you. I was thinking about spending some time out there."

"It's your day. You call the shots. Any suggestions for dinner?"

"Nope, you can choose."

After I got over the initial shock of my birthday surprise, Kincaid removed a gift from his suitcase. It was from my mother and had me bawling like a baby again. I had somehow turned into an emotional mess, but I used the cop-out of my hormonal surge and blamed our son.

My mother gave me my hospital bracelet and a stack of letters she wrote to me every year on my birthday. I called her to thank her and promised to read them all that evening. She was also an emotional mess, but it felt amazing to know that even if I hadn't been with her, she still loved me and thought of me every year. She celebrated my life when no one else did, and my heart felt full for that.

Kincaid and I both dressed in beach attire, me in a two-piece exposing my slight belly, while he wore matching trunks. We spent a little time walking along the beach, treading in and out of the water but only going about knee-deep before settling into one of the lounge chairs behind the house. I read through my mother's letters while Kincaid remained quiet, allowing me the space to deal with my emotions. His hands moved gracefully across my skin, mainly my stomach, reminding me he was there, supporting me while I got to know my mother a little more. Some letters were pages long, and the others were simply handwritten statements saying, "*Happy Birthday, I love you.*" Regardless, each meant the world to me, so I called her when I was done. The two of us cried once more, but it was a release we both needed.

Kincaid ordered dinner, which we ate on the balcony before retiring inside for the evening. After a shower, he was all over and in me. I was blessed with my first round of orgasms by way of his tongue, then the fun really began.

"I'm obsessed with your body. Every curve, the softness of your skin, your stomach."

I grinned, watching through lazy, lustful eyes as Kincaid traveled up my body, pausing at my stomach. He peppered my skin with kisses while balancing his weight so it didn't rest on me. I should have been ashamed that something so sweet felt erotic. He was honoring our son, and my horny ass felt my sex clenching from the petal soft feel of his lips.

"Everything about you is beautiful. I'm so fucking blessed."

By the time his face was hovering above mine, his mood had shifted again. His eyes were low as he pushed my thighs open a little more, making room for himself. When I felt the pressure from his head then the thickness of his length easing into me slowly, my body relaxed. It was a natural reaction because his hardness, in contrast to the softness of me, felt so damn amazing. He widened me with ease. My body belonged to him and he was an expert on how to please me.

Kincaid retreated and returned again and again until he located that place that had my muscles clenching and my back arching away from the mattress. He handled me with small movements, which amounted to gentle thrusts that heightened my experience. My body has been so sensitive lately. Something as simple as my T-shirt brushing against my nipples could have my thighs clenching and my panties soaked. This only excited and amused Kincaid. He seemed to use it to his advantage. I didn't mind because my climaxes were dangerously intense. I could feel everything, like at the present, I would swear to feeling the exact position of his mushroomed head when he reached its destination. I could literally feel every inch of him.

After allowing his tongue to explore my mouth, his lips found my nipples, followed by his eyes on me again. The way he looked at me caused my body to shiver. Kincaid cherished and loved everything about me, making my emotions go haywire again.

When I came, he came in such an explosive way that I couldn't begin to explain the way my mind and body took flight. My entire frame vibrated to the pulse of his dick, which was still embedded deep within me. The two of us remained connected, panting and touching misted skin like it was necessary to regain our conscious minds. After a few minutes, Kincaid was on his side, with arms open, requesting my presence. I didn't hesitate because I needed it just as much as he did. He held me as if he needed to protect me from the world, from anything or anyone that would do me harm, and at the core of my soul, I knew he would. That feeling of peace allowed me to close my eyes and drift. I was asleep in no time.

What an incredible first birthday!

CHAPTER 15

KINCAID.

My guys surrounded the beach house. There was not a chance in hell that anyone could get to Nari, but I still kept the security app open, occasionally checking to ensure she was safe. I promised to be gone only a few hours but hoped it wouldn't take that long. My goal was to spend our time here celebrating her birthday. To know she had never once experienced something as menial as a grocery store cake and that annoying-ass song not even once in her life had me wanting to track down every family she'd spent time with and physically show my displeasure with them for depriving her of such a simple privilege. Instead, however, I promised to make sure each birthday from here on out made up for those she lost over the years.

"You need to focus. She's good, fam. That place is secured like Fort Knox."

I locked my phone, dropped it in my lap, and flexed my fingers, causing my knuckles to crack when I balled them into fists.

Cast was right. I made Nari promise to stay in until I returned, and my guys were instructed to shoot first if even the slightest thing felt off. No one would have a chance to get near her, but still, I couldn't temper the anxiety of not being there.

"We're in and out," I said instead of addressing his comment about Nari. "If anything feels off, you put a bullet in anything moving. This has the potential to go left."

"You already know how shit's going down. Even if I don't make it out of there, you damn sure will." His voice did not have an ounce of uncertainty, which confirmed what I already knew. Cast was loyal and would trade his life for mine. With a nod and no words, I acknowledged his declaration. It wasn't necessary to handle things any other way.

I delivered one last look at the building where we were parked, and I spotted four sharpshooters without having to do any heavy inspection. Medina was an important man, so his movements were heavily guarded. Even something as simple as a meeting with O'Neal about his bullshit handling of the city put hittas on the roof. Unfortunately, that had me thinking about the minor details of what I was doing, which would mean me taking over the city. Those details would be handled later, and I would have to make it work.

Cast and I approached the restaurant. I carried what I had planned on using as leverage with Medina. We were stopped at the door, and one of Medina's men had to send word that I was there and wanted to see him. There was a chance that he would decline, then I would have to figure out my next move. There were nothing short of ten trained guns outside the building and half as many inside.

When one of Medina's foot soldiers returned, extending a hand, I shook it then pointed to Cast. "He comes with me, or I can leave."

His eyes narrowed and moved to Cast before returning to me. "You don't come here making demands, Akel. We respect you, but The Family has to be cautious right now. I'm sure you can understand."

"I do, which is the reason for my visit. I assure you, I'm only here to offer a solution, but as I'm sure you understand, I have to consider my safety the same as Medina has considered his own."

With questioning eyes bouncing between Cast and me, he eventually nodded. "This way."

We followed him through the restaurant to the back corner, where a table was set up filled with food. Three men were seated: Martinez, Medina, and O'Neal, who didn't look too happy to see me.

"Akel, I must say I'm not happy about the last-minute visit." Medina was the first to speak. Martinez kept a stoned expression. He didn't like me but was curious about my impromptu meeting. It was uncharacteristic of me, which had all their guards up.

"I apologize for not reaching out first, but this was a delicate matter which needed to be handled accordingly. Had I given a heads-up, it may have offered the opportunity for some involved to shift the narrative to protect their ass. I couldn't risk that." I stared at O'Neal, who seemed extremely concerned about my presence.

"Please, have a seat."

"No, thanks. I feel it's best if I stand. However, I have something for you." I lifted the box and Medina's brows inched in closer as he frowned. He was a full-blooded Cuban in his early seventies with hard features, thick salt-and-pepper hair, and a body resulting from too many years of eating for pleasure and not health. On his pinky finger, he wore a ring that matched the one on the hands in the box I carried. He motioned to one of his guys, who accepted the offering, placing it on the table. They all watched as Medina slowly lifted the lid. Within seconds, three guns were aimed at me, while Cast had his on Medina. *Take out the boss; don't worry about the soldiers.* I was sure that was his thought process.

"Is this some type of joke?"

"Unfortunately, no."

"Then you better start explaining—now."

"That was delivered to my home the night my wife and I celebrated our marriage with family and friends. O'Neal must explain the reasoning behind it, considering he's responsible. I have my assumptions, which I'm positive will give you the answers you need. But I think he should explain why he killed one of your top-ranking men."

All eyes moved from me to O'Neal.

"You can't possibly think I would be that careless. To kill one of your men—what would be the point?"

He was already sweating, and his pupils dilated with fear. As I suspected, he hadn't planned on me piecing things together.

"You wanted to start a war between me and the Gallardo Cartel. Likely because I called you on the fact that you hold the title, but Martinez holds the power."

Martinez growled under his breath, now extending his gun toward O'Neal. "*Es esta la verdad?*" (Is this the truth?)

"Hell no. Why would I—"

"*Silencio!*" (Silence!) Medina's fist slammed hard against the table, causing the china to rattle from the impact. Seconds after, his angry eyes found mine.

"What proof do you have?"

"I need to reach into my pocket without one of your men putting a bullet in me." Medina nodded and allowed his eyes to sweep the room, confirming that he approved my request. I pressed play on the recording from the night we pulled up on Darian. The recording was cued to the section where she mentioned O'Neal's name.

"*The tattoos, he had them on his face too. There was a cross on his left temple. Oh, and when he was leaving, he called some guy named*

O'Neal and told him it was done. That's all I heard because he was walking away from me while he finished the call."

I ended it there, and all eyes were on O'Neal within seconds. Martinez rushed him, knocking O'Neal backward so he tipped over in his chair but didn't move because the barrel of a gun was then pressed against his head.

"*No aquí, primo.*" (Not here, cousin.) Medina was quick to speak up as he stood, adjusting his jacket. Martinez struggled to keep from pulling the trigger, but he obeyed orders and backed away. O'Neal, being the pussy he was, tried his best to cover his ass.

"How do you know that's real? He could have gotten anyone to make that recording. It could be his fucking wife, for all we know. Are you *really* going to take his word and make it final?"

"Yes. Akel is an honorable man. I don't have to like him, but I've always respected him. He's fair and has never been an issue for our Family . . . unlike you." Medina's eyes went dark and O'Neal kept his mouth closed.

"You give me your word?"

Medina was offering me one last chance to validate what I presented. I looked at O'Neal, and he was clearly spooked. Something was off about this, especially considering how Martinez reacted so quickly. It was as if he already knew the outcome and had been waiting for this moment. That's when it clicked.

Muthafucker! O'Neal wasn't behind this. Martinez was.

He had more reason to get rid of O'Neal than I did and was using me to make it happen. It was too late to change the course of things, and it would be too hard for me to convince Medina that his own blood was behind the loss of another Family member. I decided to play along and use this to my advantage. I would eliminate O'Neal and force Medina's hand with the strong-arming the Cubans had been attempting over the past year.

"I do."

He extended a hand, but I hesitated. My eyes briefly cut to Martinez, and that was the minute I knew for sure.

"One last thing." Medina's sharp stare was hard on me as I continued. "I've handed over the man who disrespected your Family. He took one of your own. I need something in return."

"I'm not in the position to negotiate with you, Akel. Respect will only get you so far."

"Understood, but what I'm asking is fair. Your Family has been pushing hard lately. That creates a problem for me."

"I will not back down. This is our city."

"I'm not asking you to completely back down, only that you not be as visually aggressive. There has to be a level playing field, or it creates a rift with the other Families."

"I don't give a damn about them."

"But I have to. I want us to agree amicably, but I will not hesitate to use force if required. That will cost us both. Can you agree to back off some? That's all I'm asking."

"Fuck that. *Esta es nuestra ciudad, primo. No negociamos con él ni con nadie más.*" (This is our city, cousin. We don't negotiate with him or anyone else.)

Medina delivered a look to Martinez that had him silent once more, but he was seething because he wasn't the one calling the shots.

"I will agree. War costs time and money. It's not beneficial to either side. My people will back off *some*."

I extended a hand. "As long as you honor your word, we have a deal."

The two of us shook before Cast and I left. I didn't miss the fact that Martinez realized I'd had the final say. The only way he could bypass Medina's promise to me was to kill him, and he would never take it that far. His disloyalty would only extend so far.

Dumb fucker. How often do I have to prove I'm smarter than you'll ever be?

"They're going to make O'Neal an example."

"They are, but that's his fucking fault."

And the poor fucker was innocent. At least with this. I decided to keep that detail to myself.

"And The Families?"

"I didn't kill him. They can't say shit to me, and even if they did, I wouldn't give a damn. He fucked himself. Saulo was there at the last meeting. He saw what I saw, and that was that O'Neal wasn't fit to be in charge of such a huge part of their operation."

I left it at that. Cast would fly home within the hour. I was done with business, and the next twenty-four hours here in Miami would be dedicated to reminding my wife just how important she was to me.

I stood in the doorway of our bedroom, watching Nari sleep peacefully. I had only been gone for a few hours, but based on what I saw, she hadn't left the bed after I woke her that morning to let her know I was going. I didn't mind because even if she wasn't experiencing the worst that pregnancy seemed to bring most women, she was extremely exhausted all the time. I wanted her to rest as much as possible with the understanding that no matter how hands-on I planned on being, our son would rely primarily on his mother for the first few months of his life.

Nari was hot and cold. She would be sweating one minute and freezing the next, and currently, the covers had been tossed to the side, exposing her beautiful brown skin. My eyes traveled from her ankle up to her thighs, pausing at the curve of her hip while her hand rested on her stomach. The other was tucked beneath the pillow, and her hair was a spiraled mess that crowned her head, sprawling across the pillow in a sort of soft, brown chaos. She was beautiful, and not just because she was mine. Nari was the type of woman men would sell their souls for and give their last to keep close. I was in that number. This woman owned me, controlled me, and with little to no effort. She was considered in every fucking move I made.

As I entered the room, I began stripping out of my clothes, and once I was down to nothing, I pressed my knee into the mattress and eased my hand between her thighs. My thumb stroked her nub a few times, and she moaned softly, still partially asleep. I grinned as I watched her body awaken before she was able to. Pushing one finger into her sex, followed by a second, I began a slow, steady rhythm that had her eyes slowly peeling open and connecting with mine.

"Good morning," she mumbled, adjusting so she was on her back and her knees landed gently outward, providing me better access.

"Good morning," I returned, hooking my fingers and applying more pressure with my thumb just before I lowered my head and added the third element . . .

My tongue.

It didn't take long to get my intended result because she seemed to be in a heightened state of arousal lately. While she attempted to recover, I got comfortable behind her, lifting one leg to enter easily. Nari was ready for me. No matter what happened in my life, if I could come home to this, to her, to our son, my world would feel complete. After providing my wife with several orgasms, I allowed my first to take flight then slid to the side of Nari, forcing her into my chest.

Easing my hand between her legs, I grinned when she flinched because her body was still sensitive from the damage I had done.

"We have plans for lunch. Are you going to be able to leave this bed anytime soon?"

"How do you do that to me then expect me to be functional?" she mumbled in a lazy tone that had me smiling harder and kissing her shoulder.

"It's a late lunch, so you have a few hours."

"Mmmmm," she groaned under her breath, snuggling closer to me in the process. "How was your meeting?"

I thought about how I left things with Medina and O'Neal. If I had to bet every penny I was worth, I would be willing to wager double or nothing that O'Neal was currently in a lot of pain if he wasn't already dead.

"Good, but we're not about to discuss that. We'll be flying home tomorrow, so this is our last day. What would you like to do?"

"I'm a cheap date. As long as I'm with you, it doesn't matter."

The two-point-eight million I spent on the pieces I gifted for her birthday would certainly contradict that statement. However, Nari would never know the bottom line of how much I spent. She would likely demand I return the jewelry, but that wasn't an option, considering I enlisted Gian to custom-make the pieces for her.

"You're anything but. However, we can keep things simple if you'd prefer. How about we start with lunch then see how you feel?" My fingers glided across the smooth skin of her stomach while I kissed the back of her head. Her shampoo's key lime and coconut scent gave me the euphoric scent of home. She was definitely my safe space.

"Mm-hmm, now can I go back to sleep?"

"You can do whatever your heart desires as long as it includes me."

"Good, I sleep better when you're with me."

So do I.

I landed one last kiss on her shoulder, allowing Nari to drift again. I found myself doing the same. Hopefully, I would be up in time to make our scheduled lunch date, but if not, I would send my apologies and regards. My only priority was my wife. Everyone else could wait.

"Your home is lovely. Thanks so much for inviting us."

"No, thank you for coming. My husband would have pouted for weeks if you two had declined."

"Grown men don't pout, baby." Troy kissed his wife on the cheek, handing me a glass of cognac. It was a unique blend I sent him every so often. He pretended it was too expensive for his taste, but I was sure he simply appreciated it more when I gifted it. His net worth mirrored mine.

"Then I don't know what else to call it because you seem more disappointed when you can't see this guy than when you miss me."

I chuckled, lifting my glass and taking down some of the smooth liquor while he shrugged. "You're beautiful, baby, but look at this guy. How can I not be disappointed when I miss the opportunity to see that pretty face of his?"

"Easy, Troy," I warned, forcing a smile from my old friend and business partner.

"You two have an odd bond."

"Don't be jealous, baby. You'll always and forever be my first love," he teased, bringing Nicolette into his chest.

"So you say."

"Aww, I see she's finally realized you're full of shit. Took her long enough."

Troy shot me a dirty look before grinning. "I might be, but she already has my last name, so she's stuck with me." He winked at Nic, and she rolled her eyes.

"Nari, would you like wine? I have a bottle I've been dying to open for months now, but I needed a good reason. You two being here feels like the perfect occasion."

Her eyes quickly shot up to me, and I offered mine in return. I didn't mind sharing the news about our son, but it had to be her decision. She was more private and reserved where the baby was concerned. I was ready to formally announce to the world that I had been lucky enough to expand our family.

And forever tie me to the woman who wants to run every chance she gets.

"Uh, no, thanks. No alcohol for me for a few more months now," she offered, allowing her hand to rest protectively over her stomach. Her loose-fitting jean shirt hid evidence of our son unless she brought attention to it like she was currently doing.

"Oh, wow, are you . . ." Nicolette paused and grinned wide. "You're pregnant?"

"We are," I confirmed, and she lunged at me, offering a tight hug.

"Congratulations, Caid. Wow, first, you're married, and now a baby's on the way."

"Shit, man, congratulations. You should've told me." Troy was next in line.

"Thanks. We have been waiting for the right time to make a formal announcement."

"Yeah, to people who don't fucking matter. I'm family." His words were light, but I sensed he felt a bit slighted by being out of the loop. I was sure Nari also picked up on it because she attempted to smooth things over.

"Kincaid was only honoring my wishes. I wasn't quite ready to share the news with the world. It was something I wanted the two of us to share in private for a bit longer. I'm positive he would have let you know if I had not insisted on keeping the news between us."

I kissed her cheek after she lifted her eyes, offering me a soft smile.

"Well, it doesn't matter. Now we know. This is exciting news, and so soon. First, we find out that you're married, and you're already working on the little ones."

"Things moved rather quickly with us, and no, she didn't marry me because I got her pregnant. We did things the good old-fashioned way. *Kind of.* I think she actually likes me, but the jury's still out about that one."

Nic and Troy both laughed, and Nari blushed. "Nah, man, she more than likes you. I see the look in her eyes. That's love."

"I certainly hope so."

"Wow, Kincaid's having a baby. Yeah, I need to open that wine."

We spent the next few hours catching up. Troy and Nic apologized for missing the reception, but I understood. He was out of the country on business. They did, however, send a gift, which wasn't necessary. Nari seemed to relax around them, which I appreciated. Nic and Troy weren't like most people I had introduced her to. They had no idea of the full scope of the life I lived. They were simply good people to whom I'd grown partial over the years.

While Nic and Troy left us out on their deck to refresh everyone's drinks, I noticed Nari's eyes moving between all of us until they stepped through the sliding doors leading to their kitchen. I touched her leg, gently massaging her thigh to check-in. As comfortable as she presented, my friends weren't technically hers, and ensuring she was okay was important. We'd been here for several hours.

The connection of my hand on her body had Nari looking up at me. I leaned in closer and kissed her cheek. "You all right?"

"Yes, I'm fine. Just trying to make a connection. You two seem close, but you're so very different from each other. He's definitely not Cast or Darius."

I cracked a smile and nodded. "They are different. Neither knows anything about the life you're familiar with. All they're aware of is that I'm a business associate and a good friend."

"They really don't know about *that* stuff?"

"*That* stuff, like I'm into things that would likely have them questioning my presence in their lives?" My eyes lowered to Nari's, delivering a loaded gaze, and hers softened.

"Yes. I mean, I'm not saying—"

I chuckled at her fumble. "It's cool. I know who I am, but a small part of me craves an escape and needs to share a meal with friends who know nothing about the heaviness of my life. Nic and Troy are those friends. They see me, and only me." I covered her hand with mine, lifting it enough to place a kiss on her wrist. "And now, they see you. You've added another layer to the man they know."

"Which is?"

"Husband and father. For that, I'm truly grateful."

"So, then, how did the two of you meet?"

"On the playground. Your husband tried to steal my husband's favorite toy, and Troy stood his ground and told him no."

"Damn sure did, and I'm pretty sure I'm the only one who's ever gone toe-to-toe with this guy. He's pretty determined when he has his sights set on something he wants, but I'm just as tough, so I handed him his ass."

I threw my head back and laughed while Troy and Nic returned to their seats. Nari looked confused as her eyes bounced between all of us.

"Wait, so you've known each other since you were kids?"

"Oh God, no. I don't think we'd still be as close as we are if we had. There's only so much pushiness one can take in a lifetime. Wouldn't you agree? You're married to the man." Troy grinned at Nari, whose beautiful smile expanded.

"I plead the Fifth."

"Good answer," Nic returned before sipping her wine.

"This doesn't make sense then."

"The very beautiful and cunning Nic, here, is using an analogy. The playground she's referring to is a conference room at Lux Flight, which he owns."

"And *he* tried to steal from up under me." Troy pointed a finger my way.

"It was business, nothing personal," I shrugged.

"Well, it turned personal. The two spent weeks negotiating, or rather, *arguing* over the company. However, Troy won." Nic winked at me, and I chuckled.

"Indeed, he did."

"I was having trouble keeping things afloat. It was stressful, and to make matters worse, this twenty-something, arrogant-ass kid bulldozed his way into my office, telling me I had a week to sign over my company to him. He showed up without an appointment, carrying a stack of papers, offering me money for my blood, sweat, and tears."

"And what did you do?" Nari seemed too intrigued by this story, but I was sure it was because she wasn't prepared to hear that someone had gotten the upper hand on me.

"I told him to get the fuck out of my office before I beat his ass." Troy laughed, shaking his head, likely remembering that day.

"And what did he do?" Her eyes shot up to mine before she waited for Troy to answer.

"He left and came back a week later with a better offer. Truthfully, I should have accepted, but Lux Flight was my baby. I couldn't imagine handing it over. That night, I invited Kincaid to dinner at my home to meet my Nic, and he agreed. We didn't talk business; we just shared a meal and a good old faithful glass of brown. The next day, he returned and asked if I would be willing to allow him to help me rebuild my company as an investor. I agreed, and we shook on it. Now, he's my business partner."

"But how did you go from full-out war to being business partners?"

I looked over at Nic, who grinned and shrugged. "I explained to Caid how important this business was to my husband and me. He had a change of heart."

Troy kissed his wife's cheek. "The fact that my wife was the one who forced a change of heart was a blow to the ego, but I've learned over time to know we're a team. This woman loves me enough to fight on the front line without question or reservation."

"You're damn right I do. When you love someone, you go the extra mile."

Nari nodded and smiled softly, but I could sense her uncertainty when her eyes met mine. I wondered what that was about but chose to wait until we were alone to explore her thoughts. The conversation shifted to our new addition to the family, and Nari seemed to settle back into a comfortable space. We ended up with Troy and Nic until just after nine that evening, and by the time we made it back to the beach house, showered, and climbed into bed, I was grateful for the downtime. I never really knew how exhausted I was until the opportunity for me to be still presented itself.

While Nari sat Indian style next to me, tackling her hair with some sort of twist style to prepare for bed, I allowed myself to settle for the evening. When I occasionally looked up at her, I could see the thoughts heavy on her mind. It was still odd how I could feel her moods and see those frustrations in the simplest gestures. Right now, it was the way she stared blankly, chewing the corner of her lip while her eyes were slightly squinted. As adorable as it was, I knew my lady had something on her mind.

"What's got you in your head?"

"Huh?"

Those brown orbs found their way to me in a matter of seconds.

"You're lost in your thoughts. What's up?"

"Troy and Nic are older than you?"

"Yeah, Troy is fifteen years my senior and Nic is maybe ten. Why?"

"How long have they been married?"

I was curious where this was going but decided to answer and allow her to get there without me expediting the process with my own questions.

"If I remember correctly, their twenty-fifth wedding anniversary will be at the end of this year. It's supposed to be a big deal, according to Nic. She's planning a huge party."

"Is that the type of wife you want?"

"Excuse me?" I frowned, lifting myself and scooting back so I was upright against the headboard. She turned enough at my side to face me.

"The way she talked about stepping in when you were bullying Troy over his business—"

"I wasn't bullying him, sweetheart. The situation was no different than any other acquisition I initiate."

She grinned and shrugged. "Sounds like it was quite different considering the outcome."

Nari was teasing me, which was a good thing, but I needed to get us back on track.

"I was young and out of my league with that one. I didn't know shit about a business producing a luxury jet line."

"Then why go after his company? I thought your thing was failing restaurants and hotels?"

"I wanted a jet, so why not own a company that provides them for leisure? It's the best of both worlds, but can we get back on track? Why are you asking me about Nic? I've never—"

Her eyes quickly rolled. "No, that's not where I'm going with this. I know you've never slept with her or even been interested in her. I can tell from how the two of you interact. You do, however, admire her as a friend and also as an example of a wife to your friend."

The explanation allowed me to release. I was sure Nari still struggled with her insecurities about me and other women despite her working on it. The feelings were still potentially there.

"I agree to all of those things, but I'm still at a loss about the direction of this conversation."

"What I mean is her dedication to Troy. Is that the type of wife you want? Because, if so, I haven't been anything close. At least not the way I should."

"The wife I want is the one I have, Nari. You can only be you, and I'm okay with that because it's who I fell in love with."

"I feel like I've been so focused on me, trying to find my place with all this, that maybe I'm not being what you need, and I want to be as committed and supportive to you as you are to me. I can see the way she is with him. They seem so . . . perfect for each other."

I chuckled at the thought before motioning to my lap. "Up here."

She moved without hesitation, taking a minute to get settled. "They're anything *but* perfect. Yet, they work well together. Their union is one I admire because it's genuine. But no marriage exists without conflicts or struggles. Not theirs, not my parents, or even Darius and Alisha. Nic and Troy have been through rough times, but they've survived because they honored their commitment to each other. They also have years of navigating their marriage, which is why they're comfortable in the space they're currently in. We'll get there, but not without days, weeks, and even years that have us questioning ourselves and our marriage."

"You worry about that stuff?"

She seemed concerned, which meant she took my words to mean I was second-guessing our future.

"I do because I always want to give you the best of me, knowing there will be times when I fail. But never do I worry in a way that means I feel as if I've made a mistake or we won't have a marriage that survives our struggles."

I could see her body relax. "Me either. I just wonder sometimes if I can be everything you need. There are so many layers to your life that it's hard to keep up. Nic seems to have it all together. I want to be that for you."

"Her role in his life is much different than yours in mine. Troy and I are not the same man. Your challenges with me are experiences Nic can never begin to understand."

"I get that. I'm just making a point."

"Nic is Troy's wife. I need you to be mine. I'll never expect or require you to be anything other than who you are."

"Well, just for the record, I think the fact that Nic stood up to you for her husband is badass, and I would totally do that."

I laughed at the thought. I could see Nari going hard on my most challenging competitors to ensure my victory. "I have no doubt in my mind that you wouldn't."

"Good. As long as you know. I might only be an Akel by name, but the weight it carries is kinda growing on me."

She leaned in, placing her hands on the headboard to balance her weight while delivering a kiss. One of my hands gripped the back of her neck, and the other rested at the small of her back, bringing her chest to mine.

"You wear it well, sweetheart. You certainly wear it well."

CHAPTER 16

NARI.

"Do I look pregnant?" I turned away from the mirror, allowing my arms to rest at my sides while I waited for Kincaid's input. He smiled handsomely, arching his brow at the same time.

"I'm not sure how to answer, sweetheart. That sounds very much like a trick question and one that could potentially get me in a lot of trouble based on how I choose to respond."

I laughed, playfully rolling my eyes. "I didn't say fat, just pregnant."

"Is that not the same as far as pregnant women are concerned? I'm still navigating dangerous waters here."

"My God, how are you this timid with a simple question and still able to be as successful as you are?"

This time, he was the one who seemed amused, throwing his head back and laughing. "With business, I have an intended goal, and I don't give a damn about their feelings, but that's not the case here. Different terms apply, but our son is gracefully making his presence known to answer your question. It's a sight I rather enjoy.

However, it will be a lot harder to avoid the conversation with others." His eyes lowered to where my hands now rested.

"We can make an announcement, and you can tell whoever you want. I simply needed to be selfish with the news for a little while."

"How about we just stick to confirming when asked?"

"That works. I'm sure it will be a topic of discussion today."

"Today?" He frowned, trying to remember what he missed about my day.

"I see you've forgotten that I have plans, which means I need to hurry. I'm sure those vultures . . ." I paused to grin, and he chuckled. "I mean, *wives*, would have plenty to say if I showed up late. Can't have the boss looking bad on my behalf."

"You're not obligated to anything."

I had decided against having them in our home, at least for now, so one of the other wives hosted this meeting. I also wanted to get a feel for things before taking on the responsibility of planning.

"Oh, but see, I am. You, sir, have created an expectation. As your wife, I have to do my part. Just don't assume I'll be as poised as you are. They give me shit, I'm giving it right back."

His cheeks hiked before amused eyes met with mine. One of those long fingers hooked my chin right after and his tongue began to explore while his body leaned into me, allowing that thick impression to be a reminder of why I struggled to get out of bed most mornings.

"I expect nothing less." He winked and stepped away. I followed him from the closet back inside our bedroom, where he was collecting his phones. "You can drive, or Conner can take you."

"Drive? Unless you know something I don't, that would be kind of hard, considering I don't have a car."

"You are correct. You don't have *a* car; you have *several* vehicles. Check the garage. The keys are to the left of the door in a glass case."

"You trust me to drive your vehicles?" I raised my brow in amusement, following him through the bedroom into the hallway.

"*Our* cars, and yes. Use what we have until you decide what you prefer. I'll order whatever you want."

While I leaned over the railing that overlooked the foyer, Kincaid took the stairs, pausing briefly with his brows slightly pinched. "You do have a license, correct?"

"I thought you did your research, Mr. Akel." A teasing smile filled my face. He chuckled and started moving again.

"That's the one thing I didn't give much thought to. Maybe I should rethink this and insist that Conner drive you."

"Nope. Too late, buddy."

I was well aware that I would be guarded. However, there was some sense of normalcy in my life when I could at least drive myself. It was a knock-down, drag-out process to gain that inch, but I needed the small victory because I was beginning to feel stifled by my lack of freedom.

"He and Floyd will both be shadowing you. I'll check in later." Kincaid paused at the door, and I nodded.

"Have a good day, *honey*." My sarcasm brought a smile to his face just before he was out the door. I had a little over an hour before I was to meet the wives for lunch. At least Alisha would be there because Lord knows I had a feeling this wouldn't go well.

Alisha grinned from the passenger seat of Kincaid's G-Wagon. After exploring the six-car garage, I found an array of foreign vehicles. They were all equally tempting, but I was sold the minute

I sat inside the G-Wagon. I had fallen in love with the one he kept in Miami and this one was identical other than its color. It was a brand I knew, considering the mileage was under 2,000 miles driven, and it smelled like new leather instead of his cologne, so I assumed it wasn't his preference. *Rich people!*

Knowing Kincaid, he likely purchased it just to have, considering the only vehicles he drove were his favorite babies: a custom i8 or the equally obnoxious McLaren Roadster. He had a thing for dangerously fast cars. Both were extremely nice, but this little baby was my new favorite thing. The exterior was a matte black finish with a black and red interior. I could tell it was custom, which meant he put a lot of thought into a vehicle that spent most of its time in the garage collecting dust. After twenty minutes of fiddling, I figured out how to adjust the air and turn on the radio before I left to pick up Alisha. We had just arrived at the restaurant where we were scheduled to meet the other wives, and I was already feeling my mood change.

"This truck is totally you. I swear it's a perfect fit. I never really liked them because they drive like shit, and I'm so short, but this is definitely you."

"It's a'ight." I shrugged, sticking out my tongue. She laughed, narrowing her eyes toward the building.

My phone lit up with a notification, making me stare at the device and frown.

J1928: Wants to send you a message.

I clicked on the notification and went to my requests, already knowing who it was from. *Joey.* This was his third fake profile in the past two weeks. Each time I realized it was him, I would block him. Just after we were married, Kincaid insisted I change my number to one that couldn't be traced, so the only access Joey had was through my social media accounts. I likely should have mentioned it to Kincaid, but the last time he crossed paths with Joey behind me, it ended with crushed bones. I didn't want to be responsible for what the next warning might be. If I continued to block him, he would hopefully get the picture. I knew one thing for certain: I wasn't getting anywhere near the man.

"I need to talk to you. It's important. Please just respond." Alisha's voice after reading the message from Joey had me quickly locking my phone. "Who the hell is that?"

"Nobody." I rolled my eyes, playing it cool. "He was one of the bouncers at the club where I used to work. I guess one run-in with Kincaid wasn't enough. I'm going to block him."

For the hundredth time!

"That man is playing with his life. Yeah, you better do that, or it won't end well."

I was grateful when she moved on.

"You ready for this?"

"Are you?"

"I'm used to it. They don't like me, but they have to tolerate me. I take pleasure in the fact that they can't figure out a way to keep me completely exiled from their precious little cliques. I only come to this stuff just to fuck up their vibes. It really shouldn't give me that much pleasure just to see them hate the fact that I'm there, but it secretly makes my day."

"You're evil."

"Maybe, but the only way to fight evil is with evil."

A few minutes later, we walked inside the building, and I was glad I'd skipped the jeans and hoodie and settled on slim-fit slacks, heels, and a loose-fitting, thin, sleeveless cashmere sweater. This place was the type of environment where the food looked better than it tasted. The whole more-plate-than-food vibe was in effect with this joint. I was sure the chef was French and had several Michelin stars.

"We're grabbing pizza after we leave here," I whispered to Alisha as we approached the hostess. She shot me a quick grin and nodded before she greeted us.

"Good afternoon, ladies. Table for two?"

"No, actually, there should be a reservation for Cynthia Tyler."

"Ahh, yes. They're in the Chalet Room. Follow me, please." She smiled politely before her heels clicked the tiled floor until we crossed into the dining area and stopped just outside a private room. She paused, sliding open one of the frosted glass doors. "Enjoy."

I offered a nod and we entered. There was a massive round table with four women. All eyes were on us, but mine landed on one person specifically. *Mya.*

"I didn't think you'd be joining us." She lifted her wrist, glancing at the watch that circled it loosely. My extra time getting acquainted with the truck had us running a few minutes late.

"Well, we're here." I shrugged. She offered a tight-lipped smile and flicked her wrist to the two empty chairs.

"Join us, please."

"Tacky," one of them mumbled, and the one beside her agreed.

"Now, as I was saying before our late guests arrived—"

"*Members,*" Alisha cut in. The five of them glared her way, sending so much heat it was only by the grace of God I didn't break out into a sweat. "We're not guests. We're members of this organization. Please address us properly." Alisha's elbows rested on the table, and her head tilted slightly.

One of the women smirked as her regard bounced around the table. "I'm sure that's what she meant. Isn't that right, Mya?"

"Yes, so, as I said, we pick a cause yearly. Last year, we donated reading materials to underprivileged schools, and the year before that, we sponsored food drives throughout the city. I was thinking this year, we'd focus on donating to foster families. More specifically, the children who are affected."

She delivered a snarky smile my way.

"I think that's a brilliant idea," one of the others chimed in. "Especially considering we have an expert on the matter."

All eyes landed on me and I produced a broad smile. Cynthia was the only one of the five women who wasn't attempting to embarrass me.

"Agreed."

Mya flipped her hair over her shoulder. "Great. So, to my understanding, it's a huge deal for these foster kids to own luggage. Typically, when they're being shuffled around from family to family, their belongings are placed in trash bags. How tragic. Is that really how they're handled, *Nair*? Is that *your* experience?"

The fact that she purposely mispronounced my name was amusing and showed her hand. All eyes were on me again, but I kept my cool. I wasn't embarrassed by or ashamed of the life I'd lived. They had a lot to learn if they assumed singling me out would somehow make me cower.

"It's *Nari*, but I'm sure you remember, considering the multiple times Kincaid had to continuously remind you why your focus should be on *your* husband and not *mine*. But let's get back on track. It was, and it's one of the reasons I respect those who have to work for what they have, unlike some who have the world handed to them and still aren't satisfied. Simple privileges always seem to be unappreciated."

"Simple?" Mya scoffed. "There's nothing simple about *your* life. I'm sure you're making good use of Kincaid's status and money."

"Ahh, I see you're still struggling a bit."

"Struggling?"

"Yes, with the fact that your pussy didn't secure you a ring." I held up my hand. "And to think, he chose me before even knowing what mine had to offer. Now, if you're done with your attempts to marginalize my life or downplay the fact that it's one you want—and *can't* have—I say we focus on why we're here."

Mya's lips parted as if she were stunned into silence, and I assume she truly was because Cynthia picked up the conversation.

"I say we donate to the cause and purchase luggage for those in need to give them a sense of belonging. Wouldn't you agree, Nari?"

"Absolutely. Most wouldn't possibly understand how something so trivial to some means the world to others."

"Perfect, then let's get started. We'll need to draft a list of resources so we know who to reach out to. I'm sure you wouldn't mind taking that on since they're *your* people." Mya just wouldn't let this shit go. I was seconds away from handing Mya her ass again, but Cynthia stepped in.

"I think Nari should be the lead on this one since it aligns with her foundation's intent. Some of us understand the value of using our experiences to make a difference by doing the work versus just looking the part and cutting a check for a photo opportunity. I appreciate those who are willing to put the time in." She then turned to me. "I understand you're just getting started. However, it would be a good introduction to your foundation. We can center the drive around it."

"I agree. I'd be more than happy to take the lead."

"Perfect, and if I can help in any way, please don't hesitate."

"Thank you, and I will certainly keep that in mind. Right now, I'm focused on securing a building."

"Oh, do you have a realtor? I know several who are really good," one of the women offered, making nice. She clearly decided it was better to be for than against me.

"I do. Her name is Annalise."

"Davenport? *The* Annalise Davenport?" one of the others chimed in with a little too much enthusiasm.

"Yes, that's her."

"Wow. I've been trying to get with her for years now. Her client list is small and exclusive. Figures Kincaid would have her at his disposal. We're about to put our house on the market. I'd kill for a shot at having Annalise list it."

"I can mention you to her. We have a meeting this week to view some properties."

"Rachel, you know I have access to Lee Roberts. He sold us our last home. I can put in a good word for you," Mya cut in, and Alisha laughed under her breath, noticing the same thing I did. It was a desperate attempt to feel important. I didn't give a damn who listed this woman's house, but apparently, Mya did.

"Lee can't get his hands on the properties I'm looking for, but Annalise can," she shot back quickly before turning to me. "Would you mind? That would be amazing, and I'd forever be in your debt. Your house is beyond gorgeous. It makes sense that it's one of her properties."

"No, I don't mind at all."

At that moment, I understood how Alisha felt about those small victories. These women were so damn caught up in the lifestyle that something as simple as getting an in with the right realtor won them over. I learned two things: never trust their intent because they would switch up if the price were right, and I was nothing like them. That was a previous concern of mine up until now. I was grateful that I wasn't the same. These women's values were all twisted.

Once the meeting was over, Cynthia approached while I waited for Alisha to visit the ladies' room.

"Hey, I apologize for how that started, but I saw you could hold your own in there." She exposed a genuine smile. From the first time we met, I felt she had no ill intent.

"I'm pretty tough when I need to be." She cracked another smile; this time, it was more of a devilish nature.

"Good because it's necessary when dealing with these women. They're presumptuous and not very appealing most days, but our association with them falls under our duties as wives of the men whose names we carry. Unfortunately for you, a few of them got passed over by Kincaid, so they're in their feelings, but they'll get over it."

"Or they won't, but I don't care. As long as there are no more surprises about them sharing a past with him, I'll be fine."

Cynthia laughed lightly. "I can't confirm or deny one way or the other, but I assure you it won't be an issue, regardless. I can make their lives miserable if they push too hard, and I have no issue with using my authority. That is, however, not why I stopped you. I wanted to say congratulations. You haven't mentioned anything, but it's a little hard to miss." She pointed to my stomach. None of the other women acknowledged that I was pregnant, so I assumed no one noticed or cared.

"Oh, yeah. Thank you."

"I get it. None of their business or mine, but I did notice, so I wanted to mention it at least. If you decide to do a shower, I would be honored to host or at the least help out." She lifted her eyes to Alisha, who was heading our way, and smiled. I assumed she felt Alisha would take on that role since we'd forged a friendship.

"Thank you, and I'll keep that in mind."

"Wonderful. Well, I won't hold you. I feel you're going to be a refreshing addition to our group, and I look forward to working with you."

"Same."

She nodded and walked away just as Alisha reached me.

"What's that about?"

"Not much. Just her way of saying a good job for how I *handled* myself today."

"You mean the way you *handed* Mya her ass? I'm sure she's somewhere reevaluating her entire life after that meeting."

I shrugged, not really caring.

"If this is what I have to get used to, I can't say I'm looking forward to being a part of their inner circle."

"Then you might as well bow out gracefully now because it gets worse before it gets . . ." She paused. "Cancel that. It never gets better, but shit, it might now that you're here. I think I'm going to be a little more active just to see them eat shit when they can't knock you off your square."

"I am not here for your personal enjoyment."

"Oh, but you are. That's what friends are for, boo. Now, let's go get that pizza."

CHAPTER 17

KINCAID.

I had three nuisances that took priority over all else I needed to handle as of late. Three things that interfered with my ability to enjoy the changes happening in my life. Manchester, O'Neal, and the person I was currently standing over. I'd recently found out he was responsible for Knotty's death.

It had been a few weeks since O'Neal's body was delivered to his home . . . piece by piece. From what I heard, his wife passed out after the arrival of the first one and had been sedated since the discovery of how gruesome the sight was. Authorities were searching for his killer, but the streets already knew it was accredited to the Gallardo Cartel. Medina wanted it known because he was sending a message. No one fucks with his Family and lives to tell about it.

"What am I doing here?" The guy's tiny, thin eyes bounced between Darius and me before settling on me. He was coming down off a high of some kind. Opioids, if I had to guess, but I couldn't be too sure.

"You created a problem for me, which is something I don't tolerate."

"Who the fuck are you?"

I tilted my head to the side and stared at him momentarily. He offered his best attempt at pretending to be hard, unbothered, but he was scared as shit. Maybe he felt it, or maybe he could see it in my eyes. Whatever . . . He was about to die.

"It would have been wise of you to fully understand what the hell you got yourself into before putting your life in another's hands, Push."

"I don't know what the fuck you're talking about, but whatever the hell it is, I ain't have shit to do with it."

"Kenneth Toussaint. Known on the streets as Knotty. You shot him and three of his guys then delivered a message that *I* was sending a warning to Knotty's people to stay off my blocks."

His eyes gave him away. I saw the recognition the minute it passed through them, but he did as I expected and lied. It didn't matter. I had the proof I needed. Since the day he'd killed Knotty, Push had been in hiding. I suppose he got antsy and decided enough time had passed because he was out on the block as if he hadn't put a target on his back by using my name. He got high and started running his mouth. After some tough love, we quickly learned the hit on Knotty was simply a fiend's dream of feeding his habit. Using my name was simply his way of keeping the trail cold and, hopefully, sending Toussaint after me. It was a dumb decision, which was about to cost him his life. Secrets were harder to maintain with a loose tongue. Lucky for us, his little habit placed him right in our path.

"I don't know anything about that."

"No point in lying. You're not here because we *think* you killed Knotty. You're here because we already *know* you did that shit." Darius sounded just as annoyed as I felt. A killer who was a coward was the worst kind. If you had balls enough to take a life, that meant you should have the balls to know it could potentially mean losing yours. Lying made you weak, and the one thing I hated more was begging, and I prayed he didn't take that route.

"You wanna kill me, then do it, but I'm telling you, I don't know shit about nobody named Knotty."

"Very well."

I turned to walk away and only made the first step before the groveling began. "Ay, wait. Look, all I did was deliver a message. Knotty ain't even your people. No harm, no foul. Can't we work something out?"

I had eyes on him again, shaking my head. "No, we can't. There was indeed harm done. My name was connected to a life I didn't take to send Knotty's people after me. I don't really give a fuck about how that affects me, but the idea that your stupid decision could have potentially caused a situation that may have harmed those close to me is a gotdamn issue. I don't make deals where they're concerned."

"Come on, man. Nobody was hurt, and like I said, Knotty ain't mean shit to you. He wasn't your people."

"But he was mine." Toussaint stepped into the room, followed by Cast. His eyes were murderous as he clutched the handle of a machete that was aligned with his thigh.

"Wait, hold on. You're not about to leave me here with him, are you?"

I looked at Toussaint, who waited. Initially, I had mentioned to him I would be the one to take the life when we found the target, but I had a change of heart and was allowing him the honor.

"Our debt is settled." Toussaint felt the need to say, as if that meant shit to me. I had respect for him, but I damn sure didn't fear him, nor did I feel any sense of obligation. If Knotty had followed the rules, he wouldn't have ended up losing his life.

"There never was a debt. I promised you, and I'm a man of my word. But don't assume this had anything to do with me feeling as if I owed you. Knotty crossed a line he shouldn't have. *That's* why you're here."

As much as Toussaint wanted to argue the point, he decided against it and offered a nod.

"This is going to be fun," I heard him growl as he neared Push.

We all stepped outside the room but could already hear the cries of torture. "Make sure you clean this up and get him out of here." I motioned to the door behind us.

"A fucking machete? I thought I was bad."

"You are bad. Shit, worse, if you want my opinion," Darius said, then laughed, shaking his head.

"Maybe I am." Cast shrugged. "He's about to make a damn mess, though."

"Yeah, good luck with that." Darius glanced over his shoulder as another tortured cry traveled our way.

"I'm out."

"Ay, before you go, you still want to keep eyes on Nari's people? Nothing's turned up."

"Keep the cameras in place for a little while longer. At this point, I'm sure he's realized Nari has no connection to them, and neither does her mother."

"Got it. You have access to the feed. You can check it whenever you want."

I tossed my chin to Cast and Darius, but he fell in step with me.

"I'm heading out too."

As we moved through the building, Darius brought up something that had totally slipped my mind with everything else going on.

"Some kid showed up at one of my clubs asking for me. He said you sent him."

I paused just as we stepped out of the building. "Shit, I meant to run that by you."

"Yeah, well, you didn't. What the fuck am I supposed to do with him?"

I grinned. "Give him a job. He's a DJ."

"You seen his work or heard him mix?"

"No, he worked at Bleu, so I assume he's decent. Put him on a slow night and bill me for his salary."

"Who the hell is this kid?"

"Not important. Just consider it a favor to me."

Darius stared for a long minute before shaking his head. "You and your damn charity work."

"It's balance. Something we both need in our lives. I'm just looking out for you."

"You need to be looking out for your damn self if he doesn't know what the hell he's doing and fucks up the vibe at my club."

"You'll make it work," I tossed over my shoulder as I headed to my car, and he moved toward his own.

"You damn sure better hope so."

After returning from Miami, I'd hooked Darian up with a job at a law firm willing to work around her class schedule. After graduation, if she passed the bar, they would take her on as a mentee, but with a full salary she wouldn't be offered anywhere else. Once she had experience under her belt, they would allow her to practice law with their firm. She was overly grateful, and I had a feeling she wouldn't accept any more offers from criminals who wanted to use her as a pawn.

After checking in with Nari, who spent the first twenty minutes complaining about her meeting and the fact that her mother was never at the house anymore, I managed to get in a few words to promise to make her day better when I got there. But first, I had to stop by and check on my mother. She had been quiet over the past few days, which wasn't unusual. But I knew she missed my father and was still settling into her new normal without him. I did my best to be there when she needed me, but sometimes, she still kept me at arm's length because of how much I reminded her of him. It was hard, seeing his face on me and not being able to have him in her life anymore. It was a painful reality we were both learning to live with.

It was quiet when I entered the house, but I knew she was home. I had security shadowing my mother but kept it discreet. She wasn't a fan of being watched or followed, but I refused to take the risk with everything that had been going on.

I found my mother in the sunroom that sat off the kitchen, flipping through a photo album. It was one of the older ones because the edges were a little weathered, and the picture she was stuck on was of one of her and my father just after they were married. It was like staring at a photo of myself. That was how much we looked alike.

"He was so handsome and stylish."

"Indeed he was." She looked up and smiled, causing me to chuckle and shrug. "I look just like him, so, of course, I'm going to agree, and my style is impeccable."

After kissing her cheek, I sat on the arm of her chair while she traveled down memory lane. I enjoyed the memories she shared about the photos as she moved through them. It was something we both needed, and once she finished, we ended up in the kitchen, where she shared a bowl of peach cobbler that she'd made the night before. It was way more than I needed, but it made my mother happy, so I indulged.

"How are Nari and the baby?"

"They're good. You haven't spoken to her?"

"Not in several days."

So, at least she wasn't just avoiding me.

"They're both fine. My son is extremely active now. I think Nari might take out a restraining order. I'm obsessed with feeling him move. She's had this special connection to him all this time, and now I can finally experience some aspects of it. At least, in a marginal way."

"You're jealous of Nari carrying your son?" She found that amusing.

"Not jealous, just feeling left out. She gets an entire journey I can only view from the outside looking in. I'm ready to have that same connection with him."

My mother laughed. "You're jealous, but that's to be expected. Your father was the same in a sense. When I was carrying you, he would get up early, sometimes before the sunrise, attempting to steal private moments while I was asleep. He would talk for hours occasionally about what he would teach you and how he was afraid of being tasked with a role as great as being your father. God, he loved you so much. I'd listen quietly to him bonding with you through my stomach. There were moments when it was so sweet that the words brought me to tears. That man was everything. *My* everything. I miss him so much at times that it makes me numb."

I dropped my fork, stood, and crossed the kitchen to reach her in three long strides. My mother became lost in my embrace while crying softly. She was not only lonely but also feeling alone, and that broke my heart. My father was all she ever knew, and I couldn't imagine how she felt losing him. It was hard for me, but I still had her, and now, Nari.

"I love you, Ma."

"I love you too, baby. I'm such a mess." She gently paused, swiping away tears. She leaned against the counter opposite me, and I allowed her the space she obviously needed. I was still learning how to be there for my mother in ways she would let me.

"You're allowed to be a mess. You lost your best friend, the only man you've ever loved."

She laughed, shaking her head. "You're so sure about that, aren't you?"

"Shouldn't I be?" I hadn't considered any men before my father. There may have been a few, but none that she loved.

"Relax, you're right. He's the only man I ever loved until you. It's just amusing to me how you wouldn't even consider the idea of there being anyone else. You and your father are the same. It's frightening, sometimes."

"Confidence is key. There's no one who can compare. You can't blame either of us for living in our truths."

She laughed harder that time, and I was simply happy to be the reason for her smile.

"Nari has her hands full. Where is she, by the way?"

"Home, sulking because Endia has been spending most of her time with Abisai."

"Well, she may as well get used to it. From what Endia has told me, she's enjoying her new beau. It's good that she's doing that, and it makes her happy. She's a wonderful person and is turning out to be a much-needed friend."

"You should take your own advice."

"And do what?"

"Whatever makes you happy."

My mother's eyes landed on me hard. "I'm nowhere near ready for that. I may never be."

"I'm not saying date, Ma. Shit, I don't know if I'm ready for that, either. I only mean do what makes you happy. Pop would want you to be happy. It would kill him to know you're not, even if it's behind him no longer being here. He was selfish when it came to you in every way, even with your happiness. He'd sacrifice his own as a promise for yours. That's all I'm saying."

She nodded. "I know, and I will. I'm not miserable, nor do I plan to be. I do things that make me happy. I just have my days."

"I know. I only worry, which can't be helped. Just promise me you'll take care of yourself, physically and emotionally. Whatever that means, just promise me you'll find a way to be happy." Her eyes pinned to mine as she closed the space between us, lifting her hands to cuff my face.

"I promise."

"That's all I need." After hugging my mother again, I returned to the table to finish my cobbler while she discussed plans for the baby's room that she would keep for him at her house. Our son made her happy. The idea of having her first grandchild definitely put a smile on my mother's face. As selfish as I already was with him, I would make the sacrifice to divide his time just to see her smile. Since my father was no longer here, it was my responsibility to take care of my mother in the best way I knew how, and I would give my last to ensure that she was good, the same as I would do for my wife.

Cast's update on Nari's maternal grandparents had me making a decision that I prayed I didn't regret. As much as I understood that my family was now hers, she had the potential to have an extended family of her own . . .

If I allowed her to.

When I entered our house, I found her seated on the floor in the living room, surrounded by her iPad, laptop, and a few open folders with her new logo printed on top of the exposed papers. The fact that she was settling into her own had me feeling a sense of pride. I wanted Nari to be her own woman who could stand independent of me. It was something I knew she needed, and I would fully support it.

"Hey, you." Her smile was genuine, which always warmed my heart. Who the hell would ever think something as simple as coming home to my wife would be what I looked forward to the most?

"What are you working on?" I slipped my hands into the pockets of my slacks while her eyes did a quick sweep of the things that surrounded her.

"Putting together a list of group homes we can contact for the drive we're heading up. They thought it was a good idea that I take the lead, you know, with me being a foster kid and all, and that's the cause we're focusing on." She rolled her eyes, and I narrowed mine.

"You don't have to commit to anything you don't feel comfortable with. I don't give a shit about any of those women or their bullshit organizations that they pretend to be concerned about."

"Hmm, sounds like you've been to a few of the meetings." She arched her brow, and I shrugged.

"No, but my mother has been where you are for years, so I know enough to say it's more about recognition than the idea of truly doing something great."

"Well, I don't mind. It will actually be a good thing because it can be an introduction to my foundation. I also plan on killing this shit so they know I'm not the one to play with or underestimate."

"Sounds like your agenda is a little more personal," I chuckled, and she nodded.

"It is, but that doesn't take away from the fact that I believe in the cause. I can kill two birds with one stone is all I'm saying."

"Then I fully support your efforts. Just let me know what you need."

"I think I have it covered for now."

"Can you take a little break? I'd like for you to come take a ride with me."

"Where?"

"I can't tell you until we get there."

"Should I be worried? Taking a ride with you could mean I end up in a foreign country."

I chuckled, shaking my head. "We'll remain stateside with this one, and it's nothing for you to worry about. I give you my word."

"I'm game then. Should I change?"

"No, you're fine as you are." She was in leggings and a fitted hoodie. There was no need for her to dress up, so her attire was fine.

A little over an hour later, we were pulling up in front of a small house nestled in a decent neighborhood across town from where we lived. Nari frowned at me after looking at the brick residence.

"Where are we?"

"Your grandparents' house."

Her eyes landed hard on me. "What? Why?"

"Because I've been watching them for months, and there hasn't been any contact between them and Eli." I still refused to call him her father.

"And?"

"And it leads me to believe he won't contact them. It's not likely that he doesn't know who they are. If he intended to use your family to get to you or your mother, he would have done so already."

"But why did you bring me here?"

I stared at the house for a long minute before focusing on her. "All you have is your mother . . ."

"That's not all I have." She frowned harder. "I have enough people in my life who matter. I know I made a big deal at first, but I'm perfectly fine with the family I have."

"It was also my decision to keep you from your mother's side."

"They don't want to know me. Shayla told them she knew where I was, and—"

"She could have lied," I amended. If I knew anything about her cousin, it was that she was jealous of Nari. It would be nothing for her to make Nari feel as if she weren't relevant to them.

"And if she didn't?"

"Then you walk away with your head held high, knowing they don't fucking matter, but this has to be your choice, not mine. Initially, I kept you from them because I wasn't sure if Eli was somehow connected to them. I don't think he is."

"And you're okay with me knowing my mother's parents?"

"Sweetheart, I want you to have a family. It simply has to be family that deserves to be in your life. If that's your grandparents, then I have no issue with you building a relationship with them."

She stared at the house a little longer before she shook her head. "I don't want to know them."

"You sure?"

Nodding with confidence, she confirmed. "They're the reason why I didn't have my mother all those years. Maybe they could be good people, maybe they're not, but that's something I can't forgive, or I possibly just don't want to. They had their chance to be a part of my life."

"If you change your mind—"

Her head was shaking quickly. "I won't."

"*If* you do, promise you'll never come here alone. Talk to me first, and I'll arrange it. I can't say that I fully trust the situation, but I'm willing to give it a try."

"As much as I appreciate that, my mind is made up. I won't be coming here again, with or without you, but thank you for caring enough to give me the option."

I was fully prepared to leave things like they were, but as if the universe were testing her, a car pulled around us into the driveway. An older woman stepped out, and I recognized her as Nari's grandmother. Nari's eyes shot over to me, searching for confirmation of her identity, and I offered a firm nod. She watched her grandmother nearing my car, and I watched Nari, gauging her reaction. For a brief moment, I noticed the conflict brewing. There was a tiny bit of longing, even after she had only seconds before decided she didn't want to explore the possibility of getting to know her grandparents. Although she had just made a firm decision not to allow them into her life, seeing the woman in person was initiating an internal battle. Unfortunately, the one thing I considered to be an option happened. She rapped on the window to get Nari's attention, and I could tell from the scowl on her face that this wasn't about to be a happy union.

"You're Endia's kid, right? Shay Shay told me you done married some rich man for his money. I can tell it's you by this expensive car." She cut her eyes at me briefly. "I don't want you around here, and you tell your mama she can stay away too. Been gone all these years, so ain't no point in y'all coming around now. We got all the family we need. Now, get away from my house before I call the cops."

The woman's narrowed eyes landed on me to be sure I understood the threat of the authorities was directed at me. Nari frowned hard, watching as the woman delivered one last glare, turned on her heels, and crossed the yard, moving toward the house. Not once did she look back or seem remotely bothered by how rudely she'd just treated her own flesh and blood.

"Wow."

"Sweetheart . . ."

Nari's brown orbs landed on me within a matter of seconds.

"Don't. I'm fine. That just further proves I made the right decision. I won't fight for the love of someone who refuses to respect me or my mother. Can we go now?"

"There is nothing *fine* about how she just spoke to you." I was seconds away from addressing the issue when Nari realized what I was thinking.

"I see that look on your face, and you're not about to say anything to her. It's not worth it, especially considering I don't plan on being in their lives."

I studied her for a moment more before she turned away from me and glanced at the house. I left Nari to her thoughts, but she further confirmed that she was okay by leaning across the seat and kissing my cheek. No words were necessary. As much as I hated the idea of putting her in a situation that could potentially harm her emotionally, I was fully prepared to take the risk, with the understanding that I would be there with all the support she required. The way Nari had just been treated had me struggling to remain neutral with my thoughts on how to react, but I settled on it being a win in my favor. I wasn't upset about her decision not to forge a bond with her grandparents. It was the selfish side of me. That might change one day, and if it did, I planned to keep my promise to facilitate the need in a way that kept her emotionally sound. That would begin with a warning that the type of bullshit she pulled today would *never* happen again. No one would address my wife with a lack of respect. Love meant compromise, and I would always do whatever was necessary to keep Nari happy.

CHAPTER 18

NARI.

The sound of a phone vibrating had me throwing my hand over to the nightstand, but it didn't take long to realize it wasn't my device receiving a call. Kincaid's raspy voice broke the silence around us, rumbling through a half-ass greeting.

"Yeah?"

"Who?" It wasn't until he repeated the name that I began to pay attention.

"What can I do for you, Melissa?"

Melissa? Who the hell is Melissa?

He tossed the covers from his body before lowering his legs over the side of the bed, leaning over enough to rest his elbow on his thighs while he listened to whomever the hell Melissa was. That tiny internal voice was telling me not to overreact, but I could already feel my annoyance building.

"I'm well aware that the baby isn't mine. I haven't been with your sister in months. Well before the timeline of conception that would grant me paternity. I only pulled strings to get her help because it was necessary for her well-being. Regardless of the imposition she posed in my life, I'm not completely heartless. If the hospital refuses to let your sister leave, they apparently think it's best that she stays."

That was when it clicked. Melissa must be Val's sister.

"Did they explain to you their reasoning for agreeing to admit her? Then you understand the severity of the situation. I may have called in a favor, but she's under a doctor's care based on their evaluation. It's not my call whether they release her. That's strictly based on their diagnosis of her condition."

He paused again, listening to her response before brushing his hand over his head and gripping the back of his neck.

"I agree and will make a call to see how I can assist in allowing that to happen. You're welcome, and there's no need to apologize on her behalf. The situation wasn't of your doing. I do, however, suggest that you and your family put the time into ensuring your sister stays on course with whatever treatment is suggested. I will not be so agreeable if she causes any more unwarranted conflicts in my marriage moving forward."

After he ended the call, Kincaid glanced over his shoulder. "That was Val's sister. She was trying to get her released, but they won't do it."

"Are you the reason she's still there?"

He snorted. "She's fucking crazy. *That's* the reasoning behind why she's still there. Melissa wants them to release her to a doctor's care in New York. She says that can only happen if I agree, but not because I've requested they keep her. She clearly needs the help even though it was the favor I called in that got the ball rolling."

"Are you going to agree?"

"To allow her to go home to her family, yes. But I will make it clear that she has to continue to remain under a doctor's care until they determine that she's well enough to be released. Thankfully,

Melissa has no plans to fight me on keeping her sister on task with treatment. She agrees."

"Is she really that messed up?"

"Apparently. One thing I've learned over time is that people's minds are fragile. It's damn near impossible to determine what one thing can cause them to lose touch with reality."

"Well, in her defense, I've experienced the one thing that sent her over the edge, so I can somewhat understand her desperation."

He joined me in bed again and inched toward me, forcing one of my legs between his to get closer. I had to angle my head back to see him because mine aligned with his chest.

"I'm glad you find this amusing."

I grinned at the thought. "Either I find humor in this extremely exhausting situation, or I pick a fight with you."

He chuckled, lowering his eyes. "That would undoubtedly be a waste of your time because I wouldn't engage. But I do have a few ideas of what I *will* engage in."

"Don't you need to be leaving soon?"

"I do, so stop talking so that I can commence with *engaging*."

Within a matter of seconds, I was on my back, and Kincaid's head found its way between my thighs. I had no objections to what his current plans were, and neither Melissa nor Val were taking up space in my mind any longer.

Shortly after Kincaid left the house, I found myself in the kitchen and was greeted by my mother. She smiled, and I pouted.

"Oh, wow, this is a surprise."

She lifted her eyes from the book she was reading, offering a subtle grin.

"I know I've been gone a lot, and I apologize. I'm supposed to be here spending time with you."

"No, I'm just being my typical emotional self. I'm glad to see you happy because, apparently, Abisai makes you happy. I just miss you, that's all."

"He does, and I miss you as well. I mentioned to him that maybe we should slow things down a bit . . ."

"Oh God, no. Don't stay away from him because of me. It's not that serious."

"It is if it bothers you. We've already missed so much time."

"No, it's really not a big deal, I promise, but I am curious to know why you would have to slow things down if you're only *friends*." I delivered a smug grin before removing the bowl of fruit I was sure she'd prepared for me.

"We are just friends. However, he wants more."

"Well, what do *you* want?" I plopped down in the chair across from hers and she closed her book, using a folded piece of paper beside it to hold her place.

"I don't know. He's a really nice guy. Sweet, attentive, mature. I enjoy spending time with him, but I can't say I've ever desired anything past companionship."

"Why not?" I frowned at the same time her eyes fastened to mine.

"Truthfully, I'm a lot to take. I have my good days, but the bad days can be really bad. Depression comes with highs and lows, even when I stay consistent with my medication. It's hard for most people to understand, better yet, deal with my depression in a long-term commitment."

I considered what she was saying. She'd been happy for the most part since she'd been here, but there were times I recognized a difference. It was like the light in her spirit dimmed a little.

"Does he know?"

"Of course. We've talked about it. My condition is a part of who I am. I can't separate the two, so I don't hide from it, and he's very observant. He senses when I'm unbalanced."

"And how does he feel about it?" If he couldn't accept her as she was, then he most certainly wasn't the one she needed to be with. I felt a sense of responsibility to my mother, and even though I was the daughter, I wanted to protect her from anyone who didn't have her best interest at heart.

My mother's smile blossomed. "He insists he can handle anything. He even went as far as expressing his offense that I didn't trust him to be man enough to love me as I am."

"Really?" This time, my smile blossomed.

"Really."

"Then I don't see an issue."

"People are quick to say what they can handle until it becomes their reality. I don't want to put anyone in the position of feeling obligated."

"I don't see him as the type of man who would feel obligated. He seems like the type to know what he wants with the understanding that not everything will be perfect."

She stared at me for a long moment before shaking her head and laughing lightly.

"What?"

"Shouldn't *I* be the one giving *you* relationship advice?"

"I mean, yeah, and you have, but it goes both ways." I popped a few grapes into my mouth and she nodded in agreement. After swallowing, I continued. "All I'm saying is, don't create problems that don't exist and don't tell him what he can handle. He knows himself better than anyone else, right?"

"Right, and I'll take that into consideration, but there's still no rush."

"I agree because I can't necessarily say I'm ready to hand you over to him anyway. I kinda like the idea of you being here."

"I love being here as well, but I also don't want to wear out my welcome."

"Not possible. This house is big enough for everyone to have their space. Trust me, it's not a big deal. Speaking of houses, Kincaid took me to your parents' house last night."

"You spoke to them?" Her expression was stoic, so I couldn't tell how she really felt. I did, however, assume that was intentional.

No, but she definitely spoke to me with all the hate she harbored for you.

"I didn't need to. He wanted me to know that he no longer felt as if they were a threat and left it up to me to decide whether I wanted to get to know them."

"Have you decided?"

"Yes. I have all the family I need. I'm perfectly fine *not* knowing them."

"Because of me?" She seemed concerned.

I could have easily told her how hateful my grandmother reacted, but what was the point? My decision had been made before I ever laid eyes on the woman. Her lack of acceptance only further confirmed I had made the right decision.

"Yes and no. I'm angry because they made you give me away. I'm not at a place where I feel like I can forgive them for the relationship they cost me with you. I don't think I ever will be."

"They're not bad people . . . well, my sister and your cousin may be, but my parents aren't terrible. I don't hate them. I just choose not to allow them to be a part of my life."

"And I'm making the same choice, not for you, but for me. Like you said, sometimes, things are better left alone. I'm happy. I have a circle I trust and know truly cares about me. That's enough."

My phone vibrating had my mother lifting her things. "I'm going to go sit out by the pool for a little while."

I nodded and answered, smiling, until Alisha spoke.

"Apparently, I'm selfish."

"What?" I frowned at the first thing out of her mouth.

"Darius thinks I'm selfish."

"Well, you kinda are." I tried humor because she seemed genuinely upset.

"Nari, I'm serious. He wants a baby and says that I'm selfish."

I paused with my mouth hanging open just before I was about to take down a few grapes. They landed back in the glass bowl as I frowned.

"A baby? I thought you couldn't have kids."

"I can't, well, sort of. I personally can't have kids, but I can carry one. It would just have to be someone else's. I had one ovary removed after the accident and the other one was damaged to the point where I'm not fertile. But my uterus is in perfect working order."

"Wait. I'm lost. Why are you selfish?"

She released a harsh breath. "He's been bringing up kids a lot lately. I mean, we've talked about it before, but it's been a recurring theme over the past couple of months. We've considered adoption all the other times, and I was okay with that if it's what he really wanted."

"You don't want kids?"

"I mean, I do, but I would also be okay if we never have them. It's not like the topic hasn't come up over the years, but this time, he mentioned using his sperm and another woman's egg so I could carry the baby. Like one that's donated. I told him no, that I would be okay with adopting, and he called me selfish."

I opened and closed my mouth, trying to decide what the hell to say to that.

"Nari, are you listening?"

"Yes, I'm listening."

"Well, do you think I'm being selfish?"

Hell no! Darius tried it!

"That's not a simple answer, Lish."

"Why the hell not? How would you feel if Kincaid asked you to carry a baby that belonged to him and another woman? He's the one being selfish. Why can't he be okay with adoption if he really wants kids that bad? It's not like I'm saying no completely."

She seemed extremely emotional and I understood why. Truthfully, I could understand both of their sides, but I couldn't honestly say I would feel any different than she did about the situation.

"Lish, I get it, and you're not selfish. I also see why he would feel the suggestion is a viable option. It's not like him cheating or—"

"Oh my God, you *don't* get it. It will be his kid with another woman and *not* mine. How am I supposed to be okay with *that*? I can't believe he's even arguing with me about this. He's been okay with no kids all this time, and now that you're pregnant, he can't stop fucking talking about us having a kid. But the thing is, it *won't* be mine. Just his and some other woman." She was damn near yelling to the point where I briefly removed the phone from my ear.

"Whoa. Sounds like you're saying this is my fault."

"Because it is! I don't even know why I called you. I have to go." She hung up in my face and I sat there stunned. Did she *really* just make this *my* fault? What the hell?

Before I could even think of reacting, she called me back, and I almost didn't answer, but I gave in. She and I had become close over the past months, damn near family. I was sure she only blamed me because she was lost in her emotions.

"Shit, Nari, I'm sorry. I really am sorry. It's not your fault. It has nothing to do with *you*. I'm just, it's just . . ."

She paused, and I could tell she was emotionally overloaded and crying. "It's okay, Lish. I get it."

"No, you don't." She sniffed a few times before releasing a harsh breath. "I don't want another woman to give him something I can't. If that makes me selfish, then I am because I don't think I can do that. I really don't."

"Did you explain things to him that way?"

"No, because it makes me the bad guy. I'm the one who can't give him a baby. He can produce a kid; I can't."

"I know, baby, but he knew that before he married you. It's unfair to throw this on you now and without considering your feelings about what he's asking. You need to really explain what the issue is. It's deeper than you're admitting. You feel like you're not enough."

"Because I'm not if he wants another woman to give him what I can't."

"But you are. He loves you so much, Lish. You're definitely enough. If you explain to him that you feel you're not enough, I guarantee he'll prove you wrong. Be honest about why this bothers you so much."

"I want to, but I'm afraid he'll decide that maybe I'm not and . . ."

"And what?"

"Leave me."

"You know better, baby. There isn't a damn thing in this world that will ever make me leave you, Alisha. How the hell can you think it's even a possibility?"

Darius's voice was so clear that he had to be near her.

"I thought you left?"

"I did, but I didn't feel right about how we ended things. Can we talk without all the yelling?"

"Hey, go talk to him and be honest. I love you, okay?"

"Love you too, and I'm really sorry. I promise I didn't mean it," she said softly.

"I know, babe. Call me later."

"I will."

CHAPTER 19

KINCAID.

"Gentlemen." I stood and greeted Saulo and Kafi as they entered my office. It was an unexpected visit, meaning there had to be a concern. A number of issues could have brought them to my door, but I assumed O'Neal was the reason.

"Good to see you, Kincaid. I hope all is well." Kafi offered his hand and initiated a hug after we shook. Saulo offered a similar greeting before we shook and both men sat in front of my desk. At the same time, I returned to my position behind it, extending both arms to adjust the comfort of my suit jacket before I allowed my hands to rest comfortably in my lap.

"To what do I owe the honor?"

Saulo cleared his throat before he straightened his posture. "We have come across some information regarding your father."

My brows inched in closer as my regard moved between both men. Much like myself, The Families were still investigating all avenues in an attempt to find out who was behind the shooting. Unfortunately, I had come up empty, so I prayed they were more successful. It was unsettling that I wasn't able to put an end to the person who cost my father his life.

"You know who was behind it?"

"Regretfully, no."

"So, why are you here?" What the fuck was the point of being here if there were no new leads?

"We don't have any firm evidence, but we've recently come across information that leads us to believe that Kaber was involved."

I snorted at the name. I was fucking positive he was involved, but I also had enough sense to know he wasn't the one who put in the order. Kaber was a fucking coward. The type to throw a rock and hide his hand. This was bigger than him, but he knew something. My only regret was that someone got to him before I could.

"A lot of good that's going to do any of us. There's no doubt in my mind that he played a role in what happened, but as I'm sure you both know, he wouldn't have the balls to do it himself. So if you're not here to tell me you know who actually pulled the trigger, then you can leave."

My expression was stern. As much as I respected them both, the topic of my father wasn't one I cared to discuss. A man as protected as he was shouldn't have been so easy to reach. The thought plagued me daily, especially now, considering that I not only had myself to consider, but also Nari and our son.

"We haven't been able to find the persons responsible, and we likely never will. Kaber's desperation behind his pending status caused him to make some lethal alliances. We have pictures of him parked outside the restaurant the day it happened. He pulled away seconds before your father and Razi ended their meeting and stepped outside. We also have photos of him days before, meeting with two men we believe to be responsible for the shooting. Their faces were concealed as they entered one of his warehouses.

Similar photos of those two men were captured of them exiting the building across from the restaurant and also leaving Kaber's home the night of the shooting, the night he was found dead. Again, their faces were concealed. They knew the exact angle of the cameras. Based on the build and movement of the bodies, we determined they were the same men in all of the footage. Unfortunately, there's no way of identifying who they are. We can only assume it's one of the many bad alliances Kaber made due to his desperation after you ended the deal with him. He made many promises that he could not follow through on."

"Again, what's the point in bringing this to me if there is no resolution?"

"The same way we got our hands on the footage, we knew it was only a matter of time before you did. Whoever was behind this put a lot of effort into concealing their identities. It's taken some time for us to get a hold of what little we have, but it still leaves us with no answers, only a long list of people who would have placed a target on your father's back because of the money that was promised."

"My father didn't owe anybody a damn thing!" I roared, feeling frustrated about my hands being tied behind this situation.

"He did not, but Kaber would have made it appear that he did. We have no way of knowing the conversations he had on your father's behalf, but I'm willing to bet that he commissioned the death of Yusuf, and they killed Kaber as well to cover their own tracks."

"Then I go down that list until I get to the right person."

"And do what? Put yourself in a situation that places not only us but also you and your family at risk. Be smart, Kincaid. You are only one man."

"Who fears no one and nothing."

"Not even the loss of more lives of those you love, like your wife and son? Is retribution worth that much to you? Are you willing to take that risk because if your father could, he would tell you to leave it alone? Live your life."

"But he's not fucking here, is he?"

"He knew the risks the same as you. All I'm asking is that you consider the weight of the decisions you have to make." Kafi's regard landed on me, further expressing his feelings on the matter with a stern look.

"Is that your way of demanding that I leave this alone?" I leaned back, massaging my chin, watching them both silently warring with what they wanted and what they knew I deserved.

"It's our way of saying your plate is full and you need to focus on what you can currently control."

I didn't respond, but they knew I wouldn't. I refused to make a promise I wasn't positive I could keep. I also understood I couldn't play vigilante without creating consequences beyond my ability to keep confined.

"Is that all?"

Saulo nodded. He was the first to stand, followed by Kafi. "It was a great loss for us all. Do not for one minute think we don't understand the magnitude of your loss, Kincaid."

"As much as you feel you do, you never will. Send me what you have. It's the least you can do." I looked between the two men, making sure there was no option for them to deny my request.

"You will have it within the hour. Please send our regards to your mother," Kafi stated before both men left my office. Saulo paused at the door, turning to face me one last time.

"I would assume you will be expediting the matter of finding a replacement for O'Neal?" I could sense from his tone he had some idea that I played a role in handing him over to Medina.

"Someone will be in place no later than the end of the month. Until then, I will be the point of contact."

"*Bien* (Good), and Manchester?"

"What about him?"

"I assume his replacement will be expedited as well. His services, although minimal in the scope of things, are still very relevant to our needs."

"His services aren't invaluable."

"I agree, which means, should it be deemed necessary, you won't have any issues finding someone to fill the void."

I frowned but didn't respond. Saulo's expression conveyed his thoughts, but it wasn't appropriate for him to actually deliver a verbal confirmation.

"It was good to see you, Kincaid," was the last thing he said before leaving. Saulo wasn't able to hand over the name of the person who took my father's life, so he was offering me a pass with Manchester. At this point, he was still breathing, but my guess was they all knew that wouldn't be for long. Not that I needed their approval or remotely cared what they thought, but I did appreciate the effort.

An hour after they left, I received a call from Nari asking if she could come by when she finished her meeting with Nathan. As fucked up as my mood had been since Saulo and Kafi left, I knew a visit from her would help with the frustration that had been building since it was confirmed I would likely never know who was behind my father's shooting. It was in my nature to protect and solve problems others wouldn't otherwise be capable of solving, so to be lost with no options weighed heavily on me.

As soon as she stepped into the office, Nari had my attention. She was dressed in designer sneakers and a black cotton dress that hugged her body, exposing her curves and stomach. It was still small and round and only visible from the front view, but it was enough to put a smile on my face. As she approached me, I smiled, leaning back until she stopped between my widespread legs.

"This is a welcomed surprise."

She grinned as I extended a hand and placed it on her stomach.

"It can't be classified as a surprise since I called to tell you I was coming."

"I wasn't speaking of the visit itself but more so how quickly you were able to turn my day around."

The second I looked past her toward the door, she rolled her eyes. "Your assigned handlers are accounted for. Conner's with the truck and Floyd is out there standing guard."

I chuckled at how quickly she read my reaction. "How did it go with Nathan?" I pulled her down until she was forced to get comfortable on one of my thighs, and she took it a step further and leaned into my chest with her shoulder.

"Good. I'm officially trademarked. He received the final paperwork this morning."

"Congratulations. I'm extremely proud of you."

"Thank you. I will meet Annalise tomorrow. We have several properties to view, but I think I've already decided on the one I want. I'd like for you to go if you can."

"I'll make time."

"Now, let's discuss what has your mood so tragically misaligned."

I snorted, feeling my mood shifting again. I didn't want to travel down that road. Having Nari here was supposed to take my mind off my current issues. "I'd rather discuss you." I moved her face closer to steal a kiss, which she granted before revisiting the topic. She wouldn't let me off the hook as easily as I'd hoped.

"No diversion. Tell me who I need to see."

"Who you need to see?" I frowned and her smile grew wider.

"Yes, whose ass I need to put my foot in for messing up my husband's day."

I chuckled at the thought. If only she understood how impossible a task that was. "It's not important. I'd rather hear about your day."

She stared for a moment longer before deciding to let it go. "Well, my day was kind of interesting. I got into a fight with Alisha which lasted for all of maybe ten seconds before she called back and apologized."

The idea of them arguing didn't sit well with me, but with women, it was inevitable. They had a bad habit of overthinking issues that could be resolved with a simple conversation.

"What was the disagreement about?"

"Did you know she and Darius were considering children?"

"I did. He has mentioned it to me, but why would that cause a disagreement between you and Alisha?"

"They had an argument and she called to ask my opinion about it. I didn't necessarily give her the answers she wanted and she got upset and blamed me for him wanting kids. She hung up but called right back to apologize, then he came home and apologized to her so they could discuss it with level heads. Did you know he wanted her to carry a baby?"

"Yes, he came to me for advice."

"And what did you tell him?" Nari frowned hard, like she had already assumed the worst.

"I did more listening than anything, but I mostly told him it was a topic he needed to discuss with his wife. The two of them together should be in one accord with whatever decision they chose."

"He wants to have a baby with another woman and for Alisha to carry it." I could tell from her tone whose side she was on.

"It's an option, as well as adopting or Alisha carrying a child who doesn't have either one of their DNA. That's a decision the two of them must make together without our input," I warned, hoping she knew enough to stay out of it.

"I agree, but it's a lot to ask."

"It is, and I pray they find a middle ground that makes them both happy, but what I know for sure is they love each other and they'll figure it out. You stay out of it. Be supportive without your opinions. Meddling in others' marriages never fares well for the outside forces." My eyes fastened to hers, delivering another warning.

"I was very supportive and kept my opinions to a minimum because I really wanted to tell her she wasn't being selfish. Darius was, for asking her to carry another woman's child that he fathered with *her*."

"Sweetheart, their situation is delicate and requires—"

"Wait, so you agree with him wanting to do that?"

I chuckled, bringing her mouth to mine. "That's not what I said. I'm only agreeing that they should consider all options if they truly want to have a child. However, what's decided should be the option which works best for both of them."

As I leaned toward my desk, reaching around Nari to answer an incoming call, I heard her mumble I had better not ever expect her to *do some shit like that*.

"Akel," I greeted and waited.

"Kincaid, how are you? It's Carlton Adams. I was just getting back to you about the plans for the Martin Suites renovations. If we can extend the budget to 1.8 million, I'm positive we can get everything you're asking for and finish ahead of schedule. I know that was a concern of yours."

"That's half a million more than I expected, Carlton."

"It is, but it cuts your timeline by six months, which means you can get a faster return."

Nari attempted to ease from my lap, but I gripped her thigh until she mouthed *bathroom*. I let her go, and she placed her phone on my desk, crossing the room. I watched until she shut the door behind her.

"Sounds like you're attempting to be more of a financial consultant than my contractor, Carlton."

He laughed, amused by the accusation. "Hell no. I'll let you be the moneyman and stick to what I know. All I'm saying is I've worked for you long enough to understand that you appreciate an expedited timeline whenever permitted. I'm offering you that option, but it's gonna hit your pockets a little harder."

"And you can assure me that you won't cut corners and I'll get the quality I need?"

"You have my word. It's not just your name on the line with this. I guarantee my work, Akel. You know that."

"All right. Send over the requested changes to the budget and I'll sign off on it after I've had time to review everything."

"You'll have it first thing in the morning."

"Sounds good." When I leaned toward my desk to hang up the phone, I noticed a message notification light up on Nari's phone.

> **J1928:** I'm willing to take that risk for you. I understand you chose him, but I still care about you, Nari. What's wrong with just being friends?

My eyes lifted to the bathroom door in an effort to give myself a minute to consider the possibilities. If I expected Nari to trust me, then I would have to offer the same in return.

Fuck that.

I keyed her password, which I wasn't even sure she was aware I had, and went to her social media app, going straight to the chain of messages.

> **J1928:** I need to talk to you. It's important. Please, just respond.

> **NariAkel:** You either have to be crazy or you have a death wish. Please stop contacting me because I'm only going to keep blocking you. He fractured your hand just because you touched me. You claim to know so much about him and the kind of man he is, yet you keep pushing. Leave me alone!

Some of the tension left my shoulders with her response, but still. This muthafucker was really testing my patience.

That was the last message she sent, but he returned several more.

> **J1928:** I miss you

> **J1928:** As a friend. I know you're married. I respect that, even though I think it's a terrible mistake.

> **J1928:** Just let me know you're okay. Can you just tell me if you're really happy? I can help if you're not. You don't have to feel trapped.

There were about twenty or so more messages before those, but some had different names that she had blocked. None she'd responded to.

Nari's eyes were on me when she left the bathroom and realized I had her phone.

"What are you doing?"

"Why didn't you tell me he was messaging you?"

"Why are you on my phone? How do you even know my password?" She frowned and I laughed sarcastically.

"Is that what you really want to debate right now? Why the fuck didn't you tell me?"

"Because it wasn't a big deal. Either you're with me, or they're with me, so I'm not in danger." She motioned to the door and I assumed she was referring to Floyd and Conner.

"That's not the point. If he's this desperate for your attention, I need to know. A desperate man is a dangerous one."

"I didn't want you going after him again. It's not that serious."

My eyes narrowed as my head angled slightly to the right. "You care about his feelings more than those of your husband?"

"No, I don't give a damn about his feelings. It's not his feelings that would have been an issue had I told you about those messages."

I extended the phone and she accepted it with hesitation. "Ask him to send you his address. Tell him you can meet there tomorrow since I'll be out of town. Make sure to add it's your only chance because it's difficult for you to get away without me knowing."

She would never be within proximity to that muthafucker ever again without me being near, but I needed him to think it was a possibility. Nari had no idea just how desperate and delusional Joseph really was. However, his recent alliances painted a clear picture of the type of betrayal he was capable of. What she failed to realize was everyone had a price—including Joseph. Before me, Nari hadn't been exposed to the type of people who would rather destroy than walk away, meaning I had to deliver a crash course.

"What? No. Why do you want me to do that?"

"You know why, sweetheart. I warned him. You can't save him, but you can make his consequences less severe because if I have to waste time tracking him down, he will pay for not only defying my orders but also wasting my time. Either way, he *will* see me."

"So you're basically asking me to hand deliver him to you because I'm positive I won't be who Joey will be meeting tomorrow."

You damn sure won't be.

"You seem concerned."

"Because I am. You don't have to—"

"I don't have to *what*? Check that muthafucker yet again for disobeying my orders? I made it very clear that you were off-limits. His dreamy fantasies of you one day realizing you no longer want to be married to the monster who's holding you against your will ends now. I gave him an out. He wasn't smart enough to take it."

"What are you going to do?"

I stood, inching closer to Nari, leaning toward her face. "Send the message, Nari." After a kiss on her cheek, I bent enough to press the intercom button.

"Yes, sir?"

"Please send Floyd into my office."

"He's on his way, sir."

"What are you doing?" She frowned as her eyes met mine.

"As much as I enjoy seeing this beautiful face of yours, I have work to do."

"Are you seriously upset with me over nothing?"

"No, sweetheart. I'm not upset. I really do have a lot I need to get done. I won't be late. If you decide not to cook or don't want the chef to, I can pick up dinner on the way home. Please let me know."

She stared at me as if I'd lost my mind. When Floyd appeared in the doorway, I lifted my eyes from hers to address him.

"My wife is ready to head home now. Please don't make any stops along the way."

"Yes, sir."

"So, we're back to this now?" she gritted, and I smiled, pulling her into a hug and kissing the top of her head.

"Enjoy the rest of your day, Nari."

She shot daggers at me but didn't say another word. Nari turned on her heels and left but made a point of slamming the door as her final expression of how she felt about me sending her home.

I didn't give a damn. Such a simple mistake like not telling me about Joey's communications could be an egregious error that compromised her safety. I wasn't necessarily angry because I understood her need to preserve the man's life, but that wasn't her call to make. I also understood there wasn't anything behind her efforts other than Nari having a good heart and not wanting her conscience weighed down by the idea of playing a role in someone dying, but that wasn't to be avoided. It was, however, entirely on Joey and nothing she needed to feel guilt behind. Regardless, I knew she would. That wasn't something I could help, nor would I take into consideration. She was my priority, and he had been warned.

I sat contemplating my next move. It was time to end this shit. It had never been in my nature to allow anyone or anything to disrupt my life and I had already been extremely accommodating.

Lifting my phone from the desk, I began expediting the matter.

"Good afternoon, Mr. Akel. How can I help you?"

"I need to plan a flight for tomorrow. A day trip to Miami."

"No problem, sir. What time are you expecting departure?"

"Late afternoon. Between two and three."

"Perfect. I will arrange to have your jet fueled and ready to go by noon."

"Thank you."

"You're very welcome, sir. We'll see you tomorrow."

Every piece had to align perfectly to make this happen, but this was ending, and I would be the only one with a favorable outcome once it was over.

CHAPTER 20

NARI.

"There are twenty-four offices in the building, which all mirror this one, along with another identical to the corner suite we viewed after we first arrived. Not to mention, you can convert the three break rooms into kitchens and the lobby can be changed into a lounge or recreation center, depending on your plans for the space. It shouldn't take much to convert the offices into suites, similar to dorm-style housing. This is my top pick. I know it's a little more pricey than the others, but it's still quite a steal for the area, especially considering how newly renovated this building is."

"I don't know much about that, but I do love the space. I would have to agree, it's my top pick of all the places we've seen so far," I rattled off to Annalise while I watched Kincaid from across the room. He had his phone to his ear, like it had been all morning.

"Nari?"

"Huh?" I turned quickly after hearing my name. Annalise was busy pecking away at her phone, so she didn't look up but acknowledged she had my attention.

"I asked if you wanted to view the last two properties or if you wanted to put an offer on this one." She finally looked up, frowning slightly. "I just checked. There are two potential buyers for this location, so if you're interested, I say we put an offer in now and come a little higher."

"Um, let me see what Kincaid thinks. Can you give us a minute?"

"Sure." She nodded and held up her phone after her eyes shot over to where he was standing. "I'm going to step into the hallway to make a call."

The second she was gone, I crossed the room, standing before Kincaid. He lowered his eyes to mine while he continued talking. From the end of the conversation, I could tell the call was about one of his many business ventures. A few minutes later, he wrapped up by delivering a mild threat to *get it done* to whomever he had been speaking to before he granted me his full attention.

"Where's Annalise?" He frowned slightly sweeping the vacant office we were in.

"Making a call. She thinks we should put an offer in."

"And what do you think?"

"I don't know. That's part of the reason why I wanted you here."

He kept his expression tight before looking around once more. "It's a good area, and the space is nice. There's what, twenty-four offices? That gives you plenty of room to work with."

"Oh, so you *were* paying attention." I rolled my eyes, and his narrowed.

"It's not necessary that I pay attention, but I did my research before coming today. This is your vision, not mine. The only vote that matters is yours."

"I agree, but what's the point in you coming if you were going to spend the entire time on the phone, preoccupied?"

Kincaid widened his stance, tilting his head to the side. "I'm here to support you because I made you a promise, something I take seriously. A few matters came up that required my immediate attention. I apologize for not providing you with my detailed focus. Is there anything specific you'd like my opinion on?"

"No, never mind. I'll just tell her to put an offer in on this one."

I attempted to walk away, but Kincaid caught my arm, bringing me back to him. "Is there a problem?" His head angled slightly to the left while those intense eyes locked with mine.

"You're still angry with me about Joey." I tried my best not to allow it to bother me, but it was damn near impossible because I could still feel the distance. Even though Kincaid came home last night, had dinner with me, and worked in his office for a while before we showered together and I slept encased in his arms like he didn't have a care in the world, I knew he did. I could feel the heaviness between us, the same as I could feel it right now.

"I'm not angry with you."

"Then what are you because this . . ." I motioned between us. ". . . is off."

"I'm upset about the situation. You should have told me he had been in touch, but I'm not angry with you."

"Why does it matter? I'm not interested in Joey, but that doesn't mean I feel like he deserves to lose his life because of me."

Kincaid snorted, laughing arrogantly right after. "Believe me, I'm well aware you have no interest in Joseph. Otherwise, it wouldn't be necessary to have this discussion. Also, unless I'm missing something, his choices were his own and not yours."

"You know what I mean."

"Indeed, I do, but it doesn't change the fact that he's a grown fucking man who was warned to stay away from my wife."

"The same as Val was warned to stay away too, and she's still breathing, isn't she? As unpleasant as I'm sure being trapped in the psych ward was, she still has the promise of moving on with her life. Why is she any different?"

His eyes narrowed into slits before he rolled his shoulders back, relaxing his posture.

"And what would you have me do with Joseph?"

"I don't want you to *do* anything, but I'm well aware that's not an option. You're the one who said people's minds are fragile. Does that mean he has to . . ." I paused, not wanting to say the word. "Just promise you won't do *that*. At least give him the same chance you're giving her. Neither seems to be mentally stable."

Kincaid stared at me, his eyes tight and his jaw flexing before he nodded. "You have my word that *I* won't do *that*." His tone was clipped while he mocked me. Truthfully, I didn't care as long as he made the promise. Joey wasn't a horrible guy. He was simply in love with the wrong person . . .

Me.

"Thank you."

"Now, can we drop the subject? I really don't want to waste my time entertaining my wife's need to show compassion for a man I know wants to fuck her."

My lips parted slightly and I was seconds from arguing it wasn't Joey's intent, but it would be a lie. I knew better and the way Kincaid's head tilted slightly while his eyes challenged me to defend Joey again removed any words from my tongue. I refused to push and, instead, decided to move on.

"There are two potential buyers for this location. Annalise thinks we should put in an offer but come in higher than the others. What do you think?"

"If this is the location you want, then I agree. The other buyers may come back with a better offer because of where the property has the potential to be valued in the future, but that's a risk we take. I'll trust Annalise to move as she sees fit with this one."

Since we both agreed, Kincaid told her to do whatever was necessary to secure this location for me. I loved the space and couldn't wait to transform it into my dream.

Kincaid and I left together, and the mood felt much lighter than on the way here. Either way, I was stuck with my thoughts of what was next.

"You have a lot of work to do. Are you up for the challenge?"

"I'm nervous as shit, but I am."

He chuckled. "That's a natural reaction, but you have plenty of people in your corner who will be there for whatever you need."

I nodded to agree.

"You're still spending the afternoon with Endia?"

"No. She bailed on me to go shopping with your mother. She promised to help her find something for the *big date* tonight. Apparently, my mother wants to look *nice*."

Kincaid chuckled, allowing his eyes to cut my way briefly. "What's wrong with her wanting to look nice?"

"Nothing, really. I can tell they're getting serious even when she pretends they're just friends."

"And if they are?" He looked my way again, but I could sense he was reading me this time.

"Then I'm happy for her."

"Their relationship won't affect yours. Your mother understands the importance of being a necessary part of your life, sweetheart."

"I know that."

"Do you?"

"Yes."

He offered a nod then accepted a call. I half listened while he assured someone he would be on his way within the hour.

"You have a meeting?"

"Yes, but out of town. I'll be catching a flight after I drop you off, but I'll be home no later than nine."

"You're just now telling me?"

"I mentioned it yesterday when you were at my office."

"And I assumed you just wanted me to tell him that. I didn't realize you'd actually be out of town."

"It was last minute. You're more than welcome to join me if you'd prefer." He stared briefly, waiting, but I shook my head.

"No, it's business, and I made plans with Alisha after my mother bailed. We're going to look at furniture for the baby's room."

"Floyd and Conner will be with you." He rattled off as if I hadn't already expected to be in the company of his handlers. It reminded me of the memory he shared about being a kid and always having guards around. Kincaid noted that it became such a normal part of his life it was easy to forget they were there. I now understood how that was possible.

"Be patient with me, Nari. I assure you it won't always be like this."

"Stop trying to be all up in my head," I offered teasingly so he wouldn't obsess, knowing he was likely reading my thoughts.

Kincaid laughed, brushing a finger across my cheek. "I use what I can. You're not always forthcoming, and I have to make sure I keep that beautiful smile of yours in place by any means necessary. Just promise me you'll be patient."

"It's not like I have much choice. You kinda made it impossible for me to do anything but ride this out with you." I placed my hand on my stomach and his eyes followed.

"At least you understand the odds." He winked and I playfully rolled my eyes. Kincaid had left his mark on me. We both knew it.

There was no more running at this point and I couldn't say for sure
I'd even try any longer.

"What do you think of this one?"

Alisha angled her head to the side and stared at the grayish-
blue circular crib. It was huge, but something about the shape's
uniqueness made me fall in love. I could already start visualizing
how it would flow with the theme I had in mind for my son's
room.

"I think you and I could fit in there, but it's nice. Just as nice
as the other 4,022 cribs we've looked at in the past two hours. Let
me say that again: we've been here for *two long hours*, Nari."

"What happened to the whole 'I love shopping' thing?"

"Absolutely nothing happened to it when *it* is about *me*. I love
to shop for myself. When you asked me to go with you, this . . ."
She flicked her wrist, causing the Love bracelets that circled it to
clash against each other. ". . . is *not* what I had in mind. You know
some people do this for a living and are really good at it? I can find
ten designers right now who would gladly take over."

I rolled my eyes and she flashed a smile. "What? It's true."

"I'm sure, but I want to do this, and I bet as soon as it's *your*
turn, you're going to want the same thing."

She shoved her hand toward me, arching her brow. "Hi. I'm
Alisha. Have we met?"

I knocked her hand away and laughed. "Yes, fool. We've met,
but I'm right about this."

"No, boo, you're not. If it happens, I will most definitely enlist
a team to get it done. I already have my top three designers saved
in my contacts."

"*When*, not *if*."

"*If.* We don't know what's going to happen."

"Maybe not, but I'm speaking it into existence the same as I know you are. Especially if you already have your top three designers on speed dial ready to decorate your baby's room." I stuck my tongue out and she grinned. "How soon before you start the process?"

"We've already started. It's only been a round of tests to ensure I'm healthy enough. Next, we pick our donor. That part should be interesting. We get to read all the fun facts about them to help decide who better fits our expectations for our dream child. Sort of a 'build a baby' kind of process. Race, hair color, height, eye color. We go through the traits of the donors to craft our kid and I'm being really general right now. It's far more intricate. Just fucking weird."

"It is weird, but the end result is a baby, so it's worth it, right?"

"Yeah."

"And Darius is okay with it not being his?"

"He says he is."

"Do you believe him?"

"I do."

"Good, then that's all that matters."

The day they argued about it, Darius apologized and explained how he understood why she was against him going half with a donated egg. He swore he was the one being selfish and told Alisha he really did want kids, and he didn't care how, even if the kid was adopted. They met halfway, which meant Alisha would try to carry an embryo first, but one that was completely donated. If that didn't work, the next step would be to adopt.

"And I swear if I don't breeze through my pregnancy the same way you are, then *you're* going to pay."

"That's completely out of my hands."

"Possibly, but if I suffer, I'm giving you hell because it will be all *your* fault."

"Imagine that. You blaming me for something I have absolutely *no* control over."

She shoved my arm. "Stop. I told you I was sorry. Call it pre-pregnancy hormones."

I burst out laughing. "No, let's call it 'woman gone mad' because you, friend, had a moment of temporary insanity."

"Maybe I did, but you love me, so you can't hold a grudge."

"Fine. I agree, and I don't. I completely understand and can't promise that my reaction would have been much different."

"Yeah, but you didn't say that when it happened. You hit me with the *'try to see his side. Let him explain.'* Fuck that shit. That's not what I needed. You were supposed to be like, 'Cut his ass, Lish; he's tripping.'"

We looked at each other and burst out laughing at the same time. "You're right. From now on, I'll play my role."

"See? Problem solved." She pouted, offering me pleading eyes. "Now, can we go? I'm so over this."

"Fine. Let me take pictures of these before we go so I can call back and order this set. I think this is the one I want."

"Oh my God, this place is adorable," a woman screeched near the door. Her sentiment mirrored my own, so I looked up just in time to glimpse a familiar face.

Small world.

"See, I told you it was perfect. If you can't find what you're looking for here, then it doesn't exist. Their selection is exclusive."

As the two women traveled in our direction, I shot Alisha a look, but she was already in motion. One, whom I didn't recognize, was very pregnant but she was accompanied by Aila, whom I hadn't seen since my father-in-law's funeral.

"Look at God. I was just thinking about you while we were in here trying to decide what furniture Nari should purchase to decorate her baby's nursery."

Aila paused mid step, her eyes landing on Alisha first before bouncing over to me, where they immediately lowered to my stomach. Her lips parted and she was temporarily lost before she snapped out of it.

"Excuse me, do I know you?" She lifted her brow, frowning at Alisha. The reaction only further fueled Alisha's pettiness.

"You know, it must be truly devastating to have had everything you ever wanted right at your fingertips, only to blink, and poof!—it's gone. All that shit you gave me because you assumed your life was so much better than mine, and now . . ." Alisha grinned. "Well, I won't bother reminding you just how fucking pathetic your life is." She tilted her head to the side. "You look good, though. Maybe you'll have better luck if you lower the bar a little next time." Alisha's smile spread wider before she grabbed my hand, dragging me toward the store entrance.

"Shouldn't I be the one to check her?" I asked once Conner pulled away from the curb with us in the backseat.

"Oh, trust me, you did the minute she looked at you and saw everything she would never be or have."

"You're truly evil."

"And that hoe is truly pathetic, but God don't like ugly, and karma is a whole-ass bitch. I'm glad Caid took the ring back. She was out here in the world still posing like they were good."

The first thought I had was of Kincaid saying how fragile minds were. Aila was truly a representation of fragility.

"Prime example of lethal dick." I smirked, causing Alisha to snicker.

"*Girl*, can I testify?"

My eyes shot over to her and she sucked her teeth. "To *my own* lethal dick. I'm talking about *my* husband, *not* yours. I've had my fair share of stalkers and unbalanced hoes because of him."

"I'm just making sure. I've learned I can't leave anything to chance regarding that man. Apparently, he gets around."

"*Got*. Make that past tense or I'ma have to pull up."

"You and me both."

Alisha whipped her head around, squinting like she was searching for something.

"What are you doing?"

"I'm looking for Caid because you know good and damn well the only pulling up you're going to be doing is to that big-ass house of yours. At least until you're no longer carrying that precious cargo, but probably even after. He's not playing with you, not even a little bit."

I shot her a bird and noticed Conner grinning in the rearview mirror, which granted him the same hand motion, and he full-out laughed.

"All of y'all can kiss my ass."

"Nope. Won't be any of that happening on his watch, either." Alisha grinned harder and I couldn't help but laugh. She was right. No sense in me arguing the point.

CHAPTER 21

KINCAID.

"Twenty-two minutes. That's all you have. The second you walk through the door, the timer starts. I'm watching. Twenty-two fucking minutes, Akel. If your ass is not out of there by then, I can't do a damn thing for you."

"I'm paying you and you're threatening me?" I was amused by the exchange, but it was also one of the many reasons I kept him on my payroll.

"You're paying me because I can get the job done. There's a science to this shit. Twenty-two minutes, Akel."

The call ended and I glanced at the building one last time before stepping out of my car and tucking my gun behind my back. I wasn't taking chances. The fact that he was expecting me didn't mean I wasn't at risk. Once a week, this was his routine. The bar was closed, and he would come alone, tempting me to make a move. We were similar in a lot of ways. The same way he had been following my movements, I followed his. Eli had extended the invitation for me to get the answers I was looking for by being here, alone, once a week. It was a risk, but one he was willing to

270

take. One he was sure I would also take at some point. Today was that day.

Once inside, it took a minute for my eyes to adjust. The place was dimly-lit and appeared to be frozen in time. I could sense nothing other than the faces of those who worked there had changed in the decades that passed. It used to belong to his father. A sentimental killer was the worst kind. I chuckled, thinking about how it likely fucked with him that an Akel was in what he considered to be a sacred space, even though it was at his unspoken request. He wanted me here and had waited for the day I took the bait.

Eli sat with his back to the door, but I caught him watching me in the mirror on the wall behind the bar. There was an automatic weapon within reach, but he didn't touch it. He wouldn't, at least not right now. Eli wanted to talk, to tell me all his dirty little secrets, which would prove he had been manipulating things in my life. His ego wouldn't allow him to try to kill me until he was able to get that shit off his chest. Right now, Eli wanted to confess his sins, so I decided to grant him the opportunity, but mostly because I needed answers only he could provide. Taking a seat at the bar, I removed my gun and placed it on the polished wood surface, ensuring it was within reach.

"Took you long enough."

"I don't move on anyone else's time—especially not yours."

He chuckled, rising from the stool that held his weight. I placed my hand on my gun, finger quickly aligning with the trigger. Regardless of what I knew, I didn't trust this muthafucker.

Holding up a glass, which he placed next to the one he had been using, Eli smirked. "It's not time for that just yet, but it's coming. First, we talk. Might as well have a drink while we do. Could be a last for one of us."

I watched as he poured enough liquor to fill the bottom of the glass and sent it my way. There were two stools between us, so moving it down the bar within my reach took a good hard shove.

"You first." I motioned to the glass, and he grinned, filling his and tossing it back. I lifted mine and did the same but didn't fully empty the contents.

I wouldn't put it past this muthafucker to poison me. One can never be too careful.

"You're a clever son of a bitch, Akel. More than I've given you credit for."

He glanced across his shoulder before refilling his glass. I delivered a questionable stare, which had Eli talking again.

"Aren't you supposed to be on a flight to Miami?"

I chuckled. "Is that what Joseph told you?"

I knew the minute Joseph found out I would be out of town, he would run to Eli, who would confirm my plans. It was beneficial for him to keep track of me. The illusion of me being in Miami was never about Eli. It would give Joseph the confidence to believe he could see Nari. Like the lovesick fool I knew him to be, he'd be sitting, waiting, actually thinking she would show.

"*Joseph* is fucking useless."

A desperate man is a stupid one.

"I am curious about his role in this. The alliance doesn't make sense."

"He has no role. When I showed up at the club to do a little research on the girl, he just happened to be the one most eager to share. She really did a number on him." He laughed, shaking his head. "Dumb fuck believed anything I told him as long as I promised he could have her. He's got a soft spot for her but doesn't like you very much. Didn't take much convincing to get him to reach out to her. Turns out she's actually faithful, so there wasn't much he could do for me. He's been trying to get her alone for months, but she didn't bite. Stupid fuck's gonna die for love."

I snorted at the thought. More like a singular obsession.

"By any means necessary, I suppose."

Eli nodded, tossing back the equivalent of another shot, a clear sign he was nervous. Maybe he was more intelligent than I had given him credit for. Or perhaps he sensed this was the end and he just needed the liquid courage to confess his sins.

"Do you believe in karma?" Eli asked, cutting his eyes at me before refilling his glass.

"In some ways, yes, but with the life I live, I've come to realize what most consider karma is really just the consequences of their choices. When the outcome is not favorable, it's typically just bad fucking choices."

Eli snorted. "I wouldn't be so sure about that if I were you. I'm beginning to believe that fucking shit is real."

"How so?"

"You're married to my daughter. If her mother isn't lying, that is. I can't say I trust her all that much. The bitch did steal from me."

My jaws flexed at the reference of Nari being anything other than mine.

"I still don't follow. What does *my* wife have to do with karma?"

"Families are complicated. The secrets are what fucks you every time."

I glanced at my watch.

Six minutes.

"Can we get to the fucking point?"

"All these years, I never knew where she was. Never fucking cared after a certain point, but she is the only one who ever got away. I searched for her too. Came up empty. It's like she fell off the face of the earth, not that it mattered. Endia was one of many, but I'm sure she's already given you her version of our past. Here's mine. I fucked her. Probably shouldn't have, but a woman like that is hard to resist. I'm sure you can relate. Everything about that girl reminds me of her mother." He grinned with a twisted look in his eyes that had my finger twitching. I refused to react because it was what he wanted.

"Endia wasn't a woman. She was a kid that you took advantage of."

"Mentally, maybe, but that body belonged to a grown woman. I just had to teach her what to do with it." He shook his head as if reminiscing. I had to control the urge to shoot the muthafucker. "After a while, I never gave her a second thought and wouldn't have until you married that girl. They look so much alike that it fucked with my head some. Had me realizing she not only got away, but she also stole from me. I did a little digging and did the math. That girl could really be mine. Do you know how disrespectful that is of her to have a kid—*my kid*—without *my* permission?"

"Could be yours or not." He claimed Nari one minute, but in his next breath, he wasn't.

Eli shrugged. "Like I said, I don't trust the bitch, but I can't deny the possibility. I was a little careless in my younger years." His eyes flashed with amusement.

"Then why make Nari believe something you don't even believe yourself?"

"Because it was fun fucking with you."

As I suspected, Eli didn't give a damn about Nari being his daughter.

"You decided to play mind games with my wife just to fuck with me?"

"Initially, yes. I also knew if I made nice with her, she could hand over access to her mother. By the time I located Endia, you already had her under your protection. We could settle things now if you'd make a deal. You let me have Endia and I promise to stay out of your way if you stay out of mine."

You will never get your hands on either of them, but you will be out of my way sooner than you intend.

I laughed arrogantly. "Not happening."

"Can't blame me for trying. Her time's coming, though. Originally, I thought about killing her. Now, I think I might keep her around. She owes me and I'm curious to know if she's still as sweet as she used to be. You know, some things get better with age and time."

My eyes lowered to my wrist.

Eleven minutes.

"That's not why I'm here. Get to the point, or I leave, and you go back to looking over your shoulder, waiting for the day I finally make good on my promise."

"You're an arrogant son of a bitch, Akel. Just like your father. You should have learned from his mistakes, but I'm guessing you don't know the history between my family and yours, do you?"

"No, it was never important. All I needed to know was you and your family weren't shit and always to keep you at arm's length."

He shook his head and poured another drink, immediately tossing it back. "See, that's where you're wrong. The history is everything. It's what got him killed."

My knuckles cracked as I closed my fingers into fists.

"Now, we're getting somewhere."

"Indeed, we are."

The footage Kafi sent over of the day my father and Razi were shot might not have meant anything to them, but it gave me the answers I needed. It was also hand delivered by Eli, regardless of whether they knew it. I had a feeling they were none the wiser of the connection, but many things began to make sense for me. I was simply missing the biggest piece of the puzzle. *Why?*

"I know it was you. What I don't know is why you'd do something so fucking stupid."

Eli turned his eyes toward me. "Like I said, it's the secrets that fuck you every time. Your father had secrets and so did Razi. Unfortunately, you don't know your history."

"Which I suppose you're about to tell me."

Eli grinned. "Some of it. The rest you'll have to get from your mother."

Fourteen minutes.

"My mother? What does she have to do with this?"

His lips curled in a way that had my eyes lowering to the gun, which was inches away.

"Come on, Akel. You're not going to give up that easily, are you?"

"My patience with you is fleeting."

He snorted. "Fine. Let's have a little history lesson. Your father killed my brother."

I hadn't known for sure, but it was an easy assumption.

"Possibly."

"It's the fucking truth. Your father killed my brother, then Razi killed my father a few months later to protect his precious pawn. My father threatened yours, which wasn't a smart thing to do, but he lost a son and that clouded his judgment. None of that mattered to Razi. That son of a bitch was just as heartless as the rest of them." *Them? The Families?* "There were rules my father didn't understand. I was a fucking kid, so I didn't understand them either. I just knew my brother and old man wanted something they could never have. Respect. I lost my brother then my father. My mother wasn't far behind them because she felt she had nothing left. I was still here, but I didn't fucking matter. No one gave a shit about *my* family because of how my father handled business. It's why I worked so hard to prove we deserved respect just as much as the next man. They still didn't give a fuck about me, which means I was gravely underestimated. I had no idea who Razi was meeting that day, but it worked in my favor. The two people I hated most in the world got what they fucking deserved. No matter how great you think you are, no one is untouchable." His eyes shone with pride—the pride from knowing he made the call that killed two very important men.

"You're admitting to killing my father and you don't expect me to react?" My brows pinched as my knuckles cracked once more while the muscles in my jaws twitched.

"I know for certain you'll react. Just not now. You could easily lift that gun and shoot me, but that's too easy. *Kincaid Akel* doesn't do easy. It doesn't make a statement, and quite frankly, there's no fucking fun in this if I don't suffer, right? For months now, you've been second-guessing yourself, possibly even blaming yourself, assuming your father died because of who you chose to marry. *I* did that. I fucked with your head and that shit feels good. It's why you won't end this without returning the favor. The idea of me questioning my every move in anticipation of your next one is what feeds that ego of yours. I know because we're the same. It's why that bitch is still breathing. It keeps my dick hard to know she's constantly looking over her shoulder, waiting for the minute someone slips up and she has to face me again to answer for what she took. Don't think I couldn't have gotten to her by now if it's what I really wanted. You're not God, Akel. None of us are. This is not about you, but the minute your arrogance allowed you to believe it was . . . that was when you gave me control."

Eighteen minutes.

"And the minute you allowed yourself to believe you were smarter than me is when you sealed your fate. You and I are nothing alike, Eli. However, you are right about one thing. Neither of us is God . . ."

I paused, tossing back the last of my drink before lifting my gun. I dropped the clip and removed the one bullet lodged in the chamber before placing it on the bar between us.

"... *tamen fretus, qui quaeris, ego diaboli.*" (However, depending on who you ask, I am the devil.)

Nineteen minutes.

"I don't know what the fuck you just said, but I'm sure it's a threat."

I smirked but didn't respond. It was time for me to leave. With long strides, I crossed the room to exit before my fate was the same as Eli's. I heard his voice one last time before I pushed through the door.

"Send my love to Endia. Tell her I'll be seeing her soon."

Unfortunately, you won't.

I checked my watch one last time as I started my car.

Twenty minutes.

As I pulled into traffic, I heard the explosion, prompting me to watch from my rearview mirror as the building became completely engulfed in flames. There was not a chance in hell that he survived.

My phone rang seconds later. "You were cutting it close, Akel."

"You said twenty-two minutes. I used twenty. I had time."

He delivered a gravelly chuckle. "Barely, but I expected it. As always, it's good doing business with you."

The call ended, and I tossed my phone in the passenger seat, my chest tightening with every passing second. Even though I had finally taken the life of the man who took my father's, there was no relief, and it would never come. Life was funny that way. Killing Eli wouldn't somehow erase what I felt about losing the one man who I loved and respected most in the world. It was only a temporary fix, but one I needed. Even still, I was left with the void of not having my father and there wasn't a damn thing I could do about it.

I sat in my car outside my parents' home, dreading the conversation I was about to have with my mother. I wasn't positive I wanted answers to the questions that plagued me after meeting Eli, but I had to know. Not that it would change anything for either of us. After another fifteen minutes of simply staring at the house, I brushed my hand down my face and decided to get it over with.

As soon as I entered the house, I found my mother waiting. The massive foyer divided the space with two marble staircases on either side. She sat to the right, midway down, her hands clasped in her lap.

"You were out there for a long time. It took everything in me not to come to you, but I determined you needed the space. I assume you're ready to tell me what's weighing so heavily on your mind?"

Her expression was neutral. I wondered if she knew that Eli was dead. My mother had a bad habit of watching the news. Every time my father or I left the house, she worried, so it was how she coped. Over the years, she developed the practice of searching for our names in headlines. It gave her peace each time she came up empty.

"Were you ever involved with Everett Manchester?"

Her face hardened and her eyes narrowed in a matter of seconds. "Absolutely not."

She was offended, which relieved me, but there were still unanswered questions. It was possible Eli could have lied about my mother's involvement with my father killing his brother, but my gut was leading me to believe it was true.

"Even though it was sometimes required, my father wasn't a killer. He and I were very different when it came to certain things. He saw things as either black or white. I lived in the gray areas. Those gray areas were where the tough decisions had to be made. It always weighed heavy on him, but I was okay with those decisions because they were necessary."

"You're not making sense." My mother stood and traveled down the rest of the stairs, stopping a few feet from me. Her face twisted in confusion, but I could also see her holding back.

"My father wasn't a killer by nature, but if pushed, he wouldn't hesitate. There's not much that would push him to that point, but there's one specific guarantee he would take a life without a second thought." My chin dipped so our eyes leveled. "You."

"This is not a conversation I want to have."

"Me either, but it's happening. Everett and my father were friends. That much, I know. The two were extremely close until they weren't. What changed? Why did he kill Everett? And before you lie, I already know the truth."

"Then what does it matter?" She threw her hands up and turned to walk away. I followed my mother into the kitchen, where she began moving around, opening and closing cabinets and slamming drawers in search of a distraction or possibly to release her frustration.

"That's not helping either of us." I spoke calmly and she eventually turned to face me.

"Those pictures, the ones of me . . ."

My mind rushed through multiple scenarios until I landed on the one that had my body tensing.

"He did that to you? Everett?"

She didn't answer verbally, but I had confirmation the minute her eyes found the floor.

"Why the fuck would you keep that from me?" My voice elevated, but I was unable to control the reaction.

"Because we knew what you would do. Your father made me promise never to tell you. You would have—"

"You're damn right I would have!" My body vibrated with anger I could barely control, but I regained some composure. "It needed to be done. If I had, then Eli wouldn't have killed my fucking father. *You* wouldn't have lost your husband." I hadn't realized I was moving until I noticed her flinch below me. She and I were inches apart, her eyes wide, mine tight in thin slits.

"Fuck!" I belted out, shaking my head as I stepped back, attempting to process what I was saying and what she must be thinking. Unfortunately, I couldn't redirect my anger. I had to get out of there . . .

Now.

Inhaling deeply, I slowly released a tortured breath before kissing my mother on the forehead. "I apologize. You're not to blame and neither am I. It's just really hard not to be consumed by either of those feelings, considering what I know and how this could have been avoided. We need to discuss things, but it can't happen while I'm like this. I just . . ." I paused, closing my eyes briefly. "I have to go."

She nodded slowly but didn't say a word. The minute I was in the car, my fist came down repeatedly on the steering wheel until my hand was numb. I had just blamed my mother for playing a role in my father's death and it made me feel like shit on top of the long list of things I was blaming myself for. My fist landed hard several more times in an attempt to temper my anger. I could barely feel my fingers when I started the engine and shifted to drive, but it didn't matter, because at this point, my entire fucking body was numb.

Somehow, the universe always had a way of fucking you. How ironic was it that the one thing playing on repeat in my head was the last conversation I had with Eli. One thing in particular . . . Karma or consequences.

"You good, Caid?" Cast had been watching me from the moment I entered Joseph's apartment. It was a shitty-ass, one-bedroom in a decent part of town with overpriced rent and neighbors who didn't give a damn about anything happening around them. That part actually worked in our favor.

"Yeah. I just have a lot of shit on my mind right now."

"I got this if you need to be somewhere else."

A bit of hope flashed through Joseph's eyes, which had me removing my jacket and rolling up my sleeves.

Not a chance in hell, muthafucker.

"Give us a minute," I stated, my eyes never leaving Joseph's. Cast didn't say a word, but I heard the front door open then close, letting me know he left.

I crossed the room, stopping a few feet away, stance wide, chin angled to my chest before I addressed a very anxious Joseph.

"How did you think this was going to go?"

His expression was hard and defiant. *Cute, Joseph is in his feelings. Well, so the fuck am I and you get to be my release.*

"You'll have to be more specific." His tone was just as harsh as his stare.

I'd indulge.

"Did you really think she would come? That my wife belonged here, in this mediocre apartment, living happily ever after, while you silently celebrate the victory you feel you've accomplished by getting her away from the one person you deem unworthy of owning her heart?"

His laugh was cocky as he stared me up and down in a way that expressed just how little he cared for me.

"What makes you think she doesn't belong here? Nari doesn't give a damn about any of that shit you're throwing at her. She's a good person with a good heart; all she wants is to be loved and respected. Two things you're not capable of delivering."

My chin lowered a bit more. "And you are?"

When he didn't answer, I smirked. "You're so confident in your abilities. Yet, she's not here."

"She would be if she wasn't afraid of what you would do to her."

"Come on, Joseph. You don't really believe that lie, *do you?*"

"I believe you take without giving a choice. She's no different."

"In most cases, you would be correct, and that was possibly the case when I first met Nari. However, she had a choice; still does. She chooses to love me the same as I love her. Contrary to the illusion your mind has crafted, I'm not forcing her to be with me. She could walk away right now and I would let her."

Although she wouldn't get far nor would I allow anyone else to step into the role I currently play in her life.

"That's bullshit."

"It's love. Regardless of my selfishness, I want her to be happy. It's why I know you don't truly care about her."

His eyes went dark and his lip quivered from anger.

"You don't know a damn thing."

"What I know is that if you cared so much, you would have left her alone a long time ago. Nari's choice to be with me doesn't have a damn thing to do with money. When I say she doesn't belong here with you, living like this, it's not because I feel she would ever consider herself above what you're capable of providing or too good for an average life. She doesn't belong here because regardless of what she would accept and be happy with, she deserves more than you could ever provide. Hell, if I'm being honest, she deserves more than *I* could ever provide, but I love her enough to get as close as fucking possible with the understanding that, in her eyes, none of it really matters. You're right. Love and respect are the two things she desires the most and they're what I work my ass off to provide. The other stuff is just a bonus."

Before he could respond, I removed my phone from my pocket.

"Is everything okay?" I asked as soon as I connected the call.

"Yes, where are you?"

"Out."

"Out where, Kincaid? Your mother called. She was upset and worried about you after you left her house. She wouldn't tell me what happened but made me promise to check on you. When did you get back? I thought you would be out of town for the day."

"Change of plans." I lowered my eyes to find Joseph staring. His face was tight, likely knowing it was Nari I was speaking to. "I'm in the middle of something, but I shouldn't be long. Are you sure you're okay?"

"I'm fine. I'm just worried about you."

"I'm good. Just tying up some loose ends. Nothing for you to be concerned about. We'll talk when I get home."

She was silent until I spoke again.

"Nari, sweetheart, I have to go. Is there anything else?"

"No. I'll see you when you get home. I love you."

My eyes lowered to Joseph's again. "I love you too."

Seconds after I ended the call, I put my phone in my pocket and landed my first blow. I didn't stop until I was too exhausted to continue lifting my arms. I gave Joseph one last look and walked out of his apartment. He was still breathing because I made a promise to my wife that I wouldn't take his life. I didn't, however, promise he wouldn't die. So as I exited his apartment, Cast entered and I was on my way home. *Karma or consequences.* I supposed it depended on how you looked at it. Either way, Joseph's bad choices decided his fate and he was no longer an issue I had to waste my time on.

CHAPTER 22

NARI.

There are moments in our lives when things just make sense, and even if they don't make sense, you feel the magnitude of those situations weighing you down so severely that you can't think, breathe, or feel anything except *those things*.

When I ended the call with Kincaid telling me he was fine, I knew he was anything but. Whatever was happening attached to me and I hadn't been able to settle my mind ever since.

For hours, I waited, and he never showed. I called and texted, but each communication remaining unanswered only made matters worse. *Sleep.* That was my next course of action. I decided that if I went to sleep, at the very least, my thoughts would be temporarily suspended, but that didn't work, at least not until hours had passed and I was mentally drained and physically exhausted. Only then was I able to shut off my mind, allowing me to drift, only to bolt from the bed hours later in a pitch-dark room with a panicked feeling surging through my body. My first thought was to feel the space beside me. It was cool, flat, and smooth—no sign of Kincaid. After checking my phone, I could breathe a little easier after reading the two notifications that illuminated my screen. The first alerted me that at 2:16 a.m., the front door had been opened and closed. The second was a notice that the alarm had been activated at 2:17 a.m.

He's home!

I tossed the covers back and climbed out of bed, not bothering to grab anything. I wore one of his T-shirts because I needed to feel close. He'd worn it the day before with his scent still lightly lingering in the expensive, soft cotton.

I found him the first place I checked. The space was dark, but the room was dimly-lit by a slither of light creeping through the bay window, which filled one of the walls. I didn't need to see him to know he wasn't okay. His mood was palpable, covering me the second I crossed through the door. The closer I got, the stronger it felt.

"You want to talk about it?"

I stopped between his legs, my nose twitching from the smell of alcohol.

"No."

"Why not?"

"Because you already hate me." His voice was low and hoarse. He sounded tired, but I knew that wasn't the only reason for the heaviness that radiated from him. "Talking gives you yet another reason to regret your compromises to be mine."

I climbed into his lap, inching as closely as possible to his solid frame. Even in its relaxed, defeated state, it was still incredibly hard compared to mine. His muscles were clenched tightly beneath his clothes and I could feel them flex and relax as my fingers slowly glided up his arms.

"I don't hate you, Kincaid. Please tell me why you're sitting here in the dark instead of coming to bed. I was worried about you."

While we sat silently, I felt the low hum of his breathing. It was even and gentle, but the rhythm created an eerie melody that had my skin prickling. Kincaid seemed calm, but I felt the chaotic energy threatening to escape.

"Tell me," I demanded with a little more force.

"Do you really want to know?" The rumble of his voice vibrated through my chest.

"Ye—"

His hand found the back of my neck, jerking me forward until his lips met mine. His tongue lashed forward, exploring aggressively.

I wanted to talk. He wanted me. I wouldn't dare tell him no, so I conceded and followed his lead. Kincaid brought me in closer and my stomach pressed against his abs while he maneuvered below us. When I realized what he was doing, my knees pressed down hard outside of his thighs, and I lifted slightly, giving him the space he needed.

My panties shifted to the side, and without giving it a second thought, I sank down on him, releasing a guttural moan. Kincaid quickly took over, lifting me until he was at risk of escaping then slamming me down once more, his length filling me as hard as his force. Each entry sent a jolt through my body, which struck like lightning.

His eyes were intense, filled with a mixture of emotions. He seemed angry, but there was something else there that I couldn't quite decipher.

"Let me help," I moaned as he slammed me down once more, meeting me at the point of impact with a thrust of his own.

"You are." A rumble vibrated through his chest following his hoarse voice. He came forward, his mouth landing hard against mine. Kincaid set one hand free, and it tangled in my hair, holding me steady, while his tongue pushed hard against mine, reaching every corner of my mouth. When he backed away, I could barely hold his stare. Looking into his eyes was the equivalent of watching the strongest force I knew unraveling. My heart twisted in pain, taking on whatever had him struggling to keep it all together.

"I'm fucked up . . ." He lost his words, and I wasn't sure why, but I jolted as his hips came up, landing him deep where he hit something in me that had me struggling to keep my eyes fastened to his. Kincaid needed me to be there with him at that moment and I did everything I could to do so.

He took me fast and hard, guiding me up and down in a way that could only be described as desperate and angry, but he maneuvered me with precision, knowing exactly how much pressure to deliver each time he brought me to his base. Over, and over, and over again, we met somewhere in the middle with hard, aggressive thrusts until we both gave in and crashed into each other. Our hands were needy, grasping onto whatever we could reach until I gave out and my spineless body rested against his. I winced when we disconnected. Kincaid lifted me, holding steady until I could manage my own weight.

He adjusted his clothes and stood, stepping around me.

"We need to talk about that."

"No, not right now. Just give me a minute," he muttered, leaving the office and me feeling alone. How could I be so close to someone and so disjointed at the same time?

By the time I reached our room, Kincaid was in the shower. I sat on the edge of the bed, waiting until he finished. We passed each other as he left the bathroom, and I entered, prepared to shower alone. When I climbed into bed, he was waiting, his body in the center of the massive mattress, not giving me the option of space. Apparently, he didn't want any, which he further proved by bringing me into his space. I shifted to find comfort after my back met his chest and his arm draped my waist. I felt his chin rest on my head, then his breathing leveled to a slow, steady pace.

"Tell me what you're thinking," I said after the silence was too suffocating.

He sighed in a way that expressed how heavy his thoughts were. "That my mother's decisions killed my father and my decisions killed yours."

I tensed behind the confession, trying to understand what it meant. Eli was dead. Kincaid was the reason. I wasn't surprised because he'd always told me it was inevitable, and I believed him. Maybe I should have felt something behind the realization of knowing that my father was dead, but I didn't know him, which, in a way, meant he technically wasn't *my* anything. Eli had done horrible things to my mother, so, in a way, it felt justified. You get what you deserve. What I couldn't make sense of was Kincaid saying his mother played a role in his father's death. *How?*

"Your mother? How?"

After a few minutes passed without a response, I tried to turn toward him, but he held me tighter.

"Not now." He inched me closer and a kiss met the top of my head. Silence took over, then I felt his chest vibrating behind me from the light sounds of his snoring. My mind moved in a million and one directions until I eventually drifted. I was too exhausted to fight it, so I didn't.

After hours of sleep, my body felt like it weighed a million tons. It took a minute to shake the groggy feeling, but when I did, I realized I was in bed alone. I grabbed my phone and checked the time.

12:38 p.m.

How had I slept that long and undisturbed?
Because you were fucking exhausted is how.

Memories of the early-morning hours rushed through me like raging waters. Kincaid's dark mood, the way he handled me then dismissed me, only to allow me back in to be his anchor while he slept, left me emotionally raw.

Once I climbed out of bed, it took a minute for the muscles in my body to work together so I could make the short journey to the bathroom. My bladder was screaming because I was well beyond my limits. The extra hours of sleep had my internal timing all off.

I cleaned up after, washing my face, brushing my teeth, then throwing on a pair of cotton shorts under Kincaid's T-shirt. Signs of him being up well before me lingered by way of his clean, spicy scent hanging in the air and the shorts he'd slept in tossed over the side of the hamper in the closet.

He was here somewhere because my phone was void of any notifications showing he was gone. I slowly dragged through the house, and after a quick search, I found Kincaid in his office, staring blankly out the window from the chair behind his desk. The same chair we'd been in hours ago. He was dressed in a navy T-shirt that exposed the fullness of his chest and shoulders, which threatened the quality of the cotton material as it hugged his upper half.

"How long have you been up?"

He turned in my direction, watching my face with hard eyes. "Not long."

"You didn't wake me." I made my way in his direction but hopped on his desk, placing the pads of my feet on the chair beside him. His eyes lowered to my stomach before they lifted to my face.

"You were up late and needed the rest."

"*We* were up late, which means you needed it too."

He grunted, leaning back in a way that disrupted his posture and forced him to slouch more. "I'm fine."

"Are you?" Our eyes locked, initiating a silent standoff. When he refused to speak, I did. "You can't disappear on me, come home all dark and dismissive, fuck me, and refuse to tell me what the problem is. We don't fight dirty, remember?"

"I wasn't fighting with you."

"It felt like it."

He snorted and turned his head away from me, giving his attention to the window again.

"We're not going to talk?"

Nothing.

"Kincaid?" My voice elevated, which brought his eyes back to mine.

"What?"

His defensive tone was clipped, and every second without him speaking, his eyes hardened even more.

"Don't yell at me. I let you release your frustrations last night, and seconds after you came, you pulled out of me and walked out without saying one damn word. You were in a bad place. I get it. But you don't get to stay there. You either talk to me or—"

"Or what, sweetheart? Tell me what my options are?" His voice was even but contained that undeniable edge—his signature style.

"You know what? Fuck it. Don't talk. I really don't give a damn." I hopped down and rounded his desk faster than I meant to, cutting the corner too sharp because my hip caught the edge.

Before I could get too far, Kincaid caught me, bringing me to him while his fingers massaged the spot where his desk assaulted me . . . or rather, I assaulted it.

"I apologize." He nuzzled his face in the space between my neck and collarbone. "You're not the one I'm angry with."

"Then tell me who."

He laughed arrogantly, falling back into his chair. Large hands brushed down his face a few times before I had his attention again.

"Myself, my mother, shit, my fucking father."

My mother's decisions killed my father and my decisions killed yours.

His words from last night came back to me.

"Angry, why?"

I leaned against his desk so we were close but not touching, sensing he needed the space.

"She told me some things she and my father kept from me. Had I known . . ." He paused, so I encouraged him to keep going.

"Had you known, then what?" I frowned, trying to make sense of what he was saying.

"Had I known then, my father wouldn't have fucking died because I would have killed Eli before he had a chance to kill my father."

"How do you know that it was Eli?"

"Because he told me, right after he tossed out that I should ask my mother why."

"She told you what happened?"

"The hell you mean *what happened?*" he rattled off so quickly I was sure he didn't have time to register what I was saying. The minute it clicked, I saw it in his eyes. "You knew?"

"She told me because she wanted me to know what type of man Eli had the potential to be."

"And you didn't tell me?"

"It wasn't my story to tell. She didn't want you to—"

"To what? To kill him? That's what I fucking do. It's how I keep order. That's who the fuck I am, Nari. My mother knows that. She fell in love with the man who promised this was who I would become. It was his life, not hers. She doesn't get to pick and choose how things play out."

"Maybe that's the problem. She didn't want any of this for you. At least not in a way that placed the burden on her shoulders. You may not understand what that means, but I do. You don't get to be angry with her because she didn't want that on her heart." I threw my hands up and his eyes narrowed as they locked with mine.

"You understand her because you two are so much alike, right? Living the same life?" His tone was even again but still clipped.

When I didn't respond, he laughed in a cocky manner. "And that right there is why I said you would hate me. You wanna know what I did last night before I came home to you?"

His eyes never left mine, but he stood, towering over me. "I paid a guy to clip a gas line in your father's bar. Then I walked inside and shared a drink while I listened to him tell me how he didn't give a fuck about you, but he would be willing to make a deal with me if I would hand over your mother. He then proceeded to tell me how he killed my father, but it wasn't even planned. But because of the history my mother had with his brother that apparently got him killed, it was a win-win situation for good old Eli. He tossed back a drink and stuck his chest out, smiling with pride, gloating, and it took everything in me not to put a bullet in his fucking head, but I didn't. I left, and two minutes after I walked out the door, the entire building exploded just as I had planned. I drove off, not giving it a second thought because he didn't fucking matter. What *did* matter was the reason I killed Eli. It didn't have a damn thing to do with my father. I did it for you, sweetheart."

"He deserved it," I said and swallowed the rising heavy feeling.

Kincaid smiled in a sinister manner, his eyes darkening by the second.

"Oh, but see, I'm not done yet. I also paid a visit to your friend Joseph."

My eyes narrowed some and his smile expanded. "Yeah, he was next on my list. We had an interesting conversation about how I didn't deserve you, but he did. That was fun, and when he finished telling me what a piece of shit I was and how he was a better man for you, I beat him until I could no longer lift my arms to deliver another blow, then I left."

"You . . . You promised." I felt sick to my stomach. Kincaid had killed before. He'd taken the lives of people I knew about but never anyone I had a connection with. Even if I didn't have feelings for Joey, he was still a good guy and I was now responsible for him getting killed.

His stance shifted. "And I kept my promise. Joseph was alive when I left him. Barely, but he was still breathing."

"He's alive?"

"No. I promised that *I* wouldn't kill him and I didn't."

But someone else did.

"So, now, you see my dilemma? You, my mother, and no-fucking-body else gets to pick and choose. *I* make the call if it creates a problem for me or anyone I love. She took that choice away and my father died. She might not have wanted the burden, but it was one she couldn't avoid, and neither can you."

He lowered his face to mine, hooking my chin at the same time, seconds before pillow-soft lips landed, delivering a gentle kiss. "I'm not perfect, and I never will be, but I made you a promise and nothing and no one can consider themselves void of being expendable in order for me to keep it. You, sweetheart, will always be untouched. Even if it means you end up hating me."

I had no idea how long I stood there alone before I realized he was gone, but what I did know was this was the man I chose and the life that came along with it. The decision had been made months ago, and just like Kincaid, I was also bound by my promises.

I stared blankly at the open space as I sat on the floor in my son's room. A week had passed since that night when everything fell apart and things between Kincaid and me were strained. We were both going through the motions, but neither wanted to take the first step to mend what was broken between us. He had been distant with me and his mother as well. She and I talked, and I assured her that he was fine. I also told the lie that promised Corinne her son wasn't blaming her for the death of her husband and his father, when I knew for certain he was. She already harbored enough guilt and I refused to add to it.

We did, however, have a heart-to-heart about everything that led up to the point of contention between the three of us. Kincaid was angry with his mother and I was angry with him. Neither of us owned the right to place blame on the next, but it was what we were all doing, and I was ready to put an end to it. I missed my husband, but because I physically had him near, more than anything, I missed the happy space we'd created. I needed us to find our way back to each other, but my pride wouldn't allow me to be the one to take the first step in that direction.

Frustrated, I lay back, uncrossing my legs, planting my bare feet on the hardwood floors while folding my arms, covering my face, and releasing a labored sigh.

"I'm pretty sure I owe you a few years as a listening ear."

I grinned at the sound of my mother's voice, peeking through my arms to find her standing in the doorway.

"You don't *owe* me anything."

"That depends on who you ask. You want to talk about it?"

I groaned, covering my face again. "No."

"You sure?"

"No."

She laughed, sitting opposite where I was, so her head aligned with mine when she lay on her back, but her legs were extended in the opposite direction and crossed at the ankles. My mother turned her face toward mine.

"Since you're not ready to talk, I will."

"Is something wrong?"

I frowned, turning in her direction, catching her eyes first, then her smile.

"No, things are really good, great, actually."

"Then what did you want to talk about?"

"I'm going to head home for a while."

"Home?"

"Yes, home, sweetheart. I still have one of those, you know." She grinned, which had my expression tight.

"You're going to Miami? Why?"

"Because I've been away for a while and need to get back to decide what's next."

"What does that mean?"

"It means I have to get back to my life."

I sat up quickly, rubbing my stomach after feeling a pull from the sudden movement.

"This is your life. Being here with us. The baby will be here soon. I thought you wanted to be there when he comes."

She also sat up, turning to face me, allowing her weight to rest on her hands, which were pressed to the floor slightly behind her back.

"I do and I will. I'm not leaving you, Nari. You couldn't get rid of me if you tried, but I don't want to get too comfortable with all this. This is *your* life, and you and Kincaid need time to settle into things. You just got married, and now, you're preparing for my grandson. That should be your focus, not me."

"You said you're not leaving me, but that's exactly how it sounds."

"But I'm not. I'm going home to pack up my place. I'll only be there for a few weeks, then I'll be back."

"Pack up your place?"

"I talked to Kincaid about finding an apartment here and he agreed it would be a good idea."

"You don't have to leave. If he made you feel like you have to—"

"Nari, sweetheart, no. He insisted that my invitation to stay in your home was open indefinitely. I decided to find my own place. He offered a few suggestions, which I think are a good idea. Some townhouses are not far from here and they're pretty nice. He's offered to purchase one, which I declined, but—"

"Kincaid does what he wants. Good luck with that." I rolled my eyes and she laughed.

"His argument was that it makes things easier for when the baby spends time with me and he refused to take no for an answer. But the point is, I'll be close, and I think it's best that we all have our own space."

"When are you leaving?"

"Tonight. Abisai is flying down with me to help get everything situated."

"Are you sure it's not about *you* having *your* own space?" I narrowed my eyes and she laughed.

She stood, brushing her palms over her jeans, extending a hand to help pull me to my feet. "That's not a conversation we're going to have. Just know I'm here when you need me and I'm not going anywhere."

"But it feels like you are." I exhaled a short sigh then hugged her. "But I'm happy that you're happy."

"Thank you, sweetheart." She tightened her arms around me and kissed my cheek. "I'm going to finish packing."

I watched her walk to the door, but she stopped beneath the frame. "Be easy on him, Nari. He's carrying the world's weight on his shoulders and he's not the type of man who knows how to be vulnerable."

"He talked to you?"

"No, but he didn't have to. He only told me I didn't have to worry about Eli anymore. I didn't ask any questions and he didn't give me any more than that. Corinne filled in some of the missing pieces."

"Oh," was all I gave.

"You guys will be fine as soon as you stop being stubborn and let each other back in."

I laughed sarcastically, rolling my eyes once more. "Got any advice on how I can make him do that?"

She grinned. "No advice you want to hear because I have a feeling that your will is just as strong as his."

My mother left and my eyes traveled around the open space transitioning into our son's room. All the furniture had been moved out and a painter was scheduled to arrive the following week. We'd decided on gray and navy. I wanted something softer, considering it was for a baby, but Kincaid insisted that the colors would be fine and the space would be suited with all the finishings to accommodate an infant. That was his soft no. I decided not to push because it was the first time he'd shown any interest in our son's room besides telling me there was no budget to complete the space.

"Your daddy is a very pushy man. I pray that trait skips you because I'm not sure I can handle two of you under one roof, bossing me around."

I smiled, moving my hands across my stomach, thinking about my appointment the following afternoon. It was a routine checkup, but it was one I was sure Kincaid wouldn't dare miss. That meant actually spending time other than how we'd been operating over the past week. We existed under the same roof and slept in the same bed each night, but we barely spoke more than ten words to each other. It was time for another truce, even if that meant I would be the one waving my white flag first.

CHAPTER 23

KINCAID.

I had been awake for hours, but instead of my usual routine of creeping out of bed before Nari, I remained on my back, arms folded behind my head, eyes closed, thinking about the past few months. When I reached the events of the past week, I felt my chest tightening as it had been since the night my entire world seemed to shift. That one moment when everything that made sense no longer registered with familiarity. That shift for me was realizing I was only one man who couldn't control everything.

Careful movement next to me had my head turning toward Nari. Her back was to me, so she hadn't noticed I was watching. Once she crept out of bed, entering the bathroom where she made a point of softly closing the door behind her, I threw the covers back on my side. After lowering my legs over the edge, I extended my arms above me, allowing my body a good full stretch. I sat contemplating for another ten minutes before I finally said fuck it and made my way to the bathroom. By then, Nari was out of her clothes and stepping into the shower. She eyed me carefully but didn't say a word.

I leaned over the sink, watching her through the mirror as I brushed my teeth. By the time I finished, she had her head completely submerged under the spray of the overhead waterfall, so when I stepped inside, she damn near jumped out of her skin when I stepped up behind her.

"Shit, you scared me."

"Has it been that long that you don't recognize my touch?" My fingers glided across her skin briefly before I forced her back against me.

"No, I just wasn't expecting you to be here."

"Should I have asked permission?"

"Kincaid, what are you doing?"

"Hopefully, apologizing to my wife so maybe she'll allow me the opportunity to get reacquainted with her body again."

"Cute."

I smirked, kissed her shoulder, and allowed my hands to glide up her stomach until I cupped both her breasts.

"Cute? That's not exactly the response I was aiming for, but I suppose it's better than you asking me to leave."

"This is your house too. I can't necessarily tell you where you can be in it, now can I?"

"You have every right to demand whatever you want. However, that doesn't mean that I will comply."

My tongue moved down her neck while my fingers pinched and twisted her nipples. Nari released a soft moan, settling against me in a way that let me know she wasn't going to object to my request to get reacquainted with her body, not that I was giving her the option to in the first place.

"What happened to my apology?" she asked while I planted a trail of kisses down her neck and shoulder.

"What apology?" I was already sidetracked. It had only been a week since I had been intimate with my wife, but that week felt like a lifetime.

"You said that you were, *hopefully*, apologizing to your wife so we could get reacquainted. It seems like you skipped that part."

I chuckled and kissed her neck again, allowing one of my hands to slip between her legs.

"I apologize." My lips brushed across her ear. "Now, can we move on?"

"No, that was too generic. What do you apologize for?" Her tone was light and teasing, so I decided to play along.

"I don't know, sweetheart. What do you feel like I've done?"

"Well, for starters, you've been ignoring me all week and keeping things from me."

I froze in place. "What have I been keeping from you?"

"Things." She turned to face me, moving damp curls out of her face before her palms glided down my chest and her fingers wrapped around me.

I chuckled, lowering my face to hers. "Then that means you owe *me* an apology as well. I'm not the only one who's been keeping *things*." My savage need for Nari hit me hard at the thought of being inside of her. "Turn around."

She looked up, and I looked down, my eyes communicating that she needed to do as I asked. When her back was to me, I lifted a hand, allowing my fingers to graze the line of her spine before I pulled her hips back so she was firm against me.

"My apology, Nari. You haven't given it yet." Greedy hands moved down her hips, over her upper thighs, then between her legs. My fingers cuffed her center, rubbing coarsely before I allowed one to push through her slick folds. It entered with ease, but it wasn't from the moisture of the water, which drenched us both. This was all Nari, her arousal, letting me know she was ready.

"I apologize for keeping things from you." Her voice was low and hoarse.

"Can you handle me, in here like this?" She still hadn't gained much weight, but her stomach could potentially create discomfort, and I planned on fucking my wife. It had been an entire week without her, so I needed to be sure she could take it.

"Yes."

"You sure?"

"Yes, Kincaid. Stop talking," she demanded, bringing a pleased grin to my lips.

My sweet Nari is in need.

I turned us, slightly lifting her leg so her foot rested on the corner seat behind us. After I guided myself in, my eyes closed tightly and I sucked in a breath.

"Fuck, Nari, I missed you."

"I missed you too."

I had planned to take things slow and easy, but our recent lack of intimacy made that an impossible task. My pace was relentless, rendering us both helpless to that first release, which she didn't seem to mind because her body worked with mine to encourage the outcome. The second came at a slower pace, and I was able to take my time, feeling even the slightest movement until our breaths became jagged, and the explosion forced me into temporary paralysis. When I recovered, I held Nari against my chest, kissing her face, neck, and shoulders. Any exposed skin I could reach fell victim to the attack.

"We're not doing that again. From now on, no matter the issue, we work that shit out. If you're mad, you tell me, and we talk about it. If I'm mad, I tell you, and the same applies. No more weeks pass without like the one we just had. Promise me."

"I promise." Nari turned, pressing her forehead into my chest. "Me too."

I kissed her gently on the forehead to seal that promise I planned on keeping, even if it meant taking the blame just so she didn't torture me with this type of distance ever again.

"Everything looks good. The baby is strong and healthy, but I am a little concerned that you've lost a few pounds since your last visit. Have there been any changes I should be aware of?"

I was standing beside the exam table and Nari's eyes shot up at me. I reached for her hand, kissing her fingers before addressing Dr. Chandler.

"We've had a rough few weeks that have made things uncharacteristically stressful for both of us. There shouldn't be any more issues moving forward, so her weight should level out. It will be my priority to make sure we're both on top of it."

Dr. Chandler nodded, offering Nari a smile. "Perfect. Then it looks like everything is in order. Do either of you have any questions about our little guy in there?"

"No, I don't." Again, Nari's eyes lifted, connecting with mine, and I shook my head while speaking.

"I think we're good."

"Great. It's a pleasure, as always. Don't forget to stop by the front desk to schedule your next appointment, and if you need me, you have all my numbers."

"We do. Thank you, Dr. Chandler. Please tell your husband I said hello."

"I will."

After leaving the office, I suggested we grab something to eat. Nari assumed it was because of Dr. Chandler's observation, but truthfully, I just wanted to spend time with my wife. We dined at one of her favorite cafes and got cozy in a corner booth, where we sat in a peaceful silence Nari eventually broke.

"So, word on the street is that you just purchased some property." Nari bit into her burger, peering over it while she chewed.

"Property?"

"Yep, a town house, I think. From what I hear, it's pretty nice."

I chuckled and nodded, lifting my own burger. "Your mother told you?"

"She did, right before she told me she was leaving for a few weeks with Abisai to pack up her place." Nari lifted her brow, as if goading me.

"Should I have discussed that with you first? I assumed your mother moving here permanently would be a good thing."

"It is, but it would have been nice if I were a part of the conversation."

"You weren't speaking to me."

"No, *you* weren't speaking to *me*."

"*We* weren't speaking to each other," I tried, meeting in the middle. Neither of us was prepared to take the blame for the past week.

"I didn't do anything wrong," she asserted, her eyes pinned to mine in a challenging manner.

"Did I?"

I was sure she had some type of feelings about what happened to Joseph, but I didn't give a fuck about those feelings *or him*.

"No."

"Are you sure?" This time, I was the one issuing a challenge.

"I don't want to fight."

"And we won't. I'm only asking for clarity so there are no misunderstandings about where we are."

"There aren't any." She held my stare as if attempting to assure me she wasn't holding on to any grievances.

"Do you want to discuss anything that hasn't been addressed?"

"No."

"Nothing at all?"

"No, Kincaid." She expelled an exasperated sigh. "I can't expect you to be anything other than you are. It's not like I woke up one day and everything about you changed. You made your point. I have to accept your way of loving me, protecting me, and keeping me—"

"Untouched."

"I was going to say *safe*, but yes. I'm not angry with you, Kincaid. I get it. Your mother also gets it, but that doesn't mean it's not something we won't struggle with."

I nodded as acknowledgment, not wanting us to end up traveling down that road again. After another few minutes of silence, Nari spoke.

"Have you talked to her?"

"Yes."

"And?"

I grinned, lifting my drink, keeping my eyes fastened to hers. "And what?"

"Did you apologize to your mother too?"

"Did I need to?" I lifted my brow and her pretty face twisted into a frown.

"Seriously?"

I chuckled. "Yes, I apologized because I was wrong for projecting my anger for something I couldn't control onto her. It wasn't my mother's fault, nor my father's, but the secrets they kept to protect me potentially prevented me from protecting them. It fucking hurts to know I could have done something had I had all the pieces."

"And as much as it hurts, there's no guarantee he would still be here if you had. I'm sure she's plagued with the same thoughts you struggle with. It's unfair to make her the focus of your misplaced feelings."

I stared at Nari, grinning, and she frowned again. "What?"

"Are you speaking from experience or just offering your unbiased opinion?"

"Both," she shrugged.

"I love you."

"I love you too." Her eyes met mine.

"And I apologize for making you the focus of my misplaced feelings. I also apologize for shutting you out when I promised never to do that again. You'll have to grade on a curve where I'm concerned. I've just recently realized I don't have all the answers, and because of that, I may not always make the right decisions. But regardless, my intent is never to do you any harm."

"Holy shit, the world must be coming to an end." A smile split onto her face.

"And what brings you to that conclusion?"

"Because my very confident and all-knowing husband just admitted he has flaws. That is dangerously close to you admitting . . ." She paused, peeking to the left and right before tenting her mouth with her hand, whispering, ". . . that you were wrong."

I threw my head back and laughed.

"I can admit when I'm wrong. Shit, I feel like with you, I'm making that confession daily."

"Could have fooled me because Kincaid Akel is *never* wrong." She flashed that beautiful smile of hers and I chuckled.

"But seriously, are you okay with us funding a place for your mother? She wants to be close, and that's a huge financial burden I don't feel she should have to take on when we're perfectly capable of handling it for her."

"As long as it's not because you don't want her at our house."

I could see how she might consider that a possibility, but I was quite fond of Endia and enjoyed having her around. She had been a great resource when it came to Nari, and beyond that, I simply enjoyed her company.

"I extended the offer for your mother to stay as long as she wanted, but she insisted that we needed space even though I assured her our home was spacious enough to accommodate us all, with the necessary privacy she somehow felt she was intruding on."

Nari grinned. "I know. I was just giving you shit, and no, I don't mind. I appreciate the gesture because you didn't have to do it."

"My commitment to you extends beyond just yourself. It's a commitment to everyone in your life playing a role in assuring your happiness and well-being."

She rolled her eyes. "Always so poised."

I chuckled and nodded. "When necessary. The property your mother decided on is a three bedroom. I figured it would make sense to have a room for the baby and one for you."

"Me?"

"You don't plan on spending time at your mother's house?" I stared and she seemed amused.

"So, you're okay with me staying the night with her?"

"Of course. We can spend as much time there as you like."

"We?"

I smirked and nodded. "We sleep in the same bed every night. Was that not one of our terms?"

"I thought the contract no longer applied."

"It doesn't, unless necessary and it works in my favor."

"How is that fair?" She arched her brow and I shrugged.

"I never said it was fair, only necessary."

Nari tossed a fry at me, and I chuckled, lifting my burger. It felt good just to *be*. The past couple of months had been so incredibly taxing on both of us that I welcomed any opportunity where we could exist without looking over our shoulders or being at war with each other. I prayed that things would remain this way, at least for a while.

CHAPTER 24

NARI.

Corinne peeked into the suite next to the one we had just left. They were all identical other than the two offices that had been converted into larger suites to accommodate the live-in resident advisors. I had already hired one and was deciding between three potentials to take the second spot. It would be necessary to have staff and security on-site twenty-four hours a day. I wanted to ensure a healthy, safe environment for the residents. Since we began promoting our services, we had hundreds of inquiries, but we weren't scheduled to open for another month. It took several months to renovate the location, and now, I was waiting for a green light from the city to open our doors. With the number of inquiries, I was already scouting our next location because what I offered proved to be a much-needed resource.

"This is coming along nicely."

"Thank you. We're pretty much done. Just waiting on the city."

She turned, offering a smug grin. "You mean to tell me that son of mine hasn't pulled any strings to get this expedited?"

"No, because I made him promise not to. I don't want anyone to think I'm not truly invested in doing the work, nor do I want them to assume this is not something I take seriously. I don't want anyone to see the name and assume we aren't here to make a difference."

Corinne's smile spread wider. "If they see what I see, then there's no way anyone can mistake your passion for anything other than what it is. A genuine heart wanting to give back."

She looped her arm through mine. "I'm very proud of you, sweetheart."

"Thank you." I rested my head on her shoulder. "I'm looking forward to working with you."

"As am I with you."

She separated and traveled a little farther down the hall, peeking into another one of the suites.

"So, how are things?"

"I can't complain." I offered a soft smile just as my little guy decided he wanted to get active. "Well, other than being ready to meet our newest addition, that is."

"We're only weeks away. I'm surprised you survived this long. Kincaid was a month early. He made a grand entrance too, which pitted the two of us at war. I thought I was going to have a nice Sunday brunch, but my son decided I would spend the afternoon in the hospital."

"Who won?"

"He did, of course. As much as we pretend we're running things, our children hold all the cards. You'll soon learn that you're simply here to serve them."

"Not if I can help it. This little guy better not have any grand ideas about running things."

My hands moved across my stomach at the same time he decided to initiate a round of somersaults or karate kicks or whatever the hell he was doing in there to disrupt my day.

"That baby boy is an Akel. You might as well give up all those fantasies of having control."

"You're really not giving me hope."

She laughed lightly, placing her hand over my stomach. "I'm simply making sure you know what you're up against."

"*Wonderful*," I mumbled.

Corinne smiled brightly. "I need to get going. I'm meeting your mother when I leave here."

"So I heard." I rolled my eyes and she looped her arm through mine again while we traveled down the hall toward the elevator.

"You're more than welcome to join us if you'd like."

"Nope. I refuse to be a third wheel. Have fun. She's coming by tomorrow to help me organize the baby's room. If your son doesn't stop buying things for him, we will have to add on to the house just to have storage space."

"This is his firstborn and his legacy. Be thankful it's not a girl, or I can assure you, things would be much worse."

"Imagine that," I groaned, and she laughed as we stepped off the elevator into the lobby.

After we exited the building, I looked up, and she kissed my cheek, promising to see me soon. Conner was waiting, helping me into the back of the SUV I was being chauffeured around in for the day before returning to the driver's seat.

"Where to, ma'am?"

"Home." I was exhausted, but my stomach was also craving something sweet.

"Oh, wait, but can we stop by—"

"Sweets-n-Stuff?"

"Don't act like you know me, Conner." I narrowed my eyes and he offered me a smug grin through the rearview mirror.

"I wouldn't dare. Mr. Akel suggested you might want to stop by there before heading home."

"I'm sure he did."

"Just following orders, ma'am."

I shot him a narrowed stare before dialing Kincaid.

"You heading home?"

"Yes, but apparently, I've been scheduled to stop by Sweets-n-Stuff."

He laughed. "It was simply a suggestion. You don't have to go."

"Oh no, buddy. I'm going, but be clear: I know the suggestion has nothing to do with me and *everything* to do with your new obsession with their red velvet cupcakes."

Kincaid laughed and I could imagine his beautiful smile as he spoke.

"I don't recall requesting anything."

"Fine. I won't bother bringing you one then."

"But you may as well, since you're going."

"Mm-hmm. That's what I thought."

"How did the walk-through go with my mother?"

"Good. She was impressed."

"As she should be. You've done an exceptional job of bringing things together. I'm extremely proud of you."

"*I'm* proud of myself."

He chuckled. "I have a few calls to make. I'll see you when you get here."

"You're home?"

"Yes, waiting on you. So hurry."

After ending the call, I felt a sense of peace while turning toward the window. If anyone had told me this would be my life, I would have laughed in their face. I was married, weeks away from delivering our first child. My mother lived a few miles away from me and we talked daily. I had a family—one who would give their last for me, same as I would do for them.

Exhaling a short sigh, I unlocked my phone and scrolled through my social media timeline. Oddly enough, the first picture that appeared was one of Shayla. She looked a lot better than she had in previous months. Oddly enough, she seemed happy. There was a time when I would have rolled my eyes at the thought of her, but the more time that passed, I actually felt sorry for my cousin. She was pregnant with twins, and from the posts she'd been making, the father wasn't claiming her or the babies. It was as if history was repeating itself in their family because Shayla shared with me that her own father refused to be a part of her life.

From a distance, I wished her well as long as she understood that offering any parts of her body to my husband anymore would not be in her best interest. I asked him several times if she'd contacted him again and he assured me she hadn't. Kincaid wasn't the type to lie. I knew it was because his arrogance wouldn't allow him to. He was a *This is what it is. Take or leave it* type of guy, which was obnoxiously sexy and annoying.

I double tapped the picture and continued to swipe. After a few more photos passed, I saw one of Alisha and Darius. Her makeup was flawless as he held her from behind with his lips pressed to her cheek. They informed us over dinner last week that they'd started the process of adoption because Alisha still hadn't had any luck with carrying a baby. She'd lost two already and he refused to allow her to continue to suffer through that devastation. Kincaid pulled some strings to get them in touch with a private agency that specialized in placing infants and I was praying they would have a little one of their own soon.

"Would you like me to go in for you, Mrs. Akel?"

My eyes bounced up to meet Conner's. We had arrived at our destination and I could already taste the delicious cream cheese icing on the tip of my tongue. I had no idea what they put in their cupcakes and I was afraid to ask. With the addiction that both Kincaid and I had, I was sure it was some type of illegal substance.

"Yes, please, if you don't mind." I pushed out a short sigh. I had been up since seven and it was well after five. This baby boy of mine seemed to drain every ounce of energy I had. Once I rattled off the order for the half-dozen cupcakes I wanted, Conner was out the door, but I caught him, delivering one last request.

"Oh, and will you please bring me a sample of whatever they have out and—"

"Two jumbo red velvets for Mr. Akel. Got it." He winked, shutting the door. I grinned, knowing Kincaid and I both had become a little too predictable. The good thing was our lives had settled into what could be considered a normal routine and I damn sure wouldn't complain about that. There was a time when I didn't know if I was coming or going and the stress of the unknown had me constantly on edge. Lately, I felt as if I could actually breathe and that feeling was priceless . . . one I'd never known I'd needed until it existed.

CHAPTER 25

KINCAID.

Our security system notified me that the front door was open, meaning Nari was home. Lately, I'd been the one who made it in first and found myself waiting on her because her days seemed to run longer than mine. With the birth of our son only weeks away, I suspended travel and managed most of my business dealings via phone and email. I refused not to be here just in case something happened. Regardless of the support system we had in place, which consisted of my mother and hers, along with Darius and Alisha, I would never forgive myself if I were away and something happened to Nari or our son, or if I simply missed the birth due to business travel.

She assured me she would understand if I needed to be away, but I could also sense she was relieved when I promised to be home for the next few months. I would have to settle back into my routine eventually, but by then, Nari and our son could travel with me when permitted. But I also had to consider she now had a huge responsibility of her own with her foundation.

"I smell you all over the house." She grinned, invading my personal space, making no apologies for the intrusion.

"I've been here for a little while." I kissed the top of her head before addressing Conner, who followed Nari into the kitchen. He placed two boxes from Sweets-n-Stuff on the counter.

"Will you be needing me for the rest of the evening?"

"No, I've got it from here," I said, offering him a nod, and Conner returned one.

"I'll call you if I need you tomorrow. I was thinking about staying in." Nari lifted her head from my chest, mumbling through thoughts of her plans for the next day.

"Have a good evening, Conner."

"You too, ma'am."

Soon after his final words, he was gone, and I gave my full attention to Nari.

"Long day?"

She pouted slightly. "Very. I want to change, curl up on the sofa, and do absolutely nothing."

"Or you can change, curl up on the sofa, and do absolutely nothing while I help you relieve some stress."

"That's an offer I can't refuse, but I'm sure you already knew that."

"I was hoping." I lifted her chin and delivered a kiss. "Go change and I'll meet you down here."

"You're not going to change?"

I was out of my suit jacket before the commute home but was still in my shirt and slacks. I also removed my tie and undid the top two buttons of my shirt.

"No, I'm fine for now. My focus will be on you."

"What if I decide I want *my* focus to be on *you*?" She arched her brow, pairing it with a smug grin while her hands began to roam, one landing just below my waist. I chuckled and kissed her once more.

"Then I'm sure my clothes won't matter, considering you're insinuating that you'd prefer me to be without them."

"Good, at least we're on the same page. What about dinner?"

"I assume you don't feel up to cooking, so I will order something. What would you like?"

"Pizza, extra cheese, and breadsticks."

She grinned, stepping away from me while I slipped my hand into my pocket to call in the order. Nari was on her way, but paused, peeking back over her shoulder.

"Get two large. I'm kinda hungry."

"When are you *not* kinda hungry?"

"Pregnancy shaming is a whole thing, you know? You better be careful with that, buddy."

I chuckled, watching as she stuck her tongue out and exited the kitchen. By the time I placed our order, Nari returned wearing one of my T-shirts. Her belly stretched the material, causing it to stop midthigh. My dick inflated from the visual as I watched her cross the kitchen to remove a bottle of water from the refrigerator.

"You want one?"

When she turned to face me, my eyes remained focused, traveling the length of her body until they made it to her beautiful face again.

"What?"

"Nothing."

"You're looking at me strangely."

"What's strange about admiring my wife's beauty?"

She blushed, rolling her eyes. "You already sealed the deal, Kincaid. Let's not overdo it." She lifted her left hand, wiggling her fingers.

I chuckled, raking my teeth over my bottom lip. "That's an impossible request with you looking like that."

Her eyes lowered to the swell increasing in my pants. "Apparently. How about we do something about *that*?" Nari pointed with her forehead before leaving the kitchen. My eyes remained trained on her body until she was no longer in sight. When I joined her in the living room, her back was propped up on one arm of the sofa while her feet were planted flat, knees pointed toward the ceiling. They gently fell outward as soon as she saw me.

I tilted my head to the side, taking in the view. "You're not wearing anything under that?"

"Did you want me to?"

I shook my head softly before nearing my wife. One finger traced the line from her ankle along the inside of her thigh, stopping just before I reached my intended destination. I enjoyed watching how her body tensed and shivered while her eyes remained fastened to mine.

After a brief pause, I allowed the pads of my fingers to graze her lips, which were already glistening from her arousal. At the same time, her back arched away from the sofa and Nari's eyes slammed shut. There was a brief moment where she trembled, and her lips parted, exhaling a labored breath as her eyes slowly peeled open, remaining low with the anticipation of what was next.

I delivered kisses along the same line my finger traveled, hovering above her center, knowing it was driving her crazy that I hadn't touched her there again. Her body shuddered while she released my name.

"Yes, sweetheart?"

"Stop playing."

I grinned, lifting my eyes to hers again. "You have to employ patience."

"Kincaid!" Her voice was low but firm.

I chuckled, landing the first kiss. This never got old. I swear I was addicted to everything about her. My tongue caressed her folds, barely grazing her sensitive skin. Her thighs moved in toward me, but I pushed them wide again before my tongue swiped her with a little more pressure. It was a warning that I was about to do exactly as promised and help Nari relieve some stress. By the time I finished, her back arched while she pushed through her second climax. I continued the busy work of using both my lips and tongue to torment Nari even more, forcing an even greater release, not stopping until her body was loose and exhausted.

"You're dangerous."

"So are you."

While she recovered, I undressed. Then my head pressed against her opening, but I didn't enter her right away. Instead, I teased her with the tip and delivered tender kisses along her spine, which trembled with each one.

Nari pushed back against me, trying to force my entry, but I didn't budge, which had a heated stare reaching me from over her shoulder. I chuckled, shifting my hips, purposely rubbing her sensitive skin once more before thrusting inside. She gasped as I felt her stretching around me, and I groaned from the depths I reached. Nari pushed back against me with each thrust, a little too eager, which let me know this round would be quick. If there were such a thing as heaven on earth, this damn sure had to be it.

A few hours later, we were both showered and changed. I dressed in shorts while Nari was back in my T-shirt. However, this time, she was wearing boy-cut lace briefs, which was a good move, considering she was straddling my waist while I stretched out on the sofa. Nari was enjoying a second round of pizza like she hadn't just finished off half of one not even an hour ago, followed by two cupcakes. My sweet Nari was enjoying the freedom of indulging and blaming our son.

"Cast invited us to dinner at his place this weekend."

"Really? Why?" She frowned, enjoying another massive bite and chewing slowly while she waited for my answer.

"He would like for us to meet a *friend*."

"A *friend*?" Nari delivered a quizzical stare.

"Yes, a female friend I'm pretty sure he's been dating consistently for the past few months, but refuses to admit she's more than a *friend*."

"Now, I'm positive the world is about to end. I was pretty sure Cast would die by the decree of *hoe is life*."

I chuckled at the thought. "I would have to agree, but it appears someone has finally changed his mind. She's older and not the type to settle for his typical behavior."

"You've met her?"

"No, but I've been around when he's talked to her on the phone."

"How much older?"

"Not sure, why?"

"Because he seems like the type to get caught up with a cougar. I'm telling you, he was crushing on my mother. You sure *she's* not this new friend?"

I laughed hard at the idea. "No, sweetheart. Your mother is practically joined at the hip with Abisai and Cast has always been respectful where she's concerned. It's most definitely not your mother and I'm sure she would have mentioned it to you if she were entertaining him."

"Maybe *your* mother, but not mine." She rolled her eyes and I grinned. Nari was mildly jealous of their relationship, which I understood because I felt the same feelings for the one she had with Endia. But we both understood the bonds were necessary.

"You should appreciate that they have each other."

"I do."

"Good because they're good for each other."

My phone rang and had me extending my arm over my head to retrieve it from the end table. I hesitated, not wanting to shift the mood of our evening after noticing the name, but if I didn't answer, that would potentially create a bigger issue.

"Hello, Melissa, how are you?"

My eyes remained fastened to Nari and her expression stayed neutral while she finished the slice she was working on.

"Great. I hope I didn't catch you at a bad time."

"No, not at all. What can I do for you?"

She fumbled a bit before getting to the point. "So, as you know, my sister has been working toward finding balance in her life."

"If you mean by receiving therapy, then yes, I'm aware."

"Yes, and well, part of that is apologizing to those who you've wronged in the past so you can make peace and move on."

"I wasn't aware that was a stipulation of therapy. I would assume that falls more under the scope of a twelve-step program. Am I missing something?"

"No, it's just a suggestion from her therapist, and I agree, but I didn't think it would be well received, so I offered to deliver the message on her behalf."

"I agree, and I appreciate your consideration, because it is a delicate matter." My eyes lifted to Nari's again and she was now frowning at me.

"Val is with me and has written out what she wants. So, on behalf of my sister, I would like to sincerely apologize to you and your wife. Val regrets any issues she may have caused due to her poor decisions and you will never have to be concerned with any future issues."

"Although it wasn't necessary, I appreciate the sentiment and will pass it along to my wife."

"Great, well. . . . won't keep you, and she really is better. I promise."

"That's good to hear. I wish her well."

"Thanks, Kincaid. Take care."

I ended the call, prepared for Nari's questions.

"What was that about?"

"Part of Val's therapy was to extend an apology to those she's wronged in the past so she could move forward with her life in a better headspace. Melissa didn't feel it was a good idea for her sister to speak directly to me, so she delivered the apology on her sister's behalf."

"Hmm," was all she offered before leaning toward the table to drop the crust of the slice she'd just finished before lifting another. I quickly moved to place my hands on her hips to ensure she didn't tumble over.

"That's it?"

"I mean, yeah."

She lifted one shoulder into a shrug. "I still don't like the woman, but at least she's smart enough to get help and move on. It wouldn't work in her favor if she didn't."

"That's admirable of you."

"Fuck admirable. That's my warning. No more passes to her or any other of your past 'space fillers.'"

"Space fillers?" My eyes flashed with amusement as I lowered my hands to her stomach. I could see the impression of one of our son's tiny limbs shifting beneath her skin. The thought of her carrying a life that we created still affected me in ways I couldn't explain.

"Yep. Space fillers. You belonged to me, even when you didn't."

I laughed, squinting. "Then why so much running and uncertainty in the beginning?"

She shrugged again, smiling behind her slice. "Because them hoes were disrespectful and I was intimidated by everything that you are."

"And now?"

"Now, I know who's running shit. It just took some time for me to settle into my role, but you know what's up," she teased, flexing.

I chuckled, amused by her newfound confidence.

"Indeed, I do."

EPILOGUE

TWO YEARS AND SOME CHANGE

"Give me the baby. They're waiting for you to speak." Alisha attempted to lift our daughter from my arms, but I turned away, delivering a few more kisses on her fat cheeks before I handed her over. Immediately, her lips puffed into a cute little pout because she wanted to stay with me.

"Your mama has to go and be great. Let Auntie Lish have you just for a little while, pretty girl."

"Where's your mini-me?"

I frowned after raking my fingers through my hair, which I decided to wear straight for today. Once I rechecked the light makeup I wore, I smoothed my hands down my wine-colored dress, removing imaginary wrinkles. The dress hugged my frame so tightly that none existed. I was close to changing only minutes ago, but Kincaid insisted it was appropriate for the event, although I was sure he was biased. I'd gained a few pounds since the birth of our daughter and I think he became even more obsessed with my body than he had been before.

Either way, I was religiously popping my birth control pills because having a toddler and an infant proved to be quite a hassle. I refused to add a third child to this chaos. Our first anniversary was celebrated in Tulum at the same villa we visited for our honeymoon. I learned Kincaid had purchased it a few months later once we realized our time at the villa left us with yet another unexpected pregnancy. The place was now sentimental to us both because it was where our children's journey began.

"She's with her dad. You know that damn girl thinks she owns Darius. I have to fight for space in his life now." She rolled her eyes, smiling at the same time.

"You love it."

"I do, but I also hate it. She clings to him, hollering 'mine' when she sees me coming, and he eats it up."

"Trust me, I get it, but it's Kincaid hollering 'mine' when he sees me coming. I swear she has him wrapped around those fat little fingers and I'm just a close second when it comes to the two of them."

"Blame yourself. She looks just like you, so how could I not fall in love?" That deep tenor had my stomach taking flight. I lifted my eyes to find the man who stole my heart and turned my life upside down standing in the doorway. The sleek black suit he wore was devilishly tempting the way it fit perfectly on his tall frame. The wine tie he paired it with matched my dress perfectly, adding just a tiny splash of color. My hungry eyes traveled up the length of him until I reached his mouth, which had me pressing a hand to my stomach when his teeth raked across his bottom lip. My uterus was reacting, and as if he sensed it, I noticed that subtle shift happening behind his eyes before his beautiful smile surfaced.

I quickly dropped my hand and he laughed.

"They're waiting for you, sweetheart."

"I'm coming."

"I'm going to head out," Alisha tossed over her shoulder, and with a dip of his chin, he reached for our daughter, who already had her arms extended toward him.

"Nuh-uh, buddy. She's all mine right now. You're on wife duty."

Alisha whisked away from him, holding our daughter protectively so he didn't have access. Kincaid closed the space between us, stopping behind me, and we stared at each other in the mirror. He kept his hands to himself for a few minutes longer, but he placed a kiss on my neck.

"You're beautiful."

"So are you."

He chuckled and shook his head. "Thank goodness I wasn't fishing for a compliment because that damn sure isn't it."

His arms encircled my waist and his hands pressed firmly against my stomach. "If I didn't know any better, I'd say you were thinking about giving me another baby."

"I damn sure was not and don't you even get that thought in your head."

His smile expanded before he created a trail of kisses down my neck. "You sure about that?"

"Absolutely positive."

"We'll revisit the topic later, but for now, you go handle your business. You look amazing."

"Thank you, but you're just a tad bit biased."

"I am, but I also don't lie."

"Is my mother here yet?"

"She is. They just arrived."

I inhaled and released it slowly. "I guess it's showtime."

"It is." I turned to Kincaid, who kissed my cheek before extending a hand to escort me downstairs to our guests. We traveled through our home and stepped out back to where everyone was enjoying drinks and the delicacies being passed around on trays.

Not long after, I had everyone's attention and began my speech about accepting donations and volunteers for my foundation. Tonight was a celebration of the completion of my second year and the opening of my third location. I had just over six hundred participants signed up for our programs, whether for temporary housing, assistance with college tuition, or just mentoring so they were better prepared to take on the world. Our guests would be a valued resource through donations and volunteer work. I never imagined something so simple to be such a valuable resource for so many people.

Once I finished my spiel, the crowd offered their congratulations with promises to assist in any way they could. My smile was wide as I looked out and saw the faces of those who meant the most to me. *Family.*

Cast attended with his *friend*, who, after two years, was still around. Alisha and Darius were watching the kids; even Nic and Troy had flown in for the occasion and were spending the weekend with us.

My mother stood next to Abisai, who had his hand protectively resting at the small of her back. They had been going strong, and although he was ready to move forward, she was enjoying the space they were in. My mother wasn't sure when or if she would accept his offer of marriage. Although it was unofficial, we all knew it was simply that way because he was giving her space and time to decide. He would have gladly given her his last name the day they met. I was sure of it.

"You were amazing." His cologne tickled my nose before I felt his body brush against the back of mine. Kincaid leaned into me but kept his hands submerged in his pockets.

"Let's hope it's amazing enough for them to cut the big checks."

"If they don't, I will, but I'm positive you'll get what you need." He kissed my cheek.

"It defeats the purpose if we're the ones funding this."

"I thought the purpose was to provide the resources. It doesn't matter where the money comes from, agreed?"

"Agreed, but I don't want—"

"Sweetheart, relax and enjoy the moment. You're doing good things. The support will be there. How about we focus on our own growth."

I felt him hard against my back, but I wasn't falling for that. "We can practice all you want, but I'm not having any more babies any time soon."

"Then I suppose I'll take what I can get."

"You're damn right because we've got our hands full with those two." I motioned to our son, who was running after Darius and Alisha's daughter. His little legs could barely hold him steady as he smiled wide, his arms extended, chubby fingers opening and closing as he tried his best to grab her.

"I think he has a little crush." Kincaid's tone was light with amusement.

"Oh, I *know* he has a crush. If she's around, he's right up under her, trying to plant those little lips of his on her face."

Kincaid chuckled. "He takes after his daddy."

"Which is definitely not going to play out well. He's too little to be chasing girls."

"It's innocent."

"For now, but that's how it starts, and it only gets worse."

"It's inevitable, sweetheart. He's an Akel. There's no denying his charm. It's how I managed to win the heart of his mother." Kincaid stepped in front of me. "Wouldn't you agree?"

"Jury's still out on that one, but I won't deny that the Akel men are indeed charming."

He leaned in for a kiss that snatched my entire soul.

"Now, let's go mingle so we can get these people out of here. I have a date with my wife to practice making a baby."

I laughed, rolling my eyes as he placed his hand on the small of my back, guiding me toward the crowd. That was one request I didn't mind agreeing to . . .

Ever!

As the saying goes, practice makes perfect, and who was I to deny this man the ability to be at his best, especially when I was the one who was technically benefiting?